D0977808

THE GIFT

"It's called inspeech," Kel said.

Kerris blushed, remembering how he had felt in his bed in the watchtower, trembling in the aftermath of a passion not his own...

"Will it go away?" he asked.

"It's yours. You can use it or not, as you choose."

"Am I—am I a witch?" Kerris asked.

Kel patted his arm. "You are."

THE DANCERS OF ARUN

BOOK TWO OF
THE CHRONICLES OF TORNOR

ELIZABETH A. LYNN

Each book of The Chronicles of Tornor is complete in itself; yet together, they form a haunting picture of a world bright with honor and dark with war, in which a new way of life is struggling to be born.

Berkley books by Elizabeth A. Lynn

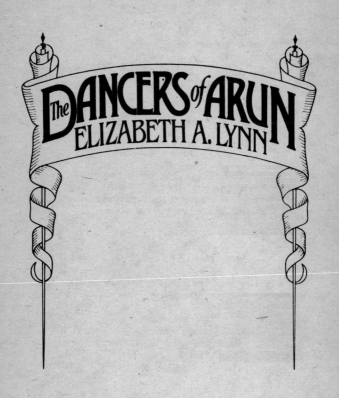

The DANCERS of ARUN

ELIZABETH A. LYNN

BERKLEY BOOKS, NEW YORK

This Berkley book contains the complete
text of the original hardcover edition.
It has been completely reset in a type face
designed for easy reading, and was printed
from new film.

THE DANCERS OF ARUN

A Berkley Book / published by arrangement with
the author

PRINTING HISTORY
Berkley-Putnam edition published September 1979
Berkley edition / August 1980
Second printing / April 1981
Third printing / August 1981

ISBN: 0-425-05189-7

A BERKLEY BOOK® TM 757,375
PRINTED IN THE UNITED STATES OF AMERICA

For Carol, of course

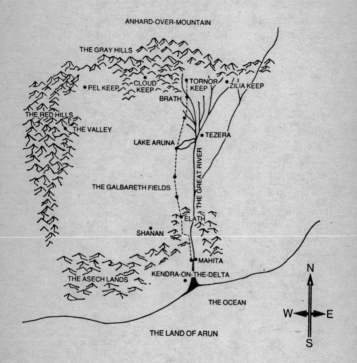

ANHARD-OVER-MOUNTAIN

THE GRAY HILLS

PEL KEEP

CLOUD KEEP

TORNOR KEEP

ZILIA KEEP

BRATH

THE RED HILLS

THE VALLEY

TEZERA

LAKE ARUNA

THE GREAT RIVER

THE GALBARETH FIELDS

ELATH

SHANAN

MAHITA

THE ASECH LANDS

KENDRA-ON-THE-DELTA

THE OCEAN

N

W E

S

THE LAND OF ARUN

GENEALOGY

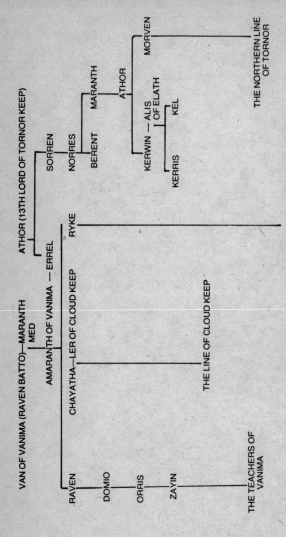

Chapter 1

Kerris woke.

He stretched. He was stiff and cold. The pallet under him was thin and prickly; he had slept far from the chimneys, in the place nearest the door. The morning sun came through the high unpaned windows of the barracks, gilding the dirty tapestries into pale color, and the sky, through the narrow slits, was gray, distant, and chilly.

Swallowing, he tasted the salt of last night's pork. Beside him an off-watch guard thrashed, caught in an evil dream. Kerris tugged his boots on. The laces flapped. He tied them. The unyielding strings kept slipping from his hand. His fingers were cold.

He blew on them to warm them. His stump ached and he rubbed it. A dog barked. Someone shouted in the courtyard. Passing his hand through his tangled hair, Kerris rose and picked his way around huddled sleepers to the Keep kitchen.

A leather curtain separated kitchen and barracks, and through it he could hear people talking. He pushed it aside and went in. The room was hot. The oven fires had been lit. An hour-candle burned in a tiled niche. Apprentice cooks, hands covered with grease and flour, hurried past him. An assistant cook wearing a white cloth apron stood over a cutting board, slicing chunks of cold ham onto a silver platter. Paula stood beside the fireplace, holding out her hands to the blaze. Kerris went to her. Bending, he kissed the top of her head. "Good morning."

She peered up at him. He was a head taller than she was. She was wearing a thick brown shawl around her shoulders. "Kerris," she said. She turned back to the pot. It held tea, honey, and milk in a great soup mixture. "Have some tea."

He looked through rows of tall glasses for a mug. "Cold this morning," he said.

"Cold every damn morning." She banged the ladle on the rim of the iron pot. "You'd never know it was spring."

Leaning by her, Kerris dunked the mug into the pot. He sipped the tea. It was hot and very sweet. "It's nearly summer," he said. "The traders'll be here soon."

Her dark eyes glinted. She made a barracks gesture. "Summer," she said, with a southerner's contempt for northern weather. "Those people upstairs awake yet?"

She meant the soldiers. She had been a soldier herself once, long ago, on the southern border. Kerris shook his head. "Just me."

A fair-haired kitchenmaid in a long linen skirt came from the storeroom. She was carrying a round of cheese. She smiled politely at Paula and with more warmth at the young cook. His hands at the board moved even faster. She did not look at Kerris. He had not expected her to. For all that he was of Tornor's ruling line, he was a scribe, a fit-taker, and a cripple, less important to the Keep than the least of its cooks.

Paula scowled. "You want more tea?" she said.

He wanted to tell her that it did not matter to him that the women of the Keep ignored him. He was used to it. He preferred it to the ridicule he might have gotten—had gotten, more than once. To please her, he dipped his mug again in the amber syrup. An apprentice opened an oven door. The smell of baking bread filled the room.

The leather curtain flapped. The chief cook strutted in. He had great hairy arms like a smith, and no hair at all on his skull. The scullions (behind his back) called him the Egg. He was a superb cook and had a temper like a fox-bitch in heat, and he hated intruders in his kitchen. He glared at Kerris. "Out," he said, fingering his square-bladed cleaver. The gesture was for show, but Kerris had no intention of challenging it. He rubbed Paula's shoulder.

"I'll see you later," he said. He turned to go.

There was smoke in his eyes and a knife in his hand. He smelled scorched food and the heavy scent of new wine. He thought, End it quickly. *He faked a stumble on a stool. His opponent grinned and stepped in for a killing thrust. Catching the thrusting arm, he looped the man's neck with his other arm and drew him helpless to the floor. A knife clattered down. Disdainfully a booted foot kicked it away. A woman screamed softly.*

He stared into the man's red and terrified face. "I could break your neck," he said. "Don't you know better than to fight a cheari?"

Ilene said, at his back, "They've burned our breakfast, Kel. Let's leave."

His vision blurred. He smelled bread. He was back. Paula stood in front of him, bristling like a mother cat protecting a kitten. The scullions were all watching. The chief cook was sputtering at the old woman. "I'll have no fits taken in my kitchen!"

Kerris said, "I'm all right."

Paula turned. Her eyes searched his face. He was sorry she had seen it. "It's nothing," he said. He walked toward the entrance to the hall. The scullions murmured, clumped together like puppies. The Egg swore at them, and they hopped out of his way.

The great hall of Tornor was big enough to hold six hundred men without crowding. Kerris rested against a wall of it for a moment. As always after a fit, he felt just slightly disoriented. He leaned on a tapestry. It showed a scene from some old battle. Josen would know which one. Kerris did not.

3

The doors to the hall were open. Men from the barracks, rubbing sleep from their eyes, and men just off watch, bulky in their layers of wool and leather, were coming in. Dogs with sleek fur and pale narrow heads ran about and around them—wolfhounds, they were, though there were few wolves left on the steppe. A hunting party last fall had brought in one mangy yearling. They had hung the skin from the castle wall and all the small boys from Tornor village had come to stare at it.

Someone opened the leather curtain. The smell of fresh bread drifted into the hall. The men elbowed each other. Kerris' appetite had gone. He walked down the lane beside one of the long tables and came face to face with the lord of the Keep.

He bowed. "Good morning, uncle," he said.

Morven, the nineteenth lord of Tornor Keep, was brisk and stocky, with the bright yellow hair and pale complexion of his line. Kerris had not inherited it. "Good morning, nephew," he said. "Did you wake as the watch changed?" Kerris nodded. Morven did not know (or pretended that he did not know) that Kerris sometimes slept in the barracks. "I wish my soldiers were as dedicated." It was meant to be praise.

"Thank you." Ousel, the second watch commander, strode up. Immediately Morven turned to speak with him. Kerris, dismissed, went on out of the hall. He thought, At least he has the decency not to laugh in my face.

Crossing the inner ward to the stair to the Recorder's Tower, he felt inside his skull for the skill that linked him with his brother. As ever, it eluded him. He could not make it work, any more than he could stop it.

In the shadow of the sundial a trio of children played the paper-scissors-rock game. Kerris slowed as he passed them. It was one of the few games he, the one-armed child, had been able to play, and he had gotten so adept at knowing what the others would choose that they had soon refused to play with him. The game dissolved into wrestling, with the biggest child, Morven's daughter Aret, on top. Kerris went on. He had never been very good at wrestling.

"Hello, Recorder."

A girl stood at the foot of the tower stair, her arms filled with

4

laundry. She wore a red gown and a brown overtunic. Her cheeks were pocked with little scars. Her hair fell down her back. Kerris felt the nape of his neck redden. "Hello, Kili," he said.

Two years ago she had approached him in the hall, brushing her breasts against him with a smile and a whispered question. "Would you like to . . . ?" No one had asked him before. He went with her to the laundry, clumsy and eager. They lay between the long wet washtubs, on the dirty sheets from the apartments. He was deeply grateful to her. Only one other person had ever touched him in that way. She had even pretended to be pleased with his efforts. Some weeks afterward he overheard her laughing about it with another girl, equating his lost limb and his sexual ability.

She thrust her hip against him. "How come I don't see you any more?"

"I have work to do."

"That's too bad." She strolled across the ward, hips swaying. The guards on the inner wall yipped appreciatively.

Kerris thought of Kel. He wondered where the *chearas* was, and what had happened to the red-faced man. No doubt the *chearis* were saddled and gone from the place. He could see them—tall Arillard, redheaded Riniard the newcomer, Jensie with the tri-colored hair. . . . He swore under his breath and pushed the thoughts away. They only made him unhappy.

He glanced across the courtyard. Kili had gone. The guards had turned back to their vigil. Kerris pictured a caravan bumping along the eastern road, blue flags flying, laden with silks and spices and wood and metal goods. The whole Keep was restless, waiting for the traders. The children played at caravans in their games.

He went up the spiral stair to the chamber at the tower's top.

The octagonal room was very old. It had been variously used: for storage, for defense, even for a council chamber when there was war in the north. It smelled of pine logs and ink. There were tapestries on its walls like the ones in the hall. The room held a clutter of furniture: two sleeping pallets, a big worktable, some stools, Josen's chair, and six cedar chests. Two of the chests held clothes. Four of them were brimful of old records.

A tall crock of *choba* oil stood in one corner. The rest of the Keep, even the lord's apartments, was lit by different kinds of candles, and the merchants did not bother to bring the heavy oil with them from the south. But Josen had ordered, and bought, on his own, the one crock. On dark winter days he poured oil into dishes, and fashioned wicks for them with wool yarn. He claimed the light from the oil was clearer and less smoky than the light from animal-fat candles. Kerris teased him with it, gently, in the evenings. "With the lamps lit, you can pretend, like Paula, that you're not really here."

"Unlike Paula," the old man would answer, "I like it here."

Kerris pushed open the door with his shoulder. Josen stood at the window, sniffing the air. He had opened one of the windows and stood looking out the crack at the view. Kerris joined him. The watchtower had been built three hundred years back by Torrel, fourth lord of Tornor Keep, "so that he might see the Anhard raiders before their kings gave the order to attack." There was no military use for a tower any more; there had been peace between Arun and Anhard for a hundred years. But the windows had never been touched, except to have new glass placed in the frames. They still looked only north.

The mountains' gray bulk dominated the landscape. The lower terraces of the peaks were stippled with green. Kerris had heard (from the merchants, who went everywhere) that in the west there were taller mountains, and that they were red, not gray. He doubted he would get to see them. The farthest he'd ever been across the steppe was half the distance to Cloud Keep.

He had been born in the south, in a small village south of the lower edge of Galbareth. Paula had told him that often enough. But he did not remember the south, nor the ride north, nor the raid on the caravan in which his mother had been killed. It was in that raid that the blow of a curved Asech blade had taken off his right arm just below the shoulder.

Josen's voice interrupted his reverie. "Summer's coming."

Kerris dragged his thoughts away from his lost past. "Paula doesn't think so," he said.

"She's a southerner," said Josen. "It's never hot enough here for them." He was a northerner, but he knew the south well, having lived there many years. He glanced at Kerris. He was tall, but stoop-shouldered. His pale eyes were deep-set and very keen. He wore the clothes of his clan: a black robe of soft wool, with a hood that fell down his back. On his left fourth finger he wore a gold ring with an ebony stone. Only scholars and lords of households wore rings: lords to indicate their rulership, scholars to show that they carried no weapons. Josen was a member of the Scholars' Guild. He had been sent to study in Kendra-on-the-Delta by Athor, Morven's father, and had returned to the Keep twenty-five years ago. "The traders are not here yet, I suppose."

"No."

Josen said something in the southern tongue.

"What is that?" inquired Kerris. He had been Josen's apprentice for five years, but he knew only a little of the old southern language.

"May they suffer seven years from piles," said the old man. "I need ink!"

Kerris grinned. He and Josen shared working and sleeping space in the tower, and as much as the disparity of age and temperament allowed (Josen and Paula were about the same age) they were friends. "May they suffer from piles after they get here," he suggested.

"Yes," Josen agreed, "that's better."

He coughed, and pulled his wide sash more tightly around his waist. He said, "I didn't hear you come in at all, last night."

Kerris' stump throbbed. "I slept in the barracks," he said.

"In case the raiders come?" said Josen, voice tinged with gentle mockery. "Even were it to happen, Morven would not let you fight. You'd be sent to shelter in the storerooms with the old, the sick, and the children. Why bother?"

"I need to," Kerris said. "I don't care what Morven thinks." He walked to the oaken worktable. Josen had already laid out on it their day's work: a pile of ancient scrolls for himself, the monthly accounts for Kerris. The scrolls smelled musty. He pulled back the chair. "Shall we get to work?"

Josen shurgged. "As you wish," he said. He crossed the little octagonal room. Kerris felt a twinge of remorse. He hadn't

7

meant to put the old man off so harshly. He pulled Josen's cushioned chair out for him. Once—before he had Kerris to help him—Josen had done the day-to-day work, tallying accounts, keeping records. But Kerris did this now, and freed from those tasks the old scholar had chosen to set about a work more interesting: recopying the histories of Tornor off the ancient scrolls. Morven had no objections. He was even willing to pay for the fine-haired brushes and the expensive ink Josen required. (The ink Kerris used faded fast, but cost nothing. Kerris made it himself out of the ink sacs of the local river eels. Josen had taught him how to do that.) He glanced at the topmost scroll as Josen unrolled it. It glinted, here and there. Some of the letters had been painted with gold, and they shone through the dust.

The old northern runes (which were really a corruption of the southern runes, Josen said) went up and down on the scrolls. Kerris could not read them. Josen had taught him only the southern script. Everyone used it now. The old records in the Keeps were the only examples left of the northern script, and when these were all copied into the southern script then no one would remember that there even had been another way to write, except a few scholars like Josen.

Pretending that nothing had happened, Josen took his brushes from their wooden, felt-lined case.

Kerris cast about for a means to mend the breach.

"Josen?"

"Hmm?" said the old man.

"What history do you copy today?"

Josen looked pleased. The hurt left his face. He loved to talk about the histories. "The history of the eleventh lord of Tornor."

"Who was he?"

"His name was Kerwin," Josen said, "like your father." He closed the brush case and put it to one side. "Most of the record is taken up with accounts of battles with Anhard. Kerwin was killed in battle. It was a common death. The Truce wasn't signed until the reign of Athor, Kerwin's grandson."

Kerris said, "Was there ever a time when there were no battles?"

Josen frowned. "Tornor was built to be a fortress. But from

Kerwin's reign to the reign of the Lady Sorren there is a gap in the scrolls."

Once Kerris had been under the illusion that it would be exciting to be in a war. He no longer thought so. "Was that the Lady Sorren who brought the chearis to Tornor?"

"There has been only one Sorren of Tornor," Josen said.

Kerris nodded. He remembered. Josen had read him the history from the scroll. Sorren of Tornor had named a *cheari* as Yardmaster, and during her reign (and after it, during the reign of her daughter Norres), Tornor had been a gathering-place for chearis.

"Where did they come from?" he asked.

Josen scowled. "You know the legend. The chearis came from the west, from Vanima, the land of always summer."

"How did the Lady Sorren get them to Tornor?"

"It's not in the record," said Josen. He snorted. "All the historians agree that the earliest chearis were southerners. Yet the legend of Vanima persists. Even now the chearis speak of it as if it were a real place." He picked up his brush and pointed it at Kerris like a dagger. "It's very frustrating."

"What is?"

"That the records should be incomplete."

Kerris took a piece of paper from his own stack. The sheets were heavy and coarse, made of pressed linen scraps and river reeds. The gray tinge of it made him think of Paula. She was getting old. He hoped the incident in the kitchen had not troubled her too much. She worried about him.... She had brought him north after his mother's death, and though she never said it, he knew she had stayed in Tornor for his sake.

"Who was the first cheari?" he said.

Josen scratched his nose with the wooden end of his brush. "We don't know," he said. "The chearis may—but they don't talk to scholars." He grew severe. "Records that are not written are not to be trusted. Spoken histories are too easily distorted into legend and myth."

Kerris smiled. He had heard this lecture before.

"For example," Josen said, "there is a passage in the history of the reign of the Lady Sorren that suggests *she* was a cheari.

9

Later in the same scroll it also states she was a messenger, a member of the green clan."

"Couldn't she be both?" Kerris said.

"It's very unlikely." Josen was stern. "Why should an heir of Tornor join the messenger clan? Some scribe was careless, and now we'll never know the truth of it—because an inattentive apprentice wrote a word wrong."

Kerris grinned at him. "If the black clan had its way, no one would do anything without writing it down."

"History is important," the old man said.

"Yes," Kerris agreed. Privately he wondered if anything would be done if the world worked Josen's way.

You will never make a scholar, said his inner voice.

Stubbornly he banished it. He would be a scribe, not a scholar, and keep the records when Josen could no longer see to keep them. He turned the tallies so that the signs all faced out. They were marked with the ancient signs: a sickle for grain, a horn for goats, a triple slash (signifying the three spikelets of the ear) for barley. The middle slash was longest. Picking up his pen, he drew a line down the center of the page. The familiar work absorbed him. The trouble smoothed from his face, and the ache drained from his stump.

When the ink began to spatter on the page, he halted. He grimaced at the botched sheet with annoyance. It would all have to be done again. He checked the tip of the quill. As he thought, it needed trimming. Laying it down, he stretched his cramped fingers. The room was very light. On the wall opposite him, the tapestry's gold threadwork was just visible. It showed a battle scene: a man with a gilt beard rallied his men. In the crannies of the tower, nesting pigeons called, flapping their wings.

"Josen."

The old man's head lifted. His hair stuck out from his skull like fine silk fringe. "Hmm?" It took a moment for his eyes to lose their glaze.

"Take a rest. My quill needs mending."

The scholar looked at the page he'd been copying. Gently he rolled it up again. He had started with the newest scrolls and was slowly working backwards. Some of the oldest records were so brittle that they fell apart to the touch. "Hmm." He picked up the quill Kerris had been using and looked at the splayed end. "You need a new quill entirely," he commented. He riffled the feathers. "Still, a rest is a good idea." He rose from the chair. "Let's take a walk on the wall to stretch our legs."

Like the other Keeps on the northern border, Tornor Keep had been built to withstand attack. It had two walls around it, one inside the other. They were toothy, smoothfaced, and formidable. Inside the inner wall were the buildings of the Keep: the hall, the barracks, the stables and storerooms, the Yard, the smithy and the apartments. The top of it was a stone walkway with room for three men to walk abreast. The outer wall was lower than the inner wall, but it too had a walkway and it was equally thick and crenellated. Both walls were broken, at regular intervals, by arrow slits.

The watchtower rose from the southwest corner of the inner wall. Originally it had had only one entrance: the door in the inner ward at the base of the stair. But during the rule of the Lady Sorren a second door, leading to the rampart, had been added. In sunlight or strong torchlight the stone of the arch glittered with mica flecks, and it was evident that the doorway had been built at a later time than either the wall or the stair.

The guard on the stairway lifted a hand as they walked beneath the arch. "Hey, Kerris."

"Tryg." Kerris smiled. Tryg was the son of Ousel's watch second. He was lithe and broad and he wore his hair in the old way, shoulder-length and unbound. He and Kerris had been best of friends when they were eight. They had shared a bed, playing at sex, as children do. "I skipped breakfast. Got any cheese?"

"Sure." Tryg turned out his pockets. He had cheese, a sour apple, a shard of linty bread. "You can have it all."

He was always generous. . . . "Thanks," Kerris said. He took the food. Josen was halfway to the guardhouse, his face a mask of abstraction. Kerris followed the old man, eating as he moved.

It was surely spring. The stones beside him were warm in the sunlight. A breeze flapped the banners. They bore the red eight-pointed star on a white field, for three hundred years the crest of the lords of Tornor. Guards leaned on the battlements, facing south, helmets off. The guard was largely ceremonial. There had been no war in the north for a hundred years. Young men from the villages came to the Keeps to learn to handle weapons. Those that liked the work went east or south, to join city guard troops in Tezera or Shanan or Mahita or Kendra-on-the-Delta. Once there, some turned merchant or courier. The remainder went back to their farms and herds. Only the old men stayed at Tornor.

Josen stopped to lean his elbows on the wall. Kerris halted beside him, licking the last bits of cheese from his palm. He heard the river music. Swollen by snow water from the mountains, the Rurian tossed and twisted in its banks. The water mill squatted beside it. Its wheel still turned, but most of the Keep's pressing and milling was done at the windmill, which was a bigger and newer building to the east of the Keep. In the field between the castle and the town, blue daisies trembled like flames.

For a moment Kerris permitted himself to think of Kel. Once, watching the tumble and sweat of practice in the Yard, taunted by some child his own age (it might even have been Tryg, but Kerris did not like to think that), he shouted that it didn't matter that he was one-armed. His brother was a cheari. They teased Kel's name from him and danced about him, mocking and vicious, calling him to fight like Kel, to dance like Kel. Since that afternoon he had coupled their names only in his mind. Paula and Josen knew, of course, and Morven. But Morven never spoke of it. Kerris did not think he cared. Morven had never met Kel, only heard of him. All Arun had heard of him. But the red clan rarely came north. It was a long journey across Galbareth to the Keeps.

Five years back a chearas had stopped at Tornor on its way from the Red Hills to Tezera. Kel had not been a part of it. They had danced in the Yard. Kerris remembered the searing, concentrated grace with which they turned and swayed and leaped. But it was not for another year that he began to experience the sudden, random moments in which he seemed to live in two bodies: his own, and his brother's. At first he had been terrified, understanding nothing, afraid that he was going mad. After a while he learned that the moments of rapport would not hurt him. They did not happen more than once every two to three weeks. When they happened in public he called them his fits.

He told Josen about them.

The old man listened gravely. "Are they painful?" he had asked.

"No."

"Unpleasant?"

Kerris tried to answer honestly. "N-no. Startling."

Josen sighed. "I'm sorry, Kerris," he said. "I don't know what they are."

Kerris felt numb. He had always thought that Josen knew everything—well, nearly everything. Stories flashed through his mind. Perhaps he was being tormented by a ghost or a demon. It would not help to say such things to Josen. The old scholar did not believe in demons.

"What should I do?" he said.

Josen pulled on his sash. It was the gesture he made when he was embarrassed. "You could talk to the village healer."

Kerris was surprised. Usually Josen had few good words for the village healer—an old woman named Tath. She was known to be ill-tempered but herb-wise. No. He knew that Tath could offer him no remedy for what ailed him, and he was afraid of what she might say. She would only feed his fears. "She can cure lung fever," he said, lifting his fore- and little fingers in a gesture he had learned from Paula. "Not this."

Josen did not ask him how he knew. (Kerris could not have told him.) He said, "If they don't hurt, don't worry about them. Let them come and let them go. They'll stop. And there is no need to resort to coarseness." He spoke with an authority that Kerris had found very reassuring, at thirteen.

Perhaps he had been wrong, Kerris thought. Perhaps he should have talked to old Tath. He scratched his stump, which had begun to itch.

"What is it?" Josen said.

A child was crying, somewhere in the apartments, and Kerris

13

found his thought checked by that high, angry scream. "I had a fit this morning, in the kitchen," he said.

Josen pursed his lips. "Worrying about it?"

Kerris shook his head. "No. Just thinking."

"You know," Josen said, "I know nothing of such things. But there may be people who do, in the cities."

Kerris laughed. "Forget it, Josen. I'm not likely to get to Tezera any time soon. Besides, I'm used to them; they don't trouble me." To himself he said, They wouldn't trouble me if I knew what they were. But he did not want to be without them. In those brief moments of rapport he knew what it felt like to live in a body that had never been maimed.

Five years back, the year he turned twelve, Kerris had been summoned to Morven's rooms. He went eagerly. At twelve a child was counted ready to join the daily practice in the Yard, to begin to learn the skills that made him or her an adult—even a cheari. Tryg had already made passage to that world: his father had given him, according to tradition, a small but serviceable fighting knife. As Kerris walked into the lord's chamber, he could almost feel on his belt the knife he expected Morven to give him.

But Morven did not give him his knife. Instead, he said, "The Yard is not for you. It would waste the Yardmaster's time to try to teach you fighting skills, let alone make you a cheari. Son to my brother you are, and a home you will always have here, for his sake. But more"—looking at Kerris' right shoulder, at the empty sleeve—"is out of your reach."

It had been Morven's idea to apprentice Kerris to Josen. It was a good idea, Kerris thought. It let him make a place.

Deep in his head a voice—his own—amended the thought. It was as good a place as any would ever be for him. He had learned to love the Keep, and the mountains that rose behind it like the spine of the earth. He loved the land in summer; he loved the steppe, windswept and thick with honey-colored grass. But it was not likely that he would ever get a chance to leave it. It was just as well he was comfortable in it.

He clapped Josen gently on the shoulder. "Come on, old man. Let's get back to work."

"Old man, indeed!" Josen pretended outrage. "Is this the respect you show your teacher? Speak well of me, or I shan't mend your quill."

Kerris grinned at him. "Yes, sir, beg pardon sir," he gabbled.

"I need more ink, too," said Josen, abandoning the play. "Blast those traders."

That night, Kerris did not go to the barracks to sleep.

Josen, as usual, avoided the morning meal. In his view food was indecent before noon. Kerris waited until he was sure that the Egg had gone to his apartments before slipping round the kitchen curtain.

Paula sat by the fire. He kissed the top of her head. Her scalp showed pink through sparse gray curls.

"Huh." Her fingers on the mug were red and swollen.

"Good morning."

"Is it?"

"Warmer today than yesterday," he said. "You should try it."

"Huh." The grumpy syllable conveyed her distrust of the north's feeble attempt at spring. "Where are you going?"

"The chicken run. I need quills." He waited a bit, to show her that he was well. "See you later." He ducked out through the scullery. As he crossed to the hen run, music came to his ears. He looked up. Idrith was playing his flute. The other guards were still, listening. The soft trills floated across the walls and the ward. Kerris sighed. Once he had thought he would like to learn to make music. But he had no voice to speak of—and there was no musical instrument he had ever seen or heard of that could be played with one hand.

The run smelled like a pasture. The hens paid no attention to him, but from the end of his tether the rooster watched suspiciously as Kerris hunted for quills.

"Be easy," Kerris told the bright-eyed bird. "I'm not after your wives." He found three white pinion feathers, and a gray goosetail feather that would suit. He brought them to Josen. The old man unearthed his penknife from the pile of papers on the table. It was a small sharp knife with a single edge, the brass handle shaped like a goat's head.

15

With short deft strokes, the old man shaped the nib. "How's the weather?" he asked.

"Warmer than yesterday."

"No sign of the traders?"

Kerris shook his head.

Josen muttered. He held the nib up to the light and scowled at it as if it were a trader. "I have been thinking," he said.

"Yes?"

"About a letter I might write. To the head of the Scholars' Guild in Kendra-on-the Delta. It might read something like: *Dear Sir, This is to introduce a worthy young clerk, named Kerris, nephew to Morven Lord of Tornor Keep, who was my apprentice and has been my colleague, in a manner of speaking, for two years.* And so on." The old man continued to hold the nib up, as if he were speaking to it. "What do you think of that?"

"I—I don't know."

"Well, think. And tell me when you have thought."

"Would the Scholars' Guild be impressed by a letter like that?"

"They would be if I wrote it," said Josen. "They might find a position for the bearer in, say, one of the great city houses, as clerk, or historian." He flicked a look at Kerris. "If the bearer wanted such a position, that is."

Kerris' stump ached. He touched the end of it, where the skin was thick and scarred. Paula had told him how they had had to sear it with the flat of a heated knife to stop the bleeding. "What great house would want me?" he said bleakly.

"Don't be a fool," said Josen. "Tornor's not the world. Do you love it so well here that you would be anguished to leave?"

Kerris had no answer.

"Consider," said the old man. "If you—"

From the wall, crisp and clear and light, a horn called.

Josen turned toward the sound. He put the knife and quill aside. Pah-pah-PAH, said the horn. *Strangers approaching.*

"At last," said the old man. The courtyard echoed with the noise of running feet. The horn blew a second time, vibrant and variant.

16

Kerris translated the pattern into words automatically. The caller had added a phrase. *Strangers on horses approaching from the west road.*

"I should have run out of ink in four more days," Josen said. He slipped the little knife into its sheath. "Shall we go out to the wall?"

They went to the stair. Tryg's voice floated up to them from the arch. "The caravans don't come on the west road," he said. "It can't be the traders."

Morven was standing in the inner ward, frowning at the young guard's words. The ramparts were crowded with soldiers and stablehands, scullions and chambermaids. Morven looked impatient. Propriety demanded that he wait within the court. It did not befit the lord of the Keep to crane over his own walls.

The horn blew again. "It's a courier from Cloud Keep," said a man's voice.

"Naw. It's a flock of sheep!" said another. Below the wall, the dogs were barking up a storm. "Hey, let someone else get a look, there."

Josen said, "Can you see anything?"

"Nothing but a lot of backs," Kerris said. He was only a little taller than Josen. The horn blared its message at the day. Kerris took firm hold of a protruding bit of stone and hauled himself up within the nearest embrasure.

"Careful," said Josen.

Kerris braced his feet against the crenel. He looked east. No wagons wallowed along the road. He looked west. He saw riders. He counted. There were seven of them, and one horse without a rider. The foremost rode a ways ahead, and sunlight reflected from his hair, which was thick blond and waist-length, and tied back with the red scarf of a cheari.

"What do you see?"

Josen's voice seemed to come from very far away. The folk on the wall exclaimed to each other. Kerris' legs shook. He knew them: Jensie, Riniard beside her, Elli and Ilene like shadows, Calwin, sturdy and small, Arillard, silent and austere.... He sat down hard in the gap between the merlons. He knew them all.

"What is it?" said Josen.

"Hey, Kerris, say something," urged Tryg.

They waited for him to answer. He lifted his chin. "It's a chearas."

There was no need for him to tell them which.

Chapter 2

Morven welcomed the chearis in the hall. Kerris watched from the tower window as they moved across the inner ward, walking with that unbelievable grace. They wore woolen tunics and supple riding pants under which the cloth of trousers showed, and tall riding boots.

In a little while a page came to the tower stairs. He bore a message: a summons for Kerris. As he walked across the court Kerris saw heads pop out of windows to stare at him. The guards on the battlement watched curiously.

Both hall doors were drawn back, flooding the hall with sunlight. The chearas stood at the head of the hall, near the commanders' table. Temeth the Yardmaster, a hardfaced, silent man whom Kerris did not know at all, save by sight, stood beside Morven.

Kerris bowed to his uncle. "You sent for me, sir."

The sunlight reflecting off the ancient tapestries seemed to flow toward Kel. The other chearis made a semicircle at his back.

"Yes," said Morven. He rubbed his hands together, a gesture

Kerris had never seen him make. "Come here, boy." He never called Kerris "boy." "It gives me great pleasure to be able to introduce you to your older brother. This is he," he said to Kel.

Funny, Kerris thought, in all the times I've shared his thoughts I've never seen his face....

"You've grown since last I saw you," said Kel.

His voice was lower and more melodious than Kerris had thought it. His eyes were gray. He was taller than Kerris, taller than Morven.

Kerris said, "I was younger then."

"You were a babe." Kel stretched out a hand. "It's taken me a long time to come north, but I always meant to," he said. "I've come to take you south with me, if you'll go. Will you?"

Kerris' breath jumped in his throat. Wetting his lips, he looked at Morven. "My lord, have I your permission to leave?"

Morven smoothed the embroidered collar of his shirt. "You're not a child. I'll be loth to have you gone, of course. It may be difficult to replace you, we shall have to write to the Scholars' Guild for a clerk—" He glanced at Kel and took a breath. "But brother is dearer than uncle. Certainly you may go."

Kel made a turning gesture of his outstretched hand and wrist. Kerris jumped as Riniard appeared at his side. "If you won't mind company," said Riniard, "I'll help you pack."

"Now?" Kerris said.

"Now," said the cheari.

Leaving Kel was like leaving the sun. Numbly Kerris led the way across the Keep to the tower stairs. Josen was not in the little room. Kerris wondered if he was still on the rampart.

Riniard glanced at the two beds and at the long table. "You live here?" he said.

"Yes," Kerris said. "I'm a scribe."

Riniard moved around the chamber like a fox in a cage. He tapped the iron window frame with one fist. "I'd go mad here," he said cheerfully. "Which is your bed?"

Kerris pointed to it. Riniard pulled the woolen blanket from the linen sheet. He knelt on the floor and folded it once the long way. "Bring a warm cloak," he instructed. "Clothing, tinderbox

20

and flints, any trinkets you want with you—"

Kerris' cloak was in the cedar chest under the windows. He went to get it. The familiar smell of cedar dust made his throat ache. Holding the heavy lid with his shoulder, he turned over the clothes in the chest. He took out a second linen shirt, a wool tunic that Paula had made him, his sheepskin cloak, and his riding leathers. The rust-colored leathers were stiff from lack of use. "Are we leaving soon?" he asked, bringing tunic and cloak to Riniard.

Shaking the cloak out, Riniard rolled it deftly in the folds of the blanket. "Immediately," he said.

"But—you'll stay to dance—"

"No," said the redhead. He patted a fold of the blanket. "The day's young, and we've ground to cover. Sefer's waiting at Elath, and Kel's in a hurry." He rolled the blanket into a tight wad. "Got a string?" Kerris found a leather lace. Riniard tied the blanket roll. He stood up, holding it under his arm. "Better put those on," he said, nodding toward the leathers. Kerris obeyed, though he disliked dressing with anyone looking on. "Where's your knife?"

Kerris pushed the metal tang of the buckle into the belt hole with his thumb, and pulled the tongue of the belt through the metal loop. When he finished, he looked at Riniard. "I haven't one." He steeled himself for a look of contempt, or pity.

Riniard simply lifted one auburn eyebrow. "Oh." He turned toward the door. "Shall we go?" Kerris followed him. His heart was beating overfast, and the leathers flapped uncomfortably against his legs on the way down the stair.

Josen had vanished; he was not on the rampart. Paula was waiting for him in the inner ward. In the open air she seemed more frail than in the kitchen. Kerris put his arm around her shoulders and laid his lips against her cheek.

She pushed at him. *"Chelito."* Her voice was soft. "It's good you're going." She passed a hand across his forehead. "You don't belong here, you never did. This is too cold a country."

He hugged her again. "Kerris," murmured Riniard. Kerris lifted his head. Morven was coming from the hall. Behind him, walking in pairs like soldiers, came the chearis.

"I'll write to you," he said to Paula.

"Hah," she said. "You'll forget me—and you should. Don't write, boy. I can't see to read."

Kel said courteously to Morven, "Thank you for the provisions, my lord. I'm sorry we can't stay, but we're in a hurry."

"We are honored by even this short a visit," said Morven. He nodded in a friendly way toward Kerris. "Good luck. If your brother sets too stiff a pace for you, come on back."

Kerris looked at Kel. His brother's lips twitched. "I'll moderate my pace," he said. "You needn't worry, my lord."

"Your horses are at the gate," Morven said.

The chearis made for the gate. Kerris glanced back at Paula. She sat like a cenotaph. Only her eyes lived. *Go on*, they said.

"You can ride, can't you?" Riniard said. He led Kerris to a glossy black mare. "This is Magrita. I trained her myself. She's part steppe horse and part desert breed: the best of both, I think. She's sweet as cream, aren't you, lady?" The mare's ears pricked forward intelligently. Kerris rubbed her jaw. She poked her nose into his palm. "She's quick, too," said Riniard.

"I can ride," Kerris said.

Riniard tied the blanket roll to the cantle of the saddle for him.

"Yo!" The cry and the sound of running feet whipped the chearis round. Tryg jogged up. "Excuse me," he said. He extended both hands. "This is for Kerris, from Josen."

Kerris went to see what it was. It was a knife in a worked leather sheath. The chearis gathered to look at it. The hilt was dimpled bone. On it was carved the southern rune for the letter "K."

Kerris held it uncertainly. There was a loop on the open end of the sheath. Kel said, "It should be worn." He held out a hand. "May I?" Kerris laid it in his palm. "Open your belt," Kel said. As Kerris worked the belt and buckle apart, Kel drew the knife. Someone—perhaps Josen—had greased the leather. The blade slid out with deadly ease. It was patterned by the hammer and honed to a fine edge on both sides—bright, beautiful. Kel slipped the sheathed blade onto Kerris' belt. He stepped back a pace to let Kerris do up the buckle.

Tryg was waiting. "Tell Josen my thanks," Kerris said. He fingered the sheath. The weight of the knife hung strangely against his right thigh. He felt tears gather behind his eyelids.

"I will," said Tryg. He smiled shyly. "Take care of yourself."

"I'll take care," Kerris said. Tryg hesitated, and then took a step toward him. Quickly, they embraced. Tryg's hands were hard and his clothes smelled of saddle grease. He strode back under the gate. Kerris watched him disappear. When he turned to face the chearas, he felt shaken.

Kel touched his shoulder. It drew him momentarily into their circle. "Let's ride, chearis. I want to make Galbareth in seven days." Kerris checked the length of the mare's stirrups. It looked right for him. Gripping the rein, he swung into the saddle. Magrita stood rock-still. He had expected her to try to sidle out from under him. He stroked her neck and told her she was a good girl.

"She is, isn't she," said Riniard, pleased.

Kel rode a tall red stallion. He turned the horse's head at the gate. "Hey, Callito," he said. The guards lifted their pikes in salute. Kel waved. "Farewell the Keep," he called. Kerris thought, I should say something. Nothing came to mind. He pressed his knees into Magrita's flanks. The chearis moved. As they swept under the arch of the outer wall, flags billowed in the wind. Kerris glanced up. Heads bobbed on the ramparts. The company reached the roadway. Dust spurted lightly beneath Magrita's nimble feet.

The road was dusty and sunny, and ridged with old ruts. Kerris wet his lips as the shifting wind blew dust across them. There had been no rain for eight days; the grass along the road was brown and limp with the heat. They crossed the bridge over the Rurian. The horses' hooves clattered on the wood. After the bridge the road curved left, following the curve of the river as it swung east. Kerris looked back. The Keep dominated the view. He looked west. Smoke from the fires of Tornor village rose into the air. Between the road and the village marched a dark bristly stand of dwarf pines.

23

Riniard had fallen back after the bridge crossing. He was riding beside Jensie, teasing her about something. Kerris heard her laugh. It was a beautiful laugh, like water running. Shyly he looked at the woman riding beside him now. She wore a yellow shirt. She saw his eyes on her and grinned. "Hi," she said. "I'm Elli."

He almost said, *I know*. He caught himself. "You know my name."

"Yes," she said. "This is Tula," she added, patting the arching neck of her dun. "But don't feel disadvantaged. We don't know much about you. Kel told us some, but even he doesn't know a lot." She cocked her head to one side as she spoke. She was straight as a spear shaft in the saddle. Her skin was creamy brown. Her hair was curly and very black.

Kerris thought, I know more about you than you do about me. He knew that she and Jensie had both joined the chearas a year ago, that Cal had been in it three years, that Jensie and Riniard were lovers, that Arillard and Ilene and Kel had fought together against the Asech, that Riniard was the newest of the chearis.

"We've been separated a long time," he said.

"Kel said that. You were taken north when you were a baby, while he was fighting on the border, and you were there during the raids, and all the time he studied with Zayin." Kerris did not know who Zayin was. "Your arm was taken off in an Asech raid, and you're sixteen? Seventeen?"

"Seventeen," Kerris said. The casual reference to his deformity had made him tense. "How old are you?"

"Oh, I'm ancient. I'm twenty."

"That's not old," called Riniard from behind her.

"Older than you, scamp!" she retorted.

"By a year, only a year!" Riniard said.

Talking was distracting; Kerris was just as pleased to let others do it. The dwarf pines dwindled at their backs, merging forest with village, village with hills. Now all he could see was steppe. It lay brown and barren on all sides. Except beside the river, the grass was nubby where the sheep had grazed it down. He smelled the earth smell. It was stronger than wine. Cicadas trilled in the grass. A hawk, wings spread, sailed the azure sky from east to west. The road coiled over the plain. They passed farmhouses, sheep, an occasional shepherd, but save for the soaring birds they were the only travelers. Steadily they moved over the flat brown world, attended by the wind and the light.

In late afternoon Kel called a halt. Kerris slid gratefully from Magrita's back. His thighs were sore, despite the protection of the leather, and his arm ached from the back of his neck to his fingertips. He sat in the tall pale grass, working his fingers to get them to uncramp.

Kel and Calwin took the horses to the river. The chearis sat in a circle. The insect murmur, which had paused, resumed.

"I've got blisters on my calluses," said Jensie. She lay flat on her back, head resting in Riniard's lap.

"I've got calluses on my blisters," said Elli.

"Complain, complain," said Riniard, stroking Jensie's hair.

"I'm sick of sleeping in fields," said Jensie. "I like beds."

Kel tramped from the river, Cal at his heels. "You can sleep in a bed when we get to Elath," he said. His boots were muddy. He folded down between Ilene and Kerris. His shirt was open to mid-chest, and the sun glowed along the fine smooth line of his neck. "Here." He tossed a pouch in Elli's lap.

She opened it. "Yum." It was filled with strips of jerky. Taking two, she passed one to Kerris.

"Thanks," he said. Slowly he chewed the salty, pungent meat.

A waterskin went round the circle. When it got to Kerris, it was half full. He lifted it to his lips. It wobbled. Kel steadied it for him. The liquid was tepid but sweet. He passed the skin to Elli.

She hefted it. "You are all pigs."

"There's more in the river," said Riniard. She drank and made a sour face at him.

Arillard lay with his arm over his eyes. Elli poked his ribs, gently. "Hey, old man," she said. "Water."

He stretched out a long arm for the skin and drank silently. He was hound-thin, the tallest of the chearis. There were streaks of gray in his long dark hair.

Cal tossed something—it looked like two bits of stone—into the air, and caught it in his palm. "Want to play?" he said to Elli.

She shrugged. "I'm not in the mood."

Kel said quietly in Kerris' ear, "Are you very sore?"

"No."

"Good."

The music of the water seemed louder. Fumbling for the pack, Kerris took a second sliver of dried meat. He sucked it pliant. The sun was warm, and the grass was softer than straw. He lay back, shading his eyes with his arm. He closed his eyes for a moment.... When he woke, Kel had vanished, and Elli was shaking him. "Wake up," she said. "We have to go on."

He blinked. The sun had moved. His eyes felt crusty. He rubbed them. "I dozed off."

"You did that," Elli said.

Riniard loomed over them. "Sluggards," he said.

"*Yai!*" said Elli. Hooking her ankle around his, she jerked the redhead's leg out from under him. He fell. Kerris yanked his own legs back. Twisting in air, Riniard landed on his side. His right arm slapped the ground. He bounded to his feet.

"Very neat," he said.

"Bah," said Elli. Standing, she extended one hand to Kerris. He gripped it. Her fingers were warm and strong. "Ready?" she said, and without waiting for his answer, pulled him up.

They passed a crossroads and a village. Women with great woven baskets filled with clothes waved at them from the riverside. A cart went rattling by them, piled with peeled logs. The road widened. In places a rock fence separated it from fields and pastures. Kerris wondered where they were. The landscape was still bare, grassy and flat. He asked Elli, "Are we close to Galbareth?"

She shook her head. "Four more days."

They did not rest again. When they stopped, at sunset, Kerris was drooping with exhaustion. His head felt too heavy for his neck, and his back ached. Someone took Magrita's rein out of his tired fingers. He did not resist. Dimly he was aware of lights, people milling around him, the smell of food and of sheep. His boot struck a rock. He stumbled. A hand closed round his upper arm and kept him from falling. It was Kel. His brother released him and patted his shoulder. "Rest soon," he said.

A dark-haired woman in coarse clothes came up to Kel. She bowed, palms pressed together in front of her chest. "May I speak with you for a moment, *skayin*?"

"You mistake," Kel said gently. "I am no teacher. But certainly."

"We need to know how many you are and if there will be room for you in the hall."

"We are seven—no, eight," Kel said. "How large is the hall? Show me." He strode away.

Kerris leaned on a post. The cooking odors made his stomach curl. A dog rushed out of an alley to bark at the strangers. "Hey," said Elli. "Are you all right?"

"Just tired," Kerris mumbled. He straightened. The gray buildings were squat and ugly in the sunset light. "Where are we?"

"It's a town, called Brath. They're going to house us and feed us." She flexed her head on her neck, and stretched her arms till her shoulders popped. A boy came running from the stable. Swerving to avoid the post, he brushed against Kerris. He backed off, eyes wide, mouthing apologies. Kerris thought, He must think I'm part of the chearas!

The hall was dark. It smelled faintly of wine. Kerris sat on a bench. A light flared near him; he shut his eyes. He felt the warmth of a body beside him suddenly and fingers poked him lightly in the ribs. "Hey," Kel said. "Don't go to sleep. You'll miss the fun."

Kerris opened his eyes. Kel had taken off his chaps. "I'm awake."

His brother's long fingers closed softly around his forearm. "Look," he said. He poised their hands side by side. "Look at the pattern." Except for the scars and Kel's hugely thickened wrist, the hands matched, curve for curve, wrinkle for wrinkle, nail for nail.

"Yes," said Kerris.

Kel let him go and leaned back against the wall. He looked

pleased about something and not tired at all. "Elli," he said. Elli glanced up. She was unlacing her riding leathers. "Do I look like Kerris?"

Elli put her head on one side. "You're taller. His hair is darker." She scratched her nose. "But yes, you do look alike."

"But—" Kerris said. "I don't think so."

"Neither of us would be a proper judge," said Kel. "You look like Mother."

"Our mother?"

"Yes. You were three when she died, but I was twelve, and I remember her very well. You have her eyes." He rose. Elli copied him. "You have to watch now," Kel said. Kerris turned his head, following Kel's passage, wondering what it was he had to watch.

The room seemed unaccountably filled with people. Candles burned in iron sconces, throwing shadows everywhere. There was a clear space in the center of the room. The chearis made their circle inside it. Stamp! A boot hit the ground. The floor shivered. Stamp! Kel loosed his hair. Stamp! It cascaded down his back in a gold drape. He touched Ilene. They clasped hands, broke apart, linked, broke, turned—each movement quick and precise as a sword cut, following the stamped-out beat. The other chearis followed, meeting, turning, joining, whirling, making a pattern, a chain of grace, brilliant as a tapestry. Kel linked with Elli, parted, linked with Riniard, fell back from him, met Ilene, followed her. Riniard spun in a fiery circle. Jensie and Elli mirrored each other's movements. Kel leaped between them. Elli linked with Arillard, Calwin teased Jensie to follow him around the swirling pattern, Riniard and Ilene and Kel met and played and leaped—whirled—pulsed—linked—broke— stamped together with a shout—and froze. They stood like statues, breathing hard, fingertips touching, faces and clothing wet with sweat.

All the hairs on Kerris' neck were on end. He was standing. He couldn't remember getting up. The villagers were shouting and stamping their appreciation. The chearis smiled. Kerris started toward them, and then sat down on the floor. His legs were suddenly shaky.

The crowd thinned as Kel strode through it. His fair skin

gleamed with sweat. He put a hand on Kerris' shoulder. "Did you like it?"

"Yes," Kerris said. "Yes, I liked it."

Elli flung herself to the ground beside him. She was breathing in great panting breaths. "Short and sweet and oh, I'm tired," she said. "What did you think, Kerris?"

Kel answered for him. "He's my brother; of course he liked it."

Shyly the villagers came in with plates of food: bread, berries, meat pies, cheese. The chearis crowded to the platters, fighting for the wine. Kel said to Ilene, "That beat can go faster." She bent her head. He drummed his fingers on the floor. Kerris listened to the laughter, awed by the chearis' resilience. He did not comprehend how they could dance after having ridden the whole day over mountains and the steppe. Elli put a chunk of bread in his hand. He ate it without tasting it. His eyes felt filled with sand. He was drowning with weariness.

"Hey, Kel!" It was Riniard, calling over his head.

A hand cupped his chin and lifted it. He blinked into his brother's eyes.

"Tired?" Kel said softly.

"Yes. I'm not used to riding." Kel's hand was warm. He was not used to being touched, either, he thought, but Kel's hands on him felt right. That was silly.

"You need to sleep. Elli, where did you put Kerris' bedroll?"

"In the corner, there," said Elli.

"Is it far?" he asked, like a child.

Kel chuckled. "No," he said, kneeling. "Relax, and I'll take you to it."

An arm slid under his knees. A second arm curled round his shoulders. The world swung dizzyingly. "Hey," he said.

"That's all," said Kel. "Lie still, chelito." Kerris lay quiet, warmed by the word of endearment. . . . Kel pulled his boots off, unlaced his chaps, slipped the knife from his belt. His blanket touched his chin. It smelled like Tornor. Fingers caressed his forehead. *Sleep*, they commanded. Kerris slept.

29

Chapter 3

Kerris was dreaming.

He dreamed that his brother had come to Tornor, and that he, Kerris, had gone with him, away from the Keep. In his dream a voice was singing. *"I am a stranger in an outland country, I am an exile wherever I go...."* The words broke off. Kerris opened his eyes. His clothes were sticky. He turned his head to one side, expecting to see Josen pottering about the tower room. Elli knelt beside him, rolling up her bedroll.

She grinned at him. "Remember us?"

"Uh." He stretched. He ached terribly. "Wuh."

"It's morning. We'll be leaving in a while. Did you hear Ilene singing?"

"Yes." Kerris propped himself up on his elbow. Riniard waved to him across the room. He was carrying two bedrolls, his own and Jensie's. He stumped out the door; Kerris heard him calling.

"Do you remember where you are?" Elli said gently.

"A town." He sat up.

"Brath," Elli said. "This is the village hall." Kerris nodded.

The benches had been pushed back to give the chearis sleeping space. The wooden walls were smooth with wear and age, and they shone like brass. The hall smelled of tallow and wine. "We danced here last night, remember?" Kerris remembered. It was not a dream, then. It was real. He caught his breath, speechless with delight and elation.

Jensie stuck her head through the doorway. "Food outside," she said.

Elli tucked her bedroll under her arm. "I'll save you some." She strode out. Kerris rubbed his face. A spotted cat sat on a bench, washing its face. Someone was still asleep, snoring softly into the folds of a bedroll. Kerris stared at the sleeper. He decided it was Cal. He looked again around the hall, half-expecting the amber walls to dissolve into Tornor's dark gray stone. He felt for his boots and touched the stiff leather of his belt. Lifting it, he felt the weight of the knife Josen had given him. It too was real, no dream. He fumbled it into place. He pulled on his boots and laced his leather chaps around his thighs. The cat leaped from the bench and padded over to Cal. It sniffed his hair. Kerris rolled his blanket into a clumsy ball. With the knife banging lightly against his right thigh, he went to join the chearas.

The chearis stood in their circle around a fire. A dark-haired woman stood with them. Kerris recognized her: she had spoken with Kel the previous night, bowing to him, calling him teacher, skayin. A short man with huge shoulders was talking with Kel. Sausages browned on wooden spits over the flames. Kerris' stomach rumbled. He let his bedroll fall and pressed into the circle between Ilene and Elli.

The short man glanced at him for a moment. Kerris wondered who he was. He wore brown trousers and a cream-colored shirt. A knife swung from his belt. The sheath was worn with handling. The dark-haired woman wore trousers, too, and soft leather boots with no heels. Her face was calm and pleasant. Her gestures were graceful as she turned the spits.

Covertly, Kerris watched his brother. His hair was tied back with the red scarf, and his chin was newly shaven. His hands danced in the air. He mimed drawing a knife. The short man nodded. They were talking fighting, then, or weaponry.

Ilene said, "Kerris, is Calwin still asleep?"

"He was when I left," Kerris said.

"I'll wake him," Ilene said. She left the circle.

Kel looked up. "Kerris. Let me introduce you to our host." Kel nodded at the dark-haired woman. "This is Sura, headwoman of Brath. This is Maroc, Yardmaster." Kerris smiled politely at them, wondering why Kel bothered to introduce him. He was no cheari. "This is my brother."

Sura handed him a spit.

"Thank you," he said. He saw Maroc's dark eyes move from his face to his empty sleeve. Quickly he bit into the sausage. The meat was hot and spicy. Grease ran down the spit and over his chin. "This is delicious," he said.

Sura said, "We are honored by your pleasure. Your dance last night was beautiful."

Elli answered. "Thank you."

"Where do you go now?"

"South," Elli said. "We'll cross Galbareth."

"Do you go by Tezera?"

"No. We'll swing west, around Lake Aruna."

The headwoman nodded. "I know that country."

"Do you know it well?" Elli asked.

"I was born on Lake Aruna." She turned her head. Something winked in her hair. Kerris glimpsed a bronze pin in the shape of a feather. "Excuse me." She left them.

Elli brushed Kerris' arm. "Lake Aruna is beautiful," she said. "Wait till you see it."

Kerris wondered how long it would take to get there. He ate the rest of the sausage. The spice in the meat made his eyes water.

Kel and the Yardmaster clasped hands. Two boys appeared, leading the chearis' horses on a string. "Let's go," said Kel. Picking up his bedroll, Kerris shook the dust from it. Elli mounted Tula and caught hold of Magrita's rein. The black mare stretched her nose toward Kerris and whickered. He scratched her jaw. Her coat shone; she looked vigorous and rested. Kerris fastened his bedroll to the saddle. Mounting, he took the rein from Elli. Sura waved from the steps of the hall.

The villagers watched from their fields as the chearis rode past.

At the boundary marker of the town, Ilene started to sing again.

They rode all morning. The countryside was steppe, bare and flat, broken by farms and barns and fields fenced with stone. Kerris' spine hurt. He wondered what he would feel like after another whole day of riding.

He looked back. The mountains thrust gray peaks into the sky as if they made a wall around the world. Birds wheeled overhead. The sun was warm. He loosened the lacings of his tunic. Magrita's gait was gentle. Slowly he relaxed into the saddle.

"The hills and stars are my companions," Ilene sang. *"And all I do, I do alone."*

"Kerris," said Elli.

"Hmm?"

"How does it feel, to be away from Tornor?"

He said, "It feels good."

They passed a cart loaded with sacks. The driver waved at the chearis. "May the peace of the *chea* be with you!" she called.

"And with you," Kel called back. It was a greeting Kerris had never heard before.

The road grew wider. Parts of it were edged with brick. On one side of it lay fields of trellised vines. Kerris asked Elli what they were. "Grapes," she said. On the other side of the road trees marched in orderly rows, their gnarled boughs thick with white blossoms. "Apple trees," Elli said. Kerris breathed deeply. The blossoms' scent lingered in the air, heady and strong as wine.

At midday they came to a river. It was shallow and swift. A broad, rutted path led to the water's edge. "This is the Narrows," Kel said. "It's shallow here, we can ford it." He led the chearas into the stream. The water was so clear that Kerris could see the bright red and amber stones on the river bottom. The water swirled in lacy ruffles around Magrita's hocks.

They rode up the steep bank. A tall peaked roof appeared ahead of them, and another, and more. Kerris smelled sheep. A cart wheeled by them, laden with bales from which came the unmistakable odor of undyed wool.

They had entered a village. The building with the tallest roof had a sign swinging from a post in front of it. The picture on the sign was of a messenger, dressed in the cloak and lined hood of the green clan. The sign's lettering read: The Green Man.

"It's an inn," said Ilene. "Shall we stop?"

The inn's windows, blue glass set in diamond-shaped frames, sparkled. Riniard said, "They'd have ale."

"I smell onions," Elli said.

Arillard said quietly, "Remember the last inn we stopped at, near Tornor."

"That was an oddity," said Elli. "It wouldn't happen here. Folk in the south are used to us."

Kerris wondered what they were talking about. He glanced at Kel. His brother was frowning.

He remembered the heavy red face of the farmboy who had challenged him. His hands tightened on Callito's rein. "Maybe we shouldn't . . ."

Kerris' vision blurred. He held hard to the pommel of his saddle, fighting the weakness that threatened to pitch him from Magrita's back. I thought it would stop, he thought. I want it to *stop*. Voices babbled at him. Magrita moved uneasily. He fumbled for the rein. The back of his neck was wet, and his head hurt as if it were about to split.

Two hands gripped his shoulders, hard. "Kerris. Kerris." It was his brother's voice. The separation reestablished itself. He caught his breath and lifted his head.

Kel had muscled Callito next to Magrita. "It's all right," he said. "It's over."

So Kel could feel it, too! Kerris pulled himself straight. He said, "I thought—when you came—it would end."

"That's not the way it works," Kel said. "Do you know what it is?"

"No."

"It's called inspeech."

Behind him, Riniard said plaintively, "What is this?"

"Shush," said Ilene.

Inspeech. Kerris said the strange word to himself. "I—I never

35

knew. Josen couldn't tell me what it was. He's a scholar."

Kel said, "He wouldn't know. The name is not well known. Have you ever heard of witches, or witch-gifts? Inspeech is a witch's skill. Our mother Alis had it. You have it from her. Don't be afraid of it."

His voice was gentle as if he were reassuring a child. "I'm not afraid," Kerris said stiffly. "I was surprised."

"I've known for years you were an inspeaker," Kel said. He grinned. "I remember the first time I felt you reach to me. I was making love. I was dumbfounded. I didn't know what had happened. Sefer had to tell me."

Kerris flushed. He had forgotten. He remembered now—lying in his bed in the watchtower, trembling in the aftermath of passion not his own, terrified and confused, not knowing what was happening to his mind or his body. Only later had he come to know that what he had experienced could be had another way, that it had nothing to do with the fits, or with Kel.... He grew conscious of the chearas overhearing every word. "Will it go away?" he said.

"It doesn't usually," Kel said. "It's yours. You can use it or not, as you choose. When we get to Elath you'll understand more. I'll take you to the school."

"Am I—am I a witch?" Kerris said.

Kel patted his arm. "You are."

A dog wandered out to the porch of the inn. Baring its teeth at the strangers, it began to bark. A man with a soiled apron around his waist came out and kicked the animal solidly in the ribs. Yelping, it scrambled from the steps. The aproned man eyed the travelers, smiling broadly. "I've room for eight!" he called.

Ilene said, "Since we're here, let's stop."

"All right," said Kel. He dismounted. Kerris slid from Magrita's back to stand beside him. His spine ached, and his legs felt permanently bowed. Kel touched his shoulder. "Don't worry about it," he said. "We'll talk later." When there are not so many ears to listen, his tone implied.

"Yes," Kerris said.

Kel looked him up and down. "Tired?"

Kerris straightened his back. "Not really," he said.

Kel's nod was approving. "Morven underestimated your endurance."

As they walked toward the inn, Kerris grew aware that Riniard was looking at him oddly. So his friends in the Keep had looked at him, when they pranced off to join the fighting circles, and he could not.... Lifting his chin, he stared back at the redheaded cheari. Riniard looked away, blinking nervously.

I am a witch, Kerris thought.

The innkeeper came down the porch steps. He bowed with his palms pressed together. The top of his head was bald. Kerris thought of the Egg. Did all cooks lose their hair? "Welcome, chearis! You honor us." A tall boy came round the corner of the house. "We will see to your horses. Come in." He beckoned the chearas up the steps. The doors swung inward, hinges squeaking. The room was hot and noisy and smelled of onions. As the chearis walked in, there was a sudden lull in the talk.

The innkeeper covered it. "Welcome to The Green Man. You'll have heard of us on the road, we've a good name. Cora, bring ale!" he called. Kerris gazed curiously at the people at the tables. Dressed in traveling boots and cloaks, they looked very like the folk of Tornor village. The innkeeper led the chearis to a round table and brought chairs for them himself. An aproned girl—his daughter by the look of her—set a pitcher of foamy ale in the center of the table. The innkeeper brought mugs. Ilene poured. Kerris lifted his mug to his lips. The foam made his nose itch. The ale was tart and creamy. When he set the mug down, he found Kel smiling at him across the table.

The smile emboldened him. "That man—at the inn. The one you fought."

"Yes?"

"Did you kill him?"

Kel shook his head. "No. Chearis don't kill."

The food was mutton and onions, served in a savory sauce. The chearis ate quickly. The innkeeper would not accept the coins Kel offered him for the meal. "We are honored by your visit. Come again," he said.

As they rode from the inn, Kerris noticed a youth in the street staring after them, eyes bright with wonder. "Is it always like this?" he said to Elli. "People bowing, and not letting you pay for food?"

"It varies. In the cities folk are less awed by the red clan. And there are always those who think we deserve no honor at all, like that fool in the inn near Tornor, who thought that anyone could be a cheari."

"It wasn't always like this," Ilene said, turning around. "Once dancers had little honor in Arun, and the Yards were only for combat. The chea was unknown, or forgotten. We were more intent upon killing than upon building and learning."

Kerris remembered the thick stone walls of Tornor, holed with arrow slits, and the faded legacy of the tapestries on the walls. "The killing stopped when the chearis came," he said.

Arillard, at the back of the procession, lifted his voice. "Wars stopped," he said. "The killing only lessened."

Elli said in an undertone to Kerris, "Arillard's family, his wife and children, were killed in an Asech raid ten years ago, near Shanan."

Kel said, "There are Anhard soldiers in the city guard at Kendra-on-the-Delta."

"The truce between Anhard and Arun was not made by chearis," said Arillard.

"But it was kept by chearis," said Kel. "We fought Anhard for three hundred years."

"We have fought the Asech for at least that long."

"Border skirmishes," Kel said. "Caravan raids."

The exchange had the feel of an old disagreement. Neither man raised his voice. But Kerris sensed a tension in the chearas that had not been present a moment before.

Ilene said, "Kel holds with the scholars, who say wars ceased in Arun when the armies went home."

Arillard said, "I don't think such distinctions matter—especially not to the dead."

There was a little pause. Kel said, "We all have our dead."

Arillard was gazing down. Kerris could not see his face. He said, "That's true."

A butterfly with orange wings dipped across Magrita's

withers and fluttered into the trees. Kerris thought of his own dead. He supposed he ought to hate the Asech for killing his mother. It was hard to hate a whole people, especially people he had never met.

"There are no more armies in Arun," said Elli. "That dream held."

"Whose dream was it?" Kerris asked.

She hesitated, and then said, "We say it was the vision of the first cheari, that there would be no armies in Arun."

"Who was the first cheari?" He had asked the same question of Josen. He did not expect an answer.

To his astonishment, Elli looked at Ilene. "You tell him."

Ilene stroked the neck of her bay. "This is clan history," she said. "We do not often tell it to outsiders. The first cheari was a warrior and a scholar. His family name has been lost, but we know that he came from Kendra-on-the-Delta."

If Josen could only hear this! Kerris thought.

"He made a home in the Red Hills, and built a village in a valley. The men and women he gathered to him became the first chearis. The valley took his name, and became Van's valley, Vanima."

"I thought it was legend!" Kerris said.

"No," said Ilene. "It's history. Before he died, Van named a successor, and she named hers, and so on. Zayin is sixth in succession to Van, and he still lives in the valley. I don't think he has ever left it. Kel and I trained under him for four years. He named us chearis."

A whip cracked behind them, and they moved to the roadside to let a wagon pass. Riniard said, "Are you still talking about the old man, Ilene? Give over!"

Ilene's lips pressed together. Kel frowned. Elli said, "Riniard's jealous, that's all. He didn't train with Zayin."

Kel said, "Perhaps so. Riniard, would you say that to Zayin's face?"

"Not likely," said the redhead.

"Then don't say it to mine."

There was a small pause. Riniard muttered something that might have been *I'm sorry*. The wagon waddled by them, laden with barrels. The driver called greeting. "May the peace of the chea be on you!" A light wind riffled the trees and a petal floated to Kerris' knee. I am a witch, he thought again. He reached out his forefinger and touched the fragile blossom.

At sunset they forded the second river. "This is Broad Rush," Kel said. The water was indeed broad and swift and it looked very deep.

"Do we swim it here?" Kerris asked, trying not to show how nervous the prospect made him. The water had a flat green hue.

"We don't swim it at all," said Kel. He pointed across the stream. In the red twilight Kerris had to squint. He saw what looked to be a man standing on a large flat rock.... The man waved and cried a cheerful halloo. The rock detached itself from the bank and became a boat, a barge. Swiftly the ferryman poled across the water and brought the barge neatly under the chearis' noses. There were two ferrymen: a tall man and a boy. They were both barefoot. The barge was big, with sides to keep loose cargo from sliding. It was easily big enough for eight people and their horses. The ferrymen threw looped ropes over stumps to hold it fast against the bank.

"Hai, chearis," said the man. He wore a dirty rag twisted around his hair. "You honor my barge."

"Can you take us all in one trip?" said Kel.

"Easily, easily. Hai, it's been busy this day. We took a whole caravan of the blue clan across on their way to the Keeps."

"That was yesterday, Pa," said the boy.

"Was it? So it was. Ai, just bring the beasts on, steadily now."

The chearis dismounted. Kerris took firm hold on Magrita's rein. The wet rocking planks made him nervous. Ilene's bay did not want to move and had to be coaxed on. The barge smelled dank. The ferrymen pulled the ropes from the stumps and pushed off. Water leaked up through cracks in the flooring. Kerris wondered if the others could swim. He watched the dark water swirl past. From the middle of the river it looked much broader than it had looked from the bank. The ferryman talked about the caravan. Kerris wondered if it would eventually arrive in Tornor. He felt a little stab of homesickness for Josen, for Paula, for Tryg. Magrita nudged him, impatient to be away from this odd place, and he stroked her to quiet her. The barge scraped bottom. He tensed. They had reached the other side.

The far bank was steep; they led the horses off one by one onto a rickety wooden dock. It smelled rotten, and the planks were covered with moss.

Punctiliously Kel offered payment. The ferryman waved it away. "Na, na. It's bad luck. Peace to you!"

Night birds called from the fields. Kerris slumped over Magrita's neck, hoping they did not have far to go. The river noise faded. He smelled the perfume of the apple trees, stronger now than in daylight. He wondered why they were still riding in the near-dark. Ahead of him Kel and Ilene consulted in low tones.

Kel pointed. "This way," he called, turning Callito off the path.

In a little while they were sharing food and water round a fire in some farmer's fallow field.

"Fine silks, light silks, who'll buy my silks, scarlet ribbons, blue ribbons, gold thread, silver thread, light silks, fine silks, who'll buy, come buy...."

"Tough pots, see my pots, no scars, no stains, no dents, no cracks, copper pots, iron pots, stone pots, clay pots, come see...."

"Fresh fish, river fish, silverbacks, trout, carp, red eels, mudfish, fresh fish, come see, who'll buy my fish...."

"Fine ale, red wine, white wine, sweet wine, come taste, come smell, come see, fine pots, light silks, no stains, no scars, red eels, fresh fish, gold thread, come see, come taste, who'll buy...."

The crossroads was jammed. Kerris tightened his knees on Magrita's smooth sides. Everywhere he looked, and down the road as far as he could see, were caravans, with throngs of people ringing them round, and men and women shouting, each calling the virtues of their wares. The smell of fish frying steamed in the hot air, mingling with the scents of men and horses and wine. The caravans gleamed blue, their wood freshly painted, ribbons rippling in the breeze.

A woman tugged at Kerris' foot. "Fine grapes, new grapes,

pennies a bunch—" He shook his head and urged Magrita onward, trying to stay at Callito's back. He had never seen so many people in one place. He saw a tall man swinging a long bladed sword for an admiring crowd, a woman with bells on her wrists and ankles dancing on a piece of red cloth, a juggler spinning plates on sticks, a man with smoke, blue smoke, coming smoothly out of his mouth.... Callito paused. Kerris drew Magrita up beside the big red horse.

"Where are we?" he shouted.

Kel grinned. "This is the Tezera crossroads. That way"—he swung his arm east—"leads to the city. The whole Tezera road, from here to the city gates, is lined with traders and players of all sorts. Here." He tossed a coin to a woman tending a stall. She flung something up to him. He caught it and passed it to Kerris.

It was a fruit of some kind, with a hard green rind around it. Kerris tore the rind away with his teeth. He sucked at the fruit. It was pulpy and tart. He spat a seed toward the ground.

Kel was watching him. "Like it?"

"Yes."

Kel bought a bag. "They're better than water when you're thirsty," he said.

The merchants' chants—*"fine ale, white wine, come taste, red eels, no dents, fine silks, who'll buy"*—made Kerris' head rock. He sucked some more of the pulpy fruit through the hole in the rind. He looked around for the others. Ilene was behind him. Elli and Cal were watching the juggler. Riniard was over under a blue canopy, near the man with the smoke coming out of his mouth.

"What's that?" Kerris said, pointing toward the man with the sword. "What's he doing?"

Kel laughed. "He's showing off. He's from Anhard."

Magrita's ears went back and she snorted. Kerris grabbed the rein. A dark-haired woman with rings in her ears slid past. "Sorry," she said. She wore a scarf of red and mottled gold around her neck. The scarf moved. It was a snake.

Kerris said, "That woman has a snake on her head."

"She's from one of the Asech tribes," said Kel.

Kerris swung round to stare at the woman, but she had vanished. Involuntarily his left hand went to his stump. His rein

42

lifted. Obedient to the signal, Magrita stood still. Kerris dropped his hand, but not before Kel turned and saw it.

He pointed in the direction the woman had taken. "There's an Asech tent over there. You can see the poles sticking out of the top." His voice was casual but clear.

Kerris craned his head, but could not see through the press of riders. He was not sure what a tent looked like, anyway.

Kel went on. "The Asech live in tribes, in groups, and each group does what it wants. That woman comes from a tribe that trades with Tezera. They bring their goods all the way up the River Road in caravans, just like the traders. We've probably never had to fight them. I don't think they carry weapons. Then there are other tribes, who never come out of their hills except to make war."

Kerris' mouth was dry. He licked his lips. "Their swords are curved," he said.

"When they wear them, yes," Kel said.

"How can we trade with them and fight them, too?" Paula had told him what the swords looked like, so different from the straight weapons of the north.

Kel said, "We trade with some of them. They do not know the chea. They are not one people, as we are."

"What do we sell them?" Kerris asked.

"Pots, cloth, choba oil, leather goods."

"What do they sell us?"

"Herbs, spices, dyes. Horses."

Kerris touched Magrita's neck. He remembered that Riniard had said she was part desert stock.

"You fought them," he said to his brother.

"Yes," Kel said. "I fought them six years ago, and ten years ago. I was in the border guard. Arillard was my captain."

"He hates them, doesn't he?"

"He tries not to," said Kel.

"Do *you* hate them?"

Memory and pain moved in Kel's eyes. "I did," he said. He looked at the place where Kerris' right arm had been.

Finally they left the crossroads. The chearis had scattered all over the market and it took some time for them to meet again.

Jensie had bought a tunic with silver braid down the side seams. She insisted they stop while she put it away.

Kel sat Callito, frowning.

"Hey," Ilene said, "what's wrong with you?"

"I want to reach Lake Aruna before nightfall," he said.

"Well," Ilene said, "you don't have to look so fierce about it." Kel didn't answer her. Kerris wondered if their conversation about the Asech had anything to do with Kel's ill temper. When the chearas reformed into its lines, he fell back to ride with Elli. She looked at him curiously but did not speak.

They halted once to let the horses rest. The road remained crammed with travelers. Riniard walked back and forth, commenting on the passing scene, but the rest of the chearas was silent, affected by Kel's mood. Grim, he sat by the side of the road, plucking grass stems.

The sky turned bright blue. Clouds like feathers, tinged with lavender and rose, made translucent patterns on the horizon. The traffic halted altogether. "One side! One side!" voices bawled. The chearis pressed against each other.

"What is it?" said Elli.

Kerris turned from side to side. All he could see was a rocking sea of wagons and fluttering indigo ribbons. Kel's hand closed on his shoulder. Startled, Kerris looked up.

His brother's face was smooth, no longer troubled. "There," he said. "See the green?" Kerris stared. He saw—or thought he saw—a green flag. Kel was taller than he and could see more. Suddenly the people ahead of him shifted. He saw a rider on a dark horse, wearing a green cloak, carrying a green banner.

"Yes."

"That's a messenger for the Council at Tezera from the Houses in Kendra-on-the-Delta."

With the passage of the courier, traffic began to move again. Kel patted Kerris' wrist. "Ride with me." Kerris moved Magrita up beside Callito. "Here." Kel tossed him another of the hard green fruits.

Riniard pulled out of line. His horse went into a canter. "Meet you at the lake," he shouted. A sunset haze shimmered in the west. Riniard's red hair blazed in the light. He disappeared around the road's curve. Kerris wondered how far they'd traveled that day. Ahead of them a yellow wagon pulled to the roadside. Children tumbled from it, shouting. Kerris patted Magrita's neck. Her proud head drooped.

"Will we camp soon?" he said.

Kel said, "We'll camp at the lake." They plodded by another wagon. Somewhere out of sight, a woman was singing. Voices called to them, inviting and gay. Kerris saw flames, and smelled the distinctive odor of peat. The firelight reflecting off smiling faces made him aware of his own aches and pains. He straightened in the saddle. The sky was blazing red in the west.

"Soon," Kel said, out of the dusk. They rounded a bend. Kerris gasped.

A sheet of gold spread out on their left, tranquil, unmarred, a brilliant glaze of fire reaching to the edge of the horizon and beyond. . . . Over it a few stars glowed. A crescent moon splayed its horns overhead. Elli exclaimed, an oath too faint to catch. Kerris closed his eyes. When he opened them, the lake was still there, no end to it. A heron called from somewhere. He looked at the horned moon. It too reflected flame: its configurations shone more copper than white.

Elli said, "That's worth coming all this way for."

Riniard said, "Well, you made it!" He swaggered out under the shade of one of the droopy trees that lined from the lakeshore. "I've found us a resting place." Kerris dismounted. He felt Elli take his arm and turn him toward the water. Arillard was already kneeling beside a pile of sticks, hands busy with flint and wool. Ilene and Jensie rubbed the horses down. Sparks drifted in the night air. One fell past Kerris' head, and he saw it was a winged creature with light in its tail. It spiraled slowly upward and vanished into the evening.

Kel passed the bag of fruit around. Kerris stretched his legs out toward the leaping flames. Ilene sat cross-legged, back straight, just touching the stump of a log. The sunset light gleamed off her brown skin like rain.

Riniard was laughing loudly, teasing Jensie about her shirt.

"Rini, will you shut up, please?" said Elli.

He frowned at her, sulky. "Why the hell should I?"

45

Elizabeth A. Lynn

"Because I asked you to," said Elli. "Be still, look at the lake."

Ilene said, "Feel the chea, Riniard. It lives here. You can talk to Jensie any time."

"If I can talk to Jensie any time then I can talk to her now," said Riniard. He pulled Jensie into the crook of his arm. "Can't I, love?"

She brushed his lips with her hand. "We can talk later," she said peaceably.

"Riniard." There was an odd note in Kel's voice. It brought Kerris' head up.

"What?"

Kel rose, and stepped around the fire to where Riniard sat. Suddenly there was tension in the air. Jensie pulled out of the crook of Riniard's arm. The heron called again, a screech like an ungreased iron hinge. . . . "Did you buy anything at the bazaar?" Kel said.

"Like what?" Riniard sounded sulky and defiant, like a child caught out in a lie. "Jen bought a shirt."

"You went ahead of us," said Kel. "And you're talking too loud, and you're being quarrelsome." In a movement too swift for Kerris to follow, Kel bent and when he straightened Riniard was standing, too, with both Kel's hands fisted in his shirt. "I can smell it. I thought I smelled it when we rode in but I wasn't sure." He dropped his hands. Riniard staggered. "Your reflexes are slow and you can't keep your balance worth shit. You've been smoking heavenweed."

Riniard took a step backward. "Yes," he said.

Kel hit him. The slap rocked Riniard's head back. He brought both hands up reflexively and Kel caught his wrists. "Rini, what's the matter with you? You promised you'd stop!"

"Let me go," Riniard said. Kel let him go. Riniard sat down. After a moment he sighed and shook himself like a cat waking. He touched his cheek. "It's been six months," he said, folding his arms around his drawn-up knees. "There's only us here, so I knew I couldn't get into any—trouble. It was only a little, Kel, there's no harm done."

"You broke a promise," said Kel, standing over him, hands on hips.

Riniard scowled. "So I broke a promise. Have you never broken a promise?"

Ilene drew a quick breath. Kel glanced at her, and then at Kerris. "Yes," he said softly. "I have." He knelt beside Riniard. "Give it to me."

Riniard fumbled a packet out of a hip pocket. Kel tossed it on the fire. The flames flared crimson for an instant. A sweet, heavy smell filled the air. Riniard's face twisted for an instant, and then relaxed.

"Will you promise not to buy more?" said Kel.

Riniard looked down at the ground. "I promise not to buy more," he said. He looked up. "Kel, I'm sorry."

Kel ruffled the redhead's hair. "No matter." He went back to where he had been sitting and pulled his blanket around him. "I'm going to sleep," he announced. "I want to get an early start in the morning."

Kerris watched as the chearis settled themselves for sleep. The stars burned their patterns into the sky; the night was windless and warm. He had understood very little of the scene he'd just witnessed. What was heavenweed? He felt left out, isolated, a stranger.

He rolled over to his right side to find Elli watching him, the whites of her eyes brilliant as stars in the firelight. She lifted an inquiring eyebrow, and then jerked her head in the direction of the horses. In a moment, Kerris understood. He rose, and began to pick his way toward the silhouetted animals. Elli followed him.

They shared a drink of water from a waterskin. "What's heavenweed?" Kerris asked.

"It's leaves of a plant, like tea leaves, except that you don't drink it, you smoke it. You put it in a pipe or roll it in a paper and breathe it in."

"What does it do to you?"

"It's nice, sort of dreamy and pleasant. It does slow you down. Most chearis won't touch it, except at feasts or festivals. But it makes Riniard quarrelsome, mean as a snake. When he first rode with us, he would fight all the time, with anyone. The heavenweed does that to him. It's too bad, because he likes it.

When he joined us, he swore not to smoke it. I guess it's hard, to give it up."

"I suppose," Kerris said.

"Is that what was bothering you?" said Elli.

"Yes. Thank you."

She grinned. "No trouble." They went back to the fire. Elli was quieter in the woods than he. He lay in the cocoon of blanket. He wondered what heavenweed tasted like. He wondered how Elli had known his feelings. He wondered what promise Kel had broken. He wondered if he could ask.

Josen, he thought, the world is wider than you ever told me it was. The thought left him just a little frightened. For a moment Tornor seemed a haven, a place of peace.... He could not go back, he knew that.

Away by the lake, a heron called, like a horn blaring a tuneless challenge into the darkness.

Chapter 4

At dawn the sky was gray as ice.

The lake was still, except at the shore, where it rippled lazily against the sandy bank. The air was moist and chill. There were dewdrops on Kerris' blanket. He shook it awkwardly and folded it into a shapeless lump. He put on shirt, breeches, boots. He wrestled his wool tunic on over his head. The wool was damp and it stank. He ran his hand through his hair; it came away moist. His arms prickled with cold-bumps.

Elli came to the clearing. "Hey," she said. Kerris blinked. She was stark naked. "Aren't you coming in the water?"

Now he heard the splashes and the laughter from the lakeside. "No. I can't swim." It was not true; he could swim, though not well. He tugged a fold of the tunic straight.

"It's shallow. You can wade."

He hated taking his clothes off in front of strangers. "I just dressed. It's too much work to do it all again."

Disappointment was plain on her face. "As you like. Brr, it's too cold to stand around. I'm going in." She whirled and ran toward the lake. Her hair blew back as she moved. Her body looked all of one piece, like something carved but living. She had a white line, a scar, on her right hip.

Kerris heard a monstrous splash, and Jensie laughing. His bladder was full. He unbuckled his belt and went around a tree to piss. As he came back to the clearing he glimpsed the swimmers. They had made a circle with Elli in the middle; they were playing some sort of game. Kel's hair was tied on top of his head in a knot. Jensie's was braided and tied with her red scarf. Elli lunged at Kel and he slid away from her, agile as a river eel. He was laughing. Elli fell flat on the water. The water leaped upward in a silver spray.

A twig snapped. Kerris turned swiftly. Cal was coming up behind him. They stood to watch the swimmers. Cal's dark thick hair was standing up on his head. He smoothed it down with both hands. "Foolishness," he said. "If the chea had meant for us to swim, we would all have been born with gills."

The swimmers had ceased playing. Jensie was out of the water. Where her clothes had screened her from the sun, her skin was milk-white. It made the brown of her face and arms and throat darker. She had freckles across the tops of her breasts. She looked angry. Riniard called to her. She did not turn.

On the horizon the sun was showing over the rim of water, gilding it. Kel strode up the bank. He too looked all of a piece, and he moved like the wind. The rising sun turned the droplets on his shoulders to diamond. He stretched, long in the light. The muscles jumped in his thighs and across his groin. His body hair was thick there. Ilene came behind him and caught his wrists, pinning them behind his back. He took a step forward and then whirled. One hand was free. Ilene bent, anticipating the counterthrow. Holding hands, they walked up the beach.

Kerris' pulse jumped in his throat. He took a long deep breath, as if the sweet damp air by the lake had suddenly grown thin. His cheeks felt hot as wax.

At the clearing something was evidently amiss. Riniard was sulking. He saddled the horses, his face hang-dog, stealing looks at Jensie, who scowled and would not look his way.

As Jensie passed Kerris she put a hand flat on his chest. "Ride with me today," she said.

"But—"

"Please."

He shrugged.

A light steam rose from the lake as they left it. They rode through a bed of feathery curling plants that Kerris had never seen before. They looked woven, like cobwebs or lace. He asked Jensie what they were called. "Ferns," she said. "I don't know what kind."

"Thank you." Kerris felt strange. He was very conscious of Riniard riding behind him.

Jensie said, "Can you really not swim?"

"Not very well."

"We'll teach you when we get to Elath."

We—that meant all of them. For a moment Kerris envied that easy "we" of the chearas. Jensie looked very young, scarcely old enough to be a cheari. "Have you been to Elath before?" he asked.

"Last year. We were there for the summer harvest. There were six of us then."

A red fox whisked across the path, brush tail flying. It grew hot. Kerris took off his tunic. "Where are we going today?" he said.

Jensie said, "Into Galbareth."

A rider cantered past them: a girl, black braids streaming behind, riding bareback on a big roan gelding. Voice a treble note, she called greeting to the chearas. The road lifted; they went up a gentle rise, and halted on the summit.

Kerris shivered with excitement. Before them lay the wide green and gold heartland of Arun, the Galbareth Fields, stretching like wings on each side of the Great River. He looked down. Haze overlay the grainfields. Angular roofs broke the stunning monotony of fields—barns, storerooms, stables, and homes. Far to the west, a windmill lifted stubby arms. The road wound into the dust and vanished in it.

Kel said, "Kerris, do you remember?"

"Remember?"

"You've seen it before."

"No," Kerris said. "I have no memories of that journey."

51

Cal moved round the others to take a place in front, riding next to Kel. He lifted his voice so that they could all hear. "We have to stay together. It's easy to get lost in the grainfields. Riniard and I were born here, but the rest of you are strangers. Galbareth doesn't like strangers. Keep your horses from foraging, and do no hurt to beast or folk." The chearis nodded gravely. Kerris looked behind. The mountains were gone. He felt a tremor of panic, as if the earth itself had trembled. Clenching his knees, he patted Magrita's arched neck.

"Why are we going this way?" he said to Jensie. "Why not stay by the river?"

"If we took the river way we'd have to dance at every village between Tezera and Elath. This is faster." She sounded subdued. A light hum, barely audible, lifted out of the grainfields like a voice. Kerris thought, It's the wind in the wheat. Tall stalks on either side of the path sang and whispered. The wind bent them down in great rhythmic sweeps, like the strokes of a giant's hand.

"Let's go," said Cal.

They descended into the gold ocean. The land seemed barely to notice them, yet Kerris had a sense that they were under scrutiny. In Tornor he had heard merchants talk of the Galbareth as if it were a living thing. He had not understood it. He did now. They passed horses, cropping grass in a field left bare. The animals lifted their heads and gazed after the riders with liquid eyes. Crows flew over them, and, higher in the indigo sky, hawks wheeled in deadly hunting circles. Colorful ribbons fluttered from poles. They passed two women, straw-hatted, gowned. The nearer of the two straightened to watch them go. Her face was sun-browned and her eyes were black as a crow's wing. She spoke no greeting.

Thunderheads began piling up in the west in the afternoon. The wind picked up. Slate gray and amethyst, the clouds rolled at them. The chearis halted to consult. Cal looked worried. "I doubt we'll find shelter," he said. "Buildings in Galbareth have a habit of moving about, so that farms you thought were right at your elbow are two fields away."

"Perhaps the storm will rain itself out before it reaches us," said Elli.

"We're riding into it," Cal pointed out.

They went on. The sky darkened. Drops of rain oozed from the sky, as if squeezed through a cloth. Lightning leaped from cloud to cloud. The horses quivered at the approaching thunder. Kerris laced his tunic tight about his throat. The grain hissed, a frightening, malicious sound. Something scuttled across the roadway under the hooves of Jensie's steed. It bucked and she swore at it.

"Stop." It was Ilene. She pointed southwest. "The wind bent the grain—I thought I saw a space. It could be a barn."

"It could be an illusion," said Cal. He looked at Riniard. The redhead shrugged, biting his lower lip. "How far away was it?"

"Not far," Ilene said. "There's a path to it." She pointed to a break in the lines of wheat. A narrow path led to the right.

Cal, Kel, and Riniard talked. Finally, Cal led them off the main road to the narrower way. Roused, Galbareth spat dust at them, like an immense cat waked from sleep.

The horses balked, and had to be led. Single file they tramped through the grain. Dust flailed at their eyes and rasped in their throats. Lightning jumped over them. The very air smelled scorched and burned.

"Here!" called Calwin. Kerris led Magrita out of the punishing lash of stalks. He looked around for a barn, but there was no barn, only earth, and some scraps of wood heaped in a circular clearing.

The storm broke.

The rain was cold. They shivered under it. Kerris heard Jensie swear. He crouched beneath the wet. The world dissolved, changed, and blurred away. He was lost in a country he did not know, and the people around him were insubstantial as shadows, ghosts—strangers. He did not know them. He did not know where he was. He was small, and alone. The mountains had vanished and he was lost without them. His hand cramped painfully on Magrita's rein. He was afraid. He was afraid.

He heard his name being called, and ignored it. He did not know these people. He did not want to come out.

"Kerris!"

"What's wrong with him?"

"Kerris, listen." He turned his face away. The voice followed him. *Listen*. It was Kel's voice, ringing inside his mind. *It will pass. Don't fight it. We are here. You know us. We care about you, chelito, don't run from us. We're your friends.*

Kel's hands were firm on his shoulders, holding him, and his voice was clear, inescapable, and unshakable as the mountains. Kerris' vision blurred and cleared in waves. He waited for the waves to stop.

His mind felt bruised. He looked into his brother's face. "What—" His mouth was dry as the dust. The chearis ringed him, watchful and silent as cats.

"Get some water," Kel said. Someone moved and came back with a waterskin. Kerris tried to hold it but his arm shook. Kel lifted it to his lips. The water smelled of leather. Kerris drank until his belly filled. Kel gave the waterskin to Elli. His left hand rested still on Kerris' shoulder. "Better?" he said.

"Better. Yes." Kerris could barely talk. HIs head throbbed. "I heard you—"

"Inspeech is not my skill," Kel said, "but I have learned a little of it from Sefer and you have no barrier to keep me out. I hope I didn't hurt you, chelito."

Elli knelt. She put one hand on his knee. "Kerris, are you all right?"

It took effort for him to turn his head her way. His neck ached. His headache dulled. "I think so." He looked at Kel again. "I *was* frightened," he said.

"It's no big thing," Kel said gently. "What frightened you?"

"The space..." He gestured toward the vast, fluid land. He tried to stand. Kel brought him upright with an arm around his back. His muscles creaked. The storm had stopped. The sky gleamed lavender and blue. The last of the thunderheads was hurrying ponderously east.

"We should have talked before," Kel said. "How does your head feel?"

"Tired," Kerris said. His hair and clothes were soaked. The seat of his pants was muddy.

"Can you ride?"

He lifted his chin, conscious of the chearis listening. "I can ride."

Kel smiled warmly at him. "Good." He turned. "Cal, find us shelter. Kerris needs a roof over his head tonight, and we could all do with a bed."

"I'll try," said Calwin. His hair was up on end again.

"I'm sorry—"

"No," said Kel. "Don't say it." His grip was a hug. "It's my fault, if anything. You should have been at Elath, among your own kind, five years ago. Come now, let's leave this place." Letting Kerris go, he strode to Callito. Riniard was holding Magrita's rein. Kerris took it from him. The rain had washed the dust from the air, and the wheatfields steamed with a heavy, pleasant odor.

You should have been among your own kind five years ago.

Somewhere in the south he had family—even friends. His head throbbed. The edges of the world vibrated alarmingly. He wondered how far they would have to ride to shelter.

Not far. His brother's voice was gentle in his mind. Cal was leading the way back to the main road. Ribbons fluttered on a pole in the middle of a field. At the back of the line, Ilene was singing. Kerris touched his heels to Magrita's sides. The black mare quickened her pace.

The village Cal found was small, smaller than Brath, and it appeared so suddenly out of the fields that Kerris imagined it had grown there in response to Kel's demand. As the chearas rode into it, Kerris picked out a stable, a pigpen, a well with a peaked wooden roof.... The buildings were of wood, too, but their roofs were thatch. He smelled chickens. He counted six houses and one building that looked as if it was used for storage. The rhythmic pounding of metal on metal betrayed a smithy. The street was largely empty. The ground was wet, puddled in places from the storm, but drying fast. Three women swayed by, with baskets on their heads, their backs straight as arrow shafts. They held the baskets easily in place with one hand. Their skirts fell to midcalf. One of the women wore sandals with leather laces that went up past her hem. The hem of all three skirts was

trimmed in gold thread. The other two women were barefoot.
The apparition of eight strangers in their midst seemed not to
interest them at all. One woman turned her head, without
breaking stride, to glance with casual curiosity at the chearas.

They halted in the middle of the street. "Where is the—" Elli
began, and then fell silent, at Cal's gesture. A woman appeared
on a doorstep, moving so quietly that Kerris was startled. She
had a smooth, unlined face. Her hair was long and streaked with
gray, and she wore it down her back, as young girls did at
Tornor. A small colorful triangle of fabric was pinned to her
hair. Her gown was brown and gold. She was barefoot, and the
skin on her arms (which were also bare) was almost as dark as
Elli's.

"I am—headwoman—of this village," she said, hesitating
over the word headwoman as if she did not use it often. "It's
seldom we see travelers here, and more rare that those travelers
are chearis. Where do you come from, and where do you go?"

"We are not lost, *damisen*," said Cal. "We were caught in the
storm, and we beg shelter."

"You are of us," said the woman to him.

"I am. My village is east of the River." He did not say its
name, and she did not ask.

"And the rest?" She looked at each of them in turn. Her eyes
were dark, like Paula's.

Kel said, "I am Kel of Elath."

"Ilene of Elath."

"Elli of Mahita."

The woman raised her hands. "That is enough." Her eyes
lingered on Kel. "From Elath—the witch town."

"Yes."

"How long do you wish to stay here?"

"One night," Kel said.

"That is well. Wait a moment, if you please." She returned to
the house she had emerged from. In a little while she came out.
She pointed across the square to a house that looked like all the
others, except for a symbol on its door, a design of beads in a
circle. "The place is vacant now, and you are welcome to stay in
it," she said.

Riniard muttered something. The woman looked at him, eyes narrowed. "You know what house that is?"

"Yes," he said.

"You are of the fields."

"Ye, damisen," said Riniard.

"Where is thy village?"

"In the west, damisen," Riniard said.

The woman made a little gesture with her right hand. Riniard returned it. She nodded. "You are welcome," she said. "Enter." She opened the door. Kerris climbed wearily from Magrita's back, unlacing his bedroll.

"You may leave your mounts in our hands. Please put your boots on the left side of the hall. There is a place for them."

The hallway was dark and sweet-smelling as an herb garden. There were rushes on the floor. Obediently the chearis pulled their boots off and lined them up in the alcove on the left side of the hall. The circular symbol from the door was repeated on both walls of the hallway.

Riniard whispered something to Cal, who spread his hands. The redhead scowled. He looked unhappy. From the alcove the hall led to a room. One half of the room had pallets. The other held a brick stove, and a wooden tub.

"If you're hungry," the woman said, "there is food in the refectory. That is the building across from this. If you need something, you may ask for me. My name is Tamis."

She left them. The door closed. With a sigh, Ilene began to strip off her clothes. Kerris counted the pallets. There were six. Riniard and Jensie would share, and two others. . . . He dropped his bedroll. He noticed a crock of choba oil under a window, with two shallow dishes beside it.

A knock sounded.

Kel opened the door. The woman handed him a bowl. "Be refreshed," she said. Green stalks poked out of the bowl, their tops leafy, like ferns.

"What is this house?" Jensie said. She shook her hair out, and put her hands on her hips. "Does someone live here?"

"No," said Cal. "This is the birthing house."

"A house for birthing?" Jensie turned in a circle. "It's

pleasant," she said. "Why does it bother *you* so much?" she said
to Riniard.

He was taking off his tunic, and did not seem to hear.

She stepped in front of him. "Answer me."

"I thought you weren't talking to me," he said.

"I'm talking to you now."

Riniard scowled. "In my village strangers are not permitted
in the birthing house, especially not men." He sat on a pallet.

Kel said, "Jen, let him be."

"But this house is not in use, or Tamis wouldn't have put us
here. What difference does it make?"

Arillard said mildly, "It makes a difference to Riniard.
Customs differ."

Ilene took off her shirt and threw it on the floor. "Must we
quarrel?" she said.

"No," Kel said. "Jensie, be still. Ilene, look." He pushed the
bowl at her.

She glanced at the leafy greenstuffs, and grinned. *"Fetuch!"*
Choosing a stalk from the bowl, she took a bite of the leafless
end. "Kerris, taste it."

Kerris sniffed. "What is it?"

Kel took a stalk and handed it to Kerris. "Have some."

Kerris nibbled the piece. The green weedy stuff crunched
between his teeth. It was good, but odd. He took a second bite
and gave the stalk to Kel. Sitting on the pallet, he took off his wet
and muddy shirt. As he pulled his spare shirt from the bedroll, he
realized that he had forgotten to bring a second pair of pants.

"Here," said Elli. She threw a pair of cotton pants onto his
lap. "Wear mine."

"Thanks." He put the dry clothes on. It still made him feel
strange to dress and undress in the presence of strangers, but he
pretended not to care.

Cal gathered the muddy clothes and blankets into his arms.
"Give them all to me, I'll wash them," he said. Kerris felt his
blanket and his wool tunic. They were both damp. He handed
them to Cal. He lay down. His arm ached, and he was so worn he
could barely keep his eyelids open.

The chearis wiped their weapons. Kel sheathed his knife and

started to scrape his chaps clear of mud. Ilene sat beside him. "It'll be good to sleep on a bed," she said. "This reminds me of home, you know."

Kel grunted.

"Don't look so sour. It's two days' ride; we'll be there soon."

The warm clothes were gentle on Kerris' bare skin. He smiled at the ceiling. He was very glad to be indoors.

Kel said, "I wish we were there now." He sounded grim.

The scraper noise checked and resumed. "Why?"

Kerris closed his eyes. He didn't want to listen.

"I feel a break in the pattern," Kel said. "Something's wrong."

Ilene said, "A big thing, or a small thing?"

"I. Don't. Know." The words seemed to keep time to the scraping rhythm. Kerris put his arm over his eyes. "I. Don't. Know. What. It. Is."

Just before sunset, Tamis came for them.

She brought them to the refectory, which turned out to be a common eating hall, like the hall at Tornor, attached to a kitchen. It had twenty round wooden tables in it. Shallow dishes filled with choba oil spread light across the tables. At the back of the hall was the serving window from the kitchen. Cal went to it. He brought back a platter heaped with food: soup, bread, cheese, ham, fetuch. There were long curling string-like things in the soup. Kerris did not know what they were. Softly, he asked Cal.

"They're made of wheat paste. They're called noodles."

The villagers paid little attention to their guests. Children ran up and down the long room, calling to one another. Kerris glimpsed a woman with smoke coming from her mouth. A sweet smell eddied through the hall.

"Hello."

Kerris looked around, and then down. A child stood at his knee, staring at him. He had a dark face, dark eyes, and long black hair which looked as if it had never been cut, or even combed.

"Hello," Kerris said.

The boy's brown shirt was decorated with scarlet thread. "What's your name?" he said. He did not seem very old.

"Kerris."

He walked all around the table and returned to Kerris' side. He tilted his head. "Where's your arm?"

Kerris' skin prickled. He said, "It got cut off a long time ago, when I was a baby."

The child digested this. His forehead wrinkled. "Who did it?"

"It was an accident," Kerris said.

"Did it hurt?"

"I don't know. I can't remember."

"Can I touch it?"

Elli, beside Kerris, took a breath.

Kerris said, "Surely." Gently he turned on the stool and pushed his dangling right sleeve back with his left hand.

The child ran light fingers over the scarred end of the stump. He patted it. "Bye," he said. At the other tables the adults were watching, faces impassive. Kerris let the sleeve drop.

Tamis came out of the shadows. "Are you comfortable?" she asked.

"Yes, thank you," said Kel.

She ran a hand over the child's thick hair. "That is well. You must forgive our children; they see so few strangers. This is Pito, my sister's son." She pushed him gently. "Go thou, chelito." A woman's voice called and the boy ran toward it. "I have a favor to ask of you, chearis. This village is small, as you see, too small to have a Yard. We use our knives for skinning and cutting, and our young folk learn to milk and plant and weave, not fight. But some of them have ridden to other villages, to learn what they can about the chearis' art. Would you speak with them?"

"We would be pleased to," Kel said. He smiled. "We were all young once. Are they here? Ask them to join us."

The woman spoke rapidly in the old language. Nobody moved. Then slowly the young folk began to make their way to the chearis' table. Kerris counted them, six, seven, eight, ten. Dark-eyed, with dark hair, they stood shyly in a clump. Two of the girls and three of the boys wore knives.

"You don't have to be afraid of us," said Kel. "We won't bite."

Kerris watched them approach with a tightening feeling in his stomach. He did not want to sit while the chearis talked fighting.

Elli indicated the sheath of one of the knives. "That looks like Tezeran work," she said. "Is the knife Tezeran, too?" The girl who wore it nodded. "So is mine." She drew her own knife. Its blade glittered. "I got it from my mother when I was sixteen, a gift. It was made in Varin's smithy, though I doubt Varin himself ever touched it. Would you like to hold it?" She held it out, hilt foremost.

"Oh, yes," the girl breathed.

"Let me see yours." The girl drew her own knife. "Yes, that is a fine blade. You take good care of it, I see. Lay it on the table. Here." The girl laid her own knife on the table and took Elli's from her hand. Arillard was showing one of the boys how to get out of a wrist grip. Jensie had taken off her scarf, and was demonstrating to three of the boys how she tied it.

Kel's hand fell on Kerris' shoulder. "Come," he whispered. He nodded toward the door. Awkwardly Kerris freed himself from the table.

As they walked from the refectory, an owl hooted. The fields rippled softly to the wind's caress. Kerris looked up. The crescent moon sailed the sky like a boat. He picked out the star-figures Josen had taught him to see: the red Eyes, the brilliant, curling Tail. He watched Kel out of the corner of one eye.

Kel said, quietly, "I didn't think you were comfortable in there. Did I do wrong?"

The question was disarming. Kerris' stomach stopped tying itself into knots. "I wasn't. Thank you."

"Let's sit," Kel suggested. He felt the grass. "It's dry." They sat. The murmur of the voices in the refectory reached them, a wordless sound. Kel took something from his pocket. It was a wine bottle. He drank, and held it out. Kerris imitated him.

"Is your head still tired?" Kel asked.

"No." Kerris handed back the wine. He wiped his mouth.

"Then speak to me," said Kel. "Not with words. Use inspeech, as I did this afternoon."

"I don't know how," said Kerris.

"Have more wine." Kel shoved the bottle into his hand. Kerris drank. His throat tingled. "Now reach to me with your thought."

"I can't—"

"You can," Kel said. He touched Kerris' shoulder. "You've been doing it for four years, Kerris. Do it now. Try."

The wine burned in Kerris' blood. He took a breath. He thought, What if my mind were a hand, how would I move it . . . ? The sky blurred. The earth spun. He was suddenly inside Kel's head, looking out at a slim, dark-haired, one-armed stranger. . . . That's me! he thought, and at the same time felt the press of other thoughts, not his own—*He did it; he's going to be good, as good as Sefer; how pleased Sef will be!*—and the image of a slender, white-haired man with eyes like green ice played across his consciousness.

He shuddered, and went back into his own head with a jolt.

Kel was holding his shoulders. The wind on his cheek was warm. He leaned on his palm, waiting for the world to coalesce. It did. He looked into his brother's face. "Was that what you wanted?"

"That was exactly what I wanted," said Kel. "You can do it deliberately, Kerris, it doesn't have to happen by accident! It's your gift, you can control it. I wanted to show you." He dropped one hand, but kept the other on Kerris' shoulder. "Are you angry with me? I didn't give you much time to think."

"No," Kerris said. "I-I'm not angry. I'm surprised." Elath is the witch town, he thought, and I am a witch. "Tell me again what it's called in Elath—my gift."

"Inspeech," said Kel. He crossed his legs, tailor-fashion, and rested both hands in his lap.

"Can you do it?"

"No. I am a patterner."

"What's that?"

Kel's voice was soft. "To me, all acts are part of a pattern, in balance and in opposition, in flux and at rest, and there is no act

62

to which I cannot see the right response, the move that completes the pattern. That's why I am a cheari. The scholars say the whole world dances, and the name of the dance is the chea. I see that dance, a bit. The whole pattern—that I can't see."

"Can anyone?" Kerris asked.

"Those who see into time are called foreseers. I foresee just enough so that where a man's knife will be in the next moment is made clear to me by where he is putting it now—" The starlight touched his waterfall of hair with silver. His arms went out in a flying dance, blocking, countering an imaginary thrust.

Kerris said, before his mind could stop his tongue, "What was the promise you didn't keep?"

Kel bowed his head over his suddenly stilled hands. "Can't you guess?"

"I don't want to guess."

"I was thirteen," said Kel. He lifted the wine bottle to drink. His throat muscles moved in the light. "I promised our mother, the day the caravan left Elath for the north, that if anything happened to her or to our father, I would take care of you. Father was south of Shanan, fighting the Asech. I never saw him again. I joined the fight the next year. Word came finally from Tornor that the caravan had been trapped on its way north, that Mother was dead, but you were alive.... I should have gone then to Tornor and brought you back to Elath. I didn't. Even when you called to me four years ago, I delayed."

Kerris recalled the years of exile, the times of pain and frustration and contempt. He felt a rush of rage, like no anger he had ever felt. It streamed from him—and he felt it touch his brother's mind. Kel winced. At the same time, Kerris felt pain lance through his forehead. Chilled, Kerris caught the anger back. He hadn't known it could hurt. He would have to be careful....

Kel said, "You have the right to be angry, Kerris."

Kerris could almost hear Josen's voice. *Let it come, and let it go*, the old man said.

As he said it, fear closed round his heart like a fist.

His head blurred. *Kel?* he thought, and heard his brother answer— *What is it? What's wrong?* Terror whipped at his nerves, mingled with anger like his own, but not his own. . . . He pulled back into himself with all his force. The contact broke, like a string snapping. Someone in the village was young, angry, and afraid. He willed his eyes to focus. The grass prickled on his palm. He pushed to his feet, Kel with him. He sniffed the drifting scent of heavenweed across the road.

"Let's go back," he said.

Chapter 5

They went into the hall. The adults had left, except for three old men blowing puffs of smoke at each other in the refectory's warmest corner. Kerris stretched to match his brother's stride. Cal, shirtless, was showing wristholds to a boy about his size. Elli and Arillard were demonstrating a turn in a dance. Ilene talked quietly to the oldest girl. Jensie was laughing, surrounded by three admiring boys. Her tricolored hair was a froth around her face. No one looked hurt, angry, threatened. Cautiously, Kerris extended his new sense into the dark. Through the laughter and delight in the room, the fear blazed like a beacon.

"Someone's in trouble," he said to Kel.

"Here?"

"No, somewhere else, but close." He wondered how he knew that it was close. It didn't matter; he knew.

Kel said, "You thought it was here and it isn't."

"Yes."

"Try to find it."

"How?"

"Reach out farther this time," said Kel. "Don't be afraid. You

Elizabeth A. Lynn

can always come back, and it can't hurt. I'm with you."

The smell of heavenweed tickled his nose. He closed his eyes, willing away the noise and laughter. Kel's arm was round his shoulders, steadying him. He leaned against it. His concentration wavered; he forced it outward, like a mole nosing into a burrow....

The smell of heavenweed thickened. He stood in the starlight. His blade lay on the ground at his feet. His wrist was scratched. He swallowed, tasting his own fear. The man in front of him gestured with his knife. His voice was slurred; he sounded angry. "I'm not finished with you," he said. "Pick it up." His red hair fell in front of his eyes. With a scowl, he brushed it back.

Kerris came back into his own mind. The noise had stilled. The chearis were all watching him. "It's Riniard," he said. "He's fighting someone."

Kel swore "I'll break his neck. By the chea, why couldn't one of you have kept an eye on him?" He glared at the chearis. They looked at one another and did not answer. Cal pulled his shirt on over his head. "Who's he fighting?"

"Some boy." Kerris grabbed for the name. "Jerem."

The oldest girl said, "But Jerem never fights."

"You fight when you're attacked," said Kel. He jerked his head toward the door. "Come, we have to find them."

A boy said, "Is Riniard the one with the red hair?"

"Yes," said Jensie mournfully.

"He and Jerem went out together to work on knife technique. I think I know where they would be."

"Show us," said Kel. At the other end of the hall, one of the old men giggled. "Quietly."

They went into the street. Kerris followed Kel. He was very conscious of the knife banging at his hip. Desperately he wished that he could use it. He had felt Jerem's fear, shared it, tasted it in his own mouth. He had been Jerem. The irony of it made him grimace. If he were truly Jerem, he would be dead, dead as mutton, dead as his dead mother.

"The rest of you wait here," Kel said to the would-be chearis. "We'll be back soon. Which way?" he said to their guide.

The boy pointed south, into the grain. "There's a path," he

66

said. "It comes out in the pasture west of the old barn." Wind bowed the fragrant wheat. Kerris shivered, feeling the brooding power of Galbareth around them. He wondered if the others felt it, too. He did not want to walk into the field.

Ilene said gently, "Take us there." The boy nodded. He was barefoot. The moon silvered the tips of the wheat. The wind brushed the ears to sibilance. As they walked toward the grain, red eyes lifted in the darkness and vanished. Kel's fingers closed around Kerris' wrist.

They plunged into the field.

They went in single-file, the boy first, then Ilene, then Kel. The chearis moved as they always did, serene and silent as cats. Kerris stayed at Kel's heels, trying not to stumble. A foraging rabbit squeaked, unnerved by the invasion. The wheat sang. Kerris' chest ached. A thought trickled through his skull, in a voice not his own: *Don't be afraid. You're not alone.* Kerris strained to see ahead of him. He saw the starlight on Kel's hair, and that was all.

They were out of the wheat. Kerris heard a rhythmic sound, *whuf, whuf;* the wind, he thought, and then he saw the two shadow figures circling and circling. The points of light that were the knife-blades gleamed. His throat contracted and he thought, Not the wind but breath. Kel let him go. He froze. The other chearis passed him with a rush.

Riniard heard them and turned, but Kel and Ilene were on him, bearing him down, pinning him to the cool, stubbled soil. He hit hard, and his breath rushed out with a sobbing sound. There was an abrupt, shocking silence.

"Make light," said Ilene.

Kneeling, Arillard made a flame in his tinderbox. By its light Kerris saw Riniard on his back. Kel stood over him. The rage back of his eyes was bright as heated iron.

Cal and Jensie were both bending over the boy. He sat on the ground, holding his right arm. A knife lay at his feet. "It's just a scratch," he said. His voice was high and young. "It's j-j-just a scratch."

Kel said to Ilene, "Keep him there." He went to the boy's side. "You're Jerem." He knelt. "My name is Kel."

Jensie used her own knife to slit the boy's torn sleeve from wrist to shoulder. "It *is* just a scratch," she said.

"Ye, skayin," said the boy.

"How old are you?" Kel said.

"Four-t-teen."

In the flickering pale light from the tinderbox, the blood on the boy's arm was a black line against his skin.

Kel picked up the knife. "This is a good blade," he said, turning it in his fingers. Lightly he tucked it into the sheath at the boy's thigh. "Tell us what happened."

The boy said, "We came to t-t-train." Jensie did something to his arm, and he gasped.

"I want to pad this," Jensie said. "Have we cloth?"

"Go on," Kel said to the boy. He took off his shirt and began to tear it into strips.

"We smoked some heavenweed. I had some with me. We started to fence—I don't know what happened. I must have said something stupid. He got angry."

"And yet you held him," Kel said. "You did well." He fed Jensie the strips. She folded two of them into pads and laid them across the wound, and tied two more strips across the pads. "Not many grown men could hold a cheari."

"I don't think he meant to hurt me," Jerem said. The flame went out. In the darkness his voice continued, painfully clear. "I dropped my knife once. He made me pick it up."

Kel's bare shoulders lifted and fell. He rose. "Take him back to the house," he said to Ilene, not looking at Riniard. "Can you stand?" he asked Jerem. The boy struggled to his feet, his arm puffed with its bandages. "Good. Cal, take him home. Tell his family we will provide whatever recompense they think is proper. Jensie, go with him."

Jensie's head jerked. "Why should I—" she stopped. "All right. Yes." She did not look at Riniard, either. "My name is Jensie," she said to Jerem cheerfully. "Jenézia, really, but no one calls me that but my mother." She slipped her hand under his left shoulder. "Do we go this way?"

"Yes," the boy said. He added, "My name is Jeremeth." They started toward the path. Ilene had one hand on Riniard's shoulder, urging him up. He rose. For a moment they faced each other, boy and man.

Riniard bent down. When he straightened, he held his knife between his hands. He sheathed it. He said softly, "Jeremeth. I'm sorry I hurt you."

The boy swayed. Jensie tightened her hold on him. He stammered something too soft to hear. Ilene and Riniard disappeared between the wheat rows, and Jensie and Jeremeth followed them. Elli was talking to the boy who'd led them to the pasture. Still talking, she drew him to the path. A night bird made a weeping sound. Kerris heard a click from Arillard's tinderbox. The little flame showed Kel standing, looking at the earth. The wind played across his loosed hair. His muscles gleamed like polished stone. The flame blew out.

"Well," said Arillard.

Kerris wondered if he should go, too.

"What do we do?" Kel said. He flung his hands out, palms turned up to the sky, poised as if he were dancing.

Arillard said, "What can we do?"

Kel dropped his hands and his voice went flat. "I can yell at him for breaking a promise, and for fighting as if he were a *rocho,* a thief, not a cheari."

"You've yelled at him before," Arillard said. "We all have. Ilene is probably yelling at him now."

"I can beat him," said Kel.

"Would it help?" Arillard said.

"He would remember it," Kel said grimly. "And it would help relieve my temper." His voice rose. "Arillard, he might have killed that child!"

Kerris turned to leave. "Kerris, don't go," Kel called. He beckoned. Kerris went to him and Kel looped an arm about his shoulders. "What do *you* think?" he said.

Kerris remembered Jeremeth's terror. He temporized. "Riniard said he was sorry."

Kel said, "He was sorry last night, at the lake. What will he have to be sorry for next time, and the time after that, and the time after that?"

The wind sang in the grain. Arillard knelt. Slowly he filled his tinderbox with tufts of dry grass. "He was named cheari too young," he said.

Kel's arm flexed. "I was cheari at twenty-two. Elli is twenty."

"You are you. Elli is Elli. Neither of you is Riniard."

Kel sighed. Leaving Kerris alone, he walked toward the black, silent barn, and back again. "I wish Sef were here," he said.

Arillard said, "Kel, there are only two forks in this road. Either we keep Riniard with us, or we don't."

Kel's shoulders hunched. "Would you advise me to send him away?" he said.

Arillard said, "I would hate it."

"So would I," Kel said. "He belongs with us. He makes the pattern right." The light from the quarter moon fell on his face. There were tension lines around his mouth.

Spontaneously, Kerris reached out mentally to his brother. He recoiled from the mingled pain, fury, and helplessness.

They walked back through the field and across the square. Kel said nothing all the way. Arillard said only, "I wonder what the village will demand as recompense for the boy's wounding."

The door of the birthing house was open a crack. A candle burned in the hall alcove. They stopped to remove their boots. Kerris took a deep breath of the sweet herbal scent.

They entered the sleeping space. The double room seemed close and hot. Cal and Jensie had not yet returned. Ilene was standing by a window. As they came in, she cocked her head to one side and made a sour face. Elli sat on a pallet, sharpening her knife with quick strokes. Her face was grave. Riniard faced Ilene. The light from the oil dish at Elli's knee did not reach him: he looked like a shadow, or a ghost. The silence smouldered.

Arillard found a second candle. Stooping, he lit it at the flame of the dish and stuck it in a wall-sconce. Kerris looked at Riniard. The redhead was pale, and there were dark half moons under his eyes. He looked at Kel. "Well?" he said hoarsely. The misery in his voice and stance struck Kerris like a blow.

Wait! he sent to Kel. Then, focusing his strength on Riniard, he extended his mind past the outward play of feeling, sense, and thought to the hidden sentience below.

He felt shame, misery, defiance, and fear.... A sluggish, sullen knot, the fear snaked and twisted back upon itself. *It's no good, I'll never be what they desire, I'm weak, unworthy of them, it hurts, I love them and it hurts, they'll have to send me away, they'll have to, better sooner than later, better now, better now, who are you??? get away from me, get out!*

Kerris got out.

He leaned on the wall. His head ached, and his vision wavered familiarly. He reached for his brother, linked with him, and turned once more toward Riniard's mind. It was like going into a nest of snakes. *Look,* he said to Kel. He held them both there as long as he dared, and then pulled away from Riniard, and broke the link to Kel. His knees shook. He wondered if he was going to fall. An arm came out of nowhere and helped him to sit. Someone was sobbing. He waited for the world to cease whirling. The person on the other end of the arm was Elli. The person weeping—kneeling, head in shaking hands—was Riniard.

Kel went to him. "Riniard." He caught the redhead's wrists and forced his hands down from his face. "Young fool." Riniard would not look up. Kel stroked his hair. "Ilene, Elli, Arillard, help me." Kerris felt Elli squeeze his hand, and leave him. The chearis gathered in a tight little circle with Riniard in the center. Steadily, Kel stroked Riniard's hair. "You're one of us, Red. You, yourself, not some imaginary person with all the virtues that we've never met and wouldn't know if we did meet him. We chose you. You hear me? We chose you. We love you. We won't send you away, Red, no matter what you do, unless you ask it. Do you, Riniard? Have you tired of us so soon?" His hand stopped its steady movement. "Tell us. Do you want to leave?"

"No," Riniard whispered.

"Idiot," Kel said. He cupped Riniard's chin in his hand. "Look at me." Riniard lifted his head. His cheeks were wet. "You'll stay with us, because we want you, and love you. Next time you want some heavenweed, tell us! We'll stay with you and keep you out of trouble, and when your eyes close we'll put you to bed to sleep it off. All right?"

"All right," Riniard said. His voice was shaky, but the color had come back to his face.

"And next time you try to start a fight, I'll beat you silly. You know I can."

Riniard assayed a smile. "You can. Any time."

Kerris crawled onto a pallet. His head had ceased to ache, but he still felt cold, and tired, more tired than he had ever been in his life. He rolled on his back. Cal and Jensie came through the arched doorway and stopped, both looking at the chearis surrounding Riniard. Kel said, "Comfort him, Jen." His tall figure passed in front of the candle. He bent over Kerris. He, too, was tired, but the tension lines were gone from around his lips, and his eyes were tranquil, without rage. "That was a difficult thing you did," he said quietly. "You did it well. I don't know what would have happened if you hadn't been here. I'm glad you are." He went through the doorway and disappeared down the hall.

Elli sat down beside him. "Hey," she said, "what did you do? I know you did something."

"I showed Kel what Riniard was feeling," Kerris said.

Elli frowned. "I don't suppose you can explain it more," she said.

"I would if I understood it." The answer came out more sharply than he'd meant it to. He was too exhausted to apologize. His mind felt bruised, as it had the day before in the storm.

"Never mind," said Elli. Lifting her arms, she slid her shirt over her head. "I probably couldn't understand it even if you could explain it. I don't always understand when Kel talks about patterns." She lay down next to him. The edges of their pallets touched.

Jensie murmured from the corner, a soft, loving sound. Ilene stood, naked, and snuffed the ensconced candle with her fingers.

Elli said softly, so that only he could hear, "I won't keep you awake much longer. I just wanted to say—I like you. I liked the way you let that child touch you today. I like it that you helped Riniard. I like the way you're not afraid to ask for things." Her hand crept across the pallet and clasped his palm. "I mean it."

He swallowed. "I like you."

"Don't forget to give me back my pants tomorrow."

"I won't forget."

Kel came back. He stepped around the pallets and spoke to someone Kerris couldn't see. "Move over." Kerris heard the sound of shifting cloth. Then Elli blew on the oil dish, and there was only the soft sounds of breathing, and the wind in the grain, and the rhythmic cries of the lovers.

The chearas was up at dawn.

Kel sent Calwin and Elli to the stable for the horses. "We'll find morning meal on the road," he said. "We've trespassed enough on the good will of this village."

Sunlight patterned the walls of the birthing house. Kerris looked out the window. A man and woman walked toward the fields, carrying hoes. A child laughed somewhere in the square. Clouds billowed, chased by an eastward wind. A midden-smell blew across the square from the pasture. It was very peaceful.

Arillard said, "I wonder what they are likely to ask as payment for last night."

Kel reached for the straw broom in the corner. "We'll give it, whatever it is—as long as it doesn't delay us."

Jensie and Ilene shook the pallets clean. Kerris looked for a task. Riniard tapped his shoulder. "We can get the clothes," he said. They stopped in the alcove for their boots and then went behind the birthing house to the drying line over which their cleaned, dry clothes were pinned. Slowly Kerris unpinned them from the hempen rope and piled them in Riniard's arms. They smelled of soap and sun.

Riniard said, "Last night—" Kerris waited. "I felt you in my head. That was real, wasn't it?"

"Yes," Kerris said, "that was real."

"I felt Kel, too. It was terrible."

"I'm sorry if I hurt you," Kerris said.

"You didn't, and if you had I would have deserved it," Riniard said. He shifted the weight of the clothes. "I'm not angry. You helped me. I don't know what would have happened

73

if you hadn't done it. I just want to tell you that it was terrible."
He licked dry lips. Kerris remembered the first time he had
touched Kel's mind. He had been terrified.

"I won't do it again," he said, not sure if this was what
Riniard wanted to hear. The redhead nodded. All the clothes
and blankets were off the line. They walked back to the house.
Riniard sorted out the clothes. Kerris took his pants and blanket
from the pile. He rubbed his face against the fabric. There was so
much about himself he didn't know. His stump itched. He
scratched it. He didn't know the limits of this gift he
had—inspeech—nor even where to learn them. Kel—he glanced
across the room at his brother. Kel could not tell him. But surely
he was not alone, there were others who could do what he
did.... The image of a man with silver hair and green eyes
shimmered in his skull. *Sefer*. He knew without knowing where
the knowledge came from. Perhaps Kel had said it, or thought it.
Sefer, at Elath, Kel's lover, was like him.

Cal and Elli came in. Cal said, "The horses are outside, and so
is Tamis. She's waiting for us."

Elli crossed to Kerris' side and began to roll up her blanket.
"What are *you* scowling for?" she said.

"I didn't know I was," Kerris said.

"Well, you are. Give me my pants."

Kerris took the borrowed pants off and pulled his clean ones
on. "Where do we go today?" he said.

"Through Galbareth," said Elli, twisting a tie around her
blanket. She started to speak, and stopped. "We should reach
Elath tomorrow." She knotted the tie with exaggerated care.

Kerris balanced his own bedroll on his knee and tied the lace
with his hand and his teeth. He picked the roll up. "What were
you going to say?"

She sighed. "I was going to ask you if you were still afraid of
Galbareth."

Kerris glanced out the window at the golden fields. He said
truthfully, "I don't know."

He breathed deeply as they went through the long hallway.
He wondered what herbs the villagers grew to make it smell so
good. He had never smelled anything like it in Tornor. Tamis
was waiting for them outside the door. Gathered in their

semicircle, the chearis faced her. She wore gold and brown, and the gold-threaded triangle she had worn the day before. On her left wrist a copper bracelet caught the light and winked like a star.

"Damisen," Kel said (he did not say the word as smoothly as had Cal and Riniard), "we regret the trouble we have brought upon this village. Tell us, please, how we may amend it."

The headwoman folded her arms under her breasts. "It is not great trouble," she said. She looked at Riniard. "Though it may bring trouble to the one who made it. What comes to a cheari who mocks the chea?"

All the chearis stiffened. Riniard flushed red. Kel said, "That is our concern, damisen."

She inclined her head. "Jeremeth's wound is small. Our *lehi*, our healer, says it will mend in eight days. But for eight days Jeremeth must do a child's work. Therefore we ask that the eight of you take his place in our fields, and do his work for one day."

"But we—" Ilene bit her lip.

"Yes?" said Tamis. "You refuse?"

Ilene looked at Kel.

"No," he said. "We do not refuse. It's fair. But we have a prior promise to keep, in Elath, and we cannot wait, not even for one day. Let us come back. Let us return when the harvest moon rides and the spring planting is ripe. We will work the harvest. That way both promises may be kept. We swear by the chea to return."

"Do you?" said Tamis. She gazed at each of them in turn. Kerris thought, I am not a cheari—but she was looking at him, eyes like the earth itself, without mercy or malice.... He bowed his head like the others. The horses snuffed the breeze, regarding the strange tableau with liquid eyes. Tamis moved gracefully to one side. She made a little gesture with her left hand. "That will suffice."

With the sun streaming over their left shoulders, Cal led the chearis back on the road. Jensie and Riniard took the lead. They rode side by side, apart from the others, touching, talking, laughing aloud.

The other chearis did not talk much. The sense of

Galbareth—the feel of a living presence in the grain and in the earth—kept them still. No one disturbed their passage. They rode like ghosts through a golden landscape. Home, Kerris thought. I'm going home. But the word did not touch him. Home was Tornor.

That night they camped in a barren field. The grass was scorched in places as if fire had passed, and where it was unscorched it was grazed to the stone. "No fire tonight," Cal warned.

Elli spread her blanket. "Why not?"

Calwin plucked a tuft of grass and let it blow away on the wind. "There've been fires here before. The smallest spark might set it blazing. The wheat's as dry as bone."

"Smell the dust," said Ilene.

Elli rubbed her hands together. "I can't smell anything but cowshit," she said. "I'm cold."

Kerris said, "You want my sheepskin?"

She grinned. "No, that's all right."

Kel crouched at the edge of the circle, staring at the endless fence of grain. His hands moved, pushing at the earth, making hills and roads and ridges, a miniature world in the dust. A fox barked in the wheat. Kerris guessed he was thinking about Elath, worrying about Elath. *Something's wrong.... I don't know what it is.* He tried to find words to help his brother's mood. Nothing came. A scribe should be good with words, he thought.

Arillard seemed to be asleep already. Riniard and Jensie lay whispering lovers' secrets under two cloaks. Kerris lay down, wishing for the warmth of a fire, wishing that at least the ground was softer. His spine ached. Suddenly Elli exploded at his elbow, "Ai, I'm sick of the fields! I want to see water and green hills again." She wrapped her blanket around her shoulders and sat hidden in its folds, scowling like some crabbed and ancient woman.

Ilene said, "I want to see my family." Her knife lay bared in her hand. She sat cross-legged. The rasp of the whetstone on the blade melded with the crickets' whine. "I haven't seen my son in a year."

"You have a son?" Kerris said.

Her wide mouth curved. "His name's Borti. He's two. He lives with my mother and sister and my sister's children. Sometimes I worry that he'll forget me, he sees me so seldom. When he's old enough, if I haven't settled down to be Yardmaster in some village, I'll take him traveling with me."

"Where does he live?"

"In Elath, of course. I was born in Elath. You think only witches live there?"

"I didn't know," he said.

"You don't remember it at all?" Ilene asked.

Kerris shook his head.

"It's a beautiful town," said Ilene.

"Is it big?"

"It's bigger than Brath. Smaller than Kendra-on-the-Delta, or Tezera."

"Smaller than Mahita, too," said Elli.

Riniard poked his head between the cloaks. His hair was tousled. "Elli compares all the places we go to Mahita," he said.

"*I* have the proper respect for my birthplace," Elli said.

"You weren't born in my village," said Riniard. "Something for which you should give daily thanks."

Cal said, "If you like Mahita so well, Elli, why aren't you there, inside of marching around the countryside?"

Ilene chuckled. Elli rubbed her cheek with her hand. "Oh. You know. I like Mahita to go back to, the way Kel likes Elath. I get restless staying in one place."

Ilene said, "Zayin says, A true cheari is like a note of music: only happy in company with others of its kind and on the move."

"*I'm* not a piece of music," said Riniard. "I'm a person."

Kel had not moved during this exchange. The moonlight touched his fair hair and his fair skin—he looked like stone, like a statue. Suddenly Kerris could not hold back. He reached out with his mind—and found himself sharing in a fierce and terrible longing, a desire so strong that the sweat prickled on his skin and the blood rushed to his head. He withdrew at once, shamed. He hadn't meant to pry. He felt a fool.

"Hey," Ilene said. "Why so still?" Leaning back, she tweaked the sleeve of Kel's tunic.

He looked away from the dust. "I'm thinking," he said.

She sheathed her knife and stood lithely. "I know what you are thinking, too," she said. Crossing to him, she bent and whispered in his ear. He half-smiled. He ran his hands up her arms and drew her head to his, an easy, loving gesture. They kissed: a long kiss. "Come on," she said, "get up. Walk with me."

Kel sighed and stood. Ilene took his hand. Hips brushing, they walked quietly towards the dark privacy of the furrows.

"Good," said Arillard from the shadows.

Kerris watched them stride between two rows of grain, and disappear. His senses stirred, remembering the extraordinary beauty of Kel's naked body in the light, by the lake.... A sour voice in his mind commented, So much for a lover at Elath! He knew that was unfair. Chearis rarely stayed in one place for very long, and he'd never heard that their discipline insisted they stay celibate on the road. Kerris pulled his blanket tighter round his legs. What difference did it make that Kel and Ilene were lovers? It was none of his, Kerris', concern.

The answer filled his head. *He can dance, and fight, and he has always had a home to go to, and someone waiting for him there. He is loved and beautiful. I am*—the images of what he was seared his mind and he fought them away, praying that no one could see him, that Elli would not notice and ask him what was wrong.... Tears burned his eyelids. Setting his teeth against sound, he laid his cheek in the dirt.

At midday the next day, they came to the end of Galbareth.

One moment they were riding between tall rows of grain and the next moment they were out of the grain, and in front of them the hills were green and soft, sprinkled with trees.

Kel whooped. He reined from the line and tore down the road, bending low over Callito's neck, urging the red stallion into a blistering gallop. Far away he slowed and came cantering back. His eyes, as he grinned at them all, beamed triumph. His hair had come loose. It tumbled down his back. "At last," he said. He looked at Kerris. "We'll be in Elath before sunset," he promised.

"Good," Kerris said. It was hard to meet Kel's eyes. What, he thought, was there for *him* in Elath?

Kel said gently, "What's troubling you, chelito?"

The affectionate diminutive made Kerris angry. I'm not a child, he thought, knowing at the same time that he was being unfair again. He said stiffly, "It's nothing."

Ilene said, "He's nervous, that's what's troubling him, Kel. You'd be nervous too if you'd been shut up all your life behind the walls of some damned Keep!"

Kel nodded slowly, still watching Kerris, his eyes uncomfortably keen. "Is that it? You have family in Elath, Kerris. Cousins. Besides, you belong there—you have the inspeech. You won't feel out of place." Then his own excitement overcame him. He brought Callito's head around in a standing leap. "Let's ride!" They followed him. Kerris' anger dissipated. He gazed with pleasure at the green hillocks. Goats grazed on the slopes. The road wound up and down again through gentle valleys. Tall white flowers lined the sides of the path. From the summit of a hill they looked across a dell to another hill. Between them, in a sunlit cleft, rested the patterned streets and pastures of a village.

Kerris' heart thumped. But they rode by it. Ilene was singing. *"In sunlight we must part, my love; in starlight we may smile; The moon is shining bright, my love, O let me stay a while; Sing hey and a ho for lovers, sing hey for the setting sun, Sing hey for the girl who makes me smile when the harvest work is done!"*

They stopped for a meal. Kel's impatience drove them back to the road. The meadow grass coarsened. Rocky outcroppings jutted over the path: huge blocks of weathered, angular stone. Kerris thought, There were mountains here once. The rocks were oddly impressive. They threw great shadows over the path, and once or twice Kerris thought he saw faces carved on them, eyes, nose, a mouth....

His mind twitched.

He felt it, and then felt it go.

He thought at first that he had imagined the sensation. His stump itched. He scratched it. Ahead of them the road curved and narrowed. He felt it again, a sting within his head, like someone plucking a string.

Kel? he thought hesitantly. Kel did not seem to hear him. Magrita sidled and shook her head at nothing. Kerris soothed her. His trepidation grew. The dark rocks made him nervous. He could not free himself from the feeling that there was something hidden nearby, waiting for them. . . .

"Stand!"

The brusque command stopped them in mid-pace. Kerris looked up. A woman stood poised in a cleft in the granite. She held a strung bow, like a figure out of Tornor's tapestries. She wore coarse brown pants, boots to her knees, a leather tunic. Her face was heavy-featured, skin weathered and red. Her hair was black. She looked like a farmwoman, and not a young one. But she held the bow in sure hands, arrow loosely nocked.

"Kel," she said. "Ilene. Welcome."

"Cleo?" Ilene said. "What the hell?"

The woman smiled grimly. "We guard the way to Elath." A man's face peered over her shoulder. He lifted a hand in greeting to the chearas. "It's like old times."

"What is it?" said Kel. "What's happened?"

"War has happened," said Cleo. "The Council will tell you all about it." She unstrung her bow. "Go on. Go in."

Chapter 6

The town of Elath lay in a shallow bowl. The rocks fell away as the chearas rode up the final curve of the northern road. They looked down. Kerris' hand ached, he was gripping the rein so hard. He flexed his fingers. He glimpsed silver-gray houses, a patchwork of pastures, gardens, and fields. Veins of blue water decorated the gold meadows. On the rim of the bowl, trees whose branches stood straight up against their trunks lined the horizon like fenceposts.

They went down toward the village. A woman waved from a meadow. She was shepherding a squawking flock of geese to a pond. "Eyah, Kel, Ilene," she called. "It's well you've come, we can use you."

A bird with scarlet feathers darted under Magrita's nose and into a flowering beech tree. Kerris stared. He had never seen one like it. It strutted on the pendulous branch, brilliant and cocky. "Kerris!" said Kel. He beckoned. "Come up, come ride beside me." Kerris clucked to the mare. Kel pointed to a gray peaked roof on the eastern side of the bowl. "That farm belongs to Ardith, our mother's brother. We have cousins there."

The road widened. It became a square, with posts for tying horses to, and a tiled trough. At one end of it sat a red brick building whose chimneys belched black smoke.

"What's that?" Kerris asked.

"That's the smithy."

They rode by a house with a sign swinging from it. The sign showed a painted picture of a shoe. A little farther on a tanner and a butcher shop leaned against each other. From the butcher's racks hung sides of lamb, beef, and pork, fish still in their glittering skins, two huge turkeys, a necklace of pigs' feet, and strings of fat plucked quail.

The tanner's shop stank of boiling oak bark. Kel waved away the drifting steam. "Whew." Magrita stepped fastidiously over the wagon ruts. There were a lot of them. "This is where the caravans come," Kel said. People were poking out of windows, watching them. A few waved.

A man staggered by under the weight of a carp big as a baby. His shirt was slimed from holding it. Kel halted to let him cross the road.

Kerris asked, "Who rules in Elath?"

Kel smiled. "This is no Keep," he said. "There's a Council."

"Like the Council of Houses in Kendra-on-the-Delta?"

"A little like that. It was patterned after that. But we are not so grand in Elath. Anyone who owns land can be on the Council here. There are no great families, as in the city."

They rode by a burned and blackened house. A voice shouted, the words muffled. Kel reined in.

A man walked around the charred boards. "Yai!" he said, holding a hand up, palm out.

"Yai," responded Kel. "What happened, Emeth?"

The man grinned. It was not a nice grin. "We were raided."

Ilene leaned over the pommel of her saddle. "Anyone hurt?" she said.

"Noro was burned. She's healing." He pointed his chin to the other side of the street. "The stove blew apart in Thiya's house." Kerris looked. One of the houses had a wall made of two kinds of wood: the silver wood which seemed common, and a dark red wood. The red wood looked newly cut. Yellow curtains covered the windows. The red and silver made a strange pattern. "Killed him."

Ilene muttered an oath. "Anyone else?" she said.

"No," said the man. He wore a blue shirt, and dark brown pants tied with a leather belt. His hair was braided like a woman's. "Your family is well."

"I thank the chea," Ilene said. She gathered her reins in both hands. "Take Kerris to the school," she said to Kel. "I will join you later. I want to see my son." She urged the bay stallion out of line and into a side street.

Kel touched his heels to Callito's sides. Kerris wondered why he had not asked if Sefer had been hurt. *If I had a lover I would ask,* he thought. Yet another house sat scorched and soiled in the sunlight. Fresh boards lay on the ground in front of it next to a huge pile of soiled ropes. From the rear came the sound of hammers. Kel slowed but did not stop.

"Who lives there?" Kerris asked.

"Moro and Sevrith, and their children." Between the beats of the hammer Kerris heard the shrilling of children's voices. "Moro is ropemaker for the village."

"How many people live here?" he asked.

"In Elath? Thrice five hundred."

It seemed a lot. It was nearly twice the number of folk in Tornor village.

Kel reined in abruptly. He pointed at a house. "The house you were born in stood there," he said.

It was just a small silver cottage, with leather curtains at the windows. "That house—"

"No. That one is new. The other was destroyed in the war, ten years ago."

Kerris gazed at the cottage. Something—memory?—stirred in his head. The line of the street began to look familiar. He told himself that these were Kel's memories, not his own. His memories began with Tornor.

Kel said gently, "Kerris, you don't *have* to come with me to the school. Would you prefer to go to the farm? Ardith and Lea are anxious to meet you. I'll take you there."

"Would you rather I went there?" Kerris said.

"No," said Kel. "I like your company, and I want Sef to meet you, and you him. But you must do what you want."

Kerris wondered if Sefer would like him. He gazed up the slope of the bowl to the farm Kel had pointed out to him. It seemed very remote. "I'll stay with you," he said.

Behind them, Elli and Jensie were pointing out the village sights to Riniard, and Kerris remembered that the redhead, too, had not been here before. A brindle goat trotted across the road.

The street seemed to end in a forest. Kerris said, "Is the school a building?"

"Certainly it is," Kel said. "It was Sefer's idea. We built it seven years ago." He pointed into the trees. "You'll see it soon. Look for silver."

At the edge of the trees Kel dismounted. Kerris copied him. He thought he heard water. "Is there a river here?" he asked.

"There's a stream by the Tanjo," Kel said. To the others he said, "Wait for us, we won't be long." He gave Arillard Callito's rein. Kerris handed Magrita's to Elli. The word *Tanjo* puzzled him. It was a southern word: it meant a hall where apprentices were trained.

"Come," said Kel.

The grove was dark and silent. Partway through it Kerris heard the music of water clearly. It reminded him of Tornor. He glimpsed a silver roof, silver walls. The water fell across a patterned barrier of rock in a steady, directed stream. Kel touched his shoulder. "Open your mind," he said. Kerris took a breath. If my mind were a hand . . . Slowly he slipped from the body's confines. He touched the mind of some scaly predator in the grove: it seethed with a cold ferocity. He left it quickly. He touched Kel's mind. It trembled with barely contained eagerness. He reached toward the silver building, wondering who was learning what within its walls.

He touched the mind of a stranger. . . .

A boy sat in a corner. He was staring at a pale white surface. The surface danced with flecks of color. His mind ranged outward, toward the water sound amid the trees. He wrapped his thought about the water and scattered the current into a high, joyful mist, beading the cypress needles with wetness.

"See!"

"Good," said a man's voice. *"That was good, Korith."*

Kerris blinked as the wet glory of the fountain leaped in his mind.

He put his hand to his cheek. His face was cool with the fountain's spray. He looked at the water, running once more in its accustomed grooves. "Did it—?"

"Yes," said Kel. "It did."

Something shone blue in the grove. A man came running around the tree trunks. He was slim, tall, though not as tall as Kel. I know you, Kerris thought. His hair was white, held off his forehead by a blue band; his clothes were brown, trimmed with blue thread. His eyes were green. He came to Kel, and they embraced.

"Sef," said Kel. "This is Kerris." He drew the white-haired man around. "Kerris, this is Sefer."

"I'm glad to meet you," Sefer said. It was he who had said, *That was good, Korith.* He was a fingersbreadth taller than Kerris, no more. Their eyes met. Kerris' skin prickled. He felt as if every thought in his skull, every hope, every desire lay bare to that intense green gaze. Frightened, he backed up.

Kel slipped his arm to his lover's waist. "Stop that," he commanded. "He's not ready, Sef." They kissed. Kerris turned his head away. It was like seeing two flames joining in the dark.

Sefer said, "It's good you're here, *nika.*"

"So I've been told," Kel said. He touched the hilt of his knife. "Cleo spoke of war."

"No," Sefer said. "It isn't a war. Not yet."

"The others are waiting in the street. Can you leave the Tanjo?"

"I shouldn't," Sefer murmured, "but Tamaris is there, so I suspect I shall be forgiven." Kel stroked his lover's back with one hand. A flush of rose touched Sefer's pale skin. They strolled to the street. Kel shortened his stride to match his lover's. Kerris, behind them, felt his back muscles twitch.

Elli and Arillard greeted Sefer with laughter and ribald comments. Kel introduced Riniard. "It's good to meet you," Sefer said. Riniard mumbled a greeting. He looked apprehensive. Leading the horses, the chearis walked south along the main road. They passed a Yard. Men and women sparred inside the fence. A few shouted greetings, but they did not break the fighting circles.

The stablemaster was waiting for them in the doorway of the horse barn. He was a big man, black and bearded, with spadelike hands and crooked teeth.

"Eyah, Kel. Glad to see you." He grinned gap-toothed. "All of you. We've got a war on our hands, you hear?"

"We heard," said Kel. "We're going to hear more."

"It's like the old days. Lalli, Sosha!" His shout brought a girl and a boy tumbling from the hayloft. They were dark as Ilene. "Take the chearis' horses and rub 'em down good, or I'll feed you to the bears." The children seemed unimpressed. The girl made faces at him as she led Callito into a stall. "I won't keep you. Listen—I've got a horse can beat that big red one, Kel, you hear?"

Kel chuckled. "I doubt it."

"Give me a race and I'll prove it!" The man's raised voice shook the dust from the walls.

Kel patted the big man's arm. "Later, Tek."

They went to a house. It was small, a cottage really, silver, surrounded by other houses. Its roof was slate. In the entrance hall there was a small alcove for boots and shoes.

Beyond the alcove was a long room. The floor was covered with fat red pillows and reed mats. The walls were hung with soft wool squares in many colors. A low table stood to one side, decorated with a copper vase filled with branching sprays of flowers. There were several chamberpots on the floor. In one corner stood a bright red washbasin on a carved wooden stand.

"Be at home," said Sefer. "Are you hungry? The spring harvest is in; there's plenty of food."

Jensie unlaced her riding leathers. Tossing her bedroll into a corner, she put an arm around Riniard's waist, her thumb hooked into his belt loop. "I'd forgotten this place was so pleasant," she said.

Kel grinned. "Nika, you know better than to ask that. Chearis are *always* hungry."

"Wait," Sefer said. He disappeared through an arched doorway. He returned bearing a platter heaped with cheese and fruit, a flagon of wine, and a dish filled with fetuch. The dish was green with blue flowers. "Sit." The chearis sat. Sefer put the tray on the table and went to the arch again.

"Where's Ilene?" he called.

"With her family," Kel said.

Sefer brought in a cluster of copper cups. "Then you're six. No." He smiled at Kerris. "Seven."

Elli picked up one of the cups. She held it to the light. It was dimpled, and engraved with a simple, flowing pattern of a horse's head that went all the way around the bowl. "This looks like Asech work," she commented.

Sefer sat. "It is."

Arillard said, "We saw Asech traders bearing the snake sign at the Tezera crossroads."

Sefer said, "I will say it one more time. We are not at war with Asech." He poured wine into a cup and passed it to Kel.

Kerris glanced at the placid room. The hangings on the walls reminded him of Tornor's tapestries. He ran his fingers along the braided mats. Sefer handed Cal a cup of wine. This is my birthplace, he thought. I was born in this valley, in a house like this one. . . . He closed his eyes, trying to summon a memory, one memory. Nothing happened. He had memories of cold and stone and ice. He had no memories of trees that grew in the shape of flames, of red birds, or of silver walls.

Kel said, "Tell us what *is* happening, then."

Sefer said, "We were raided, three nights ago, the night of the quarter moon. They came in the middle of the night—with torches." He poured a third cup of wine and gave it to Arillard. The oldest cheari looked grim. Kerris had a sudden moment of vision. He saw the peaceful, sleeping streets lit by torchfire, saw horses rearing, smelled pitch, heard the shouts and the terrible crackle of flame eating at dry boards. . . . He shivered. Sefer put a wine cup in his hand.

Arillard said, "Isn't setting homes to the torch an act of war?"

"They carried weapons and did not use them," said Sefer.

"So?" Cal said.

"So they did not wish to kill, only to frighten."

"Thiya was killed," Kel said. "Emeth told us."

"Thiya was killed by accident, not design. They want something from us—something more than spoil."

"Who are they?" Kel said.

Sefer took a moment to answer. He sipped his wine. "We don't know."

Kel's head snapped around. He stared at his lover. "How can you not know?" he said.

"We know they are Asech, that's all," Sefer said. "We could learn nothing from their minds, Kel. They were barriered. They are like us."

Cal said, "Witches?"

Sefer nodded, his green gaze enigmatic. "Just so."

"And you think they mean no harm?" said Elli.

"I didn't say that," Sefer said.

There was silence. Kel murmured a question in which Kerris caught a name—Terézia. Sefer nodded. "Where is she?" asked the cheari.

"With the guard."

Arillard said, "The folk on guard—Cleo—and Tek at the stable spoke of war. So did Emeth."

Sefer turned the copper cup between his palms. "Most people will. It's simpler." He put the cup down. "But we've sent riders south and west. No other towns have been attacked. Just Elath."

Arillard shook his head. "That makes no sense. How many raids have there been?"

"Just the one."

Kel growled. He looped his arm around Sefer's chest and fell back with him into a heap of pillows. "Damn the Asech and their raids," he said. His hands moved on Sefer's hips. "I didn't come home to fight." He leaned forward to touch his lips to the back of Sefer's neck.

Kerris looked at the mats on the floor. His body felt too hot for his clothes. A hand touched his knee. He looked up. Elli smiled at him.

Kel said, "If the raiders want something, nika, then they will have to come back to tell us what it is."

"Yes," said Sefer.

"Do you want help? Guards on the roads? We are at your disposal."

Riniard set his cup down on the tray with a bang. "A fight!" At Kel's baleful look he put both hands up, palms out. "Don't glare at me like that, Kel. I'll be good." He laughed uneasily. Kel did not drop his eyes. The room chilled into silence.

Kel said evenly, "We are chearis, not soldiers."

"I didn't *mean* it," Riniard said.

Kel stood. "Then don't say it." His gray gaze raked them all. "I want to see you all this afternoon in the fighting circles." He clasped Sefer's hand and brought him upright in one smooth heave. *"Dom a'leth,"* he said. Let's go *now.*

"Please be comfortable," Sefer said to the chearas. "This is your place." He turned to Kel. The cheari put an arm around his shoulders. They walked to the end of the room and vanished.

Elli put her hands on her hips. She said to Riniard, "You have the brains of a cricket."

"I know," the redhead said. "I really *didn't* mean it."

Arillard said, "You shouldn't say what you don't mean." He still looked grim, but his voice was calm and sad. He began to pile the cups on the food tray.

"It's all right," Jensie said. "Sef will smooth him down." She put her arms around Riniard's waist and hugged him.

Steps creaked overhead. Kel and Sefer. Jensie and Riniard laid out their bedrolls side by side. Arillard said, "I'm going for a walk. Anyone want to come?" He gathered up the food tray and cups and delivered them to the pantry on the other side of the arch.

"Nope," said Elli. The others shook their heads.

"See you at the Yard." Arillard opened a door Kerris hadn't known was there. A heavy scent drifted into the room. He glimpsed sun on grass. A breeze touched his face, like a caress. A petal fell from the flower spray to the back of his wrist. He shook it off, and began the tedious work of unlacing his riding leathers.

Cal pulled a little bag from his pack. He upended it. A pair of bone dice tumbled over the mat. "Want to play?" he said to Elli.

She grinned, and seated herself opposite him. "I've been waiting for you to bring those out."

She looked different. Kerris puzzled out how. She had plaited her hair into tight thin braids, many of them, and tied them with bits of yellow silk. He hadn't seen her do it. It looked good.

Scooping up the dice, she tossed them in the air, caught them again. "What rules?"

Cal said, "Double sixes and no dead men."

"I accept." She spun the dice to the mat. "Ha. Two and four, six doubled makes twelve. Your throw."

Kerris' bladder twinged.

He rose. He didn't want to use a pot; there were too many people about. The breeze blew across his face. The mats pricked the soles of his feet. Quietly he went into the garden. It was warm. There was a rain barrel to the left of the door, and a green lawn ending in a tangle of berry bushes. A stone bench sat under a tree. The tree's leaves were smooth as wax, and its bole was scaly silver. Kerris pissed into a berry bush. He could see the wall of a building through the snaky, thorny runners. A mole run humped across a corner of the lawn.

He sat on the bench. He felt no kinship to the place; it was pleasant, but strange. He supposed he would get used to it. He would live with his mother's brother, work on a farm (what work a one-armed man could do), go to the Tanjo.... His stump ached. He rubbed it hard, forcing sensation from the scarred nerves. He wondered if his mother's brother Ardith was anything like Morven.

He ran a fingertip along the bench. There were pink veins in the white stone. A red bird, plumage bright as blood, flew past his head. It landed on a branch, balanced, and slipped within a bush. He saw the curving clutter of a nest. Scarlet flashed behind a screen of thorns.

"Aah!" The cry rang from the upper room of the house—deep, convulsive, ecstatic. Kerris caught his breath. He looked up.... It was not repeated. A curtain wavered over a frame.

It would be easy to reach through those windows.... He heard it as if someone else had said it. It would be easy—his body heated, stiffened—to slide like a red bird (as if by accident) into

90

his brother's head.... He trembled, remembering Kel naked in the amber light of morning.

He gripped the bench as hard as he could, until his fingers throbbed with pain. When he lifted his hand it was etched with the pattern of the stone.

Elli dragged him from the garden.

"Come and watch," she said.

"I've watched the fighting circles before," he said.

"You've not seen us," she pointed out. She gazed around the garden, grinning in high good humor. Kerris guessed she had won the dice game. Seizing his hand, she laced her fingers with his. "Come on, Kerris. You've seen us dance, now watch us fight. If you aren't there it won't be the same."

Like all Yards, the Yard at Elath was a dirt-packed square. A silver fence, waist-high, kept dogs and other animals out. It was ringed with people. The chearas stood in the center. The villagers made way for Elli. "Here," she said, depositing him in the front rank of spectators. Crossing his legs, he sat, feeling conspicuous. She joined the chearis. They looked sleek and fierce, like animals. Ilene was with them. Kel had coiled his hair on top of his head.

At the southwest corner of the Yard stood a huge stone pillar. Kerris stared at it. The stone was smooth, not rough, and there was a suggestion of a face within it. It grew clearer the more he looked at it.

"Greetings," said a voice in his ear. He turned his head. Sefer had come up on his left side.

"Hello," Kerris said.

Sefer was wearing a different shirt. It had green braid along the collar. There was a purple love-bite on his neck that had not been there before. He looked happy. "Have you met your kinfolk yet?"

Kerris shook his head. "Kel said he would take me to them."

"They're here—your cousins are, at least," Sefer said.

"I can wait," Kerris said. Anger, or something like it, uncoiled within him. I don't want to like you, he thought. Don't try to make friends with me. He looked away, toward the pillar.

Suddenly he did not want to meet the extraordinary intensity of those wide green eyes.

"What is that?" he asked, pointing his chin at the pillar.

Sefer said, "We made it, at the Tanjo." The implication—that it had not been made by hands—was plain. "We desired it to show the spirit of the chea. We call it the Guardian."

By now the Yard was crammed with people. But around the pillar there was a clear space. No one leaned upon it. Surely those hollows were eyes, and that curve a nose, that a mouth... "What do you see?" Sefer said softly.

"A face..." It drew him. He could not turn his head. Taller than the human figures under it, it gazed across the Yard and out across the valley, glimmering with terrible, inhuman tranquillity. He could not believe that mere human beings had fashioned it out of common rock. In a moment it would begin to move...

A hand gripped his shoulder. Sefer said, "Kerris! Look at me!"

With great effort, he turned his head. His eyes burned. Sefer's pale face and white hair shimmered. "Look at the ground," Sefer said. "Put your head down." Kerris put his head on his knees. The world grew firm again. He lifted his head.

Sefer said gently, "It can be dangerous to look at the image for too long."

Kerris turned his hips so that he no longer faced the pillar. "Thank you," he said.

Sefer let him go. "They're ready," he said. People in the back of the Yard, by the fence, were yelling at each other to sit down, be still, make room.

Kel's shout silenced them. "Yai!" The Yard grew still. Kel and Ilene were sparring: circle, kick, block, punch, glide aside—the practice blows that even Kerris knew (he'd seen them done a hundred times). But the chearis struck with dreadful speed, making a blur of hands and feet that Kerris could barely follow. Ilene kicked. Kel slid beneath the extended leg, rose, and flung Ilene backward. She rolled upright, breathing hard.

She bowed to Kel, and he to her. They separated. Kel beckoned to Riniard, Ilene to Calwin. Now there were four people to watch. Ilene hooked Cal's legs out from under him. He rolled backward and returned to the attack. Riniard sliced sideways at Kel and went flying over his hip. He hit the dusty ground with a thud.

The pairs bowed to each other. Riniard engaged Jensie. Cal took on Arillard. Ilene beckoned to Elli. Kel let them work together for a while and then joined them. They did not talk, though occasionally someone—it was hard to tell who— laughed or yelped.

"Yai!" The yell halted them. They made the circle, bowed, and separated. Ilene, Arillard, and Jensie walked to the weapons shed. They returned with *nijis*, the wooden practice knives. Again they made two pairs and one trio. The nijis were smooth, polished, yellow, nearly as long as the chearis' real knives. Kerris wondered what wood they were made from. In Tornor nijis were made only of white oak.

He watched the patterns the chearis made. Circle. Strike. Parry. Step and throw. Their shirts were patched with sweat, and their skin caked with dust. Kel shouted. Ilene passed him her niji. Arillard gave his to Riniard. Elli took the third from Jensie.

Someone tapped Kerris on the back. He turned around. A woman handed him a waterskin. He drank and passed it on to Sefer. The shadow of the Guardian extended across the Yard. A cool wind blew across the space. Again the chearis exchanged their weapons.

Jensie blocked Kel's knife thrust, arms above her head. Her muscles shook with effort. She turned him and brought him to his knees, arms extended, one on his wrist, the other on his elbow. He signaled halt. The chearis brought the knives to the shed. Weaponless, they separated, walking casually past each other. "Is it over?" Kerris said to Sefer.

Sefer smiled. "Watch Kel," he said.

The chearis walked. Kerris watched Kel. Nothing happened.... The spaces between them seemed to be getting smaller. Suddenly Kel kicked sideways at Ilene. Ilene blocked the kick with a lazy forearm. They passed each other, walking. Cal pinned Riniard's wrists from behind. Riniard whipped free. Arillard took a long step and swept Elli's legs from under her. They walked, and slowly the circle grew smaller. Ilene sparred with Elli. Kel threw Arillard. Jensie and Riniard allied to attack Cal. They separated, reformed, melted, converged, merged, switched. The circle shrank, until at last Kel was backed against the pillar, alone. Chopping, stabbing, using only his hands, he fended them off until they reached him, wrestled him down, and sat on him.

Sefer laughed. He stretched his arms above his head. "It always ends that way."

A small pack of worshipful children descended upon the chearis. Kerris stood up. His hips ached, and his legs were numb. He stamped, waiting for the prickles to stop. Kel was kneeling, talking to the children. They made a circle around him, like little chearis. Some of them might grow to be chearis, if they were strong and swift and singleminded, and remained whole, Kerris thought. Elli waved to him. He waved back. She walked across the square. Her arms, legs, face, clothes, and hair were thick with dirt, but the spring was still there in her step, in the tough long muscles of her thighs. "Did you like it?" she said. He nodded. "Good." She brushed the top layer of dirt from her arms. "Look at me, I'm a mess!" She grinned through the dirt mask. "Walk with me."

"Where are you going?"

Elli shook her head to try to shake the dust from her hair. "To the baths," she said.

There was a bath-house at Tornor: it was a long, tiled room, containing laundry tubs that could be filled with heated water. The baths at Elath were different. They were two pools on a slope. A stream fed the topmost pool, and spilled from the lower edge of the bottom one.

Elli said, "You wash in the lower pool and rinse in the upper one."

Kerris stuck his hand into the water. It was icy.

Beside the upper pool was a clothesline upon which hung long robes of every color and size. Elli said, "When you finish bathing, you choose a robe. Of course, you can't keep it, you have to bring it back."

Beside the lower pool was a structure like a house. It seemed to have no corners.... It was covered with designs made of beads. Kerris remembered the bead design on the door of the house in Galbareth. He realized that the structure was made of skins on a wood frame. The breeze blew toward him. He smelled the pungent odor of human sweat.

"What's that?" he said.

Elli said, "The steam tent."

She stripped her filthy clothes and strode naked to the tent. As she pulled a flap aside, steam billowed from it. Ilene emerged. She ran across the ground and leaped into the bottom pool. She sank beneath the surface and bobbed up again, agile as a river eel. She stroked to the side of the pool. It was edged with stone. She took something from the stone and began to rub herself with it. Kerris went closer and saw that there were pots of soap all about the side of the pool.

Another woman came from the steam tent, followed by a dark-skinned man. They went to the top pool. The woman's belly was big with child. The man steadied her as she climbed over the slippery stones, and she laughed and said something to him that made him laugh. They ducked under the water, and then stood in the shallow end with their arms about each other.

Ilene said, "Kerris, don't you want to bathe?" She pointed to the tent. "Come with me. I'm going back there to sweat the soap off."

"No, thank you."

She left the pool. Elli arrived, her skin glistening. She leaped into the water, shouting like a child. Spray shot into the air. Kerris retreated from the edge. The other chearis approached. Sefer was with them, walking beside Kel. Kel took off his clothes. He kissed Sefer on the mouth before he went into the steam tent.

Jensie and Riniard coaxed Cal into the center of the lower pool. They shouted contrary instructions to him. Sputtering, he paddled, sank, and came up swearing.

Sefer strolled to Kerris' side. "What are they doing?" he asked, amused.

"I think," Kerris said, "they're trying to teach him to swim."

The chearis carried their filthy clothes back to Sefer's house.

Elli put her arm through Kerris'. "Feel," she said. He felt the fabric of her sleeve. It was velvet, in a sumptuous golden shade. Ilene's sister had come to the baths, bringing Ilene's little boy. He was dark and chubby. He waddled beside his mother, dark eyes wide. Kel was flushed and happy. He walked with Sefer. His hair bushed out from his face. He wore a dark blue silk robe with silver embroidery on the cuffs and the hem.

A woman strode by them, carrying a hoe over her shoulder. She stopped to speak with Sefer. The tip of the hoe glinted red in the sunset light, and Kerris saw that it was a steel spearhead. He glanced around the rim of the bowl in which the village lay. He could not see the guards hidden in the rocks and thickets, but he felt their presence. . . . He wondered if the Asech would attack tonight. The woman finished her speech with Sefer and moved away, steps light in the cool evening, her broad face flinty.

Elli said, "Kerris, I want to talk with you later."

"All right," he said.

They ate evening meal at Sefer's house: hot bread with butter, cold pickled beans, strips of cheese, chunks of fish. Ilene fed Borti till he fell asleep in her arms. Next to the colorful luxury of the chearis' bath-robes, Kerris felt drab and sticky. Two dishes filled with choba oil stood in the center of the table, throwing a soft patina over the room. A cricket chirp pulsed from near the stair. Kerris wondered where it was. Paula had told him that a cricket in the house meant good luck. The chearis lazed in the cushions.

"What news of the Asech?" Riniard asked. "Are they still there?"

"They're still there," Sefer said.

Ilene rocked Borti. "You say the raiders mean to frighten, not to kill, Sef. I'll believe you for now, but it goes against my blood to let them camp so close to us and not even know exactly where they are, or how many."

"I know," Sefer said. "We cannot help it."

Arillard picked his teeth with a fishbone. "In my troop on the border there was a scout so good that she could go into an Asech camp and count the feathers in the chief's horse's mane."

Cal said, "Since when do horses have feathers?"

Arillard grinned. "O ignorant one. The Asech braid their horses' manes with feathers. Different feathers indicate different ranks."

"We can't all be aged and wise like you," said Cal. He rolled swiftly away from Arillard's elbow.

Riniard frowned. "I don't understand why we know so little about the raiders. They're human; they ride horses, they leave tracks in the night. A good scout could find them."

Sefer said, "You forget—these Asech are witches. It's hard to take a witch by surprise."

Riniard sat up. "Send a witch, then!" He gestured in the lamplight. "If you find out where they are you can send out a troop to surround them."

"Idiot," said Ilene. She kicked the redhead on the leg nearest her.

"Why?" said Riniard. "They can't be that strong. If they were strong they wouldn't need to threaten you."

Kel said softly, "A good point, Red."

Sefer said, "If they're afraid of us, they'll be extra-vigilant."

Riniard stabbed a finger into the air. "But why can't you use your witchcraft to attack them back!"

"Because our gifts come from the chea," Sefer said, "and we will not use them to make war."

"Oh," said Riniard. Deflated, he sank into the pillows and veiled his face in Jensie's hair. She tickled him and he scrambled from her reach.

Ilene said, "You know, Sef, I wonder if that's the right decision." The cricket called in the wall. "I am not a witch, of course."

Kel sat in a dune of pillows, one hand linked with Sefer's. "Tomorrow," he said, nodding to Kerris, "I'll take you to meet our cousins. They are anxious to know you."

Are they? Kerris thought. He leaned back against a bolster. Elli was watching him. He wondered what she wanted to speak with him about. His stump itched. He scratched it.

"Nika, is Kerris' gift as strong as I think it is?" Kel said.

Sefer looked at Kerris across the fish bones. "Kerris is a very strong inspeaker."

Borti snored. Ilene gathered him up. Standing, she pulled a fold of her robe around him. "I'm going to my sister's," she said. "Kel, don't forget—we are to teach tomorrow in the Yard."

"I won't forget," Kel promised. Borti's head lolled on his mother's shoulder. Softly the chearas chorused goodnights.

Kel ran his hands over Sefer's ribs. "Let's go to bed," he said. The gesture was loving, urgent, and erotic. Kerris flushed to the tips of his ears. He ducked his head, reaching for a mug of wine, to hide it.

Sefer rose. "Till morning," he said. "Sleep well."

Arillard chuckled. "We'll sleep. *You* won't."

Sefer and Kel went to the stair. Despite himself, Kerris found himself listening for the rhythm of their steps—listening for the moment when the steps stopped. The bitter envious tears were welling into his eyes again. He sat by his pallet, tracing the cracks in the floor with his forefinger.

Elli's voice said quietly into his ear, "Kerris, will you talk with me now?"

She was holding an oil dish. Bending, she set it on the mat by his knee. He wanted to say No. Go away. But he couldn't. The steps on the floor overhead halted. He told himself not to think about them. A long-legged spider ran over his hand.

"What do you want to talk of?" he said.

"What are you thinking?"

He lifted his head. No one ever asked him that, except Josen. He rubbed his eyes. Elli sat cross-legged, velvet robe glowing, hands folded in her lap.

The wine loosened his tongue. "I was thinking about my brother. How different we are."

"You look alike."

He grimaced. "Not to me. I have this." He tapped the stump. The tears returned. "He's a cheari, he has a lover, a home, all of you—" He paused. The room was so silent he was afraid the others were listening, but when he looked up he saw them by their bedrolls.

Elli said, "Have you never had a lover, Kerris?"

Kerris remembered Kili of Tornor, who had rolled with him in stained sheets. "I've had two lovers," he said. "One slept with

98

me out of curiosity." He thought, with pain, of Tryg. "The second came to me out of pity. My best friends in Tornor were an old man and an old woman." His heart insisted, They were *good* friends . . . But it was too late to keep the loathing from his voice.

Elli said, "I would love you."

He stared at her, incredulous. She was mocking him; she did not mean it. His pulse beat in his throat. "Out of pity," he said.

"No." The light from the dish flecked her hair with gold. "I like you. You may have lost an arm but there's nothing else missing." She grinned for a moment. Behind the smile, her eyes were grave and steady on his face.

He was shaken. "Chearis sleep with chearis. Riniard and Jensie, Kel and Ilene—"

"You're here."

"But I'm not one of you. I'm only here because of Kel." He had neglected to breathe. He gulped air. Elli's fingers unlaced. She touched his hand.

"Do you know what your face says every time you look at him?" she said. "I do. I wasn't lying, Kerris. I would be your lover, and your friend, and not out of pity." Her fingers on his skin burned like a brand. He knew what she was going to say before she spoke. "But it isn't me you want."

Kerris' body flamed with heat. But his thoughts flowed, pure, clear, cool as a river. . . . No wonder he had had no true lovers. There was no lover who could compete with a dream. Waking and sleeping, from the day Morven forbade him the Yard, he had dreamed of his brother, until the night he had sought him out, across distance, through time, using a gift he still did not understand.

Through numb lips, he said, "It's funny, isn't it."

"Kerris—" Elli gripped his wrist hard enough to hurt. "Why do you hold back? Kel cares for you. At least you could say it—say something!"

He wondered if she'd lost all sense. He pointed upward.

"Oh—" she shrugged. "Sefer knows that Kel loves other people. He doesn't care. How could he? It makes no difference to what happens between them."

Arillard reached from his pallet to blow out the light. The room darkened. "Does everyone know?" Kerris said. "How I—that I—" Elli shrugged again. "Does Kel know?"

Elli said, "I don't think so." She licked her thumb and forefinger.

Kerris did not think so either. For a moment the urge moved in him to be sure . . . as if without volition, he reached into the dark house, seeking to touch his brother's mind.

And was stopped, by a seamless mental barrier. A thought came through it, a clear, compelling warning. Kerris' head throbbed. He withdrew. The communication had not come from Kel. His skin prickled, recalling the intensity of Sefer's gaze at their first meeting. Sefer knows, he thought. He hated Sefer for that certain knowledge.

"Will you tell him?" he said.

Elli blew the last lamp out. She pinched the wick with damp fingers. "Not if you don't wish it."

"I thought there were no secrets in a chearas," he said.

She answered, "I can keep silent." Her tone was even and courteous. He considered what she had offered him, and was ashamed.

"I'm sorry," he said.

She nodded. They sat in silence. The moon's glow ripened in the window. Night sounds filled the room: birds, crickets, the bark of a fox. A board creaked in the chamber over Kerris' head. His raw nerves quivered. He said, "He wouldn't want me." But he remembered what she had said. *Kel cares for you.*

Elli stood. Briskly she drew the gold velvet robe over her head. "Maybe not," she said softly. She slid into her blankets. "There's one way to find out. Ask."

"I *can't.*"

"Don't wait too long," she said, as if he hadn't spoken. "If he doesn't know, he will. Your face will tell him." Warm in the cool room, her fingers laced with his a moment. "He's a patterner, remember, and a cheari."

"I know what he is," Kerris said.

She took her hand from his and rolled over on her stomach. Light from the lifting moon touched her skin. She muttered something—he could not hear the words.

The white crescent appeared over the windowsill. Kerris moved from its range. "What?"

Elli lifted her head from the pillow. She repeated the words. "He's not blind. He knows what you are, too."

Chapter 7

When Kerris woke in the morning the chearis were scattered across the dim chamber, blanketed lumps, still sleeping. He had been awakened by the piercing warbles of the birds, so different from the pigeon noises of Tornor's flocks. He pulled on tunic and pants and went into the garden. The grass was thick with dew, chilling his bare feet. He rubbed his eyes and watched the red bird dart back and forth in the welling sunlight.

In a little while the others would rise. Kel would take him to his uncle's. He wondered again if this, his maternal uncle, was anything like Morven. He went back to the chamber and put on his boots. On impulse, he left the knife and sheath that Josen had given him by his bedroll. He had no use for it. He was not quite sure what he was doing. He didn't want to see his brother—and Sefer—not yet, not until he had time to think. . . . He was still bemused and a little tremulous from his talk with Elli.

He went into the street without looking at the upstairs windows of the house. *He's not blind*, said Elli in his memory. *He knows what you are.* Kerris rubbed his hands over his face, feeling stubble. He would need to shave soon. What am I, then?

Kerris thought. I'm a scribe, a cripple, a witch. . . . A bird flew past his head. This one was blue with black bars on its wings. He walked by the Yard. The top of the Guardian gleamed with the sunrise. He passed a well. He retraced his steps. Dipping up a bucketful of water, he rinsed his mouth and washed his dusty face.

When he lifted his head, he saw a woman at his elbow. Her hair was white: it sprang curling out of her head like unsheared wool, thick as northern fleece. She wore gold, edged with green. Her face was lapped with wrinkles.

"May the peace of the chea be with you," she said.

"And with you," he answered. He looked up the terraced slope of the valley, seeking the farm Kel had pointed out to him the day before. "Can you tell me which of the farms is Ardith's?"

The old woman put a surprisingly strong hand on his shoulder and turned him eastward. "Follow the line of white birches," she said. "Ardith's farm is the one with the steepest roof."

"Thank you."

"You are welcome." She had pale pink skin and a wide mouth. When she smiled, wrinkles rippled from her lips to the borders of her face. Her eyes were dark and very powerful. "My fingers are not as agile as they once were. Would you dip me a bucket?"

"Of course," Kerris said. He lowered the bucket into the well and cranked it up again. He left it, brimming, in her weathered hands. Squinting, he strolled east. Paths tracked upward to the valley's rim. Cows grazed in unplanted fields. Groves of cypress, pine, and birch marked the farms' borders. A good fifth of the fields were nubbly as a sheared sheep, showing where the winter wheat had been scythed. It was gathered and husked now, milled, packed into sacks, laid in the village storerooms. But elsewhere the grain grew tall, almost ripe, awaiting the autumn harvest.

A woman rode down the slope on the back of a piebald mare. Kerris caught, in the misty morning, the glint of metal. He could not tell if she was carrying a hoe or a spear.

The curve of the bowl made distances deceptive. The farms

were bigger than they looked. Halfway up the slope Kerris passed a clear, shallow stream. It fed into a pond. In the pond's depths bright red fish swam in circles and figures through fronds of underwater greenery.

It was pleasant to be alone, unobserved except by an occasional stranger. It seemed easier to walk without the knife's weight bobbing at his thigh. The ground was moist and rich. It clung to the soles of his boots. He sniffed. The air smelled of cow dung, pinesap, and wet earth.

He saw a doe and two spotted fawns nibbling the new leaves of a birch tree, and stopped to watch them. There were few deer in the north. The doe's coat was red, like clay. The fawns' legs were stick-thin as the bones of birds. He took a step in their direction. The doe saw him. Her tail flicked white as milk. She nudged the fawns ahead of her into the deeper recesses of the forest. This is home, Kerris thought. It did not seem as preposterous as it had the day before.

Through the sun-dazzle he glimpsed a man ahead of him. He was wearing brown, and a straw hat like the hats the women wore in Galbareth. Kerris caught up with him. He carried a brace of rabbits in a rope net. "I'm looking for Ardith's farm," Kerris said.

The man said, "You've found it." He had a good voice, calm, comfortable. "I'm Ardith." He pushed his hat farther back on his forehead. Stout leather gloves poked from his belt. His hair was brown. His eyes were gray-brown, like rock. "You're Kerris, Alis' son. Heard you'd come in with Kel. The children said they saw you at the Yard. Thought you'd be up here." He gestured toward the slate-roofed farmhouse. "Come in. Lea wants to meet you."

"Thank you," Kerris said.

"Thought Kel might come with you."

It took a moment before Kerris realized that he'd been asked a question. "I didn't wait," he explained. "He was asleep when I left."

The farmhouse was built much like Sefer's cottage, but larger. Just inside the front entrance was a rack for boots and shoes. The downstairs chamber was wide and airy, floored with mats, strewn with thick cushions. In the center of the room was a low wooden table. There were soft leather curtains at the windows.

"You must meet the *abu*," Ardith said. He led Kerris to the rear of the house. There was a brick hearth with an iron pot set in it, a pan rack, and a tiled stove. A chair with a striped blanket across it sat just in front of the hearth.

"Abu," said Ardith. The blanket moved. There was someone beneath it. A head lifted from the colorful folds. An old woman gazed at Kerris. Her hair was white. The pink of her skull showed clearly through the strands. Her eyes were milky and bulbous. The blanket fell from her bent shoulders. Her lips curved. "Abu, this is Kerris-no-Alis. Reach your hand to her," he murmured to Kerris. "She is blind and wishes to touch you. She is Lea's mother's mother." Kerris held out his hand. The crone extended a hand from the blanket. She rested it in his. Her fingers were knobby and shrunken, and her nails were very long. She mumbled something. "She says she is glad you have come," Ardith murmured. The dry hand was like a claw. She drew it back within the blanket and dropped her head. Gently Ardith adjusted the folds of the blanket around her shoulders.

"She built this house, she and the *anu*," he said. "She remembers a time when all this valley was streams and trees."

Footsteps rang overhead. A tall, dark-haired woman sped through a suddenly twitched-aside curtain. "Nika," she said, "Tazi is in the girls' room and will not let me open the door!"

Ardith held out the rabbits. "I will see to her," he said. "Lea—" but the woman was already coming toward Kerris, arms outstretched. Without hesitation, she put her arms around him and hugged him. She was tall as he. She wore dusty brown pants, and a cream-colored shirt embroidered with geometric patterns in threads of many different colors. Her hair was thick and flecked with gray.

Releasing him, she stepped back. "Ai," she said, "you look just like Alis."

Kerris did not know what to say to this. Ardith laid the rabbits on the tile stove and went up the curving stairway.

"Have you met the abu?" said Lea.

"Yes," Kerris said.

"She is my mother's mother, no kin to you," Lea explained. "But she knew your mother's family." She pointed at the table. "Please sit."

"Thank you," Kerris said. He sat. Now that he was here he was not sure why he had come. He said diffidently, "Did you know my mother well?"

Lea said, "She was as close to me as my older sister would have been. We grew up together. I was eight when she had her first child. I thought all babies looked alike. It took having four of my own for me to learn otherwise."

The stairs shook. A small, sullen-faced girl raced down them. A door opened: Kerris glimpsed green plants in sedate rows. The girl skidded through the door. It slammed with an ear-shattering bang behind her. Lea sighed. Ardith came downstairs, fanning his face with his hat.

"That's Tazia," Lea said. "She's my youngest. Meda, my oldest, is eighteen. Reo and Talith are between them." She turned to her husband. "What is she angry about now, nika?"

"She wants to be with Meda."

"Yesterday she wanted to go with Reo to watch the chearas." Lea lifted both hands toward the ceiling. "She is ours, I remember bearing her, but I never thought to have such a grudgeful child." She laughed then. She had a deep and tuneful laugh. "Forgive us, Kerris. She is only eleven, and already the gift is strong in her. Did she say where she was going?"

Ardith was gutting the rabbits with swift, skillful motions, tossing the innards into a crock by the stove. "I told her to go to the Tanjo. Tamaris is there."

Lea said to Kerris, "When it first came, your gift must have been a trouble to you, so far from anyone who could tell you what it was."

The matter-of-factness of her tone made it hard for Kerris to answer. He thought of the curiosity, revulsion, and scorn with which the folk of the Keep had greeted his fits. He remembered how hard he had tried to make them go away. "Some," he said.

"You are an inspeaker, aren't you, like Sefer," she said. "That's good. He is a good teacher, I have heard."

Kerris said, "I know I have a lot to learn." It came out stiff. A look that he could not interpret passed between Lea and Ardith.

Lea said, "I am sorry. We forget that outside Elath people do not speak easily of the witch-gifts." She went to the pantry, and returned with the inevitable plate of fetch. She laid one stalk in the old woman's hand before she put the food on the table.

Kerris wondered if mealtimes in the south were different from mealtimes in the north. Perhaps food was so abundant—in spring and summer, at least—that it could be freely offered to a guest at any time. In the north only the lords of the Keep offered food to a visitor without first counting stores. For politeness' sake, he took a stalk of fetch. The bowl it lay in caught his eye. It was of a rich orange color. He wondered who had made it. He had never seen clay work so fine, at Tornor.

He touched it. The glaze was smooth as water. "This is nice."

Lea reddened like a girl.

Ardith smiled. With quiet pride he said, "Lea made it."

"It's beautiful."

The door to the garden slammed open. Tazia stood in the doorframe, her face contorted with fury. "I don't *want* to go to the Tanjo."

She wore brown, like her father. Thick black braids, tied with red silk, stuck out over her ears. She thrust her chin out, glaring. The curve of her small cheekbones copied, in little, the curves of Lea's broad face.

Lea said, "Tazi, don't make noise with the door."

Tazia stamped her foot. "But I want—"

Ardith said, "Tazia. That's enough."

She tilted her head to look at him, as if considering disputing the gentle command. Some of the anger went from her face. She looked at Kerris. "Who are you?"

Lea said, "You know very well who he is. He is your cousin Kerris, come from the north to live at Elath."

Kerris thought, Is that what I came for?

Tazia said, "Oh." She scratched her chin, tapping her big toe on the matted floor. Her feet were very dirty. "You came with the chearas."

"Yes."

"Do you know my sister Meda?"

Ardith said, with patience, "There is no reason why Kerris should have met your sister."

"She is with the guards." The small face scowled. The small fists knotted. "I want to go there."

Ardith squatted, as if to reason with the child. "You cannot. You are too young, you would be in the way."

"I could help," Tazia asserted. "I'm strong. I can throw stones. See!" The sunset-colored plate lifted from the table and swooped like a bat to the silver beams of the chamber. Pieces of fetuch went flying to all the corners of the room. Kerris ducked as the plate sailed by his ear. Lea made a grab for it with both hands. Suddenly it ceased to move. It hung, quivering, aloft, and fell without shattering to the table. The fetuch stalks hopped from their corners and landed at Tazia's feet.

Ardith said, "Tazi, pick them up."

By the hearth, the abu lifted her head and cackled, a sound like stones tumbling.

Tazia looked stubborn.

"Take them to the well and wash them, and bring them back. You've done enough mischief for one morning." The door at Tazia's back opened, though no one touched it. "When you've brought them back, you will go to the Tanjo."

Braids eloquently drooping, Tazia gathered the dusty stalks from the mats. She went through the door and it closed behind her. Lea picked up the orange bowl. and ran her fingers over it. "It's not cracked." She laughed. The merriment playing over her face strengthened her resemblance to her daughter. "I remember the time she tried to use the gift to milk the cows. Ai, that was funny!"

Kerris said, "She is a witch."

"She moves things with her mind, as you saw. She is surely her father's child. Thank the chea none of the others are so gifted. It came to her young. Usually a woman's gift does not come until she bleeds. Alis' gift did not come till then."

The door opened. Tazia plodded in. She put the dripping stalks of fetuch in the orange bow. Silently she went, closing the door. Suddenly it sprang open again. A pair of small fawn boots

109

soared through the air and landed with a plop outside. The door shut. Lea laughed her lovely deep laugh. She rose. "Come," she said. "You like my work. Let me show you my workroom."

Across the little garden (which was indeed an herb garden, steaming with mingled fragrances) stood a shed. Kerris guessed that it had once been a stable. A faint smell of horse lingered in it. The floor of the shed was covered with white dust. "Clay dust," Lea said. "It's impossible to avoid." Three barrels stood beneath the windows, each covered with a damp cloth. Lea lifted the cloths for Kerris to look. Each was filled with clay. The first clay was red, the second whitish, the third gray. Jars, plates, and bowls lined a shelf on the opposite side of the room.

Lea showed Kerris her worktable. "I mold the pots on the wheel." She pointed to a potter's wheel in the corner. "I bake them in the kiln, the potter's oven. That is just behind this shed. If you like I'll show you. Then I decorate them." She pointed to a score of little pots lined up along the worktable. "There are my paints: enamels, lacquers, and glazes. Some are powder and some liquid, some have glass in them. Some do not." She lifted a blue jar and turned it for Kerris to see the pattern. It was covered with white flowers. "This design is made by painting around the flowers with the blue glaze and letting the clay's natural white bake through."

"What do you do with them?"

"Trade them to my neighbors. I make most of the pots and plates for the village. The best of them I save and sell to the blue clan. There is one trader from Mahita who loves my flowered jars and will take almost anything I make. I get my glazes from him." She showed him her worktools: brushes, metal pens, scrapers, tongs. Two unburned hour-candles rested in the window.

"Where do your designs come from?" Kerris asked.

She smiled. "Out of my head."

At the back of the worktable stood a *chobata*, its surface an ugly mud color. Kerris nodded to it. "Is that spoiled?"

Lea laughed. "No. It is ready for firing. When it comes out of the kiln it will be a brilliant red, and I will lacquer it with black."

"How did you learn to do this?"

"From my mother. Women in my family have always been potters." They went behind the shed. Kerris admired the kiln. It was bigger than he had thought it would be, brick, with an arch through which logs could be fed. Lea opened the metal door to show him the shelf on which the pots rested. There were perhaps twenty pots on it. The earth beneath the shelf was littered with pink sherds. "All those need firing," Lea said. She closed the door and pushed the metal bolt. "But I've been busy, and it's hard to find the peace of mind to work within the trouble."

"Tazia?" ventured Kerris.

"No. Tazi's my joy, even in mischief." Lea's gentle voice took on an edge. "No, I mean the Asech raid."

In the garden, Lea bent over a tall plant with small blue flowers. She flicked a red-shelled insect from the serrated leaf. "I lost friends and family in the last raids," she said. "Elath was attacked, you know. The raiders were beaten back, but we haven't forgotten. This isn't the first time we've had to rebuild our homes."

Kerris said, "Did you know my father?"

Lea turned over more leaves. She looked sideways at Kerris. "A little. He was everything that Alis was not. She was slim and dark and quiet. Ardith is like her. She tired quickly, because of the gift. Sometimes I thought she was quiet because she was an inspeaker. . . . I was dreadfully jealous of Kerwin." She brought her hands together. "They met in Kendra-on-the-Delta. He was escorting his father, the lord, to the Council of the Cities, and needed a new cloak. She was walking in the market. It was a chance meeting. The old lord wasn't happy. He wanted Kerwin to make a city match, with a daughter of the great families, Med, Hok, Batto. But Kerwin was stubborn. He was tall—" her voice trailed off for a moment. "As I remember him, he was very much like Kel."

Kerris did not want to think about his brother. "How did my father die?" he said.

She lifted her thick, dark brows. "Don't you know?"

"They told me only that he was dead in the war. I never knew when, or how."

"He died on the border, a year after Alis was killed."

111

They walked back toward the house. At the last row of plants Kerris noticed an oddly shaped rock, partly overgrown with runners. He hunkered down to look at it further. The face, mouth, nose, eyes, of the Guardian, showed through a screen of white blossoms. He straightened hurriedly.

Lea said, "Don't worry. This one is flawed. That's why it's in the garden."

"How did it come here?" he asked.

"I made it," she said.

"Did you?" He hunkered down again. Warily he touched the smooth face. At this distance he could see that it was clay, not stone. "Why?"

"Sefer wanted one for the Tanjo. I made several till I got it right. The others are in other people's homes. Lara—she is headwoman here, you may have met her—has one; so does Tamaris."

A bee lighted on one of the white blooms. Gently Kerris pulled his fingers back.

They returned to the house. Two boys stood over the iron pot. The lid lay on the stovetop. The rich odor of stew steamed upward toward the roof. Kerris' mouth watered.

Lea grinned. She advanced toward the intent boys. Suddenly the pot lid rose from the stove and landed firmly on the pot. Ardith came down the last few steps of the stair. The boys spun around. The taller one said to his father, "We were only looking—" The smaller one laughed and stuck an elbow in his brother's ribs.

"You can't fool Poppa, don't you know that by now?" He looked at Kerris. He was dark, like his father. He wore dusty clothes, a leather belt with a knife on it, a straw hat. His feet were dirty as Tazia's. "I'm Reo," he said. His voice was deep. Kerris realized that he was the older of the two. The other boy moved with the lanky carelessness of boyhood, and he wore no knife. "That's Talith."

"I'm Kerris," Kerris said.

The younger boy turned. "Hello," he said. His skin was redder than his brother's. "I saw you at the Yard yesterday." His gaze slid uneasily over Kerris' stump and returned to his face.

Ardith said, "I thought you were weeding."

Reo said, "You said you were coming right back." Man and boy smiled at each other. Their smiles were remarkably similar. Kerris guessed that Reo was his father's favorite, as Talith was his mother's. Casually, the older boy leaned to the table and took a stalk of fetuch from the bowl. It twisted from his fingers and landed back in the bowl with a plop.

"I'll bring some with me," said Ardith. "Get out of here." Talith giggled and made a teasing face at Reo.

"Did you meet the baby?" said the younger boy.

"Don't call your sister names," said Lea. "She was here earlier. She's at the Tanjo."

"Learning to throw rocks at the Asech. Pom!" Talith mimed aiming an invisible rock. Reo caught his brother's belt and pulled. Talith squawked and folded in the middle, and Reo towed him out.

Ardith said, "I should go back to the fields."

"Go, then," said Lea.

"Care to come?" Ardith said to Kerris.

"If you like," Kerris said.

Lea put her hand on the front of her husband's shirt. "Tell me where you'll be," she said.

"In the wheat, on the high slope, mending a fence," said Ardith. He touched his wife's cheek with one palm. "They won't come in the daytime, nika."

Lea's voice was bleak as the winter wind. "They have before."

The broken fence was made of stone. Chest-high, it ran between the field of winter wheat and the pasturage where the black and white cows grazed, their heads all facing in one direction, their backs to the sun. A small pile of stones had spilled from the wall in one place and rolled a little down the slope. Kerris helped Ardith collect them. "The cows rub against the stones to scratch, and also because they want to get at the wheat," the farmer explained. "The rubbing loosens the stones." He picked up one stone, turned it, and laid it back on the wall.

"Can I help?" Kerris asked. The dark man shook his head. Carefully he replaced the spilled stones in the niches from which they'd fallen. A few of the rocks took some effort to lift. Ardith did not stop to put his gloves on. When he fit the heaviest one in, Kerris could see blood trickling from under a torn nail. Ardith sucked the cut clean.

"It's nothing," he said.

"Couldn't you do that with your mind?" Kerris asked, shyly.

Ardith half-smiled. "Stones don't turn weightless if I lift them with my mind." He pointed to the ground. A pebble spiraled up from the dust like a quail from its nest, hung in the air in front of Kerris' nose, fell back. "That's easy. Heavy things are hard. They tire me."

They went down the slope again. The wheat ears lifted from the haulm, taller and more golden than the pale northern wheat. Creepers of blue flowers ran up the stems. The smell of cow dung fertilizing the plants was everywhere. Kerris said, "Could you really throw stones at the raiders?"

"I suppose," Ardith said. "Stones, or a spear. But even Tazia knows we don't do that. It would be terrible to use the gifts of the chea to make war."

They joined the boys in the field. Ardith opened his sack and passed out pieces of fetuch. Both boys had taken off their tunics. Reo's chest was patched with clumps of hair. He grinned at Kerris. "Poppa dragged you into working, huh."

"I'll do whatever I can," Kerris said.

"Tali," said Ardith, "give Kerris your hoe and go get another." Talith passed Kerris his hoe and danced off through the row.

"You know," Reo said, "it will take him forever to get back here. He'll go and sit with Mother, or play in the stable."

"I know," said Ardith. "Let him be, Re."

Kerris held the hoe uncomfortably against his side. There seemed to be no convenient place for him to brace it. The soil was rich and dark. He chopped at the roots of the weeds, imitating Reo's smooth steady motions. In Tornor at the harvest, when the guards of all the watches went back to their villages to help their families cut, sheaf, and stook the wheat, he had never done so. Sweat tracked down Reo's naked back. Kerris unlaced the throat of his shirt. He did not want to take it

114

off, but already he felt the sweat starting under his arms. Reo whistled, one row away. The straw hat bobbed in the next row as Ardith bent and stroked, bent and stroked.

Talith returned with a short-handled hoe. He wriggled through the tall stalks and handed it to Kerris. "Mama said you might find this easier to use." Kerris took it. It was easier. He looked down across the terraces to the peak of the farmhouse roof. Smoke curled from its chimney.

In the next row, Reo yipped. "Coney!" Kerris looked up in time to see a gray lop-eared shadow spurt right between the boy's spread legs.

At noon they went back to the farmhouse. The abu snored before the fire. Lea spread food for them: bread, cow cheese, sausage. Kerris' arm and hand burned along the lines of the muscles. He ate slowly, savoring each bite. It seemed to him the field work was the hardest work he had ever done.

Talith said, "Kerris, what do people do in the north?"

Kerris smiled. "The same things people do in the south."

"Farm, you mean." The tall boy sounded disappointed.

"Yes. Farm, and herd sheep and goats."

"Are there chickens, pigs, cows?"

"Chickens and pigs. No cows. There isn't enough for the cows to eat. The soil in the north is thinner, and harder."

"What did you do?" Reo asked.

"I was a scribe. I did accounts for the lord of the Keep. I copied records." Both boys nodded, assimilating it.

"Are there wars in the north?" said Talith. He made a skewering motion with his breadcrust. "Pom! Uh!"

"There were once," Kerris said. "We fought Anhard. But the Anhard folk come now just to trade."

Lea said, "Tali, it goes against the chea to speak of war as if it were *fun*."

The afternoon was just as busy as the morning. Ardith, Reo, and Talith mended tack in the stable, mixed slop and fed it to a pen of spotted pigs, raked cow dung into piles in the pasture—Ardith explained that, mixed with weeds and chaff, it went on the fields—and (with the help of a stolid mule) dragged a fallen tree from a grove and chopped it into firewood. Most of the work took two hands. Kerris felt superfluous. He had never done any of it. He didn't know how. Ardith had to show him how to use an axe. He watched, and did what he was told.

At sunset work stopped. In the west the sky was fiery; in the east it darkened. Silhouetted cypresses stood like spikes along the rim of the bowl. The weeders sat on the farmhouse steps.

Softly, Ardith talked about his sister. "We were always close. The year she died the Asech were bold, raiding the roads as well as the villages. I didn't want Alis to leave Elath. But Kerwin insisted she go north, as much for your sake, Kerris, as for hers, and he wouldn't listen to the foreseer, who said that she ought not to go. He hired guards for the caravan, though—men and women from the city guard in Mahita who were willing to leave their own homes to travel north."

Paula had never said what town or city she came from. "Were they all from Mahita?" Kerris asked.

"I think so. A few of them were *skuthi*, deserters. But they swore loyalty to Kerwin and they kept their word."

Kerris said, "One of them carried me all the way to Tornor Keep."

"So we heard—but that was much later."

Kerris said, "When did you first hear of the attack?"

Ardith turned a stone between his thumb and forefinger. "There's a bond between siblings, witch-children, especially if one of them is an inspeaker. When the attack began Alis linked with me across the fields. I was here, standing guard on the rim as Meda is doing now. They tell me I fell, and would not speak for hours. I saw it through her eyes as it happened. And at the end I felt her die."

Fireflies drifted like small stars over the wheat. They went into the house. The room was warm, bright with the light from three oil dishes, and steamy with cooking smells. Tazia was home. They ate around the table. In the middle of the meal Meda returned. She was tall and slim and fierce. Greeting Kerris politely, she ate and then sat by the hearth, sharpening her spearheads. The abu snored.

"How is it out there?" Ardith said.

"Quiet, for now," Meda answered.

Kerris leaned against the cushions, stomach filled with rabbit stew. He was feeling very content, when Reo approached him. "Cousin?"

He explained that a friend of his, from Elath, was in Kendra-on-the-Delta, apprenticed to a silversmith. "I wanted to write him a letter. I was going to ask Meritha to do it. She writes the records for the Council. But I thought—you might not mind—you could do it now."

"I don't mind," Kerris said.

"Meritha is old, and her hand shakes."

"My hand won't shake," Kerris said. He smiled, thinking of what Josen would have said to shaky lettering. "Can your friend read?"

"No. But he can ask someone to read it to him. I just want to say hello, and tell him I miss him."

"Do you have ink, and a quill, and something I can write on?" This proved more difficult. Tazia ran to the chicken coop to find a turkey feather for the quill. Lea suggested using one of her dark blue glazes. Meda contributed a piece of white cloth that she had been saving to embroider for a shirt panel. In the yard the sleepy chickens clucked their fury at the intrusion. Tazia came triumphantly in with two red tailfeathers clutched in a grubby fist.

Lea brought out a rag for Kerris to experiment with. Reo sharpened the quill point into a nib at Kerris' direction. But the glaze would not sit on the point. In desperation, Kerris turned the feather around and used the vanes, as if they were a brush. The strokes showed thick and clear on the cloth. Reo cheered. "What do you want me to say?" Kerris asked. Even Meda ceased her work to watch. Talith, fascinated, leaned both his elbows on the table. Reo batted him back.

"You'll jiggle it," he said.

"I will not!" Talith flushed with fury.

"For Dev-no-Demio, apprentice to Smith Tian, of Goldsmith's Alley, Kendra-on-the-Delta." Reo's voice softened and deepened. *"From Reo of Elath."*

"Wait a moment, let me catch up." Using the feather end of the quill was more like painting than writing. "All right, go on."

"Dev—My cousin Kerris is writing this for me. He is from Tornor Keep. He came from the north with the chearas that my cousin Kel is in. We are all well. Your family is fine." He paused.

Ardith said, "Say nothing of the Asech raid. We don't want to alarm him—or anyone."

Reo nodded. *"I went to your farm yesterday. Your spotted mare foaled a he-colt. It is white but I think it will be spotted when it grows up."*

"I've only room for one more line," Kerris said.

"I miss you. I wish you were not so far away." The boy's voice grew somber. "That's all," he said.

Kerris put the quill down. He blew across the cloth. He wondered how long it would take the script to dry. "Tomorrow you can seal it with hot wax."

Ardith rose. "I'll take the abu to bed," he said. Gently he tucked the folds of blanket close and picked the old woman out of her chair.

Lea said, "Maybe when Dev comes back to visit he'll bring the cloth with him, Meda, and you can still use it for a shirt."

Meda chuckled. "I can get more cloth."

Reo said, "He won't be coming back, not for a long time. He said so when he left."

Lea's lips pressed together. Meda cocked her head on one side as if she would say something, but didn't. Tazia seized the still wet quill and began to draw designs in blue on her shirt front. The leather curtains were still open. The air was warm. An herb smell came from the garden, and the smell of bread from the oven. *I would have had a family like this,* Kerris thought. *If war hadn't happened, if my father had not sent us north, if the Asech hadn't raided the caravan, if my mother had not died....*

He smelled a heavy, sweet scent, stronger than the bread, stronger than flowers: the scent of heavenweed.

"Here," said Ardith. He held out a small wooden thing with a stem and a hollow and a coal glowing in the hollow. The scent came from there. Kerris had seen other such tools in the wagons of the southern traders at Tornor. Cautiously he held the thing at the tip of the stem, farthest from the dark bowl. The wood was warm.

"What do I do?" he said.

Talith giggled. Reo cuffed him. "Don't laugh at a guest," he said. He sat next to Kerris. "Put the end in your mouth," he said, "and breathe in, as if you were taking a breath of air. Hold it, and then let it out."

Kerris did as he was directed. The smoke was less pleasant in his lungs than it was to his nose. With effort, he did not choke. He remembered the name for the implement: it was a pipe.

"Now pass it," said Reo.

Kerris passed the pipe to Lea. He waited for an effect. His eyes throbbed, and his fingers tingled.

"Do you like it?" said Reo.

"I guess."

The pipe returned to him. He took a second mouthful of the smoke.

"I used to smoke heaven with Dev," said Reo. He let the blue smoke trickle from his nostrils.

Kerris' mouth felt dry. "Is there wine?" he said.

"I'll get it," said Reo. He went to the pantry alcove. Kerris studied his cousin as he went across the room. He wondered if Reo and Dev were lovers. He flexed his fingers. They still tingled. He felt infinitely older than the farmboy. He thought of Kel, with Sefer, and his heart contracted.

Lea said, "Kerris." He looked up. She and Ardith were holding hands. They looked much younger than he knew they were. "Have you thought about where you are going to live, in Elath?"

"No."

Lea glanced at Ardith. He nodded. "You may live with us, if you like."

He knew they spoke it for his mother's sake, and in her memory. But he was touched by the offer. They need not have made it. "Thank you," he said. His tongue felt thick. It had to be from the heavenweed. "I—I don't know—"

"Don't have to tell us now," said Ardith. "The offer stands." His eyes were warm. Kerris thought, He's nothing at all like Morven. He leaned into his cushions, feeling lazy and sad at the same time.

Tornor seemed very far away, farther than the bare measurements of distance and days. In his mind he could hear what Josen would say to this offer. You're wasted on a farm, Kerris. Go to Kendra-on-the-Delta. You are a scribe.

I am a witch, he said into his head, as if the old scholar could hear him. I have family here, and people who care for me. He heard Reo's feet against the dry mats. The face of the Guardian—serene, unfathomable—came into his mind. It made him think of Kel. He thought, Suppose I speak. He'll laugh. But he knew his brother would not laugh at him. He stared out the window at the star patterns. He was almost resolved to say to his kin, I'll stay, and we'll see what happens. He put up his hand to take the wineskin from the crook of Reo's arm.

And the stars exploded.

Chapter 8

Fire—Fear—Fire—Fear—Fire—the words shrieked and stormed in Kerris' mind. He was standing. He could not remember rising. Smoke and the smell of flaming oil were bitter in his nostrils. Lea was soothing Tazia, "Hush, babe, hush, chelito, it's well, it's well." His head thrummed with the force of the warning. Sweat rolled down his sides. The message beat on. *Fire—fear—fire—*

"It's the raiders," Ardith said. His voice was strained. "They're coming."

Reo's face went colorless. Kerris realized that he had not heard the warning, nor had Talith. Meda flashed by him, spear in hand. Ardith went up the stair with long strides. He returned carrying two belts with sheathed weapons hanging from them. One was a longsword. He gave Lea the other. It was a knife.

A horn blew. The notes were sharp and pure, the same melody that the horn might blow at Tornor to warn of attack. Pah-PAH, pah-PAH-pah.

Reo said, "Father, may I go with you?"

"No," Ardith said. "If the raiders come this way there must be two people here, one to guard the children, one to carry the abu. If they come, get to the trees. Blow out the chobata. It will make the house harder to find." He buckled the longsword on. Kerris watched. He had seen, at the Yard in Tornor, men and women train with the wooden swords, but he had never seen anyone wear a real one. Ardith saw his gaze and said, "I used a sword in the fight on the border."

They left the house. The horn still sounded, painfully clear. Ardith ran lightly down the path. The sword bounced, and he put a hand on the hilt to steady it. Kerris ran at his heels. He felt agile as a goat. He guessed that, too, came from the heavenweed. The light of the crescent moon made the dust glitter. The cypresses loomed over the path, dark, shadowy, and tall. Where the moonlight touched the birches they gleamed.

Kerris' boots were not made for running. His left heel began to blister. He forced himself to stay beside his uncle, knowing that if he fell behind he could lose his way and blunder in among the trees. They ran to the village. Figures brushed by them, purposeful shadows, hurrying to posts. Ardith slowed as they entered the streets. Kerris dared to whisper. "Where are we going?"

"The smithy."

Weapons glinted in the dark. A woman gave orders in a quick fierce whisper. Kerris thought he saw Arillard running. Ardith seized his elbow. "Look," he said. Kerris looked up.

Light flared on the rim of the bowl.

The raiders came. They spilled into the valley, shouting and screaming, torches burning in their hands. They did not stop at the farmhouses. They came straight for the village, howling like wolves in the chase. Torchlight glittered on their weapon-hilts. They bristled with metal. Their horses were huge and sleek. They wore gray-brown cloaks that waved into the wind and faded in the darkness to the color of earth. It made the riders harder to see.

Sparks leaped from the torches. Kerris backed against the wall of the smithy. He wished he had his knife. He tried to count the raiders. There did not seem to be very many of them. It would only take a few good archers, he thought savagely, to bring the horses down. On foot the raiders could easily be killed or captured.... Bloody images overwhelmed his thoughts. Horrified, he caught himself. War was vicious, ugly, a cruel occupation; it broke the chea—but he could not stop the images. The Asech dashed through the narrow village streets, shouting, circling, making their horses rear. The man on Kerris' right muttered something, part oath, part plea.

He heard the crackle of flames. A house was burning. He pulled himself together, ready to run, but the men beside him made no move toward the fire. Kerris leaned his mouth to Ardith's ear. "That house—" he gestured.

Ardith said, "There are others there."

Suddenly the square in front of the smithy was filled with plunging horses. "Witch people!" It was a woman's voice. She urged her horse forward, and the other riders drew their steeds back to give her room. "Witch people, do you know us? We are the Asech, the desert riders. My name is Thera. I speak for my people."

The horses stamped and were stilled. The only sound in the space was a child sobbing somewhere in a house. The Asech swung their torches like flags. The man on Kerris' right said, "O Guardian of the chea, curse them."

A woman moved out from the line of villagers. Her hair was white. Her long robe was gold. She moved with care, as if her hips pained her. Kerris recognized her.

She faced the woman on horseback. "I am Lara," she said. "I am head of the Council of Elath."

There was a burst of speech among the riders. Thera leaned down. "Do you speak for your people?" she said.

"No one does that," Lara said. "But if you wish to parley, you may speak to me."

Thera laughed. The torchlight showed her face, thin and bronzed. "We do not parley, old one. We command. We are the desert riders." The boastful words had a ceremonial ring. "Look!" Thera flung an arm toward the slopes of the bowl. The villagers murmured and gripped their weapons. The fields were bright with pinpoints of yellow light: torches. "If you gainsay us we will burn your fields."

Lara said, "We see. Very well. We will use your language. What do you command of us?"

Thera said, "In the cities, even in the desert, they tell stories of the witches of Elath. They say you make water gush from stone. You hold fire in your bare hands, and take no hurt. You move rocks without touching them."

"We know these tales," said Lara.

"Listen. We too, have power. We are witches. You know this, people of Elath. You have tried to touch our thoughts, and you have failed. Is this not true, old one?"

Again the crowd murmured. Again Lara lifted a hand. "It is true," she said. "You have power. We feel it."

"You have a school in this village," said the Asech woman, "where you teach your children to be witches. We have heard of this school in the desert. You teach your children to hold fire. We come to learn. Teach us to hold fire, people of Elath."

Lara said, "You have burned our homes. You threaten to burn our fields. Why should we teach you anything?"

Thera threw back her head, and yelled.

A horseman cantered forward, leading a second horse. Limp over the horse's saddle, tied, face down, lay a man. His red hair shone in the torchlight like spilled blood.

"He is young and fair," said Thera. "Foolhardy, too, to approach an Asech camp alone. He will not tell us his name. He has courage. Who is he—a loved son? A father? A brother? We have him now. Do you wish him to remain unmaimed, unharmed? Then you will do as we say."

The burdened horse pranced a little. On its back, Riniard did not move. Lara's ancient face was impassive. The man on Kerris' right was cursing again. The smoke from the torches made Kerris' eyes tear. He lifted his hand to wipe the tears away.

"Each day you deny us," Thera said, "something will be taken from him. Perhaps just a finger. Perhaps an eye."

A growl rose from the streets. "Barbarians!" called a voice. Thera scowled. "We are the desert riders," she said. "We do not live by city laws." Her horse tossed its head. Its mane and tail were braided. There were feathers in the braid on the mane. Kerris wondered if they meant that Thera was a chief. Some of the other riders had feathers braided into their horses' manes as well. Thera's horse tried to rear. Easily she held it down. Leaning forward, she patted its arched neck. With her glossy hair and sharp-boned features, she reminded Kerris of a bird, a hunting bird, a bird of prey.

The horseman leading the second horse said something brusque and angry to her. She replied in a soothing tone. The sound of the fire in the nearby street had lessened.

"Come to us in the sunlight," Lara said. "Come tomorrow. We will teach you."

"If there is treachery our captive will suffer," said Thera. She was now so close to Kerris that he could see the curved sword on her hip, and the fringe on her boots.

"There will be no treachery," said Lara.

"We will come," said Thera. "Expect us when you see us. It will be soon." Her horse reared. "Iaah!" The riders swung their torches, yelling and shouting. They raced from the square to the road, riding hard, brilliant against the dark fields as a falling star against the sky. Kerris thought of Riniard. Perhaps the young cheari was already hurt. Bile came up in his throat. He swallowed.

His knees were unsteady. He leaned against the wall. Ardith was gone, vanished into the crowd. Kerris wondered where the chearas was. Everyone began to talk. A familiar voice rode the noise: Sefer. Kerris went toward him. He saw a brown face in the moonlight. It was Elli. He touched her shoulder. She whirled to face him, one hand fisted, the other holding her knife. "Did you see—?"

"I saw."

She sheathed her knife. "Poor Riniard," she said.

Lara, Sefer, and three other Elath folk who Kerris did not know were standing together, listening to a woman in brown. She was holding a bow. Kerris remembered her: Cleo from the rocks over the road. Ilene stood at her elbow. Cleo said, "We let them through, as you directed, and counted them. We counted fifty-four, including the ones left on the rim. But there may be more. If they have the gift, they could bring an army through Arun and no one would notice till they had gone!"

"I know," said Lara. She touched Cleo's face. "Daughter, you did well. Go back. Tell your troops that the Asech will return in daylight, and to let them through again."

"How many will there be?" said Cleo. "When will they come?"

"I don't know," Lara said.

Kel appeared out of the darkness. "Elli," he said "Ilene. Come." The other chearis were gathered behind him. He wore boots—not heeled riding boots, but tough-soled trail boots. His knife hung at his hip. His hair was braided and pinned to his head with an ebony comb.

The stink of the torches still soured the air. Elli said, "Where are we going?"

"To get Riniard back."

Cleo said, "Six of you?"

Kel looked at her. His eyes were granite. "That's right. We'll follow their trail to their camp." He stared at Elli and Ilene. Wordlessly they moved to join the others. "We'll be back. It may take us a little while." He turned. Kerris glimpsed Arillard's face. It was tense and troubled.

A man came up. "Lara, shall we—" he started to say, and then his voice trailed off. Uncertain, he glanced from Lara to Kel.

"Nika," said Sefer. "No."

Kel turned. Sefer faced him. Kel walked to him. Sefer did not move. He tilted his head a fraction, to meet his lover's eyes. The noise of the street seemed to fade. Thoughtlessly, Kerris reached for his brother with his mind. It was like touching heated metal.

At his sides, Kel's hands fisted until the knuckles turned white.

He spun from the chearas and walked away. Elli said, "Should we—"

"No," Sefer said. "He won't go."

"We should have attacked their camp."

"They could pick us off in the rocks."

"Not all of us, they couldn't. We should have fired their camps. The witches could have done it."

"We could do it now."

"They'd kill the redhead, or worse. I'll not be responsible for *that*."

"Damn them. Ten years ago we'd have attacked their camp and killed them in their beds, as they killed us."

The chearis walked silently through the streets to Sefer's cottage. Around them the villagers' angry voices rose and fell. As they entered the long room, Jensie shivered and let out a cry.

Ilene went to her at once. "Ai, chelito, he will be all right. Don't think of it." She put her arms around the girl's shaking form and drew her down into the cushions, rocking her as she had rocked her son.

"Soon?" said Elli to the darkness. "What does *soon* mean?" No one answered her. Calwin brought an oil dish from the table. The cricket whined from the stair.

Taking the tinderbox from his pack, Arillard lit a lamp. Kerris sat on his bedroll. His eyes ached from the smoke, and his left heel was raw.

Jensie lifted her face from Ilene's breasts. Anguish hollowed her face like age. "Why did Sefer stop us?"

"It was a stupid idea," Ilene said gently. She stroked Jensie's hair. "If the Asech are witches, they would sense us coming. They would have hurt Riniard, perhaps killed him."

Jensie trembled again. Arillard said softly to Ilene, "You knew Sefer would stop him."

She turned her head to answer him. "Of course. Didn't you?"

Cal said, "The people in the street are angry. They might decide to do something stupid."

Ilene shook her head. "They won't."

Kerris wondered where Kel was. His heel stung. Rising, he limped to the pantry. He found a waterskin by feel. Moonlight through the window illuminated a row of plates and bowls. He took a bowl. With the waterskin under his arm, he went back to the chearis. He gave Elli the waterskin. When it came back to him it was less full by a good deal. He poured some water into the bowl and dipped his heel into it. The scent of the garden blew through the window curtains. His head felt thick and stuffy. Maybe Kel was with Sefer, he thought. Envy spurted in him. He told himself not to be a fool. . . . Jensie was weeping now. Ilene rocked her. The girl's misery clawed at him.

Elli said in his ear, "Kerris, where's Kel?"

"I don't know."

She sighed, and made a signal to Calwin. He rummaged in his pack and brought out the white dice. They hunched over the mat. "Mahita's rules," Elli said. "Dead man throws again." Cal nodded and flicked the dice across the mat.

"Four and three. Your throw."

Elli threw. "Three and three."

Over Jensie's head Ilene was frowning. "Arillard. Maybe you should go look for him."

Arillard said, "You heard Sefer. He won't go."

"I hate it when he goes off like that."

"He has to."

"I know."

"He always comes back."

"I always think—someday he won't."

Violent, ugly pictures cavorted through Kerris' head. *He saw the Asech camp in flames, he saw Thera ringed with archers, struck with arrows, screaming.* . . . He shuddered. These were not his thoughts. He was taking them from other people's minds.

"Six and one," said Elli.

The front door opened and closed. Everyone looked up except Jensie. A woman walked in. She surveyed them with her hands on her hips. She had a flat copper face. "Ilene," she said, "where's Sef?"

Ilene shrugged.

"Out in the street somewhere," said the woman, answering her own question. "And Kel?"

"Walking off a rage," Ilene said.

"Ah. Well, if Sef comes in, tell him I'm here." She walked across the room to the stair, head bowed, legs dragging in a flat, tired gait. She went upstairs. Kerris heard her moving overhead.

The pictures came back. He did not know what to do to make them stop. They came from his companions, from Elli and Arillard and Jensie, most of all from Jensie. . . . "Who's that?" he said, trying to distract himself.

128

Ilene answered. "Terézia. She's Sefer's housemate. She's in Cleo's troop. Cleo must have sent her in."

Kerris wondered if all inspeakers spent their days wrestling other people's thoughts and fears and dreams out of their heads. *He hung from the horse so limp, like a corpse, maybe he's dead, maybe they lied to us, the murderers, O his bright hair, and his eyes were closed....* He forced the brutal litany away.

He rose. "I'm going into the garden."

Ilene said, "We should stay together."

"I won't go far." He limped across the mats. The texture hurt his heel. The grass was cool, damp, and soothing. There was a scent of smoke in the breeze. He sat on the bench. He could still feel the thoughts of the people in the house. Ilene was worrying about Jensie, and about Kel. Jensie was tormenting herself with images of Riniard.

The breeze lifted bumps on his arm. He contemplated going back inside to fetch his tunic. The thoughts of the others wafted to him. Elli was dicing; part of her mind was on the game, part on Riniard.

Leaves rustled. Someone moved in the moonlight. Kerris leaped to his feet, his heart thumping.

"Kerris." It was Kel. He crossed the garden in four strides. "What are you doing out here?"

"I got restless."

"Ah." Kel turned toward the light-filled windows of the house. "Sef isn't there," he said.

"No."

Kel's lips pressed together. "How's Jensie?"

"Ilene's comforting her."

"That's good. Where were you today?"

"With Ardith and Lea."

"If you'd waited I would have taken you there."

"I wanted to see if I could find it myself," Kerris said.

Kel frowned. His hair was still pinned to his head. He looked sleek and fierce as a mountain cat. "Did you like Ardith and Lea?"

"Yes," Kerris said. "They—they offered me a place to live."

"I thought they would," Kel said. Suddenly he stepped

forward, very close. He felt Kerris' waist with his hands. His voice sharpened. "Why aren't you wearing your knife?"

"I took it off."

"I can see that. Why?"

"I can't use it," Kerris said, "why should I wear it?" His voice lifted, and he realized that he was angry.... He saw Kel's mouth twist and straighten, and felt pain bore through his own temples, and knew that he had hurt him.

"I'm sorry," he said, appalled. "I didn't mean it."

Kel looked gravely at him. His fingers brushed Kerris' shoulder. "I wouldn't want anything to happen to you," he said. "Kerris." The word was a caress. "I'll teach you to use the knife."

"It's too late," Kerris said.

"It's not too late. I know, this is my skill, remember? Trust it. Will you let me teach you to use the knife?"

Kerris couldn't breathe. In a voice that barely seemed his own, he said, "I would let you teach me anything."

Kel's fingers tightened on his shoulder, moved to his neck, cupped his chin. "Would you?" said the cheari. His thumb pressed against Kerris' throat, over the racing pulse beat.

Daringly, Kerris put his arm around his brother's body. Kel's face bent to his. Their lips touched lightly. "Hmm." The murmur was speculative. Gently Kel ran his fingers down Kerris' ribs. Kerris stroked Kel's side. He felt awkward and clumsy. Kel's body was beautiful, strong, whole. His back was ridged with muscle.

Kel kissed him again, more firmly. His lips were cool. He tugged Kerris' shirt free of the belt. He lifted his head. "I can't get to you with your clothes on."

Kerris took his shirt off. Kel stroked his ribs and his chest. He pulled his own shirt over his head. The moonlight turned his body white. "Touch me," he said. Kerris did. "Lie down." Kerris lay down on top of his clothes. Images of Tryg, of Kili, littered his mind. He thought, I'm a fool. This isn't going to work.

The grass tickled his back. He started to sit. "Kel, I—"

"Don't talk," said Kel. He took off his pants. "Lie still. Let me."

He shook his head. His hair fell down and coursed over

Kerris' belly. Kerris shivered. He made himself touch Kel's shoulders, chest, his nipples.... They were tense. Kel lifted over his body blotting out the light. Kerris wished for two hands with which to hold him. He tried not to think of his stump, lying useless and ugly in the grass. He tangled his fingers in Kel's hair. Kel lowered himself between Kerris' thighs His body was powerful and warm and fluid as sunlight.

He shifted his weight. Now he was kneeling. "Stay right there," he said. Kerris tried to laugh. Kel teased him, with hands and lips and tongue. His memories of Tryg dissolved. He arched his back. His breath clogged in his throat. He gasped for air. A convulsion of pleasure wrung his nerves like fire. He cried aloud at the burning, and dropped into the grass.

When he opened his eyes, he could see the moon. His head lay on Kel's arm. "Awake?" said his brother.

"Yes."

"Are you cold?"

He would never be cold again. "No. You?"

"No."

He was still lying on his back. His thighs were wet, sticky. Kel was on his side. He ran his fingers over Kerris' face. They smelled of sex. "You've been out here a long time. The others may come looking."

"I don't care," Kerris said. "Let them." Suddenly he thought—Kel might care, might not want the others—Sefer—to know.... "Do you?" he said.

"Care if they come looking? Don't be silly." Kel trailed the tips of his fingers over Kerris' thighs. Kerris jumped. "Was it your first time?" Kel asked gently.

"It was the first time like *that*," Kerris said.

"Good." Kel's tongue traced a pattern on his chest.

Kerris wrapped his hand in a lock of shining hair and tugged his brother's head up. "It wasn't much for you, was it?" he said.

In answer Kel's mouth came down hard on his. When he lifted his head, he said, "It was fine."

Kerris touched his lips. His mouth felt bruised. "Are the others awake?" he asked.

131

"The lamps are out. But you can tell that more easily than I, chelito."

That's true, Kerris thought. He reached to the house with his mind.

Jensie, mercifully, was asleep. Ilene and Elli were drowsing. Calwin was snoring, as usual. Arillard was awake. He touched a stranger and retreated quickly. That was Terézia. Sefer was not there. He said so.

Kel said, "He will be."

For the first time since he had entered Elath, Kerris thought of Sefer with no envy whatsoever. "You love him very much," he said.

Kel nodded. His hair stroked Kerris' chin. "We grew up together. We've been lovers since we were children—before we knew what sex was, or how to do it. We learned fast, though." He laughed. "Sef's the only person in the world who can tell me what to do and make it stick. Except Zayin."

"Like tonight."

"Yes. He was right, of course. And if he hadn't stopped me I would never have come back to the house through the garden, hoping to sneak by Jensie—and look what I would have missed!" Bending, he ran his tongue over Kerris' eyelids.

Night noises filled the garden: the rustling of hunting creatures, the call of an owl, the throbbing croak of a tree frog. Kerris felt the damp through his clothes. Reluctantly he stretched. His heel twinged. "Let's go inside."

Kel rolled upright. Kerris stood up more slowly. Kel put his hands out and laid them on Kerris' shoulders. They kissed again, a soft kiss, without hurt.

Naked in the moonlight, they went to the house. Kel went upstairs. Kerris picked his way across the mats. He found his bedroll laid neatly next to Elli's. She lay on her side, head turned away, knees nearly to her chin. He dumped his soggy clothes on the floor and rolled up in the blanket. The wool was scratchy. The floor was firm beneath him, like an arm.

Smiling, he lay back into it.

Chapter 9

He woke smiling.

Elli was sitting beside him, pulling on her clothes. Kerris reached for his crumpled shirt. There were grass stains on it. He scratched one with a fingernail. Elli's head popped through the neck of her tunic. He wondered if she knew. He put on the shirt. When he glanced at Elli, he found that she was grinning at him.

The ceiling creaked. Kerris tried to school his face to soberness. Anyone looking at him, he told himself, would think him mad, or sick. The steps moved down the stairs. He tried not to look toward them. He looked anyway. It was Terézia. "Good morning," she said. "Sorry I was so short last night. I think I know you all, don't I, from last year—" She looked at Kerris. "I don't know you."

"I'm Kerris. Kiel's brother."

"There's another one of us you haven't met," said Ilene.

"Yes. I heard—the Asech took him. I'm sorry."

Jensie said softly, "His name is Riniard." She gazed at her hands.

Ilene said, "Are you leaving, Terézia?"

"I'm going to Cleo's for morning meal, and to see that she is well. She was nearly dropping last night. Erith took over the watch, thank the chea. We didn't get much sleep on the rim."

Ilene said to Jensie, "Jen, are you hungry?" Jensie shook her head. Her face was haggard.

Ilene said, "I'd like to join you. I should return to my sister's." Troubled, she looked at Jensie. Her hand moved to touch the younger woman's hair.

Jensie said, "Go. I'm fine." Her voice was dull with pain.

"We'll know as soon as they have word of him," Ilene said.

"Yes," said Jensie. For a moment her eyes burned in her pale face, terrible to look at. She reached for the knife that lay, sheathed, to the right side of her bed, as if satisfying herself that it was still there.

Kerris stood to pull on his pants. He put weight on his blistered heel: it was tender, but clearly healing. He decided to go without boots until he could get some like Ardith's, low, with flat soles. He reached for his belt. Arillard was shaking Cal. Ilene folded the bedroll she had slept in: Riniard's bedroll. Jensie tied her scarf more tightly around her hair. Kerris raked his fingers over his head. Grass fell to the floor. It made him remember—his skin flushed, the palms of his hands grew damp, he told himself he was reacting like a child who had never made love before, and he could not help it, the reaction had nothing to do with thought.

Footsteps warned him. He sat down in a hurry and began to roll his blanket. Kel and Sefer came into the room. Despite himself, Kerris looked up. Kel was smiling directly at him, a smile so tender and clear that Kerris could only return it. It seemed shameful or cruel to be so happy in the midst of such painful uncertainty, but he couldn't help it.

Kel was dressed for the Yard, his hair coiled on top of his head. The red scarf of the cheari was braided into it. Sefer was wearing the clothes he had worn before, brown tunic, brown pants, with blue silk trim. He looked calm and rested. Kel went to Jensie and knelt beside her. Softly he said, "The sun is shining, Jen. Look at it."

Jensie raised her head. Her lips thinned in rage. "Can Riniard see it?" she said.

Kel laid something across her lap. "Here." It was a red scarf. "The troop on watch brought it to Sef last night. He must have managed to drop it before or as they took him, hoping that someone would find it and bring it to us. That means that he was breathing, and thinking. Keep it for him."

Jensie touched the scarf with the very tips of her fingers. Then her hands fisted in it. Lifting it from her lap, she knotted it into her hair.

Ilene, standing by the door next to Terézia, said, "Kel, do we go to the Yard today?"

"We do."

"What if the Asech come?"

Sefer answered. "You'll hear of it. The inspeaker in Erith's troop will tell us of their approach." He looked at Kerris. "Kerris, while the chearas works in the fighting circles, will you come to the Tanjo with me? It's time you learned your skills." There was no tension in his voice, and no anger in his face.

Kerris recalled what Elli had said. *Sefer knows that Kel loves other people. It makes no difference....*

"I would like that," he said. Out of the corner of his eye he saw his brother nod approval. "Do we go there now?"

"If you will," Sefer said. "We don't know when the raiders will come back. It could happen any time. When they do, all lessons stop."

"I'm ready," Kerris said. He stood.

Elli patted his leg. "See you later," she murmured, tilting her face up to look at him.

Kel said, "Kerris, where's your knife?" Rising, he came striding across the room. "There it is. Elli, give it to me." He pointed to the knife, which lay where Kerris had left it, near the wall. Elli made a long arm for the knife. She passed it to Kel.

"Open your belt," he said. Kerris undid the buckle of his belt. Kel slid the sheathed knife onto it. His hands brushed Kerris' waist and thigh. He did the buckle up. "I don't want you to leave the house without it on," he said. "All right?" Kerris nodded.

135

The light caresses made his heart shake in his chest. Kel kissed his forehead softly. "Go."

With some difficulty, Kerris walked to the anteroom. Sefer was doing up the laces of his sandals.

In the street, Sefer said, "You look as if you'd been standing in a fire."

Kerris felt himself redden. They walked along the street. In a garden a woman stabbed at the earth with a short-handled hoe. They passed a house. "That's the house that was burned last night," Sefer said. The burn marks were fresh in the wood.

A woman leaned from a window to call to Sefer. "What news of the raiders?"

"None yet," he called.

"What if they don't come today?"

"If they don't come today we'll wait until tomorrow!"

Birds racketed within the furry branches of the cypress trees. "It goes away, you know," Sefer said.

"What?"

Sefer looked sideways at Kerris. "That feeling of having been plunged into fire."

They passed the stables. Tek leaned in the doorway, shirtless. He held a length of iron chain in his powerful hands. "What news?" he rumbled.

"No news, Tek. We wait," Sefer said.

The big man scowled. "Are you really going to teach those murderous folk the witch-gifts, Sef?"

"We will do what we must," Sefer said.

"There are those who won't like it," said the stablemaster. "They say, if you teach the Asech the witch-gifts we'll all be burned in our beds."

Sefer said, "That won't happen, I promise it." He stopped, and laid a hand lightly on Tek's massive forearm. Tek chewed a corner of his mustache. Lalli dashed under his broad nose, a pink chunk of meat in one hand. He reached out a brawny arm and picked her up.

"What's that?" he demanded, balancing the girl on his palms.

"Pig's foot," she said, and waved it under his nose.

Sefer and Kerris went on. Their shadows marched up the street ahead of them, the legs foreshortened like dwarves'.

In the Yard there were men and women in the fighting circles, fighting barehanded and with nijis. In one corner Kerris saw the upthrust length of a wooden sword. Emeth, the man whose house had been torched by the Asech, strolled among them, occasionally stopping someone in a circle. Kerris realized he was the Yardmaster. He lifted a hand to Sefer. "Is the chearas coming?" he called.

"It's right behind us," Sefer answered.

"Any news of the Asech?"

Half the circling fighters stayed their blows to listen to the answer. Sefer simply shook his head.

At the foot of the street he laid his hand on Kerris' shoulder to turn him toward the cypress grove. He dropped it at once, as if he knew that Kerris did not like strangers touching him, and Kerris thought, Maybe he does know.

"Kel said the school was your idea," he said.

"I got it from something he said," said Sefer.

"What?"

"He was home from Vanima; he had just been named cheari. I was lamenting that there was no place for witches to learn the gifts, as chearis can learn *their* gift." He turned his palm up. "He told me to build one."

The trees' scent was rich and tangy, like pine. Their trunks were thick with moss. The grove narrowed. It became a lane: fragrant, silent, and dark. The Tanjo's roof showed through the black tree trunks: it was peaked, and covered with silver-blue slate like fish scales. At the end of the lane lay a bright green sward, patterned with flowers. Around it the silver building made a U. The construction reminded Kerris of the Keep. In the center of the grass was a circle of white, pink-veined stones and in the circle sat a painted image of the Guardian.

Kerris was careful not to look at it directly.

Sefer said, "We put the Guardian here to remind us that our gifts come from the chea and must serve the chea's end."

Kerris said, "This reminds me of Tornor—the building around a court. But there are no gardens in Tornor." Out of the

137

corner of his averted eyes he could see it: two eyes, a nose, a smiling mouth.... He wondered what made it smile.

Sefer said, "They build this way in Kendra-on-the-Delta, with courtyards and gardens."

"Do you know the city?"

"I've been there," Sefer said. "I don't like it. But my sister Keren lives there, with her family. She's a member of the black clan."

"My teacher in Tornor was a scholar."

"What is his name? My sister might have met him."

Kerris touched the stiff leather of his belt. "Josen. But he left the south twenty-five years ago."

"Then Keren wouldn't know him," Sefer said.

They entered the Tanjo through a wooden door. The silver wood was carved with southern runes. Kerris wondered if Sefer had picked them. They read: *Enter in peace; leave in harmony.* The inside of the grooves, where the cutting blade had touched, shone red. There was an anteroom for footwear. Sefer laid his sandals down. A window with yellow glass in its frame shed light into the chamber.

Beyond the anteroom was a hallway. There were doors along one side of it.

Sefer opened one. "Go in."

Kerris went in. He found himself in a light, still space. Two of the walls were red wood. The outside one had a window paned with yellow glass. The two inner walls were white. He walked to the nearest and pushed at its surface. It was smooth and cool and it gave a little to his touch.

"It's paper," Sefer said. "It comes from Kendra-on-the-Delta. It's very strong, made of wood shavings and silk. Stretched on frames, the paper makes screens of any size you want. They're so light that three people can carry them."

There were flecks of color in the screen, like the bits of colored silk that Elli tied her braids with. Kerris rubbed the ball of his thumb over them. He thought, Walls like this would never be practical in the north. It's too cold in a Keep.

He turned away from the paper walls. The room was floored with matting, like Sefer's house, and piled with cushions. In one corner there was a small wood table and a clay pitcher.

You belong here, he told himself. He was a witch, he was among family and friends in the village he'd been born in. He belonged where he was. He sat on a mat. "I'm ready," he said.

Sefer sat opposite him, legs crossed tailor-fashion. "Tell me what you know of your gift," he said.

"I know what to call it," Kerris said. "It's called inspeech. A person who can do it is called an inspeaker."

Sefer smiled. "One can hear that you were trained by a scholar. Keren talks like that—very exact. What can you do with it?"

"I can—" Kerris paused. "I can touch other people's minds with my mind, so that I can know what they are thinking and feeling."

"Describe it," Sefer said.

Kerris felt foolish, describing inspeech to Sefer, who already knew it well. "When it's strong," he said doggedly, "I feel as if I were sharing the other person's body. When it's not strong I just hear their thoughts, as if I were listening to them."

"When did it start?" Sefer said.

Kerris felt himself color again. "I was thirteen. I was asleep. I touched Kel's mind. It woke me."

"Were you frightened?"

"Yes. I thought I was mad. It kept happening. I knew that I was doing it but I couldn't control it, either to make it happen or to make it stop. Finally I realized that it wouldn't hurt me."

"Did you know at once who the other person was?" Sefer asked.

"Not at once. But soon."

Sefer folded his hands in his lap. "You're not the first inspeaker to have wakened to a gift that way. That is a kin-link. It often happens between siblings when one is an inspeaker and the other has a different gift."

Kerris said, "It happened to my uncle and my mother."

"It happened to Keren and me," Sefer said. He rubbed a hand across his cheek. "You don't remember your mother, do you?" Kerris shook his head. "Nor any of your life before you were brought to Tornor? I wonder why. Never mind, go on—was Kel the only person whose mind you linked with?"

"Yes—until he showed me that I could link with other people. He showed me how to control it. That was only a few days ago."

"And can you control it?" Sefer said.

Kerris remembered sitting in the house after the raid, feeling the chearis' feelings, thinking the chearis' thoughts. The memory was vivid and unpleasant. "Not entirely," he answered.

"It will come," Sefer assured him. He rose, circled the room, and returned to his cushion. "Let me tell what we know of the gifts," he said. "We don't know exactly what they are, or why some people have them and some not. There are five kinds of witch-gifts that we know about—some say seven." He held up a hand and ticked the gifts off on his fingers. "Mind-speech. Patterning and foreseeing. Some people claim that these are two separate gifts. Far-traveling. Far-traveling seems common. Many people do it in dreams. Weatherworking. Mind-lifting. Weatherworking is a kind of mind-lifting. Healing. Healing is very rare. There are only three healers now in Elath."

Kerris wondered who they were. He thought of a question that Josen would ask. "How long have people known about the gifts?"

"That depends what you mean by 'known.'" Sefer said. "I asked Keren to look through the black clan's archives for stories about witches and witch-gifts."

"Were there any?"

"A few. I think there have always been witches in Arun. But until now witches have not themselves been sure of what they could do, and so did not use their gifts—or, if they did use them, kept such use a secret. From what Kel and Ilene tell me of the history of the red clan, I think that Van of Vanima was a patterner, maybe a foreseer. But there's no way to know. Even now there are scholars who claim that the gifts are mere trickery or superstition."

Kerris thought of Josen. "In the north only the very ignorant believe in witches."

Sefer smiled. "And they are right to do so, and the very wise are wrong."

A door opened and closed beyond the room. Someone called down the hallway.

Kerris said, "In Galbareth they call Elath the witch-town. They're afraid of the gifts."

Sefer sighed. "I know. Even Calwin, when he comes here, grows nervous. Some of the trading caravans won't stop here any more. But people fear new things. Even some of us." A rueful look shadowed his face for a moment. "Keren is a patterner, like Kel. But she has chosen—like Kel—to limit the ground of her gift, to use it only to pore over dusty records, as Kel has chosen to use his patterning to dance, and fight, and nothing more."

"What would you want him to do with it?" Kerris asked.

"Oh—" Sefer scratched his chin. "To study. To learn. To explore! We know so little about this world. Think of what the gifts could show us! We might far-travel to the ends of the earth, to lands beyond Arun, beyond Anhard, beyond the ocean. There must be people there. We could speak with them. We might see into the future, and even into the past. We might learn to heal, not just fevers and wounds, but age, decay, and even death. Do the stars have a pattern, as the superstitious claim? We can learn it. The more we know, the greater grows our understanding of the chea, and the closer we come to the heart of harmony, to the order that underlies and infuses and springs like breath through all things. We made the Guardian to show us the chea. But we know too that it is imperfect. The gifts come from the chea—surely we are meant to use them!" His voice shivered like a horn calling an army to the field, and then softened. "We know so little. Imagine a time when messages fly from Tornor to Kendra-on-the-Delta, say, as easily as I speak with you, when crops do not fail, when rivers do not flood, when no one goes hungry—" He smiled. "Can you?"

"Not—not easily," Kerris said.

"Ah, well. I cannot always see it either. But I hope that one day people will come to Elath to study the gifts as they now go to Tezera to learn blade-making, or Kendra-on-the-Delta to learn silk-weaving."

"Do the other teachers here feel as you do?" Kerris asked.

"More or less," Sefer said. "We argue. Most people, like Keren or Kel or your uncle, are concerned with the practical aspects of the gifts, with making the gifts useful."

"How are they useful?" said Kerris.

"Surely you can see that," Sefer said. He leaned both elbows into the cushions. His hair fell behind his shoulders. "Healing, weatherworking, being able to lift an object without touching it, truth-seeing—"

"What is that?"

"Knowing if someone is telling the truth, or not. Mind to mind cannot lie. It would be a valuable talent for a diplomat. Imagine if the Council of Cities, or the House Council in Kendra-on-the-Delta had an inspeaker in its pay, as it has guards and scribes."

It made sense. Kerris' stump itched; he rubbed it lightly. He could feel the scars through his shirt sleeve. An inspeaker did not need two arms, only a mind. What would it be like, to possess a skill in which his deformity was no hindrance, none at all? As a scribe he would always need someone else around to mix his inks, sharpen his quills.... He said, "What do I need to learn?"

"You already know a great deal," Sefer said. "Reach to me, Kerris."

Kerris started to do so. He had to shut his eyes. The sight of Sefer calmly watching him was a distraction. *If my mind were a hand....* He extended his thought to the man in brown, expecting to be stopped, or warned away. Instead, he felt a subtle warmth, a welcoming. It drew him in. His sight dimmed, as he expected it to. His awareness of his body faded. It was like falling, no, like diving into a hole, a bright cool space.... He felt the welcome again, clear as song, and amusement, judgment— *he is strong*—compassion, curiosity, and over all of it an easy, confident, completely self-sufficient control. He touched memory. Images flicked across his consciousness: *a field ready for harvest under a glassy sky, a woman's face, the taste of fetuch, Kel's smile, a line of song too brief to follow, the smell of smoke in winter, the curve of fingers around the weighted haft of a scythe....*

He probed deeper. He felt the memory of pain—*a childhood*

slight—and deeper still—*a loss, a death*—he retreated from that rush of grief. He could see himself, his body, slumped among the pillows. He directed Sefer's eyes to close. They did. He directed them to open, and they did. He wiggled the fingers of Sefer's left hand.

Enough, said Sefer. *Your link with your own body is growing tenuous.*

Slowly, Kerris withdrew. His own body was cold. His nerves felt numb. His eyes and mouth were dry. He breathed deeply. Feeling shimmered through him. He touched the mat, the soft wool of the pillows, the seam of his shirt. His mind was filled with light.

Sefer brought him a drink in a glass goblet: water flavored with lemon. He sipped it cautiously. The lemon taste tingled on his tongue. Compared to what he had just done, the other times he had made use of inspeech were trivial. He wasn't sure he had done anything. Maybe Sefer had done it all.

He cleared his throat. "Did I do that?" he said.

Sefer nodded. "I simply let you in."

"What was it?"

"The deep-probe," Sefer said. "It's not an act to undertake with impunity. If you're careless, you can hurt someone."

"I didn't—"

"You didn't," Sefer said. "In fact, you did it very well. Your technique's a little clumsy, but as I said, you didn't hurt me. If you had, *you* would have felt it too. That's one of the properties of the gift that prevents misuse—it echoes—and when you are in pain, you can't use inspeech, except in reflex. That's the reason, if you over-use, you'll get a headache. The pain destroys your concentration and forces you to relax."

Kerris said, "I used to feel dizzy after linking with Kel. And my eyes hurt."

"Those are common effects," Sefer said. He patted his stomach. "Some people get sick."

Kerris sipped the lemon-water. He was awed by the buoyant lucidity of Sefer's mind. "Thank you for trusting me," he said.

Sefer said, "I have no reason not to trust you. You're not a cruel or violent person. I didn't think you would be careless."

"But I'm not—" Kerris thought of all the things he was not: not graceful, not skilled, not whole....

Sefer said, "Kerris, you're not a fool or a weakling. The folk of Tornor did you a wrong if they made you think that of yourself. You're competent and clever—and attractive. If you won't believe me—" his grin had a measure of pure mischief in it—"ask your brother." He linked, a light firm touch, with Kerris, and fanned a succession of images through Kerris' mind: *Kel smiling, Kel naked, Kel striding across a room, hair like a fiery cloak down his sleek back....*

Kerris shivered. "Don't."

The images stopped. "I'm sorry," said Sefer gravely, but his eyes were amused. "I shouldn't tease you."

Sunlight through the glass window pane made a yellow stain on the white wall. Kerris wondered if Sefer had done that deliberately to disconcert him. Grimly he pulled a pillow over his lap. "Can I do that?" he said.

"Think pictures into someone else's mind? With training you can. What seems to come easiest to inspeakers is sensitivity to others' feelings, and a kind of awareness we call the scan. It's like running your hand over materials, silk and wood and dirt, and feeling their differences, while the rest of your thought remains outside, detached—only instead of touching silk and dirt you are really touching someone's feelings with your mind."

"May I try it?"

"That's what we're doing here," Sefer said. He made a beckoning gesture with his hand. "Go ahead."

Kerris extended his thought.

Sefer met him. *Keep your touch light,* he directed. Kerris touched the cool bright surface of the teacher's mind. Gingerly he made contact, drew back, made contact again—like a water spider on a puddle, he thought—he felt Sefer's laughter. It drew him. He felt the familiar dimming of his senses.

Is this right?

No, Sefer answered. *Withdraw.*

Kerris obeyed. "What did I do wrong?" he said.

Sefer rubbed his cheek. "It wasn't wrong, precisely," he said.

"Your sensitivity is acute. It draws you into other minds. Can you make a barrier?"

Kerris did not have to ask what it was. "I've never tried," he said.

"Try."

"How do I do it?"

"Imagine a wall, an endless wall, between us. It has no cracks. It can be brick or stone, anything you like. It cannot be broken and it cannot be climbed. Think of that wall."

Kerris shut his eyes. He imagined a wall, gray like the stones of Tornor. The image wavered in his head as if he was looking at it through water. The effort made his head hurt. He stopped.

"Wait," Sefer said. "Rest a bit. You'll get it. It isn't hard."

Kerris waited till his head stopped aching. He tried again. The image coalesced and shattered. He felt a sudden pain. "Unh."

Stop. Sefer's command rang through his skull. He tensed. The pain had frightened him. He opened his eyes. The silk flecks danced in the screen.

He rubbed his eyes. "That was wrong."

"It shouldn't have hurt," said Sefer. "Nothing you do should hurt you." He rose. "Come."

"Where?"

"We'll go outside and sit in the garden," Sefer said. He began to stack the cushions in a neat line. "We can both do with a rest."

Kerris stood, pushing the pillow off his lap. When he took a step, his knees popped.

A plump man with broad features was standing in the hallway.

"Korith's looking for you, Sef," he said. His hair was braided in one long braid down his back and tied with a silk ribbon. His shirt was rose silk. His hands were fat and soft.

"If you see him tell him I'm in the garden," Sefer replied.

"Who is that?" Kerris asked, when the man was safely behind them.

"That's Dorin," Sefer said. "He is a teacher here, a far-traveler. He can visit other places in thought." He halted. "Are you hungry?"

"A little."

"Wait." To Sefer's left was the arch of a doorway, partially concealed by a striped curtain. Sefer twitched it aside. He returned from whatever lay behind it with a flowered plate of fetuch.

They sat on the grass just outside the ringed circle. Kerris kept his back to the image of the Guardian. He ate the fetuch; he was beginning to like the light, sweet taste. Sefer combed his hair off his forehead with his fingers. The silk on his shirt glittered like water in sun.

Kerris' stomach rumbled. Embarrassed by his greed, he rolled on his belly. He put his elbow on the grass. A lizard rustled in the dirt.

Sefer pushed the plate at him. "There's plenty. Have more."

Kerris nibbled a second stalk.

"Skayin!" A boy moved from the Tanjo. Coming to Sefer's side, he crouched in the grass. He was slim and dark, with a thin, curious face. Reproachfully he said, "Where did you go? I went into all the rooms, looking for you."

He closed his fingers over Sefer's right sleeve. His pointed chin and high cheekbones reminded Kerris of the river otter. Sefer smiled at him. "Korith, this is Kerris, Kel's brother. Kerris, meet Korith. He can mind-lift, like Ardith and Tazia."

Korith smiled. "Hello," he said.

Kerris recalled a fountain leaping into the cypress branches. "Hello," he said.

"You're Tazia's cousin," said the boy. He wrinkled his nose. "When I looked into *that* room, Tazia was throwing pillows."

"Was she alone?" Sefer asked.

"Oh, no. Tamaris was with her."

Sefer looked relieved. "Korith is also my nephew, and a nuisance," he said. He riffled the boy's hair. "What did you want with me, chelito, that caused you to disturb the entire Tanjo?"

"I didn't," said Korith, with dignity. "I was quiet. I looked for you yesterday but you were busy. I have been practicing all morning, by myself—and you are not busy now, are you?" He glanced from Sefer to Kerris. "I wouldn't want to interrupt you."

"Korith is learning to mind-lift over distance," Sefer explained. "No, chelito, as you see, we are resting. How far did you reach this morning?"

The boy waggled his fingers. "To the ribbons on the pole in Oril's field!"

"That is very good," Sefer said. "Your mother would be proud of you. Korith is Keren's middle child," he said. "When she realized that he was a witch, she sent him here from the city."

Kerris said, "Do you like it?"

The dark boy smiled. "Oh, yes. I miss the city sometimes. I miss my mother." His voice was wistful. "I'd like to see her."

Without meaning to, Kerris caught the feeling that radiated from the boy—*pride, love, loneliness, fear* (quickly suppressed), *homesickness*—and an image, of a quiet, plump woman with dark hair beaming at a shadowy figure that seemed to be Korith himself.... Korith seemed oblivious to Kerris' presence. But Sefer was looking at him, as if he had sensed the contact being made. Kerris bit his lip. The little pain jolted him back inside his own head.

Sefer said, "Family is a net we are all part of. I miss Keren too, chelito. When the trouble is over, perhaps I'll leave Elath, and we'll ride to Kendra-on-the-Delta together."

A shadow fell across the grass. "*You* leave Elath? Not likely." Kerris looked up, shielding his eyes. A woman stood over them, hands crossed beneath her breasts. Her hair was dark and long, and it made a cloud around her face. She wore a bright green gown, cinched at the waist with a copper belt.

Sefer said, "Kerris, this is Tamaris. She teaches mind-lift. She's also on the Council. How is Tazia, Tam?"

Tamaris said, "She's a little demon this morning. She threw a tantrum because I would not tell her she could go to the rim with Ardith. He was bringing supplies to the guards. I let her wear herself out; she's asleep. Are you stealing my students, Sef? I thought I would work the rest of the morning with Korith, and I find him here."

"I am not," said Sefer. He freed his sleeve from Korith's grip. "Korith, go with Tamaris."

"But I want you to watch me!" the boy said imperatively.

147

Sefer sighed. "Very well, chelito. I am watching. Show me what you can do."

Korith closed his eyes. His thin nostrils flared. Kerris' vision dimmed. *He was looking at a field, at a wooden pole. The pole had ribbons tied round it. They hung motionless in the breezeless day. The grain stood in long rows, dreaming of sickles and ovens. Suddenly, the ribbons snapped and rustled. Four startled ravens sprang out of the grain. Warily they circled the dancing ribbons.*

"See!" said Korith.

"Yes," said Sefer, "I see. That's very good."

Tamaris said gently, "Korith, you must not be so insistent that people will think you rude."

"Was I?" said Korith. "*Inanu,*"—the word meant "uncle" in the southern tongue—"was I rude?"

Sefer did not answer. His eyes were glazed and lightless. His face twitched, like a man with a fever. His lips moved. "Yes," he murmured, "Yes." He drew a deep, sluggish breath. "I will tell her." He tilted his face upward, toward the sunlit hills.

Chapter 10

The hair lifted on the back of Kerris' neck.

He looked at Tamaris. She was watching Sefer. Korith sat folded down on his knees, hands clasped in his lap. The pose changed him from otter to squirrel. Sefer muttered again. His vivid face was blank. "Sefer?" Kerris said. The inspeaker's head did not turn. Kerris reached for Sefer's shoulder, to wrest him from the seizure.

Tamaris' fingers closed on his wrist. "Let him alone," she said softly. Her hand was cool. "He's being spoken to."

Kerris thought, This is how I looked, in Tornor. His nerves jangled.

Sefer shuddered. His eyes focused. He put his hands to his cheeks as if they burned him, and then laid them in his lap. He cleared his throat. "That was Beria on the rim."

Kerris did not know who Beria was. "What did she say?" Tamaris said.

"A messenger came from the Asech. It was not the woman Thera but a man. He said his name was Nerim. He spoke with a heavy accent; Beria said it was difficult to understand him. He came with a green flag. He said the Asech will leave their camp tomorrow and come to the village. He asked that the message be passed to Lara."

Tamaris' hands clenched on her gown. "How many will come? All of them? As many as came on the raid?"

"Beria didn't know."

"We must tell Dorin, and Kel."

"Yes," said Sefer. Taking off his headband, he wiped his forehead with his sleeve. He stuffed the band into a pocket.

Kerris said, "Did the message say anything about Riniard?"

"No," Sefer said.

Korith scrambled up. "I'll tell Lara," he said, breathless, his dark eyes wide with excitement.

"No!" Sefer's swift syllable halted the boy in mid-leap. His face twisted in pain. So did Sefer's. He caught Korith in his arms and pulled the boy against him. "Ai, chelito, I hurt you. I'm sorry." He stroked the boy's hair.

"It was only a little," Korith said. He stood straight. "Shall I not tell Lara?"

"I will—or Tamaris."

"Can I tell somebody?"

Sefer looked at Tamaris. "You can go to the Yard and tell Kel," he said. "But go quietly, chelito. Be discreet. Don't shout it."

Korith bounced with barely subdued delight. Whirling, he sped for the cypress grove.

Tamaris said, "What difference does it make, who knows?" She picked a stalk of fetuch from the plate and bit into it.

Sefer said, "There are still hotheads in this town who would like to attack the Asech. A message from their camp may act like salt on a wound."

"They couldn't find it," Tamaris said. "An army of Asech might be marching to Elath from the desert, Sef, and not one of us would know it until they arrived. Their barriers are so strong, they might as well be invisible!"

Sefer stood up. "I know, Tam," he said. "I've touched those barriers. It makes me wonder—"

"What?" she said.

150

"How have they been living, that they have learned to barrier so strongly—and have learned *nothing else*?"

"I don't know and I don't care," said Tamaris.

"Ah." Sefer glanced toward the white painted figure of the Guardian. "But we must care, Tam."

Tamaris' tone grew dangerously soft. "Don't preach to me as if I were one of your students, Sefer of Elath!" She glared at him. He said nothing. Tamaris sighed. "Ai, you are right, of course." She ran a hand down the crumpled fold of her dress. "Shall I speak to Dorin?"

"If you would."

She grinned. "Since you have sent my student running your errands, there is no reason why I should not do the same." She spat out a morsel of fetuch and strolled toward the school, hips swaying.

A red bird with a beetle in its beak swooped over the garden. The sun flashed on its wings. Kerris said the first thing that came into his head. "Who is Beria?"

"Berénzia," Sefer said. "She is an inspeaker." He rubbed his chin. "I must give Lara the message. Do you want to come with me?"

"I don't want to be in your way," Kerris said.

"You won't be," Sefer said. He took a step, winced, stopped. He lifted one foot and picked a burr off the sole. "Wait a moment, while I get my sandals."

After the bright garden, the cypress grove was fragrant and cool. The streets were hazy with dust. They passed a woman pulling onion bulbs from a garden. She wore a straw hat, like the women in Galbareth. A squat man staggered by under the weight of a water yoke. Two buckets hung from its arms, and water slopped from the sides of the buckets with every step he took. Red-faced, he grinned at Sefer. "Any news?" he asked.

Sefer shook his head.

Lara's house was near the well. On the door was a bronze knocker shaped like a bull's head, hanging by the horns. Sefer tapped with it on the wooden door. A small pink boy wearing no pants opened it. "Chelito," Sefer said, "is thy abu at home?" The boy stuck his thumb In his mouth and stepped backward. Sefer gestured to Kerris to go in. There was an alcove for shoes. Sefer slipped off his sandals. The child toddled on ahead of them.

They followed the boy into a wide light room. Hangings like the ones in Sefer's cottage brightened the walls. Cushions covered the mats. A flowering vine poked through one of the windows. There was a screen, like the wall screens in the Tanjo, to one side of the room, and stairs at the back. The stairs creaked. A woman came down them. It was Lara. "May the peace of the chea be with you," she said.

Sefer put his palms together and bowed to her. "And to you, lehi."

Lehi meant healer. Sefer had said that healing was a rare gift, that there were only three healers now in Elath. Kerris wondered if he should bow, too.

The old woman smiled at him. "Do you know the way now to Ardith's farm, Kerris?"

"Yes, lehi," he said. "Thank you."

At the end of the room, near the stairs, was a niche in the wall. Inside the niche was a statue of the Guardian. Kerris turned his right shoulder to it.

"What brings you here, Sefer?" said the old woman.

"News from the rim," Sefer said. "A message from Beria. The Asech will come tomorrow."

The boy child wandered in. Lara stroked his dark curly hair. He fisted his fat hands in her skirts. "So," she said. "Who knows this?"

"Beria, and Erith, I'm sure. Tamaris, Kerris, and my nephew. They were with me when Berénzia spoke to me. I sent Korith to tell Kel. Tam will tell Dorin. No one else knows."

Lara fingered the boy's head. "Do you think to keep it secret?" she said. "You have lived in Elath thirty years, Sefer, you know you cannot hide things from this small a town."

"People are restive," Sefer said. "I want no excursions into the rocks tonight, no daring young nitwits rushing off to spy on the Asech camp."

"Tell the steady ones," Lara said. "Tell Ilene and Moro and Ardith, tell Hadril and Terézia and Dol. Tell them to watch and listen and stay alert. And then tell everybody exactly what you know. Otherwise there will be fifty rumors, each of them less true than the one before it, and the chea only knows what people will choose to believe."

Sefer smiled. "You are right, lehi."

The boy tugged at Lara's dress. Chuckling, she fished in the pocket of the skirt and took out a bit of apple. "Here, chelito." The sound of a bell ringing halted her smile. "Excuse me," she said. "That is Meritha calling; I must go to her."

The name was familiar. Reo had said it. Meritha was the Council record-keeper. Reo had said that she was old.

Sefer said, "Let me go, Lara. Why tire yourself going up and down stairs?" The bell rang again, a tinny sound.

Lara said sadly, "No, Sef. I thank you, but her mind wanders. A strange face might frighten her." She walked to the stairway. She put a hand on the stair railing and hauled herself up to the first step. The bell rang a third time.

Sefer sat on a cushion. After a moment, Kerris sat beside him. "My cousin told me that Meritha is the Council scribe," he said.

Sefer teased a bit of the mat with his toe. "She was," he said. "She's very old. Old age is the one illness even a healer cannot cure."

"Kerris." It was Lara's voice. She stood at the turn of the stairway. "Will you come up? Meritha would like to meet you."

Kerris' spine prickled. He wanted to ask "Why?" and was afraid that if he did so Lara would think him rude.

She said, as if she had read his thought, "She knows you are a scribe. That's why."

Kerris followed Lara up the stair. The treads were not matted. The boards were worn and smooth. He entered Meritha's room at Lara's back. It was a small chamber. The pallet took up most of it. One side of the ceiling slanted in. The room smelled of urine and age. Meritha was sitting up in a bed. The look of her startled Kerris. She was a big woman; the flesh hung loosely on her, but her shoulders were broad, and her hands were huge. He had expected a little withered woman about the size of the abu.

"Come here," she said. Her eyes were very bright, like glass. Her hair was iron-gray. The nail of her left little finger was very long. Kerris knew—Josen had told him—that scribes in Kendra-on-the-Delta grew one nail on purpose, for picking wax seals from letters. Her fingers twisted in the wool of her blanket. He knelt beside the pallet. She stared at his face, and at his stump, and back at his face again.

"Who are you?" she said.

Smoothly, Lara said, "Chelito, that is Kerris-no-Alis. You asked to see him."

The woman squeezed her eyes shut. "I did." She licked her lips. They were cracked and red. "I did." She lifted her hand. "Boy, look in the cupboard."

Kerris stiffened at being called "boy." Reminding himself that this woman was sick, he turned to see what she was pointing at. Against the wall was a wooden cupboard. On top of it were a pitcher and a mug. The cupboard doors were closed by a metal bolt in the shape of a quill. He went to it and slid the bolt aside. The door swung outward. "Look on the top shelf," Meritha said.

He had to kneel to see into the cupboard. It smelled of ink. The bottom shelf was strewn with odds and ends: twine, a cracked dish, rags. On the top shelf was a square package wrapped in linen. "Take the package," said Meritha. Kerris fingered it, wondering what was in it. He took it. It was lighter than wood or clay. "Take it, take it!" called the sick woman. She pushed up in bed, leaning on one elbow. Her dry hair fell over her face.

Lara bent over her, speaking to her softly. "Go downstairs," she said. Kerris moved to obey. The sick woman's pain probed at his head. Her voice lost its rough strength: she sounded like a little girl. *Whose body is this they have locked me into, so feeble, so dry and still, I am not this, I am young and strong. . . . Larita, help me, I don't want to die!*

Halfway down the stair Kerris' knees started to wobble. He leaned against the wall to calm himself. His stomach was churning. He could not remember having been so close to death before. It hurt. Meritha's whine continued in his head. In the room downstairs, Sefer was waiting for him at the door. "Come on," he said. "Our errand's done."

154

It took a little while before Kerris could talk. He was grateful for Sefer's silence. Finally his stomach ceased heaving. He settled the package more firmly in the crook of his arm.

"What is it?" Sefer said.

Kerris braced it on his hip. "I don't know. You open it." The linen was very fine, fine as silk, and it was golden-yellow, the color of Kel's hair. Sefer unfolded the cloth. Within it was paper, smooth eggshell-colored paper, marked with the characteristic herringbone pattern that meant it had been made in Kendra-on-the-Delta.

On the way to the cottage Sefer stopped at several houses, to tell the folk in them that the Asech would indeed be coming the next day, and to urge calm. Kerris trailed behind him, half-listening. Hadril, the cooper, volunteered to tell several other people, among them Ardith. Moro the ropemaker was not home, but his oldest son, a thickset boy who seemed about Kerris' age, dragged Sefer into a corner to ask him, "Is it true the Asech are coming tonight?" The corner smelled of heavenweed.

"No," Sefer said. "It's not true. They'll be coming tomorrow, in daylight, as they said, and we will teach them, Perin, not fight them."

Perin fingered his knife hilt. "I've heard other things," he said darkly.

"So have I," Sefer said. "They're not true."

Perin looked disappointed. "Is—is the cheari still alive?" His voice cracked on the last word.

"We don't know," Sefer said.

Sefer's cottage was empty when they got there. Sefer said, "They must still be at the Yard."

Kerris nodded. He put the writing paper by his bedroll. There were things other than paper in the folds of yellow cloth: a quill with scarlet vanes, a stick of red wax, a cake of ink, a brush. Already a letter was forming in his mind. *To Josen of the Black Clan, Recorder of Tornor Keep, from Kerris....*

"Kerris."

"Hmm." Kerris glanced up. Sefer was sitting in a patch of sunlight. He looked thoughtful.

"How do you feel?" he said. "Tired? Headache?"

"No." Kerris fingered the soft brown brush fibers. He wondered what kind of hair it was. He thought badger.

Kerris. Please. Sefer's voice was curiously urgent. Reluctantly Kerris remembered that Sefer was his teacher and was owed more than ordinary courtesy. He laid the brush down.

"I'm sorry. I thought we were finished with lessons for the day."

"We will be if you're tired," Sefer said.

"I'm not tired."

"Then I think we should take advantage of this privacy," Sefer said. "In the garden—I felt you in Korith's mind."

"I didn't mean to do that," Kerris said.

"I know," Sefer said. "But you need to learn to barrier, soon, or that will keep happening and you won't be able to stop it." Brusquely he thrust an image into Kerris' mind, of a bright candle and a moth with green, lacy wings. "The emotions of people around you will draw you in." *The moth circled, circled, and dived into the licking flame.*

Kerris winced. He thought briefly of Meritha. "That's unpleasant," he said.

"Inspeakers grow more sensitive, not less," Sefer said. "You're my student now. I don't want to be responsible for anything happening to you."

Inconsequentially, out of memory, Kerris heard the words of a song. Ilene had sung it. *I am a stranger in an outland country, I am an exile wherever I go.* He put the thoughts of Josen and letterwriting from his mind. "You don't think it can wait?" he said.

Sefer said, "The Asech come tomorrow. I don't know what will happen then, except that I shall be busy."

"All right," Kerris said. He remembered the pain he had felt trying to make the barrier before. He told himself that was a fluke and would not happen again. "What should I do?"

Sefer stretched his legs out. "I'm going to extend to you," he said. "I want you to stop me by making the wall."

Kerris took a deep breath. He closed his eyes, trying to imagine himself in Tornor, standing in front of the stones of the inner ward.

His stump itched. He scratched it, trying to concentrate on the blackness behind his eyeballs. The wall trembled in his head. The back of his neck stung. His concentration fled. The wall dissolved as if it were made of sand.

He opened his eyes. "No good."

"Try again," said Sefer.

Kerris closed his eyes and tried again. Patches of sweat formed under the arms of his shirt. His head began to ache. *Nothing you do should hurt you.* Sefer had said that. He decided to ignore the pain. The wall formed. It seemed clearer than before. He persevered. It broke apart with a snapping sound, scattering like shards of glass. A sharp pain shot through his skull. He could not quite control the cry. "Unh."

"You're hurt," Sefer said.

"No."

Let me look.

Yes, come ahead, he said. *I could hardly stop you,* he added. He tensed at the touch of another mind. But Sefer's examination was brief and gentle and did not hurt. His concern was very plain. He did not conceal his thoughts or his feelings, and something else was plain. Kerris waited until the teacher withdrew before he faced him with it.

"You said you wouldn't want to be responsible for anything happening to me," he said.

"Yes," said Sefer.

"It isn't *me* you care about. It's Kel."

Sefer cocked his head to one side. His look was quizzical and direct. "I *do* care about you," he said. "I care about all my students. If you were to be hurt, somehow, because I failed to teach you to barrier, Kel would be furious with me, and it's true, I don't want that to happen. But I promise you, Kerris, I would work just as hard to teach you if you were not Kel's brother. Reach to me, and see." He made the little beckoning gesture with his left hand.

"No," Kerris said. "No." He felt ashamed of himself for having doubted.

Sefer said, "If you don't trust me, Kerris, we must stop."

"I trust you."

Sefer rose. He wandered to the window and stood pushing on the leather window curtain with one finger. "I want to try something," he said.

Kerris turned to watch him. "What?"

The curtain swung rhythmically to the prodding hand. "I want to link with you, very tightly, in deep-probe, and while we're linked, I want to build the barrier for you. That way you can see how it's done, and how it feels."

Kerris' stump itched. He scratched it. "Will it hurt?" he asked.

"It shouldn't. If it does, I'll break the link." He hunkered down, back against wood, so that their eyes were on a level. His hands dangled between his knees. "Do you want to try it?"

"All right," Kerris said.

He felt Sefer touch his mind. The teacher slipped into his head as easily as a fish slides through a current, swift-gliding, untrammeled.... Kerris remembered the red fish he had seen in the depths of the blue pond. Suddenly he was blind. His bones felt soft. He could not move. His head turned. Sefer had made his head turn. His eyelids shut. He was thrown back into his skull. *Look*, said Sefer's voice. *Look*. It was the only thing he could look at: a landscape, green and blue, grass and water.... A bird called, piercingly sweet. He looked down at the landscape, as if from the tower windows, and then, with no warning, he was standing in the grass. It reached to his knees, bowing under the wind's warm hand. He was standing on the steppe, looking out into a far country.

He saw the wall.

He was facing it. It was dark stone, higher than his head. He pointed at it. It vanished. He pointed again. It reappeared. *This is yours. You made it*, Sefer said. His feet slid forward. He was standing next to it. He put out his hand. Dark veins patterned the lumpy stone. He felt it. It was cold and hard. He felt Sefer slip away, gliding from the deep places of his mind as a fish glides to the surface of the water.... The wall trembled, shivered, and exploded. He screamed at the enormous, snapping pain.

He was wet. He knew that was impossible. He was in Elath, in Elath in Sefer's house. But part of him was elsewhere, lost, alone, a child surrounded by strangers. The world was colorless and frightening and he was bereft and hurt, so hurt....

Kerris! The mental shout resonated inside his skull.

He sobbed. He *felt-saw-knew* hands reach for him, immense hands, bruisingly strong. He *was* in Sefer's house. Sefer was holding him. He clung to the teacher. Gentle hands stroked his hair and back, a comfort without erotic content, firm as a mother's touch. "Here," Sefer said. "Drink." He held a glass to Kerris' lips. Kerris swallowed. It was wine. It burned his tongue. He choked.

His head ached. He felt wretched, stupid, and incompetent. "I'm sorry," he said. It came out a croak. Sefer held the glass to his lips again. He drank, and wiped his face with his sleeve. "I tried."

"I know you did. You don't need to be sorry." Sefer put the glass to one side. "Kerris," he said, "where were you?"

"I don't know."

"Why did you go there?"

Kerris' sides were soaked with sweat. "I don't know."

Sefer gripped his shoulder. "Look at me," he said. "I felt what you were feeling, the pain, and then the fear. What was that place, Kerris? Why did you go to it when the barrier broke?"

"I don't know," Kerris said.

"I couldn't tell if it was fantasy or memory," said the teacher. "Was it familiar?"

The tears came to Kerris' eyes again. Leave me, he wanted to say, let me rest, but he knew Sefer was trying to help him. He remembered the incident in Galbareth, during the storm. "Yes. It happened before."

"How many times?"

"Once."

"When?"

Haltingly, Kerris told him. Sefer listened, and Kerris could sense his puzzlement. "I don't understand," he said finally. "I know what must have happened. In the storm something frightened you, just as now the pain of the barrier breaking frightened you, and you retreated from both fears into the memory of an earlier fear, something that terrified you when

159

you were a child. But I don't see why the barrier in your mind reminded you of the same terror as did a thunderstorm in Galbareth."

"I don't either." Kerris leaned on his arm. The muscles trembled. This was worse than the incident in Galbareth. After that he had been able to walk, and even to ride.

"The barrier stayed intact until I told you to control it," Sefer said.

"Yes," Kerris said. He pulled his knees to his chest, laid his arm across them, and rested his chin on his arm.

Sefer crouched, head cocked, eyes speculative. "I wonder—" His voice trailed off.

Kerris remembered his skill and his strength. His mouth dried. He shivered. He said, pleading, "I—can't do that again."

Sefer blinked. He touched Kerris' knee. "Kerris—do you think I want you hurt? You look as if you thought I would do something to you—as if you were an animal!"

His distress was almost palpable. Kerris felt ashamed. "No."

"I'll be back," Sefer said. He went upstairs. Kerris heard him walking overhead. He came back with a blue wool blanket in his arms. He draped it around Kerris' shoulders. It smelled of cedar and cinnamon. "Are you hungry? There's food."

"No," Kerris said. He shifted. The knife in its sheath pressed against his right thigh.

Sefer picked up the glass and brought it to the kitchen. Kerris heard him moving restlessly in the small space. He said, "You don't have to stay with me. I'm all right."

"You're sure." Sefer knelt beside him again. "Will you sleep?"

"I don't think so. I'm not sleepy."

Sefer made another circuit of the room. Kerris was sure he wanted to leave. His head smarted. He touched it with his fingertips. The hurt was all on the inside. He wriggled onto his left side. "You can leave me alone," he repeated.

"All right." Sefer went to the anteroom's arch. He hesitated there. "If you're sure there's nothing you need."

Kerris simply nodded. The sun tracked across the wall hangings. "Where are you going?" he asked.

Sefer's lips curved in the ghost of a smile. "To the Yard," he said, "to talk to Kel."

In the vacant house, the cricket spoke from under the stair. Its thin voice was derisive. You cannot do it, it said. Kerris ground his cheek against a pillow. The ache in his head was nothing to the ache in his heart. You'll never be an inspeaker, he told himself. His stump throbbed, reminding him of what he was.

The paper gleamed beside the bed. He stared at it. His eyes watered. Josen was right, he thought, I should have gone to Kendra-on-the-Delta. I could be a scribe. That's one skill I still have. He lay, watching the sunlight traverse the walls. The door sprang open. Footsteps vibrated the mats. He turned his head to see who it was.

It was Kel. His hair was wet and tousled. He wore a scarlet robe. He knelt at Kerris' side. "Chelito?" He put both hands out and then drew back, as if afraid he might do damage.

Kerris struggled to sit. "You can touch me," he said. "I won't break."

Kel held him. Strength flowed out of him, warming as a hot wind on a winter day. "Sef told me," he said, into Kerris' hair. Kerris wondered what Sefer had said to Kel, and Kel to him. He felt the pressure of Kel's thumb on the line of his jaw. Kel tipped his head up. His gray eyes were acute. "Chelito, I didn't bring you to Elath to be hurt!" His other hand roamed along Kerris's sides as if feeling for broken bones.

Kerris swallowed. He was suddenly ashamed of his weakness. "I'm not hurt," he said. He pulled himself a little way out of his brother's grip, to demonstrate that he could sit without support. "It wasn't Sefer's fault." He heard himself defending Sefer to Kel, and thought, I'm a fool.

Kel said, "No. I know that." He drew Kerris' head up between his cool hands and kissed him on the lips.

The door opened again. Others entered: Arillard, Elli, Jensie at the very end. Kel dropped his hands, without haste. "Your timing stinks," he said, not turning around.

"Tough," said Elli. She wore the gold robe she had taken from the baths. She twirled a bunch of carrots in her hand. "Hey," she said to Kerris, "we were worried about you."

Her concern made him feel good. "I'm here," he said.

"I see you are." She sauntered into the kitchen. "I hope you all want to eat. I'm cooking up a hurricane tonight."

Kerris said softly into his brother's ear, "What's a hurricane?"

Kel grinned. "A big wind." He crossed his legs and pulled Kerris to him with one strong arm. "Where's Calwin?"

Arillard answered. "He's at the baths, fleecing the farmers of their silver. Ilene went to her sister's." Jensie sat on her mat. Her tricolored hair had darkened with wet till it looked all one color. She fished a whetstone from her pack. Laying her knife on her lap, she began to hone it in a smooth, circular motion. The scrape of stone on steel made an insect drone.

Kerris' taut nerves loosened. Elli whistled in the kitchen. "Where's Sefer?" he asked.

Kel's breath tickled the back of his neck. "Talking to people. He's afraid there may be trouble this night. He'll come in later." If he was disappointed or angry, Kerris could not hear it in his voice.

"Oh."

"What kind of trouble?" Arillard said.

Kel said, "He's afraid some young fools may be getting together to attack the Asech camp."

Arillard said, "You'd think Riniard's example would dissuade them." At the sound of Riniard's name, Jensie looked up. After a moment, she returned to her sharpening. Kerris wondered what would happen with her if Riniard died. He shivered.

"Who wants to shell nuts?" said Elli. She peered around the archway. "Lots of lazy people sitting around doing nothing."

Arillard stretched out a hand. "Give them to me." She handed him a bowl and a nutcracker carved like a fish, with wide painted jaws. He put a nut between the jaws and squeezed. The shell cracked. He relaxed his hand and let the broken bits fall to the floor. The shelled nutmeat dropped in two pieces into his palm. He ate them. "Not bad."

Kel tapped the paper. "What's this?"

"Paper—writing paper—and ink, and a brush. I went to Lara's with Sefer, and Meritha gave them to me."

Kel said, "That's something I've always wished I could do."

"What?"

Arillard cracked another nut.

"Write. It's different when you have to ask someone else to do it."

"I guess it is," Kerris said. It hadn't occurred to him that Kel couldn't write. He stretched gingerly. His head no longer felt as if it would fracture if he moved. "Let me up," he said. His brother opened his arms at once. Letting the blanket fall, Kerris went into the kitchen.

His legs were steady under him. Elli saw him coming. She grinned at him. Sweat beaded her hairline. A pot shed barley-scented steam into the room. Kerris glanced around at the clutter of pans and bowls and jars and hanging spices.

"What are you looking for?" Elli said.

"Something to use for mixing."

She handed him a ragged spoon that looked as if a dog had mistaken it for dinner. He blew the dust from a dish with a nicked lip. "What's that for?" Elli asked.

"An ink bowl."

He filled it a quarter full with water and brought it back to the mat. Kel made room for him. "Tell me what you're doing."

"Making ink." Crumbling the ink cake into the water, he stirred it free of lumps. It smelled of some heavy scent, honeysuckle, or jasmine. He spread a page of paper on the table and dipped the brush into the black liquid. The brown hairs swelled evenly. He wrote: *To Josen of the Black Clan, Recorder of Tornor Keep, from Kerris of Elath, Greeting.*

He read it aloud. Kel smiled, and his hand caressed Kerris' shoulder. "Kerris of Elath."

He went down another line. *I arrived in Elath three days ago. It was an interesting journey. We stayed in a village, Brath, and in fields, and in a second village in Galbareth, I never learned its name. We spent one night by Lake Aruna.*

He read it aloud, and continued. *I have met my mother's*

brother, Ardith, and his wife, Lea, and my cousins. I have worked in a field. I wrote a letter using a feather as a brush, a piece of shirt for paper, and lacquer for ink. This paper and ink and the brush were given me by Meritha. She is the village scribe.

He read it aloud, and blew on the ink to dry it, wishing he had sand. *I hope you are well. Please give my love to Paula, and my regards to my uncle Morven.* He hesitated and then added—*and to my friend Tryg.*

"Who is Paula?" demanded Kel.

"The woman who brought me to Tornor, after—after our mother died. The old woman I said farewell to."

"I remember," Kel said. "I didn't realize.... And Tryg?"

"My friend. He brought me the knife."

"Shall I be jealous?" Kel said. Startled, Kerris looked at him. He was smiling. He ran his hands lightly along Kerris' sides.

He rose. "I'm going upstairs a moment."

Kerris watched him walk across the sleeping room.

"Hey."

He jumped, and glanced up. Elli stood over him, holding a bowl. She passed it under his nose. It was piled with plums. Kerris took one. Gingerly he bit into the hard purple fruit. Its tartness puckered his mouth.

"Who'd you write to?"

He folded the letter into threes and put it to one side. He would seal it when the lamps were lit. She sat beside him. Her bare leg, under the gold cloth, stroked against his. He moved to give her room. "My old teacher, Josen."

The corners of her wide-lipped mouth curved. Wistfully she said, "I wish you were not so shy of me, Kerris."

He didn't know what to say. "I'll try not to be."

She smiled at him. "We can be friends, I think, if you'd like. Even if—" the smile turned to grin—"even if you don't want to sleep with me!"

The house door opened. Kerris turned gratefully toward it. His ears were burning. Someone whistled in the antechamber. Calwin came in. He was grinning. He tossed something into the air and caught it. Elli laughed. "A fish!" she said. "Alas for the poor farmers of Elath!"

"It isn't a fish," Cal said. "It's something new." He strolled into the chamber and dropped the coin into Elli's reaching palm. She held the shape to the light. The silver coins of Tezera were called "fish" because they were imprinted with that symbol. This coin was round and thin and flat like a fish, but it was not silver. It shimmered like a rainbow, in flowing, changing colors.

Elli turned it over. She flicked it with a fingernail, and then bit it. "It feels like shell. Why does it have a hole in its center?"

The stairs creaked. Kel came down. He had changed his clothes from the robe to breeches and gray tunic. His hair fell loose on his shoulders.

"It has a rune in it," Elli said. "What does that mean?"

"Ask a scribe," Arillard said.

"Look, Kerris." Elli passed him the shining disc. "What rune is this?"

He held it up. It was light as shell, but clearly polished and fashioned. The rune looked carved. "It's a K," he said.

Cal took it from his hand. "It's a coin. It's called *bonta*; it's worth half a fish. The Council of the Houses at Kendra-on-the-Delta had decreed that within the city limits all buying and selling must be done with these. They're made in the city. Traders must stop at the city gates and exchange their silver and copper coins for these before they can take their goods to market. When they leave they give them back, and get back metal coins. There are assayers' tables set up at all the gates. They're overseen by the Sul Family."

"Let me see," said Arillard. He leaned close to examine the coin. He handed it back to Cal, saying, "That'll net the Sul Family a pretty penny. They must take a percentage of every coin they change."

"What does bonta mean?" Elli said.

"Shell," guessed Cal.

"Bone," Kerris said.

Cal looked very pleased with himself. He pulled something from his pocket. It chinked, a duller sound than silver or copper. It was a string with four of the shell coins on it. "This is how they carry them in Kendra-on-the-Delta."

"You won all those?" Elli said. "For shame, Cal! What kind of return for hospitality is that?"

"May I see?" said Kel. Calwin brought him the string. He pushed them back and forth, handed them to Cal, and chuckled. "I wouldn't be surprised," he said, "if the next time you play you lose those pretty things. There are people in Elath who can make your dice turn loops. Remember, this is the witch-town."

Cal strung the loose shell with the others and stuffed the string back in his pocket, looking disgruntled.

Elli leaned forward. She put her hand on Cal's knee. "Don't put the toys away," she said sweetly. "Aren't you going to give me a chance to take them from you?"

Arillard leaned far forward and picked a plum from the bowl. His eyelids drooped. "He's probably too tired to play."

"I am not," said Cal. He dragged the string from his left pocket and his dice from the right one.

"Oh," Elli said, "let's eat first." Rising, she went into the kitchen. The velvet robe trailed on the mats, making a slithering, reptilian sound.

She and Arillard brought food to the table: soup in wooden bowls, a second bowl of plums, fetuch, shelled walnuts, wine. Kel brought cups for the wine. They gathered round the table—all but Jensie.

Arillard said, "Jen, won't you eat?"

Mutely she shook her head.

Kel said, "Jen, sit with us, at least."

Jensie looked as if she would refuse that, too. But she rose, and came to sit stiffly between Arillard and Elli.

Kerris fit his fingers round the wooden bowl. He sipped the soup. It was flavorful, piquant with unfamiliar spices. There were carrots in it, and bits of meat—pork, he thought—and the soft flat strings of wheat paste which Calwin had told him were called noodles.

Arillard brought out his tinderbox and lit the lamps.

"He sleeps with that box, you know," said Kel. His warm whisper tickled Kerris' ear. "On the border we used to call him the fire-bringer." His left hand caressed Kerris' neck. The cricket belled in the stairwell.

"Remember," said Cal, "the time in Shanan when he nearly set fire to the house? First time I ever saw you get blind drunk," he said to Arillard.

"I remember the time *you* kicked a screen in, thinking it was a sheet someone had slung over a rafter," said Arillard.

"Remember the night we danced for the Council of Houses in Kendra-on-the-Delta?"

"Tell that story," said Cal. Kel and Elli told it. Kerris listened. Jensie did not speak but her head turned, listening, and once or twice she smiled. Kerris was no patterner, but as he heard the story to its end he sensed—as the melody of a song can sometimes be sensed from a few notes, carelessly whistled—the pattern of the chearas. They fit each other as a river fits its bed, or a sword its scabbard. Scholars said—Kerris had heard Josen say it—that the chea was not simply expressed by the chearis but also maintained by them, so that if the dancers of Arun ceased to dance, the world would break into discord. It would be terrible, Kerris thought, to lose this harmony, having had it. No wonder Riniard had feared that sundering. It would be worse than losing an arm.

He sipped his soup. The sense of pattern died. But he felt healed, made whole—as whole as he would ever be. For a moment he had seen the thing that holds the world together, and had felt himself a part of it, even he, who could not dance a step to save his life, and had never been within the fighting circles of the Yard.

Chapter 11

Sefer did not come in after evening meal; neither did Terézia. But sometime in the night they both returned, because in the morning when the chearis woke, they both came down the stairs. Terézia was first. She bent to take a piece of bread from the food platter Elli had put on the table. Her face was lined with fatigue, and she moved as if her legs were stiff.

Kel and Sefer followed her. Kel's chin was smooth; he had shaved. He was wearing his breeches and a butter-colored shirt with horn buttons on the collar and sleeves. Stick figures danced about the shirtfront in gold thread. He had one arm around Sefer's waist. Sefer, too, looked tired, but if anything had been wrong between the lovers, it had clearly been set right.

Kel flicked Kerris' cheek with a finger as he passed him. "Did you sleep well?" He grinned at the chearas.

Calwin stood by the wash basin, peering into the shiny silver circlet of a mirror. "If anyone makes a sudden noise I'll probably cut my own throat."

"Promise?" said Elli. Cal glared at her as he dragged his knife from the sheath. She laughed, and did up the buckle of her belt.

"I suppose I have to be content with winning all your money." She patted her pockets. "I'm glad I don't have to shave," she said to Kerris. "It must be a lot of trouble."

"It is for me." He fingered his face. His cheeks were straggly with hair. He hated shaving himself; he always ended up cut. Josen had done it for him in Tornor.

"I can help you," Elli offered. "Or you could grow a beard. You might look good." Kerris touched his face again. He could not imagine himself with a beard. Beards were for old men. "You would!" she insisted. She grinned at him. In the night he had rolled against her, and they had awakened to find his back against her breasts, her arm curved protectively (and uncomfortably) over his head.

Today the Asech were coming. Kerris swallowed back anger and worry. He recalled the stink of pitch and horse-sweat, the jangle of bridles, the gloss of Riniard's hair dragging in the dust.... It did no good to worry. They would know Riniard's fate soon enough.

Ilene came in. She kissed Jensie tenderly and clapped Sefer on the shoulder. "I'm talked hoarse and my legs ache from climbing up and down in the dirt, but the town's quiet, quiet as a sleeping babe. I hope you all got more sleep than I did."

Arillard said, "What does the Council want us to do today, Sefer? No one will come to the Yard."

"You have your choice," Sefer said. "You can do nothing. You can join Erith's troop on the rim. Or you can stay in town and help Cleo's troop maintain watch."

Elli said, "I'm going to bake today. And Cal is going to bring a lamb haunch back from the butcher's so that we can have stew tonight."

Both Arillard and Ilene looked at Kel. He shook his head. "I shall be with the teachers."

"Why?" said Ilene.

Wiping his face and sliding the knife into his scabbard, Cal sauntered from the wash basin. "How do I look?"

Elli made a rude noise. "Stunning."

Ilene walked to Kel and took him by the front of the shirt. "Why?" she said.

He covered her fingers with his. "Because of Riniard," he

said. "It's my right. And I am a patterner."

Ilene scowled. "I don't like it. I don't like it when you leave us."

Someone knocked on the front door. "Come!" Terézia called.

It opened; there was an odd scuffling noice. Ilene dropped her hand from Kel's and moved toward the antechamber. A strange man's voice spoke harshly. "Damn it, go in!"

The speaker came through the doorway. Kerris didn't know him; he was swarthy and heavyset, with thick curling gray hair and dark eyes. He had one blunt-fingered hand clamped hard on someone else's arm. He jerked. That person fell into the room. It was the boy, Perin. He looked terrified. "Good morning," said the man.

"Good morning, Moro," said Sefer.

Kerris could see the resemblance between the man and boy. "My idiot son, here—" Moro shook Perin's arm—"has something to tell you." Perin was pale under his tan. His eyes flicked from side to side, watching the chearis. "The mighty tracker. Speak."

Perin looked at the mats.

Moro let him go. His fingers had left red marks on Perin's bare arm. He put his hands on his broad, belted hips. "For this I must disturb your rest," he said. "I'll tell it, then."

"Two nights ago this boy of mine was smoking heavenweed by the stable when that redheaded cheari wandered past him." Jensie's head jerked up. "They shared the pipe. The upshot of it was they decided to sneak by Cleo's troop and get as near to the Asech camp as they could." Moro's voice lost its admonitory anger. He sounded now only troubled. He moistened his lips.

"They did that. Perin lost his nerve and ran back. Your friend kept going." The ropemaker took a step closer to his frightened son. "I thought you should know, Kel. I—I'm sorry. I don't know who egged on who."

Jensie hissed. Ilene got her by the shoulders before she could move and pulled her backward. Nobody else said anything. Arillard coughed. Kel looked at the boy. "How old are you?" he asked.

"S-s-sixteen, skayin," Perin managed.

"Old enough to remember the raids ten years ago," Kel said. Ilene said, "But not old enough to fear them."

"You did not lose family in those raids," Kel said to Moro.

"Praise be to the chea, no," said the big man.

Kel sighed. He held his hands in the air a moment and then let them drop. "What shall I say, Moro? Take him home and beat him, as I surely shall our redhead when he's back with us."

"Not if I reach him first," said Ilene, kneeling beside the seated Jensie. Relief crossed Moro's face. Swiftly he hauled his son from the house. The door was not quite closed before they all heard his voice lift, and the clear sound of a slap.

Sefer said quietly, "That was well said, nika."

Kel said, "Am I to blame that boy for Riniard's foolishness?" He crossed to Jensie and knelt beside her. She was staring into her hands as if they had words graved on them. "We'll get him back, Jen." She nodded at her fingers.

Kerris bent to take a strip of smoked fish. As he straightened, a voice range in his mind. *Ware—Ware—* The fish fell from his hand. Elli caught it before it hit the floor.

"What is it?" said Ilene.

"It's the Asech," said Sefer.

They went to the market square.

A crowd had gathered: perhaps two hundred people in all. Lara was there, in her gold gown, and Tamaris, and Dorin. The crowd parted for Kel and Sefer. The chearas, Kerris within it, trailed behind Kel.

The folk of Elath watched as the small band of Asech riders picked its way down the southern slope. There was an occasional muttered curse. The villagers were empty-handed—those that Kerris could see—but house doors and shop doors stood ajar along the main street, and faces looked out of the dark rooms, eyes grim and wary. Sunlight shafted on a knife hilt. A shadow stood by a tree trunk, holding an unstrung bow.

Kerris felt a moment's pity for the Asech. There were not very many of them. He saw Thera at their head, and a man whose face was vaguely familiar. He had blue stones in his ears. Kerris wondered what they felt, riding into a place where every hand desired to strike them.

172

They wore dun-colored cloaks with hoods folded back, and soft, fringed, high-topped skin boots. One of them was ancient, a woman. Aside from her and Thera the other riders were all men. Their hair was black and slick, their skin bronze. Under the robes they wore loose shirts and trousers, decorated with beads of many colors. The men's cheeks were scarred with knife cuts, and there were jewels in their ears, set in holes that pierced the lobes. Thera had gold rings in hers. Their leather belts were also ornamented with beadwork. They were doubly armed, with daggers and with curved scabbarded short swords.

The resentful muttering grew louder. Lara stopped it with one raised hand. The Asech paced down the street. Their horses were spirited and fine-boned, and the riders sat them as if glued to the saddle. Their harness was decorated with many colored beads. The riders' glances flicked suspiciously from house to shop to house. Against the beauty of their mounts, they seemed worn and gaunt.

There were not as many of them as there had been in the night, Kerris thought. He wondered where the others were. They halted in front of Lara. Thera spoke. Her voice was just as arrogant as it had been. Kerris' pity for the riders fled.

"We are here. Teach us."

Lara looked tranquilly into that fierce face. "First we must know how our brother fares."

"He lives."

"We would like to see him."

"No."

"Then how do we know he lives?"

"The desert riders do not lie!" Thera said.

The man with the blue stones in his ears turned his horse to speak to her and his voice rose in question. Her hands swept the air as she answered. Kerris remembered who he was. He had held the rein of the horse Riniard had been tied to. His cheeks were bare of scars, like Thera's. His black eyes raked with obvious hostility over the villagers.

His name seemed to be Barat. Thera spoke with him a little longer and then turned to Lara. "Today you will teach us—those who are here. Tomorrow more will come. They will bring a message to you from your brother, words only he could say.

When all our people have been taught and have come back to our camp, we will let your brother go unhurt. I swear it in the name of my people, *Li Omani.*" She rested her hand on the feathers in her horse's mane.

Lara conferred with Tamaris. She said, "We accept your oath. If you mean it falsely, we will know. Mind to mind cannot lie."

Barat spat a query at Thera. She responded. Kerris wondered if he was the riders' chief, and was telling her what to do. The horses stamped. They were not shod. Kerris glanced down the street. All he could see was people. There was even a small figure—a child, he guessed—perched on the peaked roof of the well.

Lara waited until the riders' conversation ended. Then she said, "There is something you must know. Only a few of us are teachers. Teaching even one person is tiring. It exhausts teacher and student. We cannot, in one day, teach all of you."

Again Barat demanded a translation. Thera gave it to him. His scowl grew more fierce; he shook his head briskly. "*Shai,*" he repeated several times. Kerris wondered if it might be the Asech word for no. "Shai!"

The old woman spoke. Her voice was cracked and metallic, but Barat stilled at once. When the old woman finished speaking he jumped into speech. A second man said something from behind him. The horses switched their tails. Kerris shifted from one foot to the other. His stump itched. He scratched it. Listening to an argument he could not understand was tiring.

Barat stabbed his finger at the second man, and at a third, and a fourth. They dismounted. So did Thera. She was no taller than Elli. Barat joined her. He was not much bigger than she was. A shrill voice spoke. One of the standing men hastened to the old woman's side, and helped her carefully to the ground.

Thera patted her horse's nose. She looked reluctantly at Lara. "Will you teach six of us?"

"Yes," Lara said, "we can do that."

"If we do not return tonight to our camp," Thera said, "the hostage will die, in as slow and painful a way as we can devise."

The crowd muttered. Kerris heard the breath hiss through

174

Elli's teeth. Arillard and Ilene were flanking Jensie: Kerris could not see her face. Kel's was impassive, immobile as stone. The Asech drew together. Barat's hand was on his sword hilt, and the sword was partway out of its sheath. "Be still," said a voice, "be still." Calming whispers rippled through the assembled villagers.

Thera spoke to Barat. The desert rider barked a command. As one, the remaining riders turned and raced for the rim, sleek and swift as hawks in the chase. They did not shout. The riderless horses surged forward. Their masters reined them in.

"Go to your homes," said the quiet voices, "go, go." Ilene's was one of them: so was Ardith's. The crowd moved away from the six Asech. Elli linked her fingers with Kerris as they stepped backward. Kel and Sefer talked, heads together. Sefer's hair fell about his face. Suddenly he looked up, right at Kerris, and beckoned.

"He's pointing at you," Elli said. "Go." She propelled him gently forward, with a push to the small of his back.

He went to Sefer's side. The teacher said to Kel, "Nika, let him make his own choice!" Kel's lips pressed together. Sefer turned to Kerris. "Kerris, I have a request to make of you. I want you with us, to make a group of six. There are six of them, and there ought to be six of us. You won't have to do anything."

Kerris' heart thumped. "Why me?" Barat was staring at him behind Sefer's back. The air fumed with a strange pungency: the Asech scent.

"Because you're a scribe and can write it down later," Kel said. His voice was tight. "That's what comes of having a scholar for a sister."

Kerris said, "You don't want me to do it."

Kel shrugged. "It's not my concern," he said.

"I want to know what you think," Kerris insisted.

"Chelito, you must do as you like."

Barat scowled. He growled to Thera.

"They're growing impatient," said Sefer. "Kerris, if you're afraid of being drawn into the Asech thoughts, don't be. Their barriers are like iron." His voice was persuasive. "Won't you join us?"

Now all the Asech were looking at him. They reminded

175

Kerris of animals, wolves or hawks, things that hunt. "Yes," he said. The morning sun heated the street. His feet were sweating in his tight boots.

He stole a glimpse of Kel. His brother's face was stony. But Kel had seen Kerris' head turn. His taut mouth smoothed to a half-smile. Putting out an arm, he drew Kerris to him. Sefer gave a little nod. They walked to where the Asech stood. Barat stared at Kerris. Kerris pretended not to see it. He made his face like Kel's, and his chin stiff.

Barat snapped at Thera. She said, to Lara, "Who is the cripple?"

Kerris' face flamed. Kel's fingers tightened on his arm.

Lara said, "He is one of us, that is enough. We have not asked who each one of you is."

Thera translated this. Barat frowned. But the old woman, who stood at his elbow, chuckled and bowed her head up and down. She patted Barat's arm. Unwillingly, it seemed, he ceased to frown. The three men he had chosen massed behind him, fanning out like the broad end of a wedge.

Lara said, "Will you leave your horses with us?"

Thera translated this for the others. They spoke among themselves. "Shai!" said Barat. He waved his hands in the air.

Thera said, "Our horses are our selves."

This made no sense to Kerris. Did the Asech think they were horses?

Sefer said, "We swear by the chea that we will not harm them. That oath is sacred to us."

Again the Asech spoke together. Thera said, "They are to be left here, not moved. But it would be a kindness if you would let them drink."

"We will."

Thera laid a hand on her horse's neck. She stroked it and murmured to it, leaning her face against it till they were nose to nose. The horse lipped her chin. Its ears pricked forward intelligently. She let its rein drop to the dust, and at once it bowed its head. "They agree," she said.

Lara said, "We will go to the Tanjo: that is the school." Barat, Thera, and the old woman walked beside her, Tamaris and

Dorin behind them, the rest of the Asech behind them. Kerris glanced back. Lalli and Sosha were coming from the well, each carrying a bucket. Tek had appeared from the shadows. He was stroking one of the horses, fingering the beaded rein.

Kel, Sefer, and Kerris walked rearguard. They moved slowly, keeping to the pace of the old woman. Her hair was streaked white and gray like an owl's feathers. Alone of the Asech she wore no sword, but Kerris had seen the hilt of a dagger curving from her belt. Under the beaded hem of her trousers her feet were flat, wide, and bare.

The Asech did not like the cypress grove. They shuffled through it, looking up and around and back at the aloof black trees.

But in the garden before the Tanjo they smiled. The brilliant clumps of color against the lush green grass seemed to delight them.

Thera said, "It looks like the desert after the rain." Her voice lost some of its arrogance. She cupped her hand against a flower's glowing petals. Barat prowled around the circle. He seemed unhappy. He spoke to one of the other men, one with red stones in his ear lobes, and jerked his head toward the image of the Guardian.

The other man asked Thera a question. The woman rider's brows drew together. She looked at the white image. "Is that—what is that?" she said.

Lara said, "That is a thing we made to remind us of the chea."

"Chea. I do not know that word."

"It is a word of the old tongue our people once spoke. It means harmony, balance, center."

The man with the red stones in his ear lobes spoke. "Chea—like cheari." He bit his lip and then spoke in the desert tongue to Thera, hands moving as if he could not talk without them. She made assenting noises. The old woman said something, her voice jumping like some ancient musical instrument. She pointed—with her chin, not her finger, to the Guardian. To Kerris' astonishment, the six desert riders faced the image, folded their hands up to their foreheads, and bowed. The crone twitched her cloak aside and curled into the grass. She spoke to Thera, who translated it.

"We will stay here."

Lara, Sefer, Dorin, and Tamaris all looked at each other. Thera saw the exchange and said, "We do not like houses that do not move." Her hands described a pen.

They sat in two half circles, Asech on one side, the witches of Elath on the other. Lara told their names. "Lara, Sefer, Kel, Kerris, Tamaris, Dorin."

The simple naming seemed to disconcert the riders. Barat spoke to Thera. Then each of the riders said a name. "Thera."

"Barat."

"Jacob." Jacob was taller than the others, slender, graceful.

"Nerim." Nerim was dark. His eyes were black as tar. The scars on his cheeks were ridged and purple-brown; they ran from the outer corner of each eye diagonally to the chin.

"Khalad." The stones in his ear were purple. A soft curly beard fringed his lips.

"Mirian."

Sefer leaned forward to Thera. "Are you the only one of your people who speaks our tongue?"

Nerim said, "I speak little." He lifted his left hand with the thumb and forefinger close together. This was the man who had brought the message to Erith's troop.

Tamaris said, "Perhaps we should have wine."

Thera translated it. Khalad's face brightened. Mirian giggled. She mimed drinking with her cupped hands. Where age had softened Lara's pale face it had leaned and withered hers. Her skin was pulled right back against her sharp bones.

"Yes," said Sefer. "Bring it, Tam."

Tamaris closed her eyes. A door opened and closed somewhere. A brightness gleamed in the air. It was a tall copper ewer. It came steadily through the garden as if invisible hands were holding it. A line of twelve copper cups bobbed in its wake. The Asech stared. The ewer landed in Tamaris' hands. The cups landed beside Sefer. They rocked and fell over. Sefer gathered them up. Tamaris poured white wine from the ewer into a cup and handed it to Thera, who peered into the cup and then passed it to Barat, who passed it to Jacob. It went to Mirian. She waited for Tamaris to drink from her own cup. Then she sipped the wine, and smiled. *"Wa'hai!"* she said.

Thera said, "That means 'good.'"

All the Asech took wine, except Barat, who folded his arms across his chest. Kerris took a swallow of it. It was astringent and dry, like a northern vintage.

Barat spoke through Thera. "Show me how to do that!" He pointed with his chin at the ewer.

Sefer said, "I'm not sure we can. Not everyone has that gift."

When Thera translated the answer, Barat scowled. He snarled a short sentence.

Thera said, "Barat wants me to remind you that the life of your brother depends on what you teach us."

Temperately Sefer answered, "We know. But we cannot change the truth. I can't do that." He pointed at the ewer. "Only Tamaris can, of the six of us."

"Then she must teach," said Thera.

"She can teach it, if you have that gift. If you don't, she cannot."

Thera repeated this in the Asech tongue. There was a brief altercation, a flurry of words, which Mirian resolved by cutting across the talk with a few shrill phrases.

Kerris wished he knew what they were saying to each other. He would have to guess, or more likely leave blank spaces on the page when he came to write it all down. He could just imagine what Josen would say about incomplete records.

He wondered if the Asech wrote things down, and what their writing looked like. The sun bounced off the yellow beads on their clothes. This close, the smell of them was strong. Except for the barefoot Mirian they wore flat-soled sandals that seemed to be made of rope. He wondered how they maneuvered on the slippery rocks of the rim, and if they had brought their tents with them.

Nerim spoke. He said, "I do that."

"Show us," said Lara.

Nerim licked his lips. He stared at the cup in his hand. It trembled and then lifted straight up. He held it at the level of his eyes for a count of ten. Jacob's slim hand was there to catch it as it hit the grass. Khalad clapped Nerim on the shoulder. The dark man grinned.

"Yes," said Tamaris. "You have the gift. We call it mind-lifting." Under her clear tones Thera spoke in a whisper. "You can throw a stone with your mind, or hold fire or water."

"Show them," Sefer said.

Tamaris held out her cupped palms. The air shimmered over her fingers, brightened, and burst into flame. She made a throwing motion. The fireball sailed upward and split into a storm of sparks.

Jacob made a noise in his throat. Barat drew a harsh breath. Nerim said, "I can cup throw. I can stone throw. I cannot other." He mimed lifting a heavy weight.

"It takes practice," said Tamaris. "Fire also takes practice. I make a shield with thought between my hands and the flame. It is difficult. Don't try it."

"It tire—I—it make tired." said Nerim. He frowned and spoke to Thera. Jacob, beside him, played with the cup.

Thera said, "Nerim wants to know why when he uses his power it makes him tired."

"Because," Tamaris said, "he is fighting himself. He is using his gift through a wall."

Again the Asech spoke among themselves. Kerris no longer found their smell unpleasant. Barat's voice was softer. In a wild, sullen way he was a handsome man. Kerris wondered why he had no scars. He shifted his legs and struck Dorin's wine cup. Wine dribbled into the grass. "Sorry."

"No matter," said Dorin. He righted it. The liquid left a pale stain on the soft fabric of his shirt.

He wore no knife. Neither did Tamaris, or Lara, or Sefer. Sefer didn't need one—he could stop a blow in a man's mind before it reached the fingers. Tamaris didn't need one either. Kerris thought, If I could use my gift as Sefer can. . . . Thera was speaking. He listened.

"Teach me," she said.

"What can you do?" Sefer said.

She hesitated. Her long callused fingers knotted together. "I can govern animals. I can sense great need. When I was small I could feel the thought of people near me. I cannot do that now."

Sefer said, "You have *my* gift: inspeech, the ability to speak mind to mind."

She thumped her hand on the grass. "I cannot do it anymore. I have tried."

"That is because you put a wall between you and other minds."

A red bird flew over the garden. The Asech all lifted their heads to look at it. Mirian's face turned like a flower to the sunlight. She lifted her hand and called something, musical as bird song. The red bird circled, banked, and came to rest on her yellow wrist. She held it there a moment, while its heartbeat shook the tiny body. Then she let it go. It flew straight up and raced for the trees. Nerim chuckled and spoke in a low tone. The old woman said something. Thera translated it. "Mirian wants to know what the wall you speak of is."

"Inspeakers construct a wall in their heads to protect themselves from other people's thoughts. Usually witches with other gifts—" Sefer jestured toward Tamaris—"don't need that wall. I have it." He looked at Thera and then at Mirian. "You have it. It's that wall which keeps you safe. Your walls are very strong, people don't even see you, unless you want them to." Thera nodded. "But you—" Sefer looked at Nerim—"also have a wall. Your gift is locked behind it. As long as you retain the wall, none of you will be free to use your gifts as they should be used."

Thera translated. Mirian's lined face grew grave. Thera said, "Mirian wants to know, if we break our walls how do we protect ourselves? They hunt us down like rats in the desert when they find us."

"Who hunts you down?" said Lara. "Not the folk of Arun!"

Mirian shook her head as this was repeated to her. She spoke. "No," said Thera, eyes fixed on the old woman's face. "Our own."

Mirian went on speaking. Thera's voice took on a ritual rise and fall. "I was ten when my father broke his leg in three places. He was hunting, and he was two lengths from the camp. I felt his pain across the salt pans. I told my mother of it, and she rode out with a litter and a mule and dragged him back. They made me swear to tell no one of my knowledge, but you know how children are. When I perceived things I spoke of them to the other children. They grew afraid of me. At last the elders heard of it. They too feared me, they called me *yamal*, demon. They decreed that I be driven into the dunes to die."

She halted. "Aaah," said the Asech voices.

Mirian rocked as she spoke. "My parents—may they be forever at peace!—hid me in a cave near the camp. For a year they brought me food and water in secret. One night they were seen. They were put to death—buried to their necks in sand, and left." The old voice broke. Tamaris filled a cup with wine and put it into the ancient hands.

Mirian drank, and went on. "I felt it. I could not help them. The villagers hunted me, but I was fourteen and knew hiding places the hunters had never seen. I lived eating rats and snakes, and raiding the water bags from the herds. I was caught by two traders. They didn't know who or what I was. They raped me, and then got drunk, and fell asleep arguing over what to do with me. I rolled to the fire and burned the ropes off my wrists." She flicked back the wide sleeves of her shirt. The inside of both her stick-thin arms were stitched with scars. "I took their waterbags and their two strongest horses, and rode east. In the middle of the great sand I found a camp, and people living there. Most of them are dead now. But they knew me—and I them. They were witch-folk, like me, shamed, deserted, driven from their tribes." She pulled the hooded cloak over her head, keening. The shrill ululation raised the hairs on Kerris' neck and spine.

Gently, Lara said, "Are you all outcasts?"

Thera's voice thickened. "They brand us now with the strokes of a heated knife before they drive us into the desert, so that we cannot join a caravan, or go to another tribe's camp. The strong ones wander until they find us. We live in a part of the desert that no one, not even hunters, comes to. When hunters do come—" her eyes burned, and her hands made a swift and murderous motion—"we kill. Our own we keep."

Sefer shook his head. "We pity you," he said, "and we honor you for what you have endured. But if you let go of your walls you will be stronger. You will see and hear and lift. No one save yourselves will ever be able to touch you or hurt you again."

Thera spoke this to the others. Khalad nodded. Jacob said nothing. He rolled a cup in his palms. Mirian mumbled from beneath her hood. Only Barat seemed distressed. He spoke rapidly, stabbing his finger at Sefer as if it were a weapon.

The old woman put a stop to his tirade. "Shai!" Shaking back her hood, she pushed herself forward, into the center of the circle, and held out her hands to Sefer. Gently he twined her bony fingers in his own. She spoke.

Thera said, "Mirian says it has been many years since she let her mind free of the wall. But she says, if you will help her, she will try."

Sefer smiled. "Good. Good." The old woman tilted her head to one side, as if she were trying to understand the unfamiliar language. There were great calluses on her palms. Her mouth tensed. She closed her eyes. Her mouth opened like a baby's. She shuddered. Her face relaxed. Tears welled beneath her eyes. Thera translated her slow whisper.

"I feel you. I feel you. I feel all of you." She dropped her hands to her lap, and looked around at her companions. "No more children hunted like rats, branded like colts, no more. We will go to them, we will find them, we will bring them home. They cannot touch us, don't you see? No more, no more." She lifted her hands in supplication. The grief in her face was terrible. Unchecked, pain surged from her thought. "O, for the dead, the many dead! O that my mother and father were still alive!"

. . . He was small. The thunder crashed about his ears. Rain soaked his clothes. The sky was a huge mottled wall of clouds. The rain had voices like birds. "Mama?" he said, and felt her arms go more tightly round him. The rhythm of the horse grew choppy. It was hard to breathe. He tried to poke his head out of the folds of cloak. The voices screamed. He pushed his fingers up and peeled the cloak from his face. Birdlike, inhuman, faces swooped out of the sky. The horse was running. He felt his mother's heartbeat pounding. He felt a jerk. The sky poured white water on him. There was a sharp pain through his right

arm. He called upon his mother and felt her falling, bringing him with her. His head filled with pictures, bright faces—Kerwin, nika, never to see you again, Lea my friend, Kel my son, O my mother—howling with terror, he thrust against his mother's body. The ground shook. His arm hurt. His mind swelled with terror, pain, loss, dreadful loss, he could not stand it, he tried to hold it back. Something built—and snapped—in his head. He screamed with the pain, but by then his mother's questing mind had left his and joined with her brother's, days away. He cowered in the white space, bereft, hurt, without recourse. "Oh, the babe!" Hands lifted him. "Ai, his arm!" He ignored the voice. He did not know it. The world was shadow and he was alone, surrounded by insubstantial strangers.

Slowly he came back. "Kerris. Kerris." Someone was calling him. It was a real sound. He moved. His muscles quivered. He smelled the sharp scent of crushed grass. He lay face down in it. He swallowed. His throat hurt; his mind hurt; he hurt all over, as if he had been beaten. He drew a deep breath. His ribs creaked.

"He's coming back." The voice was Sefer's. An ant traveled past his nose, black legs stepping high. He tried to turn his head. The world wavered in and out of focus. He saw a swath of green, a blob of gray. "Kerris, do you want to sit?" He croaked. Hands raised him.

He saw the bird faces of his dream, brown, high-cheekboned, alien. His mind froze.

"Kerris." Fingers bracketed his head. He looked into a face he knew: pale skin, pale hair, eyes like green lamps. "You're all right. Do you know me? Say my name."

"S-Sefer." His mouth felt gluey.

"You're in the garden of the Tanjo at Elath. Kel's holding you. Nika, show him."

Hands touched him, stroked him. A warm tongue lingered on his throat. "Remember me?" The explicit caresses made him shiver. He turned his head. Thera, Barat, Jacob—there were the alien bird faces of his dream—the Asech.

He was dripping with sweat. His eyes stung. He wiped them with his sleeve. Barat clamored at Thera for explanation.

He had never been so deep into the memory before. He knew it was memory now, not fantasy. This was no place of his making. His mouth tasted of ash. *Mother*, he thought. *O my mother....*

Mirian's great eyes stared at him. He wondered how much of the reaction she had caught. "Were you there?" he said to Sefer. His voice rasped.

"Only at the very end," Sefer said. "Can you talk about it?"

Kerris leaned his head against Kel's firm shoulder. "I was a baby. I was riding with my mother in the rain. I felt pain in my arm." He touched his stump. (A voice whispered: Thera, telling the other Asech what he was saying.) "My mind filled with thoughts, not my thoughts, *her* thoughts...." He closed his eyes. He tried to find, in his head, his dead mother's face. "I tried to make them stop. It hurt." He trembled, remembering the magnitude of that blow to his brain. "I was afraid." He could not see her. He opened his eyes.

Sefer was nodding. "I felt the fear, and the wave of pain, the aftershock of the barrier breaking." He covered Kerris' fingers with his own. "It was memory, Kerris, a fourteen year old memory, a three-year-old's nightmare. When your mother died, she linked with you, just for an instant. I hope you can forgive her. She was wounded and couldn't help it. You tried to wall her out and were not strong enough. The barrier broke. It damaged you enough to blot out all memory of the event and your life before it. The rainstorm in Galbareth brought it partially back to you. So did my attempt to teach you to barrier. So did Mirian's pain."

Kerris licked his lips. "That's why I could not make the wall yesterday—"

"Yes," Sefer said.

Lara said softly, "Could you feel the extent of the hurt, Sefer?"

"Not large," Sefer said, "It has mostly repaired itself, over time."

"Kerris," said Tamaris, "would you like some wine?" She passed him a goblet without waiting for his answer. His hand shook. Kel steadied it for him. He hurt, still.

Kel said in his ear, "Chelito, you don't have to stay here. Go back to the cottage."

Thera said to Sefer, "I do not understand one thing. This—your friend—was hurt because he has no wall?"

Sefer shook his head emphatically. "No. Because the—the piece of his mind that makes a wall was injured when he was a baby, and so he never learned to make one properly. He will."

Kerris drank the wine. It tasted flat. Barat was looking at him with contempt. He was not going to crawl off to rest like a child. "No. I'll stay." Kel took the cup from his hand. You're sure? his eyes questioned. Kerris firmed his shoulders. He was weak but it would pass; it had before. He felt as if a storm had shaken him in wet, cold talons, and then left him on the earth, tattered but clean.

Barat asked Thera a question. She argued with him. He insisted. She looked at Kerris. "Barat would like to know what tribe the riders you saw came from."

So Thera, too, had seen the riders in his mind. Kerris felt Kel's muscles bunch. He answered, "I don't know."

She translated this. Barat scowled. He traced the bead patterns on his tunic with one finger. Thera said, "He wants to know what the bead marks on their clothing were. Such things are different from tribe to tribe."

Kerris said with careful clarity, "I was three years old, and hurt. Tell him I don't remember." He was surprised to find that his fist was clenched. He loosened it. At his back, Kel was tense with rage.

Barat spoke flatly. Thera said, "Let us go on, then, with the teaching." Khalad spoke. "Khalad says, What is my power?" Kel relaxed. Lara's face tilted skyward, as if there were something present in the warm sunlight that only she could see. Barat fingered the beads on his shirt.

"What can you do?" said Sefer.

"I dream," said Khalad through Thera. "I dream of places I have not seen, never seen: I dream of gray mountains, and great houses of stone. I see them."

"Ah," said Dorin, "You have my gift. You are a far-traveler."

Barat nudged Thera into speech. "Barat wants to know what

use is dreaming, even of real mountains and real castles. Can Khalad fly there, like a bird?"

"Not as far as we know," said Dorin placidly. "But the gift is a real one. Don't discount it because it has no present use."

"What is my power?" Jacob's question; Jacob's turn. "My tribe drove me out when I said the words that people spoke before they spoke them. But I cannot hear thought, like Thera or Mirian. I cannot throw stones. My dreams are ordinary."

Lara said, "Have you ever touched a wound and found it healed?"

"No."

"Can you call wind or weather?"

"No."

Kel said, "Have you any skill, special skill?"

Jacob sighed, and opened his hands with the gesture of a man letting sand run out of his fingers. But Nerim said, "He fight. And he ride anything. Mule, horse, devil—anything he ride."

Jacob demanded to know what his friend had said. When it was told him, he said a swift string of sounds to Thera. She relayed it. "Jacob says that is a thing he does with his body, not with his mind!"

"No," said Kel. He rose. "It is a thing you do with your mind." He stepped toward Jacob, moving with supple noiselessness. In a blur almost too swift to see, his hand jumped to his knife. Jacob flung upward, whipping his dagger free of his belt. Kel twisted from the hips, feet gliding over the grass, hair whipping with the motion. His left hand clamped on Jacob's right. The sky darkened. Jacob's feet left the earth. He hit the ground with a thump. Kel was standing. Jacob lay on his back, dark eyes wide, cloak spread like ashen wings beneath him. Kel was holding Jacob's knife.

It had happened so quickly, no one else had time to move. Now, with a shout like a falcon's scream, Barat sprang to his feet and lunged, barehanded, at Kel.

Jacob shot upward. He stepped between them, calling on Nerim. Nerim jumped to help him, and together they wrestled Barat still. Jacob's face burned with wonder. Pulling Barat to the grass, he crouched at his knee, speaking earnestly. Barat pulled his clothes straight. He stared at Kel.

Jacob spoke to Thera. She said, "Jacob wishes to understand what you have showed him."

Kel said, "Tell him he has a gift. He is what we call a patterner. Tell him he will always be able to move first, quickest, to ride, to hunt, to dance, to find the pattern where everyone else sees chaos."

When Thera translated this, Nerim's face grew a broad grin. He pounded Jacob on the knee.

Jacob's face remained grave. Thera translated his sentence. "Jacob says, you are his master."

Kel put one arm around Sefer and one arm around Kerris. He was not even breathing hard. "Now I am. But my teacher was the finest in Arun, and I have had fifteen years to study my gift."

Lara said, "It is a matter of balance." Thera translated this, and Jacob nodded respectfully.

Barat thumped the grass with a fist. He leaned forward. *"Haraiya-na e'ka!"* By now Kerris did not need Thera's soft translation; he had heard the words too many times. *What is my power?* The Asech was breathing swiftly from the tussle with Jacob. His right hand teased the dagger handle in his belt. It was bronze, in the shape of a horse's head, with a blue stone for the horse's eye. Thera put a hand on his arm. He barked brutally at her, and she jumped back. In a slightly milder tone he repeated his question. "Haraiya-na e'ka?"

"What can you do?" said Sefer. "Why did your tribe drive you out?"

Thera did not translate his words. She touched her cheek. "Barat did not—Barat was not driven from the tribe," she said. "He chose to leave, for my sake."

Her voice took on the storyteller's lilt. "I was three years a woman when my tribe banished me to the desert. Barat and I were—" she hesitated—"*nahrebul.* I do not know your word. We had been promised to each other. After the rain I was to leave my father's home and join his father's tent. For this my father had pledged ten goats and three of our horses, one a mare in foal.

"When the elders came to bind and brand me, I was in my

father's tent, mixing wheatcake." Her hands kneaded invisible dough. "My little sister warned me they were coming. I fled to Barat's tent. He stole two horses from his father's herd and we rode. After much wandering we found Li Omani, the Branded Ones. They knew me for what I was, though my cheeks were naked. They took us in.

"Because we of all Li Omani have no brands on our cheeks, we can enter villages without fear of being known as witches. Barat has worked as herder for caravans going to your cities. We have been to the market in Shanan. That is how I speak your tongue. Barat has remained with us when he did not have to." She sat back and drew her hood down over her face, as if ashamed of having said so much.

Barat spoke to her but she shook her head and would not talk to him. Nerim finally had to tell him what she had said. A breeze brushed the cypress grove and made the flower stalks tremble. To his own surprise, Kerris found himself reaching to Sefer. *What do you think his gift is?*

I don't think he has one. Sefer's mental voice was grim.

Thera let her hood fall from her face. Sefer said, "I cannot tell what Barat's gift is. Ask him if he will let me touch his mind."

When Thera relayed the request, Barat scowled. "Shai!" He waved his hands and spoke angrily to Thera. There was a tinge of fear in his brusque voice.

"Barat says you did not ask that of anyone else."

"I touched Mirian's mind," Sefer pointed out. Mirian looked up at her name. "No harm has come to her. It is the surest way of knowing what gift you possess."

"Shai!"

Thera put a hand on Barat's arm. He shook it off. His right hand clenched around the hilt of the knife. She pleaded. So did the others, hands moving. Kel's arm slipped from Kerris' shoulders.

At last Barat yielded. He faced Sefer. *"Makhe-na."*

Sefer's eyes closed. After a moment he opened them and spoke to Thera. "You are shielding him." Her eyebrows drew together. "You are keeping a wall around his mind. I cannot touch him. Let it go."

Her fingers moved on her lap, but whatever she was thinking

of saying did not reach her lips. She bowed her head. Barat
suddenly stiffened. His eyes glazed. He trembled, and then
slumped. Sweat beaded his face. He moaned.

Thera gasped, and lifted his head to her lap. Lara said,
"Don't worry. It will pass."

Barat shuddered. Sense came into his eyes. He moved his
mouth. He spoke to Thera. She answered him. Abruptly he
hauled himself upright. His hands gripped the earth. "Haraiya-
na—" he coughed, halted, and continued. "Haraiya-na e'ka!"

Sefer shook his head. His eyes were eloquent. "You have no
gift."

Barat did not wait for the translation. Snarling, he drew his
knife.

Thera cried out. She caught his wrist. But it was Jacob and
Nerim who together forced the curved blade back into the
sheath. Barat shook with rage. He yelled at Sefer, who sat
quietly listening to the harsh and incomprehensible tongue.

Mirian screeched. The shrill sound cut across Barat's raving,
and silenced it. He answered her in a softer voice. Kel was
watching. When Barat had drawn his knife he had leaned
forward, ready to intervene. His hands rested easily on the soft
grass. He was still as water, still as the mountain before it falls.

Barat's voice rose again. He argued with Mirian. Thera,
listening, looked shocked. Kerris wondered why he was feeling
none of Barat's anger. It was intense, and very close, and he was
vulnerable.

He had no time to explore the thought. Barat was on his feet.
He leveled a finger at Sefer and spoke two or three sentences, the
words biting and filled with menace. He slapped a command at
the others. The scarlet beads shone on his shirt like drops of
fresh blood.

He whirled, cloak billowing, and strode into the trees.
Khalad helped Mirian up. She shook her clothes in order, like an
owl shaking its ruffled feathers into place. She spoke to Thera.

"Mirian says you are to ignore Barat's discourtesy."

Lara said, "What did he say?"

Thera moistened her lips. "He—he does not understand. He
thinks that you can give him power, the power to speak mind to

mind, the power to hold fire. He does not understand the power is in us."

They returned to the square where the Asech horses stood. Tek was seated nearby, peeling a willow stick in his huge hands. Lalli and Sosha were not in sight. He nodded to Lara. "There's one gone ahead." Up the southern slope a light haze lifted, where Barat's horse had shipped up dust. "Movin' like a hell-wolf."

"I hope you didn't try to stop him," said Sefer.

"Me? I know when a man's in a hurry." The Asech horses whinnied and pushed against their riders. "Those horses are like children. Look at 'em." He scratched the end of the willow stick into his beard, and lowered his voice. "Should I have stopped him, Sef?"

"No." Sefer turned to Thera, who was fondling her horse. It was a dapple with a blaze down its forehead. "You must know now," he said, "that you don't need the witches of Elath to teach you to use your powers. You five can show the others of you—those here and those still in the desert—how to dispel their walls. You do not have to hide. As long as you do not use your gifts for evil, you can be proud and fearless in what you are."

Her snapped up. "What may be evil for the witches of Elath may not be so for Li Omani. We are the desert riders. We do not live by city law."

Sefer shook his head. "The chea is not bound to place."

She frowned; her eyebrows drew together like dark wings on her high forehead. "Let us not talk of this." Her fingers smoothed the dapple's mane. "Let us talk of tomorrow." She hesitated. She rubbed her lips with one finger. "It may be true, as you say, that we do not need the witches of Elath. But what is learned today may be forgotten tomorrow. Let us see what happens. The teaching may be more difficult for us, or there may be others among us who have no power, like Barat." Her feeling for the man who had chosen exile to be with her was plain on her face.

"We will await your message," Sefer said.

Jacob and Nerim were hunched together, talking. Kerris couldn't see their faces, only their moving hands. The beadwork made a repeating triangle pattern up Nerim's sleeves. Suddenly

Thera said, "Is there nothing you can do to help him?"

Sefer sighed. "We cannot make power where there is no power. Gifts come from the chea."

Thera's hands lifted. Mirian, mounted, shrilled a few words. The gesture died. Nerim and Jacob separated. Cloaks flaring, the Asech swung onto their horses and cantered south, up the slope, following in Barat's dusty wake.

Chapter 12

The five riders had barely disappeared over the slope when Moro the ropemaker stepped out of his house. He wore a short sword in a leather scabbard. "Well?" he said. Perin came out behind him. The boy walked as if his back hurt. "What happened?"

"Let's wait," Sefer said, "so that we don't have to say it two hundred times." He beckoned to Tek. More people came out of their houses. Most came weaponless, but a few held knives, spears, and bows. Some came from the fields, hoes on their shoulders. They packed the market square. There was a clear space around Lara. Kerris edged into it. He wiped his sweating palm on his shirtfront. He was not used to so many people in one space. The swelling voices made him want to hide.

Kel muscled through the throng to the ropemaker's house. He spoke with Moro in the doorway and the big man beckoned him inside. Children circled through and around and under the legs of the adults, screaming as if the assembly were an entertainment devised for them to play in. Kel pulled back to where Tek and Sefer stood together. He was carrying a wooden box.

He set it down. Tek placed a heavy hand on his shoulder, and vaulted to the top of the box.

He shouted. The people in the square laughed. *"Hey, Tek!"* Eventually they grew still enough for him to shout the gabblers down. His voice was thunderous, loud enough to reach the edges of the square. Sefer fed him words. Tek said them. He told the restless people what had happened in the garden. He told about the branding, and the exile, and the hiding in caves. "Sefer says," he roared to the silent multitude, "that might have been us, any of us, victim or hunter."

"We are not barbarians!" shouted a woman.

Sefer slapped the stablemaster's leg. "Let me get up there." Tek jumped down and handed him up. He faced the crowd. "Then let us prove it!" he said. His voice was thinner than Tek's but it carried. "Show pity for these harried folk. I believe they mean us no further ill than what they have already done. Let them depart unmolested from our fields." He jumped down. "Tell them that's enough, Tek. We'll know more tomorrow when they come back." He coughed.

A hand seized Kerris' elbow. "Kerris." He turned as quickly as the crowd would let him. It was Jensie and Elli. Elli hugged him. He hugged back. In this press of people she was a welcome sight, even though some of the folk in the crowd were his kin, and she was not.

She grinned at him. "Hey."

Jensie said, "Kerris. What did they say of Riniard?"

"Nothing that you didn't hear." He wished there were more he could tell her.

Tek was yelling that there was no more to know, until tomorrow. "Do we have to stay in the square?" said Elli.

The stablemaster climbed from the box holding his throat. "That's thirsty work, you hear?"

A wineskin passed over a string of heads and landed in Tek's lap. "I don't think we have to stay here," Kerris said. He squinted at the shadows. Unbelievably, it looked to be not yet noon.

The chearas formed around him. Kel was busy elsewhere; he was standing beside Sefer, earnestly talking. As Kerris watched, he put both hands on Sefer's shoulders and shook the smaller man, not hard. Sefer leaned into him and nodded. They separated. Kel strode toward the chearis. The villagers moved out of his way. "I've sent Sef to sleep," he said. He put one arm around Kerris' waist.

Ilene said, "I should like to know how you managed that."

Kel said, "Told him if he wouldn't go I'd knock him out and carry him there."

"Here," said Arillard. He held out one hand filled with cheese, and the other filled with strips of jerky. "I thought you'd be hungry."

"I'm more restless than hungry," said Kel. "My muscles are all kinked." But he took a strip of jerky. Kerris took some cheese. It was mild and soft as butter. He licked it from the tips of his fingers.

Jensie said, "Let's go to the Yard."

The crowd was beginning to break up around them. "All right," said Kel. He stretched. "I'd like that." He pulled Kerris in toward him. "Chelito, how do you feel?"

"I'm fine," Kerris said.

Kel's fingers scratched the back of his neck. "No weakness? No headache?"

"No."

"Good," Kel said. "Come to the Yard with us."

A horse had left a pile of yellow dung in the street. The chearis stepped around it. "Shouldn't I be writing down what just happened?" Kerris said.

"No," said Elli. "Come with us." Arillard was walking in front of her. She skipped foward and slapped him on the back. "Bribe Kerris to stay with us while we train."

Arillard, turning, held out a piece of dried beef. Kerris took it.

"Now you have to stay," said Elli.

"Chelito, you can make your records tonight, or tomorrow. Stay with us now." It was hard to resist that plea. Kerris bit into the jerky. It was tough as an old stick.

"All right."

"Your brother bribes easy," said Arillard.

"I'll remember it," said Kel.

"Kel," said Arillard.

"Hmm."

"Do you trust their good will—these Asech?"

Kel said, "I concur with Sef's judgment, that they intend to leave peacefully. They've got what they came for. There's no reason for them to do us more harm."

Arillard glanced over his shoulder. His austere face was somber. "I hope you're right."

"So do I," said Ilene.

Arillard stopped. "You know," he said, looking at Kel, "were I younger, and more foolish, I might have done what Riniard did, that night. I contemplated it."

"Shall I be surprised?" said Kel. He touched Arillard's shoulder. "I'm not. And you didn't."

"I wanted them dead," said Arillard. His thin mouth twisted. "I, a cheari, dedicated to harmony."

"Wanting isn't doing," said Ilene.

But Arillard's face was stubborn with trouble. Sighing, he went forward.

Slanting a look at Kerris, Elli said softly, "What were they like?"

Kerris sought words. "They moved their hands when they talked," he said.

Elli snorted. "That tells me a lot. Is the old woman their chief?"

"I don't know. I don't think so. I think Barat is."

"Which is Barat?" said Ilene.

"The man without the scars. He has blue stones in his ears."

Arillard said, "He's the one who rode away ahead of the others."

"Yes," said Kel. "He's a firebrand." He was coiling his hair on top of his head. "He's Thera's lover. When her tribe tried to brand her and toss her into the desert to die, he helped her escape and then went with her."

"Good for him!" said Elli. "I'd want someone to do that for me." They turned the corner, and Kerris saw the top of the Guardian over the Yard fence.

The wide square space was empty. Kerris started toward a

place out of the way, against the southern wall. Kel pulled him gently back. "Stay. Let me teach you to use the knife."

"Now?"

"Unless you're tired."

"I'm not tired," Kerris said. "I—I don't want to waste your time."

Kel raised his eyebrows. "I don't believe it would be a waste of time."

"I'm less than a beginner."

Kel shook his head. "I thought you'd let me teach you anything," he said.

There seemed to be nothing Kerris could say to that. "I will."

Arillard strolled from the equipment shed, each hand brandishing a yellow niji. Ilene was stretching her hamstrings, bending from the waist to touch her knees with her forehead, holding her ankles with her hands.

Kel took his shirt off and draped it over the fence. "I don't want to get it dirty."

Kerris fingered his own shirt. It was grass-stained. "Should I—?"

"You don't have to." Kel sat on the dirt. Kerris copied him. "First we stretch," he instructed. "Your muscles need to loosen." He showed Kerris how to turn and twist. Ilene had finished her exercises and was sparring with Jensie. The girl's face was stone. In her mind she was fighting the Asech. Ilene chided her, reminding her it was only practice. Jensie's face did not change. "Now stand." They did more exercises. Sweat trickled down inside Kerris' shirt.

Kel went to the shed and brought back two nijis. He handled them carefully, as if they were real knives, keeping his fingers off the "blades". He pointed the knife at the dirt and waited for his brother to tell him what to do.

Kel smiled at him. "We'll work slowly," he said. "I know this is new to you. Show me how you hold your knife." Kerris held the niji as he had seen others do it, blade upright, right at his waist.

"Yes," Kel said. "Don't hold it so tightly. Point your forefinger. The grip should be firm but not so strong that your hand will cramp." Stepping forward, he angled the blade more steeply upward. "Better. Relax your shoulders. You've got good muscles in your wrist and arm, let them do the work."

He stepped back. "Turn your hips, so that the target you present is smaller. Yes. Keep your right side turned away from me." He brought his own niji up. Kerris faltered. "Don't freeze. You have a big advantage, chelito. All the fighters I know prefer to use their right hands, though some can switch." His niji leaped from his right to his left hand, and returned. "It's hard to face a left-hand fighter. Now, circle."

Kerris shuffled left, remembering to keep his right side turned away from Kel. His palm was sweaty. He feared the niji would slip from his fingers. He tightened his grip. Kel shook his head. "No. Relax." Kerris tried.

Out of the corner of his eye he saw Arillard sparring with Jensie. Calwin and Elli were practicing a dance step, arms linked. *"Look at me,"* said Kel. "Now, step in and cut me. Come on!"

Kerris stepped in with his left foot and aimed his niji at Kel's belly. Easily the cheari parried it. His left arm knocked the thrust to one side. At the same time, his right hand came up. "Keep moving," he said. "Block the blow, your arm against my arm. Quickly. Try to make me face the sun. I'm going to come in again. Block me to the outside and go for my throat. Now leap back. Right. Don't stay within reach or I'll grab you with my right hand. Keep moving."

"What if you come high?" Kerris said, puffing.

"That's simpler. Duck and slam your knife into my gut. Let's try it." The yellow niji leaped for Kerris' throat.

Kerris ducked and lunged. The tip of the knife kissed Kel's rib as he skipped back. "Good. Don't stand still!"

Kerris' fingers trembled. He let the knife fall. Kel scooped it up. Shoving it into his belt, he closed the other hand around Kerris' wrist. "Chelito?"

"I—" Kerris licked his lips. "I never struck anyone before."

Kel stroked his back. "Never? Not even when you were small, over a place by the fire, or a favorite toy?"

"Oh. Yes. But never with a weapon, even a wooden one."

"May the chea grant that you never have to use a real one," Kel said. "But if you do you'll do it right. If you ever need to stop again in practice, step backward and lay the knife on the ground, like this." He demonstrated it, a long fluid step and a dip to touch his niji to the earth. His right knee just brushed the dirt.

Pulling the niji from his belt, he held it out, hilt foremost. "Take it. Next time a strike is made, don't stop."

They continued. Kerris' chest began to burn. He panted for breath. Kel struck. He parried and cut upward, moving, swerving, keeping his hand loose on the wooden haft of the niji, keeping his shoulders down, trying to turn Kel so that the bigger man faced the sun.

Once he was late in stepping back. Kel's left hand sprang out and thumped his ribs. He kept moving. Kel smiled. The ache in Kerris' chest began to dissolve. Breathing grew easier. "Faster," said Kel. "You move too slow. I could kill you three times over. Good! Push me. Don't let *me* slow down. If I switch strikes on you—" he did so, the niji springing for Kerris' neck—"you switch your technique." Kerris ducked and sprang in. The niji grazed Kel's side, leaving a red scrape. "Yes. *Don't stop.*"

They worked till Kerris started to stumble. His lungs hurt. Kel stepped back and knelt, letting the niji brush the Yard floor. Rising, he pried the niji from Kerris' stiffened hand. Then he hugged him. He was not even breathing hard. The layer of sweat on his long torso made his body look polished. He ran his hands over Kerris' ribs. One struck a sore spot. Kerris winced.

Kel pulled the shirt away. "Let me see." A purple bruise marked where his niji had connected. "You didn't tell me."

"You said not to stop."

The others had at last worn Jensie out. She sat against the fence. Arillard and Elli were sparring half-heartedly in the shadow of the Guardian. A few of the ties around Elli's braids had worked loose.

"Let's go to the baths," said Ilene.

The baths were crowded. A gaggle of naked children played around one end of the upper pool. They danced up and down on the flat rocks and pushed each other into the water. At that end it was shallow. Elli raced for the steam tent, barely halting at the entrance flap to shed her clothes. The children splashed each other. The adults waved to the chearis. Tek stood in the middle of the lower pool. Soap foamed over his chest and groin and underarms, and down his massive legs. His hair stood out from his head in bushy spikes. His huge torso was covered with lumps and scars. He looked like an old tree.

Kerris stood by the poolside. It was muddy. Cal nudged him. "Why don't you go in?"

"Why don't you?"

The cheari showed his teeth. He danced away from the rocks. Elli sprinted from the steam tent. She dived into the lower pool, splashing Tek. He growled like a bear and lumbered after her. She chuckled and went under water, gliding like a fish through the depths, evading him easily.

She popped up at Kerris' feet. "You should take your knife off if you're going to stand there," she said. "You might slip."

"I won't slip," Kerris said, But it seemed a good idea. "Where can I put it?" The mud sucked at his boots.

"I'll hold it for you," Cal said. He leered at Elli. "Nyaa." Kerris undid his belt and handed knife and belt to Cal, who twitched his fingers challengingly at Elli and wandered toward the steam tent.

Elli scooped soap from a pot and scrubbed her hair. She had freed it from the silken ties. She ducked under the water to let the soap float away, scrubbing vigorously with both hands. She bounced up blowing water. "I told you," she said, putting a cold hand on Kerris' bare calf, "you should come in."

"No, thank you." But to please her, he took off his dirty boots and dangled his legs in the water. He had to set his teeth, not to yell. The water was icy, cold as the Rurian in spring thaw when it was swollen with mountain snow.

Her wide mouth twitched. He kicked water at her. She jumped back. Footsteps sounded in the grass behind him. "Watch!" Elli called. "Watch me." She dived backward, long body arching back like a hoop, making almost no splash as she cleaved the water. Kerris leaned forward, wondering where she would come up.

Two golden arms wrapped around his waist and hurled him into the pool.

He grabbed for the edge as it flew past, but he landed nowhere near it. He shut his eyes. Water spurted into his nose. He sank like a stone. Coughing, he kicked and clawed his way to the surface. His clothes dragged at him. When he shook his hair out of his eyes, he found Elli an arm's length away, observing him happily. "I knew you could swim."

He lunged for her, scissoring his legs with all his strength. She yelped and dived away from his outstretched hand. He chased her to the shallow end of the pool. She crouched like a brown frog amid the children and croaked at him. The children, vastly pleased, grunted in imitation. The water did not seem quite so chilly. He splashed her. She splashed him. He tried to grab her leg. She dived underwater, circled round behind him, and pushed him over.

He leaned against the mossy rocks to pull off his clammy shirt. It stuck to him; he had to almost tear it to get it off. Elli looked him up and down, as if she had never seen his skin before. He covered his stump with his left hand.

She scowled. "Don't do that."

The children hushed, scenting a quarrel. They peered avidly over Elli's shoulder, all sizes, all colors, black like Ilene, brown like Elli, pale like Jensie, freckled like Riniard.... "It's not pretty."

She waded to him and put her hands on his shoulders. "It doesn't matter." Her strong fingers nipped his flesh. "It's an arm, damn it, Kerris, that's all, just a piece of meat."

He wanted to believe her. He would believe her. Chill bumps sprang along his spine; he'd been standing too long without movement. Bending his knees, he flung himself toward her. Her eyes widened. He wrapped his arm around her and bore her down, holding his breath. The world turned liquid green, then black. Bubbles flew past his ears. He wrapped his legs around Elli's thighs. His pants flapped. Water streamed against his groin. Her nipples were hard as pebbles against his chest.

They went up. They burst through the surface, gulping air. Elli worked free of his hold and poured herself toward the deep end of the pool, swerving eel-like around the other bathers. She stayed there, laughing, till he came up, and then sank. Kerris filled his lungs and plunged to find her. She hovered fishlike beyond his groping hand, a dark blurred shape. His ears filled. He bounced up. Two strokes away, she surfaced, floating, her lean back arched, waiting for him.

At last the chill of the water wormed into his bones. He stroked into the shallow end and stood up, shaking. Elli rose behind him. She patted his hip. "You're turning blue."

They stepped out. Kel was waiting for them. His face was ruddy from the steam tent. He wore a black robe with red braid on the sleeves. His hair hung to his waist.

He handed Elli a towel and a silken yellow robe. "Cal asked me to tell you he took your knives and belts and clothing home."

"K-k-kind of him," Kerris said. Water trickled down his thighs and calves and out the legs of his pants.

Kel draped a towel around his neck. "Take those off," he said, nodding toward Kerris' wet pants.

"Here?"

Elli snorted. She bowed her head to wring out her hair. "There's nothing everyone here hasn't seen already."

Kerris plucked at the drawstring knot. His fingers were chilled. Kel brushed his hand away. "I'll do it." He took his time. His hands were warm. Their touch made Kerris shiver all over again.

The loosened pants slid down Kerris' legs and fell in the mud. He stepped out of them. Elli nudged them with her toe. "Ech. Now one of us will have to wash them. Whose turn is it to do the laundry?" Picking up the wet, soiled cloth, she held it at arm's length.

"Yours, probably," Kel said. "Give them to me, I'll carry them." He took the pants from Elli, and with the other hand settled a robe over Kerris' back. It was velvet, red as blood, with silver fish imprinted on it. Kerris thrust his arm through the sleeve. He held the robe closed. A silver sash trailed through three loops. One end of it was muddy. Elli gathered it up and tied it in a loose knot around his waist.

"Don't we look fine," said Elli. "Like lords of the city." She danced a little in the yellow silk. Kerris thought of Morven, stuck in a castle. He would not want to be Morven. "Where are Jen and Arillard and Ilene?"

"Gone ahead of us," said Kel.

They strolled toward Sefer's cottage. The sun beat on Kerris' back through the slippery velvet. After the ice-cold pool, the heat was delicious. "Why did you stay?" he asked his brother.

Kel stroked his spine. The cloth moved sensuously under his knowledgeable fingers. "It seemed fair," he said. "I threw you in."

When they reached the house, Kerris decided he was ravenous. He could barely wait for the evening meal. Ilene and Calwin shared the cooking chores. Elli coaxed Jensie to the table. She ate a little. Her head sagged; before the others had halfway finished, she had fallen fast asleep.

Kel picked her up and put her on her blanket. "Good," he said. Easing the knife from her hip, he tucked the cloth around her.

Terézia came in. She went upstairs and then came down again. "Don't you want to eat?" Ilene called to her.

Terézia shook her head. "I ate at Cleo's." A musical note trembled in the air, and another, and another. Kerris recognized the vibrant twang of a hand-harp.

"That's lovely," said Elli.

Kerris waited for the small, bitter twinge in his chest, the envy he had always felt for two-handed people who could make music. It did not come.

Terézia sat crosslegged on a cushion. "Tell me what to play," she said.

"Play the Riddle Song," said Calwin.

Terézia played the Riddle Song.

"Play 'I am a stranger,'" said Arillard.

It grew dark. Arillard lit the chobata. He laid one at Terézia's knee. "Beth, my wife, played the hand-harp," he said.

Terézia said, "You told me, last year, when I was just learning it."

"You have a light hand—your touch reminds me of hers."

203

Kel and Elli cleared the table. When there was space on it to do so, Kerris laid out the paper Meritha had given him. He put an oil dish close by, but far enough from the striped pages so that the edges would not curl. He mixed his ink in the dish with the chipped lip.

In the midst of his preparations, Sefer wandered downstairs. He had slept through the meal. His face was puffy with sleep. He went into the kitchen.

Kerris ran the soft, springy hair of the brush over his mouth. The touch was faintly erotic. He started to dip the brush in the ink, and hesitated.

Sefer emerged from the kitchen with a goblet.

"Sefer?"

"What is it?" said the teacher.

"In Tornor's records there always is a line which dates the account—like, *In the twentieth year of the reign of Morven, nineteenth Lord of Tornor*—I don't know what to put."

"Hmm." Sefer rubbed his chin. "Put the Council Year. Say, In the whatever year since the establishment of the Council of Houses in Kendra-on-the-Delta—I don't know what year it is. Arillard?"

Arillard lifted his head.

"What Council Year is this?" Sefer asked.

Arillard looked pensive. "The thirty—thirty-fourth."

"Will that do?"

It sounded good. Kerris dipped the brush in the ink. *This is the record of certain events happening in the town of Elath, in the thirty-fourth year since the establishment of the Council of Houses in Kendra-on-the-Delta, as written by Kerris of Elath*—he hesitated, and then wrote firmly, *scribe*. "What day did the Asech first appear?"

Sefer ran his thumbs across his eyelids. "On the first day of the quarter moon," he said.

In the first month of summer, on the first day of the quarter moon, Kerris wrote, *people from the desert tribes called the Asech attacked the village of Elath*—"Did they come from the south?"

"No," said Sefer. "The first time they came from the north road."

—from the north. They burned the houses of—"Shall I say whose house was burned?"

"I suppose you should." Sefer walked to the table. He stood looking over Kerris' shoulder for a moment, and then sat. "Maybe it's not necessary. Say, three houses. You'd better say that Thiya was killed."

—three families. Thiya was killed. They returned three days later and burned another house, and took captive a visitor to the village, Riniard of the Galbareth, a cheari. Through their speaker, Thera, they threatened to kill the captive unless the witches of Elath taught them witch-gifts. It was known to the people of Elath that these Asech were possessed of some witch-skills. They called themselves Li Omani, The Branded Ones. Their chief appeared to be a man named Barat. The words were coming easily. He stopped to rest his fingers. His hand was tired from the day's training.

"Does my looking over your shoulder disturb you?" Sefer said. The light from the chobata lit the underside of his face, giving his skin a waxy, yellow cast.

"No."

Kel went upstairs. Terézia put away her hand-harp, to murmured thanks. The chearis went to bed. The oil was low in the chobata when Kerris finally finished. He had covered three pages and half of a fourth with writing.

He gave them to Sefer. The inspeaker received them gravely. "Thank you, Kerris."

Kerris shrugged. He was tempted to go back over it and put in the details he'd left out. He thought of what Josen would say if he could see it. *"Inaccurate, sloppy, incomplete..."*

The night was warm. His bladder ached from sitting. He went outside and opened his clothes. He smelled the field-scents: hay, grass, cow dung, dust, horses, and the house scents—in a nearby kitchen someone was baking. The smell reminded him of Tornor's kitchen, and that of Paula. He remembered the letter to

Josen, still unsealed, still beside his blanket. He would try to remember to seal it tomorrow.

A sleepy bird sang a two-note song within the convolutions of the hedge. The urine arched out of him in a fine high stream. He grinned and shook himself, did his clothes back together, and turned to leave.

Sefer was standing at the door. The light from the window shone on his hair, turning it phosphorescent.

He gestured toward the bench. "Sit with me."

Kerris sat on the cold stone.

"How was it at the Yard today?"

The moonglow was beginning to shine over the line of the rim. Kerris watched it deepen. "It went well."

Sefer said, "I was going to apologize to you, Kerris, for what you went through this morning. Had I known it was going to happen, I wouldn't have asked you to come with us."

"I know that," Kerris said. A triangle of light showed over the jagged line of trees.

"But now I think it may have been for the best," Sefer said. He put his hand on Kerris' shoulder, turning him around a little. His face was indistinct; his eyes a shadowed, colorless glitter. "I am going to reach to you," he said. "I want you to stop me."

Kerris had no time to argue. He felt Sefer extend to him, brush the surface of his thought, probe inward—*Damn you,* he thought, *I* can't *keep you out!* He couldn't tell if the glow against his eyes was Sefer's mind or the rising moon. He raised his hand, ready to slam it against the stone bench, to use the only weapon he knew he had: pain. His hand would not respond.

No, said Sefer, *not that way.*

His heart thundered. Suddenly something slipped in his head. It felt like a bolt sliding into a new-cut groove. His hand dropped. He barked his knuckles on the bench. The moonlight blazed in his eyes. There was nothing in his head, except his own thought.

He caught his breath. He knew what he had done without knowing how he'd done it. He was unhurt. He was free. He turned all the way around to Sefer. "What—" The teacher was bending over, holding his head. As Kerris moved he straightened. There were tears on his pale cheeks.

"I—I'm sorry," Kerris said. "I didn't mean to hurt you." His knuckles stung. He put his mouth to the scrapes.

"It will stop," Sefer said evenly. He put his hands down. "I knew it might happen." His lips curved. "You did it."

Kerris closed his eyes. He could sense-see-feel his wall: it was gray stone with flecks of mica in it, like the arch in Tornor's wall, and it shimmered like a reflection in glass. "Why now? Why not before?"

"Because of what happened today," Sefer said. "In that moment of terror in the garden you reexperienced the time when you tried to make a wall and failed."

"Yes," Kerris said. *O my mother* . . .

"But you also understood it, inside—you understood that though the child in you had been hurt, the adult was strong, and would not be. I felt your understanding. You locked it away from your surface mind, but I knew I could reach it if I went deep enough. When I touched it, you responded without thought, by reflex, as a true inspeaker learns to do. You thrust me out and made the wall."

It shimmered behind his eyes, unyielding as northern granite. There was a suggestion of grass at its foot, of sky above and behind it. Kerris wondered if Sefer had taken the image out of his thoughts or given it to him. He thought the first. The steppe had been his refuge, however flawed, for fourteen years. Sefer had never seen it.

It felt natural to him as the blood running in his skin. Already he was beginning to lose the memory of what it had felt like to be without it. "Now what can I do?" he said.

"Anything you like," said Sefer.

"Shall I go to Kendra-on-the-Delta and hire myself out as a truth-finder?" He remembered his own bitter words to Josen. *What great house would want me?*

Sefer said, "You can. You can stay here and act as scribe. Elath will need one someday soon. You can even return to Tornor."

207

Kerris blinked. He hadn't thought—"No." The words came unprompted. "No."

"You know what I would like. I'd like you to stay in Elath, and teach at the school."

"I'm not a teacher."

"You could learn. It's a skill."

The door to the garden opened. Kel leaned out, holding the doorposts with both hands. "What are you doing?" He walked toward them, slipped, and recovered. "You've been out here long enough to piss a river." He put a proprietary hand on Sefer's neck. "Come in, nika."

Sefer said, "We've been talking."

Kel's hair was loose. He shook it back from his face. "Shall I go?"

Sefer raised his eyebrows at Kerris. "Have we done?"

The cold of the bench was making Kerris' knees ache. "I think so."

"Then come inside." Kel pulled Sefer up. He held him a moment and then pushed him gently at the door. "Don't slip," he warned, "there's a mole run." He tapped Kerris' shoulder. "Chelito—"

"Yes?"

The half moon balanced on the rim of the valley, its convex edge just touching the trees. Like a boat on a river it slid up the starry sky. Kel said, "What are you thinking?"

"Why does everybody ask me that?"

"Who else asks you?"

"Elli. And Josen used to."

"Because," Kel said, "your face gets a certain look to it."

"Like what?" Kerris said.

"Like a closed door."

Kerris wasn't sure he liked that. "I was thinking that the sky looks like a river." He tipped his head back to look at the stars. Kel's fingertips caressed his neck.

"It looks more like the ocean to me," said his brother.

"Have you seen the ocean?"

"Certainly," said Kel. He mimed a shiver. "It's getting chilly,

208

chelito. Come in. I'll tell you all about the ocean—tomorrow."
His smile flickered. Bending, he ran both thumbs up the inside
muscles of Kerris' thighs.

Chapter 13

Just before dawn, Kerris had a dream.

He was standing beside a table in a vast, sunlit room. He was weeping, not in fear but in anger. There was something on the table he wanted, but the top was high above his head. He pounded a fist on the table leg. The act cost him his balance. He started to totter; he saw the matted floor rising to meet him. He wailed.

Suddenly he was lifted. A woman's face smiled at him. Her eyes and her hair were brown. She patted his cheeks with something soft. "Open!" she said. He opened his mouth. She popped a bit of honeycomb in it. "Such a greedy one for sweets," she said. *That* was what he had wanted. The sweet taste burst against his tongue. She cradled him, chuckling. "Thou't'll grow so fat that we will stuff thee for dinner, like the goose!"

Her smile was loving. He pressed against her, feeling her heartbeat. Under the emerald silk of her shirt her breasts were soft and full.

Then the room began to darken, and he felt himself

awakening from the dream and from childhood. "Mother!" he called. The word made no sound. She went. He stared at the woolen hanging on Sefer's wall. The tears ran along his nose. He laid his head on his arm.

The sky grew lighter. The others stirred. After a while, when the pain had dulled, he sat up. He brushed his hair from his eyes. The cocks of Elath crowed from their yards, chiding the laggard sun.

He stumbled into the kitchen and scrubbed his face with a soaked cloth until he was sure the tear stains were gone. There were steps overhead and on the stair, and the garden door opened and closed. Arillard came into the little room, tinderbox in hand.

The chearis were in evil moods. Jensie was clumsy, a rare thing in her. She knocked a water goblet off the table. It bounced on the mats and the water spilled into the tough bound straw.

"Hell."

Arillard said, "Better lift that mat."

Jensie grunted. Alli and Cal helped her wrestle the heavy straw pad on its edge. They leaned it against a wall. In the space left by its removal the bare floor was pale and dusty.

Kel came in from the garden. He looked tired and tense. He nodded at them all and went into the kitchen. He came out with a loaf of bread, a knife, and a butter crock. He tore the bread into slices.

"Talkative, aren't we," said Ilene to the room.

Elli reached for the butter knife. Arillard shrugged. Kel sank to his heels beside the bare rectangle of floor.

Ilene put her hands on her hips. "What's the matter with you?" she said to him. "I heard you. You marched around half the night."

He slanted his head to look at her. "Something's wrong," he said.

Jensie stared at him, eyes narrowed.

"A big thing or a small thing?" said Ilene.

"I can't tell," said Kel.

Sefer descended the stairs with Kerris' scrolls under his arm.

"Good morning," he said. He lifted his eyebrows at the upended mat but made no comment.

"Sef, what's going to happen today?" said Arillard.

"I can't be sure," Sefer said. "But we should receive a small delegation of the riders, to tell us they are leaving, and to make arrangements for Riniard's release."

Ilene said, "Kel's having premonitions."

Jensie's face had whitened. Suddenly kneeling, she grabbed Kel's wrists, knocking the bread from his hand. Two red spots on her cheekbones burned like coal. "It isn't Riniard," she said. "Say it isn't Riniard!"

With a powerful swift motion Kel flipped his wrists through the junctions of her thumb and forefinger, and pinioned her in turn. "Don't, Jen," he said. "Don't come apart. We need your strength."

She bowed her head. Ilene crouched beside her. She ran her hand up the girl's back. "Come with me to Kitha's. You can help me run after Borti. He's so active I wish I were twins."

"All right," Jensie said. Kel let her go. Elli handed him the bread slice.

Kerris tugged his shirt on. He went to sit beside his brother.

"I had a dream this morning," he said. "I dreamed I was a child. I was trying to get something, some food, from a table. A woman picked me up—" he hesitated. "I think it was Mother." The word felt strange in his mouth. "She had brown hair, brown eyes . . . She wore a green shirt."

"She had one," said Kel. "With lace." He drew a circle in the dust and rubbed it out. "Maybe you're getting your memories back, chelito."

Ware—Ware—Ware—by now the rhythm and feel of the alarum were familiar. Kerris stood. Kel rose more slowly. Arillard said, "Is it—?"

"Yes."

"Shall we come with you?" said Ilene.

Kel glanced at Sefer. "No need," said the inspeaker.

Elli said, "I want to hear the arrangements for getting Riniard back."

"You'll hear them later," said Kel. He dusted his palms together. The bite of temper in his voice made Kerris start.

It was a blue, hot day. A scattering of clouds obscured the northern rim of the sky. The street was quiet, very different from the way it had been the day before. Tamaris, Dorin, and Lara stood in the square.

Two riders came under the rim of the bowl. Tek, a bulky shadow, leaned in the doorway of the butcher shop. Lepin, the smith, and Emeth the Yardmaster stood nearby. In the arch of Moro's doorway rested a tall man with a bow.

"Who's that?" Kerris asked Kel.

"That's Erith, the troop leader."

Kerris watched his brother. Kel seemed calmer now that he was out under the sky. He was wearing the shirt with the dancing figures. He walked with both hands stuffed into his breeches' pockets. Sefer walked on his right.

The riders were Nerim and Jacob. They came slowly into the deserted square. Kerris could not help admiring the way they sat their horses. They rode the way Kel walked. Nerim was wearing his long cloak, and Kerris wondered why the riders wore cloaks in the day, when it was so warm. Jacob had taken his off; it lay across his horse's neck. The beadwork on his tunic showed plainly: it was in the shape of flowers. His hair was long and shining. Kerris thought maybe it was greased. It fell down his back in a kind of club.

Nerim was holding a green square of material on a stick. It was meant to be a courier's flag. When he reached where the teachers were waiting, he dismounted. He wet his lips nervously. Carefully he said, "I bring message from my people to witches."

Lara said, "The people of Elath hear you."

"Thera tell me. I am to say, they learn. We—" he tapped his own chest, waved at Jacob—"and others, we teach to make wall down. Is slow. They much afraid. Some very learn quickly."

Lara said, "I understand. You are teaching your own people to lower their walls so that they may use their gifts. That is good."

"Thera says, if all teach, we give back—" he hesitated,

frowning, and then put his wrists together as if they were tied. "I forget word."

"Captive," said Kel. "Hostage."

"Hostage. Yes. We give back tonight, at sun end. I have message from hos-hostage. To Kel?" He bit his lip. Kel lifted a hand to indicate himself. Kerris glanced at Jacob. The young desert rider was leaning forward, eyes on the cheari. "He say, Sorry. Very sorry."

"So he will be," said Kel, "when I get my hands on him."

"He say—" Nerim's broad face twisted as he tried to remember the words—"*Elli was right. I have brains of cricket.*"

Kel's face softened. He took his hands from his pockets. "Is he well? Not hurt?"

"Well, yes. We feed, he walk—" Nerim again mimed roped wrists.

"How will you give him back to us?" said Sefer.

"We go. He stay. We tie, not hard, he can break." Nerim mimed ropes breaking apart. "He not far."

"You will leave him loosely tied so that once you have left he can break free and walk back to us."

"Yes."

Sefer's voice sounded softly in Kerris' head. *Does that seem good to you all?*

Yes, Kerris answered. Tamaris nodded. Sefer nodded to Lara.

"We accept that," Lara said.

Nerim turned to Jacob and spoke a string of words. The youthful desert rider swung from his horse. Kerris smelled the Asech body odor. Jacob's hands flexed once. His nails were pink against his brown skin. His hands were shapely and very long.

Nerim said, "This Jacob. You know. He ask, please, talk to one who fight. Kel?"

The Elath teachers all looked at Kel. He shrugged, turning both palms up.

Jacob spoke to Nerim. Nerim said, "He say, No fight. He speak peace."

Lara said, "This sounds like it is meant to be a private conversation."

On impulse, Kerris reached toward the silent desert rider. He sensed a jumble of thought, all unintelligible, mixed with a deep yearning.

Sefer said, "Nika, do you want to talk to him? He looks serious about something."

Jacob spoke again to Nerim. The older man stepped back to talk to him. He put his arm through Jacob's, an intimate gesture. Jacob bit his lip. Nerim looked unhappy. Jacob shrugged free of him, not petulantly, but sadly. He took a step toward Kel. He held both hands out, palms up. Then, very slowly, he drew his short sword and dagger. The blades gleamed in the sunlight. From the butcher's doorway, Tek grunted and came upright, hand poised on his own knife. Jacob bent and laid both blades in the dust.

Sefer said, "I think that is meant to impress you with his peaceful intentions, nika."

Kel said, "I'll talk to him." He looked at Jacob. "Tell him to pick up his weapons."

Nerim spoke. A look of pure relief crossed Jacob's face. He wiped the blades meticulously on his cloak and returned them to their scabbards.

Kel said, "We can't talk in the street."

Tamaris said, "Why not go to the Tanjo?"

Kel considered. "I can't see why not. Sef—?" he glanced at his lover. "Will you come?"

Sefer looked grave. "I shouldn't, nika. I have half a town to talk to. People must be told what's happening, they'll have questions.... Take Kerris, if you think you'll need an in-speaker."

Kel touched Kerris' shoulder. "Will you help, chelito?"

Kerris hadn't expected to be asked. "If you want me to."

Kel faced the two Asech. "We'll go to the school, where we were yesterday." He beckoned to Tek. "Tek, can you see to the horses for a while?"

The burly stablemaster gestured assent. "Lalli, Sosha!" he yelled.

The two children popped around the corner of the butcher's as if they were on strings. Lalli ran to Jacob's horse's head. It was

216

a spirited black horse with a white left forefoot; it reminded Kerris of Magrita. Nerim's horse was a roan. Sosha wound the reins around his hand. The roan swiped at him with a monster tongue.

They sat in the grass by the statue of the Guardian. Jacob's thin face was tense. The bead flowers climbed around his chest and up his sleeves. Nerim said something to him in a reassuring tone. He did not look reassured.

Kerris wondered if the two men were lovers or only friends. He crossed his legs and sat. He felt awkward. He didn't know what Kel wanted him to do. Perhaps he was just there to be a second body, a number.

He looked around the brilliant garden. A shadow in the doorway of the big carved door caught his attention. He stared at it. It was falling the wrong way from the angle of the sun. He extended his mind.... He felt curiosity, excitement, a spurt of fear. *Wait'll I tell Tazia!* ...

He grinned, and jogged Kel's elbow. "Kel. Look at the big door."

Kel squinted across the garden. The Asech turned. Kel lifted his voice. "Come out, you in hiding!"

Feet dragging, Korith came slowly across the grass. He made a wide circle around the riders. His eyes were big. He made a jerky bow to Kel. "Skayin. I was just—"

"Spying," Kel finished. He frowned at the boy. Kerris made his own face stern. "You're Korith. Sefer's nephew." Korith nodded. He was wearing brown. He looked more than ever like an otter. "Is that what you're supposed to be doing?" Korith shook his head. "Speak."

"No, skayin."

Kel's mouth twitched. "Well. Since you're here—" he gestured toward the desert riders. "This is Nerim. This is Jacob. Korith."

Nerim murmured something to Jacob. Both men smiled. They looked at the boy with friendly eyes.

"Now you've met two Asech raiders and can go to whatever you're supposed to be doing." Red-cheeked, Korith turned to leave. "Wait." The boy spun around. "You're a lifter, aren't you?"

"Yes, skayin."

"Can you lift a wine pitcher and four glasses from the pantry in the Tanjo?"

Korith gave a little hop. "I can. At least—" he looked toward the silver building, measuring it. "I think I can." He scratched his knee. "But I might spill the wine."

Kel smiled at him. "Go and get it yourself. Bring it here. Make two trips if you have to."

Korith raced for the Tanjo.

Within a short time, he was back, carrying a pitcher of wine in both hands. Four yellow glass cups trailed in the air behind him. He lowered the pitcher to the ground in front of Kel. The cheari put out an arm. The cups jiggled in the air. Korith's thin face curled with effort. He lowered the glasses to the grass without a bump.

"Thank you," Kel said. "That was very smooth." He handed the cups around and poured a measure of the amber liquid into each cup. "Now, youngling, vanish."

Korith walked off obediently. As he reached the door he leaped into the air. Kerris heard him whoop.

The Asech laughed. Kel sipped his wine. "You can drink it," he said to Nerim. "It's not poisoned." Korith's appearance seemed to have restored his good humor. "Now, what have you to say to me?"

Nerim looked at Jacob. Jacob nodded forcefully. His bound hair danced a little on his back. Nerim said, "Jacob say, I fight. I ride. I have power, *harai*, power, like you. Your power—" he made a circle in the air with his arms—"great. My power small." He made a circle with thumb and forefinger.

Kel interrupted him. "Say 'gift,' not 'power.'"

"Gift," repeated Nerim. He patted Jacob's knee. "He say, I want to learn. I want learn all, fight, ride, all. I want follow you." He clasped his hands.

Kel put the cup he was holding down hard on the grass. "Say that last part again," he invited.

"I want follow you." Nerim's voice sounded hollow. Jacob

watched Kel. Hope blazed on his thin strange face.

Kel said, "I'm honored. But I'm not a teacher. I'm a cheari. I travel, I dance. I teach only in the Yard."

Nerim repeated this to Jacob. Jacob whispered. He had not yet tasted the wine. Kerris wondered what Barat and the other riders thought of this desire. Maybe they didn't know of it.

He understood it. He tipped the glass a little and let the wine wet his lips. He pitied Jacob, and Nerim who clearly thought his friend was mad.

Nerim said, "Jacob say again, Please. He want follow to learn. He no trouble. He sleep with horse. He do anything, cook, make fire, wash."

Kerris said, "He wants to be your apprentice."

Kel frowned. "Chearis don't have apprentices! Besides, he can't be part of the chearas. No," he said to Jacob. He shook his head. His hair swung like a curtain. "No."

Jacob's lips tightened. He spoke to Nerim. Nerim took a deep breath. "He say, He follow. No matter you say no. He go. You ride, you look back—" he waved his hand—"he always there. One day you say yes."

Kel stared levelly at the slender rider. Jacob did not flinch. "An Asech alone in Arun? Not able to speak our language? He'll get killed."

Nerim translated this. Jacob shook his head. His face was intransigent. "He say, No. If try kill, he fight."

Kel's shoulders jerked. "I don't want that responsibility!" he said.

Both men looked at him silently.

Kerris said, "I think you have it."

Kel stood in such haste that the glass fell. Wine ran out into the grass. He put his hands on his hips. "Tell your friend he's a fool," he said. He closed a hand around Kerris' wrist. "Come, chelito. This conversation's over."

He went through the grove and into the street at a near trot. In the sunlight he slowed. His eyes were angry. He worked his shoulders. "Now I'm hot," he said.

Kerris said, "We could go to the baths."

"And cool down." Kel scratched his chin. "No." He tipped his head back, looking up the slope. "Are you busy, chelito?"

"Not if you want me."

Kel smiled. He slid his hand up inside the back of Kerris' shirt. "I want you. Come with me." He stroked Kerris' shoulderblades. "There's a place I want to show you."

They went up the eastern slope of the bowl. They passed houses, barns, sheds. They passed a pool with red fish swimming in the water. A horse's whinny cut the air. At the end of a pasture a prick-eared mare called to her white-coated foal. Birds exploded out of a wheatfield, chased by a running dog. The air was soft and humid.

They made a detour around nine white humps. "Hives," said Kel.

"Who tends them?" Kerris asked. He jumped back as a bee flew by, almost brushing his nose.

"Cleo's the beekeeper." Kel grinned. "Once when I was young and stupid I tried to raid a hive. I thought the bees would sting me to death. I saved myself by jumping in the pond. I almost drowned, I had to stay there so long. They stung my hands, my face, my eyes...."

A thorn hedge loomed in front of them, its branches thick with red berries. Kel reached among the thorns and picked a few. He gave them to Kerris. They were knobby, and sweet as new cream. Kel smiled at his face. "Good, aren't they. The birds get most of them."

They went into the forest. Tall cypress trees mingled with oak, birch, pine, hickory. Squirrels gibbered at the invasion. Kerris saw a red deer browsing in an alder thicket. "Where are we going?"

"Wait," said Kel. "You'll see."

The trees thinned. The grass grew dark and coarse along the narrow path. "Here," Kel said. He led the way into a round clearing. There was a circle of dark grass, and a pool. Stones ringed the water. They looked as if they had been put there, but grass grew up between in a way that showed they had been there a long time. Kerris walked around the pool. It was clear to the bottom. He could see the bare gold sand. He cupped up a sip of water. It was pure.

"What keeps the water fresh?" he said.

"Sef says there's a river that we can't see running on the bottom."

Kerris stared into the water. The golden sands did not seem to move.

The grass was checkered light and dark. A fallen log lay by the water, one end touching the ring of stones. It, too, had been there awhile; it was furry with moss. Kel sank into a patch of sunlit grass, long legs outstretched. He watched Kerris through half-closed eyelids. Kerris sat down beside him. The sun turned Kel's hair tawny. He looked like a sleeping mountain lion.

"This was our special place when we were young. Sef and I. We sat there the day I told him I had to be a cheari, the day he decided to make the school...."

"When did you know you were going to be a cheari?"

"Emeth told me. But I dithered. I loved Sefer, I wanted to stay with him always—I thought and said. I know better now. I love to travel, I get easily restless, and Sef's a stay-at-home."

"Did you see him when you stayed with Zayin?"

Kel half-smiled. He propped his head on his hand. "Once. I ran away the first year and came home. Ran all the way across Arun. When I went back Zayin beat me till I was raw. He was old, then, but he still had strength in his arm. I didn't care about the beating, so much, but he told me if I left again he would not let me back. I didn't leave again. I'd have cut my throat to stay with Zayin."

Kerris thought, That's how Jacob feels. But he didn't say it. He said, "You were going to tell me about the ocean."

Kel rolled on his back. "The ocean. Well, it looks like Lake Aruna, except it's always moving, up and back, taking the earth away with it. And there's no way to see to the other side."

"Can boats ride it?"

"A little ways. It's very strong. In the sailors' bars in Kendra-on-the-Delta they sing songs about it, how terrible it is, how deadly. Ilene knows some of them. Sometimes a storm gathers over it and you'd think the world was about to shake apart with noise and rain and lightning."

"That's a hurricane."

"Right." He moved his hand up and down Kerris' back. "Kerris."

"Yes."

"What are you going to do?"

"What—"

"Are you going to stay here and teach in the school?" His hand moved in slow patterns.

"I don't know," Kerris said.

"You can be scribe," said Kel. "You can live with Lea and Ardith. They want you."

"Yes."

"Or—" Kel paused. "You can come with us. You can travel with the chearas." He sat up and put his arm over Kerris' shoulders. "We would like to have you, chelito. The pattern feels right when you're there."

"I'm not a cheari."

"No. But it wouldn't matter."

Kerris plucked a grass stem. It lay on his palm. He could barely feel its weight. He blew it away. *I like you*, said Elli in his memory. *The pattern feels right when you're there*, Kel had said. What would I do? he thought. What use would I be? None, said his inner voice bleakly. You would be a pet. You could write Kel's letters to Sefer, and share his bed, once in a while.

He bowed his head. "I don't think—no."

Kel said, "I didn't think you would."

"You didn't?" Kerris stared at him.

"No. Why should you? But I hoped you might. We'll miss you when we go."

"When will you go?"

Kel laughed. His arm tightened. "Not till harvest, when we'll have to go back to Galbareth and pay Riniard's debt for him. Not for a while."

"Why did Riniard do that?"

"Fight?"

"All of it."

222

Kel began to work his boots off. "He had a hard time of it when he was young. The folk of his village wanted him to settle down. He couldn't. He had to fight them to let him learn to dance, to leave the village, to go Shanan.... It made him wild. It's difficult for him to do what other people want of him, even when he wants it too. He'll learn."

A bird called from the trees on a rising note.

"Tell me—" Kerris said.

"Yes?"

"Tell me about Mother."

Kel crossed his legs. "She was a small brown woman. I remember the year—I must have been around eleven—when I realized that I was tall as she was. She had gentle hands. She loved bright colors, reds, orange. She loved to see Father dressed in them, silk and velvet.... She used to come home tired all the time. I never understood why visiting other people made her tired, until I realized she was using her gift, mediating, mending quarrels. I remember when you were born." He grinned. "I was ten. I wanted to know why you were so red and fat, and was so angry when they told me *I* had been redder and fatter!"

"Father—?"

"Father was tall and blond. They say I look like him. He loved to ride; he looked like an Asech on horseback. He used to make us things out of wood, toys and such. I remember he made us stick-puppets." He waved an imaginary puppet in the air. "Mine was bald, and I liked it, but you cried when you saw yours, until Mother glued some yellow wool on it for hair. Do you remember?"

"No."

He wanted to remember. But common sense told him he could not force memory; it would come, probably when he least expected it. He closed his eyes, recalling the faint dream-taste of honey on his tongue.

Sefer might know how to wake memories, he thought.

Kel's fingers moved persuasively. "Chelito?"

"Yes...."

Kel took the red scarf from his hair, and shook his head. His hair uncoiled to his shoulders. He took off his shirt. Kerris watched him. This close, in the bright light of day, he could see scars, weals and scratches and nicks long-healed, along Kel's chest and ribs. He touched one with his thumb.

Kel felt for the buckle of Kerris' belt. "Hold still," he said. He undid Kerris' clothes, and then his own. "Turn around."

They made love. The sunlight made Kerris shy, and Kel laughed at him. This time Kerris would not lie still, and when he had his breath back he teased his brother into lying down and letting himself be handled. Kel had to tell him what to do, a little, but he persisted, finding pleasure in giving pleasure, and had the satisfaction of feeling Kel tense and tremble with sensation. His hands flexed in Kerris' hair; his hips lifted. He gasped, shook, and cried out.

They cleaned up with wisps of grass. When Kerris sat up to get his shirt, Kel held him. "No, wait. Let me look at you." He sat back on his heels. After a moment, he put his fingers on the end of Kerris' stump.

"Does that hurt?" he said.

"No. I don't feel it." Kerris swallowed. "I wish you wouldn't."

"Why not?" said Kel. "It's a scar of war, chelito. I've seen worse." He rubbed his thumb into the tissue. Kerris felt a tingle. "It doesn't disgust me, or make me not want to touch you." He kept his hand there a little longer, and then took it away. He touched the spot on Kerris' ribs where the niji had marked him. "How is that?"

"I forgot it."

Hand in hand, they went back down the slope to the village.

Except for Calwin, the chearis were all in Sefer's house. "Where's Cal?" asked Kel.

"Can't you guess?" said Ilene. "He's dicing with Tek. Last time I looked he was winning."

Elli said, "I hope so." She grinned from her bedroll. "I'm not going to ask what you've been doing."

"Very wise," Kel said. He had tied his hair back with his scarf again. Jensie sat on a mat, shirtless, holding the shirt on her lap. She was sewing a rip, with scarlet thread and an iron needle. She had a horn thimble on the middle finger of her right hand. She looked good; better than she had since the night Riniard was taken captive.

Kel went into the kitchen, and came out chewing a piece of fetuch. "Where's Sef?"

"That woman, Thera, came and got him," said Arillard.

"What?"

Arillard made a damping motion with his hands. "He said he's be back before sunset, and that you were not to worry."

"Was she alone?"

"I didn't see anyone with her."

Jensie said, "There are two other Asech in the village." She bit off the end of her thread and held the mended shirt up, head tilted. "One of them's in the stable, playing toss-up with Cal and the stablemaster. They use straws for lots. I've seen it played in Shanan with stones." Kerris wondered which of the desert riders that was. He decided it had to be Nerim.

"Where's the other one?" said Kel.

Ilene said, "He was hanging around the door a little while ago. I spoke to him—asked his name—but he just smiled."

Kel scowled. "His name is Jacob and he doesn't speak our tongue." He sat down on a mat and reached for a cushion. "Why did Sef go with Thera?"

Ilene said, "I don't know, Kel, he didn't say. It had something to do with teaching. He said what Arillard told you."

"I don't like it."

"He must have had a good reason," said Elli.

"I'm sure he had a reason he thought was good," said Kel.

Ilene said, "Even if it was a bad reason, *we* couldn't have stopped him going."

Kel's shoulders hunched. But a smile twisted the corner of his mouth. "Neither could I. Sef does what he wants. He always has."

Arillard said, "What does the Asech want?"

"Which Asech?"

"Jacob."

"He wants to be my apprentice."

There was the sound of running feet in the street. Kel lifted his head. Ilene snorted. "That's silly."

Kerris found himself wanting to defend Jacob. "Not entirely," he said. "He's a patterner—"

The door burst open.

A tattered figure stumbled in. He lifted his head. It was Riniard. Jensie shrieked. She dropped the shirt and sprang to him. He was breathing hard. He was bootless. A frayed rope trailed on the mat, and Kerris saw that his wrists were tied. "Barat!" he said. "Took Sefer. Hit him. Tied him..."

Ilene cried out. Kel went white.

He flung himself through the doorway. Riniard and Jensie got out of his way just in time. Blindly Kerris followed. Elli was on his heels. The dust was hot. He ran. Kel had turned down the street to the stable. They pounded past the Yard. People stared at them. Some shouted. Elli had gone ahead of him. His chest burned. The stable doors were wide. As he reached them he heard the sound of hooves and froze. Callito thundered past him, saddleless and bridleless. Kel leaned low over the big red horse's neck, urging him faster. Kerris went into the stable. He found Magrita in her stall and scrambled to her back. He wrapped his fingers in her mane and kicked his heels into her smooth sides.

She shot from the stable. Elli on Tula was half a length ahead of him, riding back toward the cottage. Kerris got to the house in time to see Kel erupt from it, with Riniard. Jacob was holding Callito. Kel swerved. Jacob cried shrilly and crumpled. Kel leaped onto Callito and drew Riniard behind him.

They rode up the slope to the rim. Kerris wondered why Riniard had not gone for the guard. The path was steep. Riniard gasped something. They were over the rim. Kerris heard a challenge, and Ilene's shouted response, "Stay back! Let us through!" Sun gleamed on spears and swords, but no one stopped them. They were into the forest. Suddenly Kel stopped. Callito whinnied protest as his head was dragged back. He kicked. Riniard grabbed at Kel's belt. Kel whirled the horse's head around.

Callito's mouth was foam-flecked. Kel grabbed Kerris. His lips were pulled back from his teeth. He said, "Find him. Kerris, find him." His grip sent knots of pain up to Kerris' shoulder.

"I can't if you hurt me," Kerris said. Kel let go. Kerris was afraid to shut his eyes. If he did that he would fall. He tried to blank away Kel's face, the sweating, plunging steeds, his own fear....

He extended his thought, seeking Sefer.

He felt-saw-sensed the chearis, the horses, the bright ferocity of predators in the forest—he went farther. Things grew shadowy. Sefer's mind would blaze in the shadow like a torch. He could not feel it. He felt rage—a beast—no. It was human. He felt it swooping at them through the boulders and the towering pines. "I think I've found Barat," he said.

"Can you guide us to him?" said Ilene.

"I'll try." Kel backed Callito to let him go ahead. Kerris followed the pulsing beacon of emotion.... It was slow work. He could not hurry. The branches obscured his vision. He moved off the trail into the thick trees. They had to leave the horses. Kel was swearing in a soft, terrible voice.

The trees cleared. There was a three-sided tent, made of curved branches and a beaded skin, it looked like deerskin. The sun, a red ball, shone through the trees. Kerris had no memory of its descending. Smoke defaced the air. There was a scent of burning.

They ringed the tent. Twigs cracked under their feet. Suddenly, among the trees, a woman shouted. "Barat!" A shape dodged through the pines. *"Kash'ai! Uchearis lek e'ka!"* Kel cursed. The chearis turned to see her. Kerris glimpsed high cheekbones, smooth, unscarred, and knew it had to be Thera.

She vanished in the trees. A noise from the lean-to swiveled them around. Barat was standing in front of the tent. His knife was in his hand. Its edge was bloody. He stepped forward, and crouched, eyes flicking from one side to the other.

Kel gestured. The chearis went wide. Barat had to turn his head to see them. He snarled. His lean face was ugly with rage and hopelessness. Slowly Kel advanced on him. Their shadows streamed away from the setting sun, grotesque, hugely deformed.

Something rustled in the trees. Barat turned to face it. His

227

Elizabeth A. Lynn

hand moved in a blur. The knife left his hand, glittering and turning in mid-air, just as Kel flung himself across the clearing like a stone.

There was no fight. Barat fell. Ilene walked into the trees. Kerris heard her voice and moved toward it. She was kneeling cradling Thera in her arms. The horsehead hilt grew, like an obscene flower, from Thera's abdomen.

"Is he dead?" she whispered. Her voice was very weak. "I helped him, I am sorry. He wanted—so much—is he dead?" Kerris glanced at Barat's body. Kel had left it. His head lay at an impossible angle on his neck.

Thera said, "I see it in your thought. Mind to mind cannot lie—" She choked. Her eyes grew enormous. Blood stained her tunic over the wound, bright, fresh blood. She sighed, and went flaccid. Ilene laid her down, and pressed her eyelids closed over her sightless eyes.

Kerris ran to the tent.

Sefer lay inside it. He was face down in the dirt. His hands and feet were tied. Near him was a pile of coals, still hot. There was a thin metal bar beside him. His bared back was covered with burn marks, some of them so deep the flesh was charred. His face was peaceful, almost smiling. He looked as if he were asleep, except for the great gash across his throat. Blood crusted the ground. There was no sound in the clearing but the wind, and the plangent ticking of cooling iron.

Kel touched the fair hair with a shaking hand. "Sef?" The hair stirred under his fingertips. "Nika?"

He waited for the dead man to answer, and his fingers moved over the still face as if he were blind.

He took a wavering step back. His eyes looked like marble in the dimness. He made a sound in his throat like the whimper of an animal. Then he ran, graceless, stumbling, to where Callito waited. Kerris heard the big horse whinny, and the rapid receding scrape of hooves on stone.

People came.

They broke apart the lean-to, and stamped the fire into ash, and kicked dirt over the blood. They took the bodies away. It grew dark, and cold. Kerris sat, arm around his knees. They leaned into one another, shivering. Ilene was weeping. So was

228

Riniard. Arillard said, "We must go back." Hands urged them up. Slowly they helped each other down the darkened path.

They rode into the village. Lara met them. They went to her house. Moonlight shone through the windows. The room got very cold. Arillard paced. Ilene sat right beside the door, huddled under a blanket like an old woman. Her head lifted at every sound. Kerris sat by the southern window. It looked to the rim. Once he saw a white-haired figure, and drew back, thinking it was Sefer's ghost, but it was only a man, a stranger, with the moonlight touching his hair. Once he saw a horseman silhouetted against the trees, tiny as an ant, but when he looked again the figure was gone.

Elli said, "Riniard, why did you come for us? Why didn't you go for the guard?"

Riniard roused himself. "I didn't think to," he whispered.

Ilene said, "It would have made no difference. Barat would have killed him no matter who had come."

Kerris returned to his vigil. A line in the east delineated day.

Ilene rose from her place. She fisted her hand in Kerris' shirt. "Come with me," she said. Her breath was sour. "Come outside."

He went with her to the street. A dark plume of smoke simmered on the eastern horizon.

Arillard followed them.

"It's too long." Ilene said. She looked at Arillard. "He's never been gone this long before."

"It's understandable," said Arillard. The age lines showed clearly on his face for the first time. His eyes were reddened. "He's grieving."

"It's wrong," Ilene said. "He's not whole without us. We're not whole without him. We're a chearas."

"He doesn't want us now," Arillard said.

"He has to want us," Ilene cried. "What if he doesn't come back?" She swept a hand at the circle of the rim. "He *can't* have gone far. He can't. Kerris. Kerris, you're his brother. Bring him back to us. Feel him. *Find* him."

Chapter 14

He walked up the eastern slope of farmlands to the forest. The grass was wet and glittering. Within the trees the wind blew coldly at him. It smelled of pine. Needles sagged beneath his feet. Nesting birds peered from the cypress branches. He saw the lift of a barred tail as a raccoon scuttled through the grass ahead of him. Once he thought he saw red through the fencelike trees, and moved to intercept it, but stopped himself. He'd been seeing ghosts all night. He would not be drawn after shadows.

The circle looked the same as it had the day before. It was wet, cold, and quiet. Kerris stepped to the pool. It gleamed like the iris of an eye. The water was a jet mirror: Kerris saw himself, the trees, the round hole of the sky. He picked up a pebble and tossed it into the mirror. The reflection cracked; the pool rippled symmetrically. The ripples shimmered. He took a step. A twig snapped under his foot.

Hands brushed his shoulders. A strand of blond hair fell against his cheek. He turned. His brother stood there.

Kel looked close to collapse. Night, or grief, had drained him of strength. He was white. His eyes were gray smudges. He stared through Kerris, as though he had been blinded. Kerris put a hand on his chest. His heartbeat was rapid. He was shaking with fatigue.

Kerris drew him to the water. Gently he pressed his brother down on the fallen log. He worked his own shirt over his head and soaked it in the pool, and wrung it to dampness using hand and knees. The water ran down his legs. He pressed the shirt to Kel's forehead. Kel took it from him in both hands. He buried his face in the wet cloth. Water dripped behind his collar, under his shirt.

He shivered. He lifted his head. His eyes had focused. "It's day," he said.

His voice was hoarse, as if he had forgotten how to speak. He gripped Kerris' hand. "Yes," Kerris said. "It is day."

Kel's mouth worked.

"Where were you?" Kerris said.

"I was with the Asech." His clasp was numbing. "They wouldn't look at me. I watched beside Thera's body. They walked around me. I wondered—I thought I had turned into a ghost." His voice cracked.

"You're not," Kerris said. He tried fruitlessly to free his hand. After a moment, Kel opened his fingers. They had left white lines in Kerris' skin.

"I'm not," said Kel.

"No." Kerris held the wrist up. "Ghosts can't do that."

"They can to other ghosts—"

"I'm not a ghost," Kerris said. "I ought to know." He stroked Kel's face. His brother's cheeks were cold as marble. Kel reached to him and touched him, as if making sure he was flesh. "We waited for you."

Kel shuddered. Sweat broke out on his forehead. "I rode around and around," he whispered. His hands flexed.

"I saw you one time on the rim."

Kel's face was gray with agony. "Kerris!" He crumpled, folding like a child. Kerris braced himself to hold his brother's weight. Kel was trembling as though he would come apart.

"I'm here." He stroked Kel's back. "I'm here."

"Don't go."

"I won't. Go on, weep."

He did, small in his chest, and then great sobs that fought their way through his tall frame as if they would break him apart. Kerris held him. He cried as if he had not wept all night. Sitting at Thera's bier, perhaps he had not. The dew dripped from the lowest branches of the trees. Birds came out to forage, pecking for worms in the grass. The sun rose. Kerris welcomed the heat, meager as it was, on his bare shoulders. Kel stopped weeping. He sat on the ground, curled like a baby, his head on Kerris' knees. Kerris brushed his unbound hair. "Kel," he said. "We have to go back."

Kel lifted his head. "Back," he echoed.

"To the village."

A squirrel ran around the edge of the pool. Kel stared at it, as if he had never seen such a beast before. His face was red and swollen with tears. Kerris said, "Ilene will be frantic."

Kel's head swung to look at him. A smile—barely a smile—curved his lips. "She will," he said. He leaned to the water and cupped up a handful, and sipped from his palm. "My throat hurts." Slowly he stood. Kerris' damp shirt slipped to the grass. Kel picked it up. Pursing his lips, he whistled, a two-note call. Callito's red head nosed through the trees.

Kel went to him and petted him. "He was very patient with me all night," he said, over his shoulder. "He must have thought I was mad. I was, a little mad."

They walked down the slope. Callito plodded behind them. A shifting breeze fluttered the ribbons on their poles. Smoke drifted from the farmhouse chimneys. There was no one in the fields. Brown rabbits hopped unhindered through the snareless brush.

Kel gazed at the smoke. "The Asech burn their dead," he said. His voice was charged with pain.

At the foot of the slope a group of people waited for them. It was the chearas. They gathered round Kel. Elli took Kerris' shirt from his hand. Ilene put her arm around Kel's back.

He resisted the touch for a moment, and then relaxed into her embrace. He kept one hand round Kerris' arm. "Where's Red?" he whispered.

Jensie said, "Sleeping. He's worn out."

Elli moved to Kerris' right side. She touched his ribs. He jumped. Her eyes were big with fatigue. "Thank you," she said.

Gently Kel freed himself from Ilene's arms. "Where are—where have they put us?"

Ilene said, "In Lara's house." Kel nodded. He let his fingers slide from Kerris' elbow. Quietly he hugged each of the chearis in turn. Kerris leaned wearily against Callito's flank. The big horse whickered. His coat was rough and warm.

The windows of the houses were shuttered. Shops sat silent and untended. They went to Lara's house. They halted at the stable. Calwin took Callito inside. As the big doors opened Kerris heard the sound of weeping. He glanced at Kel. Kel's face did not change, except that something moved behind his eyes. He touched Ilene. "Jacob?" he said.

"You broke his arm."

Lara's house was dark; the curtains were still drawn across the windows. The downstairs room was empty. Kel gazed around. Finally he turned to Jensie. "Riniard?" he said.

She spread her hands. "I don't know. He was here."

Ilene said, "He doesn't want to face you."

Kel licked his lips. "I'm thirsty."

Arillard went behind the screen and returned with a blue glass goblet. Kel took it in both hands. He tipped it almost to the dregs, and then checked, and handed it to Kerris. "You drink." Kerris sipped the last few swallows up. Fatigue was stealing through his veins like a poison. He remembered that he hadn't slept.

Kel walked to the stair. He stood there, frozen, swaying lightly. Kerris handed the goblet to Arillard and went to see what he was looking at. It was the image of the Guardian. "Kel?"

Kel's face was fixed, and his eyes were dangerously blank.

"Kel." Kerris got between his brother and the niche. "Come away." He pushed Kel backward. For a moment he was afraid the cheari would fight him. Arillard crossed the floor to help him. Together they edged Kel away from the statue and down to the mats.

They slept. The room grew hot and close. Kerris woke sweating. He did not know what had wakened him. He turned over. The mat scratched his bare spine. Lara was standing over them. In the hot dark room her eyes were luminous. Her gown was white with a brown pattern. Kel lifted on an elbow. Sun seeped through the edges of the windows, where the leather curtains did not quite cover them. Light like strings of yellow lace curved over the mats.

"Come," she said.

They rose. Elli took her yellow shirt from her pack and handed it to Kerris. He put it on. It smelled of her. Ilene and Arillard were standing next to Kel. Calwin opened the front door. The sunlight was blinding. Kerris shut his eyes against the dazzle.

The street was black with people. Lara went out. The chearis followed her. A woman wailed from the throng. Kerris saw his brother tremble with the sound. Ilene went to take his arm but he shook her off. Slowly they paced down the street to Sefer's cottage. The front door was open. The inside of the house gaped, ominous as a cave. Kerris twisted to look behind. The people of Elath stood like an army, waiting.

Lara spoke. "People of Elath, brothers and sisters, friends. We are here to say farewell to Sefer. We had him with us for thirty-one years; now the earth will take him back. Who will carry him to rest?"

The people shifted. A man with salt-and-pepper hair pushed to the front of the procession. He wore green and gray. His face was red. Kerris didn't know him. He looked like a farmer. "I will. I was his teacher, though he soon surpassed me. I will carry him."

"That is one," said Lara.

Terézia's came forward. Her back was stiff. She had her spear in her hand. "I will." Her voice shook. She steadied it. "I was his friend. I will carry him."

"That is two," Lara said.

"I will." It was Kel. "I loved him. I will carry him."

"That is three," Lara said.

A crow cawed from the cottage rooftop. A murmur rose from massed mourners. A voice shouted angrily. The crowd swayed and parted to reveal Nerim, dressed in his dun cloak. "Barbarian!" called someone. "Murderer!" Terézia's knuckles whitened on her spear. Nerim did not falter. He faced Lara. The dagger was gone from his belt and his scabbard was empty, limp at his side.

He said, "I carry. If you permit. My people—Li Omani—we grieve."

"No!" cried a score of voices. Nerim's eyelids flickered. He watched the crowd, face impassive.

"He has courage." Elli's whisper tickled Kerris' right ear.

Lara lifted both hands, palms to the angry people. Slowly they stilled. Kel stepped forward. Quietly he held his hand out to Nerim. "Come," he said. Nerim stepped to him. Nerim reached up with his free hand and hid his face with his hood.

"That is four," said Lara. "That is enough. Go in, bearers, and bring him out."

Terézia handed her spear to the man next to her. She stepped forward. She entered the house, followed by the gray-haired man, then Kel, and lastly Nerim. The darkness swallowed them. Kerris' throat began to ache with tears. Feet shuffled in the entrance. Slowly the four bearers emerged into the light. Between them they bore a red plank, the sap still oozing from its ends. Sefer's body lay face up on the wood. The dead face had sallowed; the body looked heavy. A net of rope kept the corpse from sliding. The bearers held rope handles. The plank swayed as they walked.

The crowd opened. The bearers moved through the village. The weeping sounds grew louder. Kerris glimpsed Kel as the bearers went by: his face was pale as the dead man's. Tears were rolling down Terézia's face.

Elli gripped his forearm. "Look," she said. "There's Riniard." Kerris craned. Through the press he saw Ardith, with Tazia on his shoulders—there was Riniard. His face was blotched. Kerris looked for Jensie but could not see her. He had lost sight of Ilene and Arillard and Cal. He wondered if the Asech were gone, or if they waited in their camp for the return of Jacob and Nerim.

Like a great serpent the procession wound through the streets, Lara at its head, the bier behind her. The ground grew soft. Kerris' knees ached. He forced himself not to slow down. He looked back once. The slope behind him was thick with people. Ahead of him an orchard gleamed, green and white. The bier stopped. The people fanned out among the blossom-laden trees.

Kerris saw Ilene carrying Borti in her arms. He jogged Elli's elbow. She looked in the direction of his pointing finger. "Yes," she said. "I see." People moved in front of them. Kerris lost sight of the bier. As politely as possible he edged forward. Lara was standing at the head of the corpse. The bearers had drawn back from it, all but Kel. He knelt, one hand extended, touching Sefer. Kerris pinched his nose. The heavy sweetness of the apple trees made him want to sneeze.

Lara lifted her hands. "Let the people who can come forward and make him a place to lie."

No one moved. Then, slowly, Tamaris walked forward. She held her hands out, palms to the ground. The earth twitched, Ardith joined her, with Tazia still on his shoulders. Korith marched to join them. His dark face was peaked with grief. More people came from the crowd. They made a circle around the bier. Kneeling, they joined hands. Kerris saw the earth lift and fracture. They were digging a place for Sefer's body. The earth rived under the pressure of their minds and a mound of dirt rose beside the corpse. Tamaris' bronze face was still as a mask. Tazia's braids stood straight out from her head with the extremity of concentration.

Lara lifted her hands. "The place is made. We say farewell to our teacher, friend, lover, and brother, Sefer. We are joyful for the time he was with us; we grieve that it was short. Let us weep and laugh, think of him, comfort each other, and be at peace, in the name of the chea."

Tamaris' shoulders hunched. Tazia's face strained with effort. The plank and its burden slid into the hole. The mound of dirt diminished. Kerris heard a soft drumming sound as the clods slid back into the closing grave.

The circle of people stood. "It is done," said Lara. A moan shivered through the mourners. Kerris found himself weeping. A white fleck floated in front of his eyes. He looked up. The petals from the apple trees were falling like snow upon the people of the village. They made a smooth carpet over the brown grave.

Kerris looked for his brother. For an instant he feared Kel had vanished up the slope. Then he saw Ilene with her arms locked around him. He plucked at Elli's sleeve. "Wait," she said. Arillard was coming toward them. Together they walked to Kel and Ilene. Calwin struggled out of the crowd with Jensie behind him. They closed the circle.

Kel's face was graven with lines, but his terrible pallor was gone. "I have to talk to Jacob," he said.

"Do it tomorrow," Ilene said.

"What should I do now?"

She took him by the elbows. "You'll lie in the sunlight, and cry, and laugh, and drink until you're drunk."

"Where's my brother?"

"I'm here," Kerris said. Kel reached for him and pulled him close.

"Tell me again I'm not a ghost," he said.

Kerris held out his wrist. The dusky bruises showed clearly against his lighter skin. "Ghosts don't leave marks." Kel grasped the wrist, very gently.

"Did I—when did I do that?"

"This morning, by the pool."

"The pool." Kel's eyes seemed to blind. "Yes."

Ilene shook him by the elbows. "Kel. Don't leave us."

He drew a breath, shuddered, and focused. "No." He looked around the circle. "Where's Riniard?" He shook free of Ilene. His eyes fastened on Jensie's face. "Jen. You know." She nodded. "Get him, bring him."

She bit her upper lip. "He doesn't want to, Kel."

Kel lifted his hands. "By the chea, he's one of us! Do I have to

hunt him down through Galbareth? What's done is done, Jen.
Bring him."

She nodded, and walked toward the trees. Her feet left a
telltale path among the apple blossoms. When she returned,
Riniard was beside her. He had not changed clothes, or washed.
His hands were dirty. His hair was tied away from his face with a
green ribbon; he was holding in his right hand the red scarf of the
cheari.

He held it out to Kel. The left side of his face was discolored.
His hand shook. Kerris felt Elli stir. The light laddered down
through the tree branches, patterning Riniard's face.

Kel said, "Idiot." Tossing back his hair, he strode to Riniard
across the whitened grass. He caught the redhead by the
shoulders. His fingers flexed, hard enough to hit bone. Riniard
winced.

Kel spoke earnestly to him. Riniard's head bowed. His hand
clenched on the red scarf. Ilene sighed. Riniard lifted his head.
He was weeping. Kel cuffed him lightly on the right cheek. His
voice was still too soft for anyone but Riniard to hear. Kel took
the red scarf from Riniard's hand and tied it on his upper arm.
The redhead straightened.

They went to the clearing by the pool. Calwin and Ilene
begged a skinful of wine from Ilene's sister. The sun was
westering, falling obliquely through the cypresses and oaks.
Insects whirred in the trees. The surface of the pool was bright as
glass.

They passed the wineskin around and around the little circle.
"I can't do this one-handed," Kerris complained.

Elli said, "You hold it. I'll squirt." Kerris leaned against a tree
and aimed the wineskin at his mouth. He got a faceful of wine.
Wiping the cool stuff from his eyes, he glared at Elli. "You've
had better ideas."

"Just hand it this way," advised Arillard. "We want to drink
it, not bathe in it." On the other side of the circle, Kel and Ilene
were sharing a blanket.

Elli lay down on the ground. "There's a stone in my back."

She arched upward. "There." She flicked the rock into the pool. "I wish I had a pillow."

"Here." Kerris patted his thigh.

"Thank you," Wriggling over to him, she settled her head in his lap. "Hey, Riniard," she called softly. The redhead looked up. He had washed in the pool; his face was no longer dirty. The swelling on his left jaw was diminishing into a purple bruise. "What did Kel say to you in the orchard?"

Arillard leaned forward to listen. Riniard's gaze swiveled to Kel, and back. "He said I couldn't run away. He said I was needed." He sounded incredulous.

Jensie stretched from the shadows and caressed his hand. "It's true," she said.

"It *is* true," agreed Elli.

Riniard said, "I guess. I need you. I know that. But I think I would rather have had a beating."

Ilene's head jerked up. "You'll get that," she said across the clearing. "As soon as the swelling on your face goes down. I promise you."

Arillard said, "You know, Red, I told Kel after you were captured, I might have done what you did."

Riniard said, "I wish I hadn't. Maybe if I hadn't—" he licked his lips—"Sefer might not—might be still—"

"No!" said Arillard sharply. A pulse beat in his neck. "Don't blame yourself. It wasn't you who killed him."

"Who else do I blame?" said Riniard.

"It wasn't anyone." Arillard's voice grew rough. "It wasn't even that poor damned devil Barat."

The name hung ponderously in the air. Elli said, "You know, old man, that's the kindest thing I've ever heard you say about the Asech."

"That Barat was a poor damned devil?"

"No. That one of them was not to blame for a death."

Arillard rubbed his face with his hands. "The girl died, too," he said. "Too many people died. A man can dwell on death too long." He stared at the black circle of the pool.

The wind rasped across the tree branches. Kerris shivered at the eerie sound. Elli drew her knees to her chest. "It's getting cold." She grinned at Kerris. "Is my head too heavy?"

"No."

The moon drove its white prow through the trees.

Jensie said, "We could gather sticks and build a fire."

"No," said Elli and Riniard in unison. Kerris shivered again. The same image was in all of their minds.

It grew colder. "Arillard." It was Kel. He was sitting up. His voice was unsteady. "Do you have tinder and flints with you?"

"Where else would they be?"

"Make a fire."

Riniard and Jensie gathered twigs and brush. Calwin cleared a space beside the pool and ringed it with wet stones. Arillard lit a fire in the rock-lined place. The pine needles hissed and snapped as the small flames reached them. In the sable mirror of the pool, a second fire flickered. The burning smell was clean and savory. Kerris glanced at Kel. He was lying on his back. Ilene was speaking to him. One arm hid his eyes.

The wineskin made another circle. Cal hefted it. "It's almost empty," he said sadly. "We *could* get another."

"You're drunk enough," said Arillard.

"I'm not drunk at all."

Kel and Ilene came from the darkness into the circle of the fire. "We're not going to get drunk," said Kel. He sat heavily in the grass. Kerris couldn't tell if the glitter in his eyes was from tears or from the wine. "We're leaving tomorrow."

"We are?" said Elli. She sat up. "Where are we going?"

"Wherever it is," said Ilene, "it can't be far."

"Why not?"

"Because we have to return to a village in Galbareth in time for the autumn harvest." The wind snapped sparks out of the fire. An owl hooted in the woods.

Elli said dreamily. "We could go to Mahita." The fire laid bands of copper across her hair. She patted Kerris' knee. "You'll like Mahita, Kerris."

"We could go to Kendra-on-the-Delta," said Ilene. "We could stop at Mahita and then ride on down the Great Road, beside the river."

Kel said, "We will. I have to go there."

Arillard said, "Why 'have to,' Kel?"

"Keren is there. Sefer's sister." It was the first time since the day before that Kerris had heard him utter his dead lover's name.

There was silence. Kerris broke it. He said, "I'm not going to Mahita with you."

Elli turned to stare at him. The fire painted her face. "I thought—"

He rode over her; he had to. "I know what you thought." They were all listening. "I'm not a cheari. I'm not one of you. I can't come. Elath is—" he took a breath—"Elath is my home, I was born here. I have family here." He stared into the pattern of the fire so that he would not have to see Kel's eyes.

The fire stained the tree trunks orange. Kel said, "You must do what you wish, chelito." The love-word tore like a claw into Kerris' heart.

A twig snapped in Elli's hand. Jensie pointed upward to the bright belt of stars. "Look! A shooting star."

"I missed it," said Riniard.

"I saw it," said Elli. She slapped the ground. Pine needles scattered. "It's a good omen. Let's go to Mahita and ride down the river. Who's hogging the wine?"

They shared the final swallows between them. Ilene sang a children's song, a lullaby. It grew darker. The fire grew brighter. "I see shapes in the fire," said Jensie. "I see a tree."

"I see a waterfall," said Ilene.

Kerris saw a chearas, riding.

They slept. Kerris woke once, sensing dawn. In the distance roosters crowed the sun awake. He felt the chearas moving, talking. The trees loomed, dark against the lightening sky.

A hand touched his forehead. *Sleep, Kerris.* The words and the hand had weight. He sank into sleep beneath it.

When he woke the birds were singing challenges across the treetops. The sky was hot and blue. He rolled over. The fire was cold, the ashes damp. Only the tracked-up earth and the lingering smell of wine showed that other people had been there most of the night.

They had left him the blanket. He sat up. He was wearing Elli's yellow shirt. His knife lay near him. He picked it up. He couldn't remember if he had taken it off, or if someone had had to take it off him.

They would be back, he told himself. He buckled the knife to his belt. They would ride back through Elath on their way into the Galbareth. They would dance in the Yard, and he would stand in the shadow of the Guardian to watch them. He might even lie again with Kel under the dark gaze of the pines.

He went down the slope to the village. The silver houses looked clean and stark against the golden fields. He passed the beehives. The mouth of one of them was black with bees. A woman waved at him. She wore a straw hat. She tipped it so that he could see her face. It was Cleo. "Good day," she said.

A black and yellow bee zinged under his nose. He stepped back. "Good day. Are the desert riders gone, then?"

"They left yesterday," she said. "There's two still in the village, the one whose arm Kel snapped and th' other one." She tilted her head toward the beehives. "You'd better go. In another minute they'll come out to find out who I'm talking to. Bees are jealous."

"Don't they ever sting you?" he asked.

She smiled. "Never." She made a shooing motion with one hand. Remembering Kel's story, he hastened down the slope, out of stinging range.

He entered the market square.

He walked by the tanner's shop, the butcher's shop. Both had doors and windows opened wide. Inside the butcher's someone was sweeping. The door of the smithy, too, was open. So was the ropemaker's workshop. On the doorstep of the ropemaker's two women were bending: one held a broom, the other an open flour sack. Newly washed clothes flapped on lines.

The women waved at him.

He wandered by Lara's house. The door there, too, was wide open, propped with a heavy stone. Impulsively, he went in. All the mats were standing on end against the wall. Lara and a woman he did not know were sweeping.

Lara stopped when she saw him. She leaned on her broom.

"Kerris. Good day. This is my daughter, Sorith. Sorith, this is Kerris-no-Alis."

Sorith smiled. She had a flat broad face like her mother's. Her hair was done up in a blue scarf. "I will ch-ch-check the bread," she said. "Exc-c-cuse me." She went behind the tall screen.

"Sorith made dough this morning, and it is rising," said Lara.

The hangings were off the walls, too. The statue of the Guardian was gone from its niche. Kerris gestured at the broom and the walls. "What is this?" he asked. "All the doors..."

"We always do this," Lara said, "when someone of Elath dies."

The word brought it back. Kerris' throat stung. He said, "It doesn't seem possible."

"I know," said the old woman. "There's no excuse for the young dying. Yet his death, too, is part of the harmony. I must believe that. He would."

The bare-bottomed boy child appeared in the garden door. "Wa?" he asked.

"Thy mother is in the kitchen, chelito," Lara said. He toddled across the room toward the screen, gazing with marked interest at the auburn floor planks. Kerris guessed that he had never seen them. "Kerris, your pack is here."

"Thank you," he said. He frowned, remembering that he had left the blanket up by the pool.

Abruptly his mind filled with Kel, images of Kel, memories of Kel, Kel loving him, Kel laughing, Kel in tears.... He closed his mind to the iniquitous pictures and waited stoically for them to stop.

"The paper Meritha gave to you is with it."

"Thank you," he said again. And remembered to ask, "How is she, lehi?"

From the kitchen came a wail, and Sorith's voice speaking softly. "No better," said Lara. "She's been the same for months. I don't think she will get much better, or much worse."

A fly buzzed across the long room. Kerris raised his hand to swat it. It looped toward the kitchen. "Lehi—" He was interrupted by the child's crow of delight.

"Yes," she said.

"Why can't you heal her?"

She did not take offense at the question, as he had feared she would. She closed her eyes, opened them. "It's the people we love best that we cannot save," she said.

Sorith came around the screen, carrying her son on her hip. Shyly she looked from Kerris to Lara. The tentative glance made her seem as much a child as her son. The boy slid down her skirt and trundled into the garden, thumb in his mouth. A bell rang.

"I'll g-g-go," said Sorith.

Lara said, "No. She'll want me. She always does." With the look of a soldier going to a war, she gave her daughter the broom.

Kerris went back to the street.

He was hunting for something. He didn't know what he was searching for. He found himself retracing a familiar path. The breeze blew through the cypresses. The dark lane leading to the Tanjo was like a tunnel. He stepped from it into the bright and fragrant garden. The sun bounced off the statue of the Guardian.

He let himself gaze at it, a bit at a time. It did not look as if human hands had fashioned it. It seemed elemental: a thing of wind, water, earth, or fire. It was not unpleasant to look at. He did not get dizzy. He looked at it for a long time, trying to recall why he had been afraid of it.

The sun spilled down the sides of the Tanjo. He heard Sefer saying, *I'd like you to stay in Elath and teach at the school.* If he stayed he could live with Lea and Ardith. There is a place for you here, he told himself.

Something glinted in the grass near his foot. He picked it up. It was a red bead. He rolled it in his fingers. A bird was singing in the cypresses. It was a silvery sound.

He had said to Elli, wanting it to be true: *Elath is my home.*

It offered him a place, a task, companions. But so had Tornor. He understood why the presence in the garden had withdrawn. He was not Sefer. He could not stay here. He dropped the red bead into the grass. The heart of it, for him, had gone.

Chapter 15

He returned to Lara's.

At his re-entrance, Sorith vanished behind the screen that hid the kitchen.

"I've come for my pack," Kerris said.

Searching amid the folded wall hangings, Lara found it and brought it to him. He unfastened the lacing that held it closed. The paper was inside it. So was his woolen shirt, one of his linen shirts but not the other, his cloak, tinderbox, and flints. His riding leathers were, no doubt, somewhere in Sefer's house. He decided to leave them there. He rolled the blanket again.

"Lehi," he said, "I'm going to Mahita."

She nodded thrice. "We shall miss you."

"I'll come back. Elath is my home."

"Lea and Ardith will be sorry. They had hoped you would come to live with them."

"I'll talk to them," he said. "They'll understand."

Her dark eyes seemed to stare as though she would see into the center of him. "May the peace of the chea ride with you, Kerris-no-Alis."

"And with you, lehi," he said. At the door he hesitated, and then, turning, offered her a deep and heartfelt bow.

On the way to the farm he stopped by the pond to watch the red fish circling and circling. His eye followed the course of the stream that fed it, and he saw what he had not noticed before—the outline of a sluice. He gazed downstream and saw another. He wondered how many of the brooks and rivers that ran through Elath ran in created channels, past ponds dug to catch the spring runoff, regulated by gates. There was so much about the town he didn't know!

He passed the wood where he had seen the deer. It was empty now. He strode toward the peaked farmhouse roof. The sun was high. A red bird flew across his path and he watched it travel up, up, over the rim of the bowl. I'll follow soon, he thought after it.

By the time he reached the farmhouse he was sweating. The bowl held the heat of the day like a cup. The farmhouse door was open wide, and all the floor mats lay propped up on end outside. The abu's chair was in the open air; the old woman sat in it, blanket over her knees.

Kerris went to her. "Good morning, abu," he said. "Do you remember me? I'm Kerris, Ardith's sister's son."

The ancient face turned up to him. The lids blinked over the milky eyes. The old fingers moved. Then the woman hunched back in her chair. It rocked slowly.

Dismissed, Kerris went toward the house door. Poles with clotheslines had been set up on the south side of the house, and blankets waved from them. Kerris peered into the house. Meda and Lea stood in the long room. Meda held a broom. Lea was stacking the cushions against the wall. Talith, on his knees beside the hearth, was sweeping ashes into a wooden bucket. Tazia was calling overhead, the words muffled by the ceiling. The table was up on end, and all the hangings had been pulled from the windows and walls.

"Kerris!" said Lea. "Come in. Leave your boots on, it doesn't matter." She rose from her knees and came toward him, arms outstretched. He dropped his pack. She hugged him. There were streaks of dirt on her broad cheeks, and she smelled of dust and straw. Her smile was warm and welcoming. Kerris licked his lips. She let him go and turned to Talith. "Chelito, tell your father that Kerris is here."

"No—wait," Kerris said, as Talith scrambled to his feet. "I—I didn't come to stay."

There was a small silence. Then Lea said, "Tell him anyway, Tali."

The door to the garden was open. The scent of herbs made Kerris' nose twitch. "Come," said Lea. She touched his arm. "Let's go into the air."

An interested cat sat in the middle of a row, nibbling at a broad-leaved bush. At their appearance its tail went up and it bounded for the shed. "Scat!" called Lea. They sat in the grass. Ardith's hat, and then Ardith, emerged round the corner of the small red building.

"So," he said. He sat beside his wife.

Kerris said, "I came to say goodbye."

Ardith put his hand over his wife's. "I saw the chearas ride out this morning," he said. "I thought, Kerris isn't with them. That must mean he's decided to stay in Elath."

"I was going to stay," Kerris said. "But I went to the Tanjo, and looked at the Guardian, and I thought about it, and it seemed to me that—that I couldn't. You want me to stay. Sefer—Sefer wanted me to stay, and teach in the school. But—" This was harder to say than he had expected it to be. He hunted for the words.

"You don't want to," said Lea.

He sensed her disappointment, and, without thinking about it, reached across the silence with his mind. *Alis,* she was thinking, *he is so like Alis*—and the image of a small, dark woman, hair in one long thick braid, wearing a green gown, stole through his head. . . . Was it her memory or his? Lea's troubled, loving face superimposed itself on the features of Alis of Elath. Kerris said, "I can't just be the person my teachers wanted me to be. I need to explore—to learn not only what I can do but what I want to do."

"If you're speaking of your gift," said Ardith, "there is no place better to be than Elath. There are other inspeakers you can learn from."

"Yes," Kerris said, "I know, but—" the red bird soared over the trees. He turned his head, following its passage. The cat mewed in the bushes. "I have to go."

Ardith said gently to Lea, "Nika, he's seventeen."

She sighed. "Yes," she said, "and you cannot build fences around the young, it breaks their hearts...." She touched Kerris' wrist. "Will you follow the chearas?"

"Yes. Kel wanted me to."

"You're not a cheari."

"No. I can't fight and I can't dance. But there must be something I can do for them." He remembered a thing that Kel had said to him and repeated it. "The pattern feels right when I'm there."

"Who said so?" said Ardith.

"Kel."

The farmer pursed his lips. "Kel is a patterner. If he saw it, it must be so." He stood. "Come. If you're going to catch them this day, you need to get started." He held out both hands to Lea. She came up into his encircling arms. From them, she looked at Kerris.

"Will you come back?" she said.

"Sometime. I promise."

They went back into the house. Reo was standing by the clean hearth. His slim face held a questioning look. "Talith said you were here." He gestured upward. "I was upstairs with Tazi."

"I came to say goodbye," Kerris said. "I'm going to Mahita."

"Oh. I thought—" Reo scuffed a bare foot on the floorboards. "It doesn't matter," he said, eyes on his mother's face. "I hope you have a good journey."

"Thank you."

"If," said Reo, "you should happen to go farther south, to Kendra-on-the-Delta, and *if* you should happen to pass by Goldsmith's Alley, do you think you might stop a moment—"

"—and see your friend?" Kerris grinned. "I'll be glad to."

"Dev-no-Demio is his name, and he works for Smith Tian."

"I remember," Kerris said. "I could even take him your letter."

"Oh, that's gone," said Reo. "Poppa gave it to the chearas this morning."

Lea said, "Do you have everything you need? Clothes, food—"

"Yes," he answered, though he had forgotten all about food. It didn't matter. He *had* to leave. He picked up his pack. "Farewell."

"Safe journey," said Ardith. The breeze blew across the room, stirring dust. Kerris nodded to Meda. She lifted her broom to him in salute. Quickly he turned and made for the open door.

He went to the stable. "Hello, pretty girl," he said to Magrita, slipping into her box. She seemed pleased to see him, and not at all dismayed by the terrible ride he had pushed her to. She blew in his ear. The stable echoed. Almost all of the stalls were empty, now. He let her lick the salt from his palm.

Her tack, neatly polished, hung from a hook in the stall. Kerris wondered who had greased it, Lalli or Sosha. He left the stall and went deeper into the stable, looking for someone to help him. The straw rustled under his feet. He would have trouble saddling and bridling the restive mare by himself.

He went up and down the length of the barn without seeing either of the two children. He went to the back entrance. As he'd surmised, it led to a pasture. A big sorrel stallion galloped in play, but there were no people in it that he could see. He went back into the clean, untended horsebarn.

He was almost to Magrita's stall when he heard a cough. He turned. Nerim was standing at the door of one of the empty stalls. He was wearing plain clothes, a cotton shirt, breeches, the clothes of an Arun farmer. Behind him sat Jacob, on the floor of the stall. As Kerris looked at him he stood. He, too, was wearing other clothing. His left arm was held close to his body by a cloth. It was wound with linen, and set between two pieces of wood. The ends of the wood protruded from the linen binding. His fingers were free. Both men smiled hesitantly at Kerris. Jacob opened his mouth, glanced at Nerim, and said, clearly, "Good day."

"Hello," Kerris said. There was a pallet in the empty stall, and a pack, and a blanket. "Are you staying here now?"

Jacob looked at Nerim. Nerim said, "We both stay. We sleep,

help with horses, work—" he mimed raking straw. The sorrel horse, then, was Nerim's. Kerris wondered where Jacob's white-footed black was.

He peeped a little farther into the stall, and saw the Asech weapons, swords and knives, lying on the ground. "The others—Li Omani—left yesterday," he said.

Nerim nodded. "They leave. We stay. He—" clapped Jacob's right shoulder—"heal, arm grow. It broke three." He said this with gusto, as if he admired the blow that had done it. "When all heal, then we leave."

"Will you go back to the desert?"

"No," said Nerim. "We go west. To fighting place. He say. Kel. Go to fighting place in mountain."

Kerris remembered Kel saying, *I have to talk to Jacob.* "He's sending you to Vanima?"

Jacob's dark eyes lit. "Vanima," he said. "Zayin."

Nerim said, "He say, Jacob, you go learn. Be cheari. If you learn cheari, come find me."

Jacob said, "Zayin." He burrowed into the stall, and reappeared with a piece of calfskin vellum. He unrolled it, with Nerim's help. On it in fine black lines, pen lines, was a map. Nerim pointed out Elath, Shanan, and the Red Hills. A broken line connected them, angling northwest on the parchment. Kerris wondered who had made it. It could not have been Kel. Maybe Ilene could draw. There were no runes on the page, just large black X's to mark the town, the city, and the valley.

With the air of a man absorbed in treasure, Jacob rolled the parchment carefully and hid it away.

"Are you going to be a cheari, too?" said Kerris to Nerim.

Nerim grimaced. "No. I no want. I not patterner. I help my friend."

"I see." Down the hallway, Magrita whickered. "Well— would you like to help me saddle my horse? I can't do it alone."

"I do," said Nerim with alacrity.

He rubbed Magrita's nose, talking to her softly in his own tongue. She accepted his presence in the stall without demur. He slipped the bit into her mouth, bridled her, blanketed and saddled her. The buckles seemed to close without being touched, the girth practically cinched itself. Kerris handed his pack to the Asech, and the lace practically whipped itself to the cantle.

"Thank you," he said.

The rider smiled. "Where *you* go?"

"To Mahita."

"Ah. You go with them."

"Yes," Kerris said. He took Magrita's rein. It occurred to him that he had no money, not a copper penny. He would have to fast on the road, or beg. He wondered how many days it took to get to Mahita. He had to go south, he knew that, and he could follow the river road.

He lifted a hand to Jacob as he left the stable. 'Good luck!" He went through the doors with the mare behind him. Tek was just striding to the doors.

"Hey," he rumbled. His muscles bulged his shirtsleeves. "You're late. The others left hours ago. They said you weren't going."

"I changed my mind," Kerris said.

The stablemaster eyed him. "You know where they went?"

"Mahita."

"You know how to get there?"

"Go south."

"What you do is, you take the southern road out of here." Tek pointed to the southern slope, where a brown ribbon snaked up to the rim and lost itself in the rocks. "You follow it. 'Bout sundown you'll hit a fork, one goes due west, the other goes southeast. That's the one you want to take. The other goes to Shanan. The southeast fork takes you to the Great River." He bit the end of his mustache. 'You got food?" Kerris shook his head. "You wait." He went into the stable, and came out with a pouch. He tied it to the cantle ring. "There's jerky there. It'll keep you going. From the fork to Mahita's just another day's ride."

"Thanks."

"You won't catch 'em on the road. They're too far ahead of you. When you get to Mahita, best way to find 'em is, ask at the stables." He slapped Magrita's flank. "Mount up." Kerris did so. "That stirrup's out." He worked the strap to the right length. "You look like Kel, some, but you're shorter. Listen, you tell him

253

from me, he still owes me a race! You hear?" His great voice lifted in a shout.

"I hear," Kerris said. He lifted his hand, and touched his heels to the mare's sides. Magrita leaped for the road like an arrow from a bow.

He had never been alone on a road. As he came up through the trees on the rim he drew a deep breath. The air was crisp, clean as salt. Beyond the settled bowl lay forest, meadows, streams, small farms, more towns. He had forgotten to ask Tek how he would know Mahita when he came to it.

Magrita settled into a brisk walk. There was a small welt on her crest where a branch had lashed her. "Sorry, girl," Kerris said to her. "I couldn't help it." She swiveled her ears back at the sound.

There were sheep in a meadow. The heavy smell of wool made Kerris think of Tornor, so far behind him. He still had Josen's letter in his pack. He had to find a caravan to give it to. A stream paralleled the road for a while before it barged off into the woodsy hills. A white crane stood delicately on one leg at the little river's edge. It fixed Kerris with a black, oblique stare. It held a struggling frog in its scissorlike yellow bill.

It grew hot. Kerris unlaced the throat of the yellow shirt. Wild beans grew along the roadside. He wondered if they were good to eat. He passed a house with a peaked roof. It was weathered and shaggy as an old mule. A black dog barked at him. In a field, two people worked among the tall rows of wheat. He could not see if they were men or women.

The road widened. Kerris saw smoke, and thatched roofs. He went up over a rise into a town. There was a small market square, hung with pennants, and a watering trough, and a well. "What town is this?" Kerris called to a passing woman. She shaded her eyes to look at him. She had a round doughy face, and round white arms. Her eyes were very blue; they looked like berries stuck in a cake.

"Warrin," she said. "Warrintown."

The smell of baking bread wafted from open doorways.

Kerris guessed it was baking day. The hot scent made his mouth water. He reined in at the southern edge of the hamlet and opened Tek's pouch. The jerky was beef, salt, and delicious. He ate two pieces. It was so tough that his jaws went numb. The sun blazed over him. He wished he had a hat to keep it off his head. Sweat trickled steadily from his hair. There were great wet patches under his stump and his arm.

A man with a straw hat was fishing at a stream. He lifted a hand in greeting. Kerris called, "Have you been here all day?"

The man was chewing a cattail stalk. He took it out of his mouth to answer. "I have."

"Did a chearas ride by here, early this morning?"

"They did."

"Thank you," Kerris said. The man replaced the cattail stalk. "Is this water drinkable?"

The man removed the cattail stalk. "It is. But go on."

"Why?" Kerris asked.

The man tilted his head back so that he could look at Kerris. His eyes showed blank astonishment. "Because," he said, "you'll scare the fish."

Kerris went on. Downstream he dismounted. The water skirled over the rocks. Magrita dipped her muzzle into the swift-running water. Kerris scooped water up in his hand and sucked it into his mouth. He had to do it several times. He wished he'd thought to ask Tek or Lara for a cup. It would make it easier to drink.

Magrita snatched at the roadside grass. He let her eat a bit. The sky was blue as flame. The half moon sat like a ghost on the eastern horizon.

He mounted. The color of the sky made him think of Sefer. He turned Magrita south again. He remembered the confident lucidity of Sefer's mind. He had not been old, thirty-one. Kerris flexed his thigh muscles. His legs were beginning to ache. The death still seemed impossible.

He thought of Thera, and then of Barat as he looked at the end, baleful and hopeless, more like an animal than a man. Thera had tried to help him, knowing it would not help. *It is the people we love best that we cannot save.* Kel had not saved Sefer. Kerwin of Tornor had not saved his wife. Alis of Elath had not saved her baby son.

His stump itched. Thoughtfully he scratched. Magrita slowed at the lifted rein. "That's not meant for you, girl," he said to her. He felt a brief moment of pity for the Asech rider. He'd spent his life surrounded by people with two arms. He knew what it was like to lack.

The stream meandered back into the hills again. The road curved up, around, and over them. He saw another house with a thatched roof isolated in a little valley, surrounded by a small patchwork of fields. A mule kicked its heels in a pasture. A woman in a straw hat was digging roots from the ground with an iron spade.

He went through yet another town. This one was larger, and the road within its boundary stones was free from ruts and edged with brick. A cart stood in front of a shop. The cart was piled with cotton bales. The banner in front of the shop showed a piece of cloth being pierced by a giant metal needle. Inside the shop Kerris heard the clacking of a loom.

The sun fell toward the west. Magrita moved at her ready pace, no longer frisking but untired. Kerris' thighs ached. In the bright dusk he saw a fox slipping through a meadow. Cicadas nittered at each other.

The Shanan crossroads reminded him of the Tezera crossroads. A few merchants were still calling out their wares to the travelers. Wagons lined the roadside. The sweet smell of heavenweed drifted from the rosy fires.

Kerris dismounted. As he led Magrita forward he counted eleven Asech tents. Lights shone behind blue glass. He smelled cooked meat, and wine. Some enterprising farmer had laid down hoe and scythe and built an inn at the crossroads, where wealthy folk could stable their horses and spend the night. Kerris led Magrita toward the building, hoping to find a water trough. It was there, near a score of ringed posts. Kerris let the mare drink her fill. From the trough he led her away from the inn, looking for a space by the roadside that was not taken by someone else's animals. Magrita would need to forage. He wondered how he could stable her in Mahita, without money. The smell of roasted fowl blew toward him. Near him, two men were dicing, calling numbers at each other. He rubbed his stump. He was feeling worn, and a little discouraged, and lonely. His stomach rumbled.

A clear voice lifted into the twilight, borne on the western wind. *"In sunlight we must part, my love, in starlight we may smile; The moon is shining bright, my love, O let me stay a while; Sing hey and ho for lovers, sing hey for the setting sun, Sing hey for the lad who makes me smile when the harvest work is done!"* He knew the song. He turned in a circle, looking for the singer. His heart pulsed in his throat.

"We ride along the river, the moon is bright and fair, it shines on the fields and the cotton and on your golden hair, Sing hey and a ho for lovers, sing hey for the setting sun, Sing hey for the lad who makes me laugh when the harvest work is done!"

He saw the singer standing over a fire. She had pale skin, dark hair. It was not Ilene. She saw him looking at her, and raised one hand. "Ho! Traveler with the black mare! Do I know you?"

He approached the fire. There were other people sitting there. A caravan bulked behind them. "Excuse me," he said. "I'm following some friends on the road, and one of them's a singer. I thought you might have been she."

"No." Her face was kind. "I'm sorry. Where were they going? We may have seen them."

"Mahita."

Her forehead wrinkled. A man holding a meat skewer said, "That is south, Hetta."

"Oh. I'm sorry. We came from Tezera."

The meat aroma made Kerris' stomach tighten. "Thank you," he said. He led Magrita away from the tantalizing smells.

He found a place between two wagons. He spread his blanket on the grass. Magrita munched the green stalks happily. He unsaddled and bridled her as she ate. It took a long time. He plucked a handful of grass and rubbed her down.

He stretched out on the blanket after tethering Magrita to a nearby willow sapling. He put his head on the curve of the saddle. The stars arched like a bridge over the world. The campfire haze was thick. He smelled wine. He wondered where the chearas was, in what town or field.

The bustle of wagons roused him. Shouting and calling, the travelers were getting ready to go their ways. The western road was dusty already. Kerris stood and stretched. Drivers swore at their horses and at each other. A mule escaped and cantered amid the wagons, with its owner running after it, waving a willow switch. Kerris rolled his bedroll. He went to find Magrita, dragging saddle and tack with him through the grass. She was waiting for him placidly, a strand of grass poking from her muzzle.

This time there was no one to help him. The buckles were damp and hard to manage, and there was no way to use his teeth on them. When he finished he was sweating.

The inn was emptying. In front of it, by the water trough, stood a tall man, surveying the crowd. His hair was light brown, and his eyes were gray as winter. He wore a patterned silk shirt and fine leathers. A red comb winked in his hair. His horse was a sleek gray stallion, fit for the lord of a Keep, its tack decorated with silver braid.

The innkeeper came out to talk with him, smiling and bowing. The tall man gave him a coin. It looked like gold. Kerris wondered who he was. A rich merchant, maybe, high in the Guild—or maybe, even, a member of one of Shanan's or Kendra-on-the-Delta's great houses.

He mounted and turned east. Magrita picked her way through the mesh of carts and travelers. Kerris passed Hetta, the woman from Tezera. She sat on a wagon seat, backing a pair of chestnut geldings with practiced skill.

Just before he reached the road proper, he saw a line of wagons with blue ribbons flying from their poles. A man in a blue cotton shirt was striding along them, giving orders. An irritated mule bared yellow teeth at a driver. It looked like the one Kerris had seen running loose. He wondered if the man in blue was the master of the caravan. He decided not to bother him. He lifted his hand to the mule driver. "Good day," he called.

"Day," snapped the driver. He cuffed the mule over the ears. "If you bite me, you lopsided monster, I'll beat your damn ribs in."

"Where are you going?" Kerris asked.

"North. Tezera."

"Can you take a letter north?"

The man swore at the mule again. "Third wagon from the top," he said, not looking up. Kerris guided Magrita to the head of the line of wagons, and then went back to the third one. It was piled with wine barrels. A man sat on top of them, kicking his heels against the barrel sides, smoking a pipe.

"Good day," Kerris said.

The man puffed. "Good day."

"Can you take a letter north to Tornor Keep?" Kerris said. He twisted on his saddle and hunted in his pack for the letter. It was curved but not crumpled. He passed his thumb over the wax seal.

"We go to Tezera," said the man. His heels thunked the sides of the barrels. Plunk. Plunk. He held out a hand. "But there'll be someone in Tezera who's riding west."

Kerris put the letter in his hand. "How long will it take you to get to Tezera?" he said.

He shrugged. Plunk, went his heels. The pipe steamed. "Fifteen days."

Chapter 16

He rounded the bend, and there was the river.

Kerris had thought it would be all one color, but it was many:
brown near the banks, gray-green, blue, even red. It was much
larger than the Rurian. He gazed across to its other side. He saw
sheds, and fields covered with rows of flowered bushes. He could
just make out the tiny figures of people walking through the
planted rows.

He gazed along the near bank. The red in the water was
saw-dust. He sniffed. The wood smell lay heavy in the air. He
rode a little further on and came upon a dock with logs stacked
on it. The water was ruddy with sawdust. More logs floated
obliquely downstream, like stitches in a swath of cloth.

South of the dock stood a big shed. A trail behind it snaked
up into the forest. Two woodcutters swung axes at an immense
log. They saw him, and straightened. Kerris called, "Is Mahita
on this side of the river?"

"Both. There's a bridge."

"Thank you." He clucked to Magrita. Her shoes clicked on
the paved road. Carts rattled by him, laden with crates and

barrels and sacks, sending loose chips of brick scuttling and flying. On his left, the river moved, gleaming like the back of a snake.

He watched the placid curves with pleasure. He found himself singing. *In sunlight we must part, my love*—He had no idea if the tune was right, and he didn't care. Neither did Magrita.

He rounded a long curve, and there was the town.

A wall of gray stone circled it, and fields of plants with yellow flowers surrounded it, lying almost flush to its gates. There was a clear space before the gateway. Guards walked the wall. Stalls with awnings lined the road before the gate, making a small market. Carts, mules, horses, and people on foot crammed into the lane. People shouted at each other. Kerris saw several Asech riders on their tall sleek horses caught within the press.

He hung back, a little frightened. A cart bustled past him and a waggoner shouted at him to get off the road. The rooftops of the town went on and on like a forest. He wondered how, amid the plethora of streets and buildings and people, he would be able to find the chearas. . . . He told himself not to be ridiculous. If he could find his brother across the whole of Arun, he could find him in a city. He urged Magrita forward. He rode past the stalls, not looking at the fruit and cheese and wine, trying not to smell the quail turning on their spits or the fish frying. The carts and riders and foot travelers resolved into a procession. He joined it. Whips cracked as the carters coaxed their teams forward. A somnolent guard outside the arched gate looked Kerris up and down and flicked his fingers to motion him inside.

The street smelled of cooking food and horses. A little beyond the gate the bustle diminished. Kerris craned from side to side, trying to see everywhere at once. This was nothing like Tornor, and nothing like Elath. Banners flapped everywhere, with pictures of shoes and bread and meat and butter, cloth and wine and candles, pots, pins, and nails. . . . The streets were brick. The buildings were part stone, part wood; some were tall, some boxy, and they leaned together like crates. On the street corner a woman with rings in her ears stood juggling six silver balls. She saw Kerris looking at her and grinned. The balls blurred through her nimble fingers.

She made a lazy, beckoning gesture with her head and started to walk away down the street, wide skirts swaying.

"I'm looking for stables," Kerris called.

A passing waggoner answered him. "That way!" He pointed with his whip.

Kerris turned Magrita in the direction of the point. He glanced back. The woman stood watching him, hands still moving, crookedly smiling.

The stable was huge; a broad, half-timber, half-brick structure. A long-legged girl ran from it as he dismounted. "Staying long?" she said. She spoke very fast.

"I don't know," he said. His own speech seemed lethargic beside hers. "I was looking for some friends. You might know where they went—they came from the north, like me, only earlier."

"Wait." She screamed into the depths of the stable. "Shay!" She waited, tapping her bare foot. "Shay!"

A second girl sauntered from the doors. "You want me?"

The first girl jerked her thumb backward at the newcomer. "You ask her. She was here this morning." She reached for Magrita's rein.

Kerris held it. "Just a minute."

Shay strode up to him. She was short and dark, with great broad shoulders like a smith's. She wore her hair in a lot of little braids, like Elli. "Help you?"

"Did a chearas ride through this morning?"

Shay yawned. "Sure. They're going to dance at the East Yard, I heard 'em talking. You know 'em?"

Kerris nodded. The other girl said, "You gonna leave your mare here or not?"

"I don't know if I can," Kerris said. "I don't have any money."

She shrugged. "You gonna get some?"

"Yes."

"Then we'll take the horse for you. If you don't pay after the first three days, we'll sell her tack." She unlaced Kerris' bedroll from the cantle, dumped it in the dirt, and twitched the rein from his hand. "Come on, pretty lady."

Shay grinned. Her teeth were yellow. "She won't sell your tack for five days."

Kerris said, "I'll be back before then." He picked up the bedroll. "Where is the Yard?"

"The West Yard is that way, about four blocks. The East Yard is across the bridge. 'Bout eight blocks from the bridge, walking east, there's a big stone building, that's the Armory. The Yard is next to it."

"Thank you," Kerris said.

"You from the north?" Her speech was slower than the other girl's, though not much.

"Yes."

"Tezera?" she guessed.

"Tornor Keep."

Shay grimaced. "That's a long way, I hear."

"It is."

"You hungry?"

Kerris smiled. "Does it show?"

She laughed. "Folk who come into town from far away are usually hungry." She pointed south. "You go that way a block, you'll come to the Hall. It's run by the town. The food's plain but there's enough of it, and they'll serve travelers for free."

The Hall reminded him of the refectory at the nameless village in Galbareth. It had long wooden tables, and a serving window. A fat woman behind the window handed him a bowl and spoon and did not ask him for money. There was meat and fish and noodles in the soup. It smelled delicious. His mouth watered at the steam. The building was mostly empty, and he guessed he had come late or early. The kitchenfolk were talking, he could hear them amid the clatter of pots. They spoke fast. He thought of Paula. She had sounded like that once, he supposed. He wondered how long it had taken her to train herself to speak at the north's slower pace.

He had forgotten to ask Shay when the chearas planned to dance. He brought the bowl back to the serving window and laid it in the big tray. The fat woman did not look at him; she was talking. He went into the street. People streamed by him in two directions. He looked for the bridge and saw it suddenly, arching over the river. He couldn't see the water. The hubbub confused him. He tucked his bedroll under his arm and walked south. A woman strolled by him with a cat on her shoulder. A man trundled past, wheeling a barrow piled high with yellow fruit. One of the yellow globes bounced from the barrow and tumbled at Kerris' feet. He picked it up and started to toss it back.

The barrowman shook his head. "Keep it!"

He looked in the window of a shop that sold spices. It was filled with jars of different colors. In one corner was a huge barrel, and a dipper on a string. A sign on the barrel said, "Salt." A man ran the opposite way, carrying a long pole hung with fresh fish. Kerris tossed the fruit in the air. It was barely bruised. He bit into its soft, fuzzy rind. Sweet juice ran out of his mouth and down his chin.

He came to a Yard.

It was very large, almost as large as the courtyard of Tornor. He put his bedroll down between his feet and leaned his elbow on the fence. Two men sparred with pikes, hair flying in the exertion of their strokes. A dark woman bent and curved alone in a corner. The Yard seemed oddly empty for a place with so many people in it. He finished the fuzzy fruit. He tossed the fringed pit into the street. His eyes kept turning toward the children's circles.

He watched them tumble and wrestle, turn and thrust, weave and dance. A bittersweet taste rose in his throat.

"Something—?" A short, stocky man stood on the other side of the fence. The clatter of a cart passing over the brick had masked his steps.

"I was just looking," Kerris said.

The man's eyes moved to Kerris' sleeve and back to his face. "My name's Charin."

"Kerris."

"New in town?"

"Yes." Something—perhaps the man's evident friendliness— made Kerris add, "I'm from the north."

"Ah." There was a note of interest in the sound. "Now I would have known you're from the north. You talk like a northerner. And that sheath is mountain work. From Tezera?"

"Yes," Kerris said.

Charin leaned his own elbow on the wall. He had wrists like a blacksmith's. His hair was short, braided onto his collar. "You traveling through, or staying awhile?"

"I don't know," Kerris said. "I'm looking for some friends."

"Oh?"

"The chearas."

Charin nodded slowly. "I saw them this morning," he said. Kerris tried not to show surprise. He had thought the man was just an idler, perhaps a member of the city guard, bound to train each day in the Yard, who decided to be friendly to a visitor and so evade practice. He had to be an instructor. "They stopped to say hello." He glanced toward the children's circles. "Where in the north are you from?"

"Tornor Keep."

"Huh. Where'd you lose the arm?"

Kerris had never been asked so bluntly before. "In an Asech raid," he said. "I was three."

"You were south, then," said Charin. "The Asech never raided the Keeps. Too bad you had to end up there. Lousy, lonely place to live." He grinned. "Give me people, lots of people, and a way to get away from them when I need to."

A flock of white birds soared over the Yard, mewing like cats. One of them had a piece of green rind in its beak. Charin was watching the Yard. Suddenly he called, "Gerri! Danu!"

In the children's circles, two small figures broke from the ring and came running. They both had knives. One of them was a boy, slender and tall, with brown hair and light blue eyes like pale silk. The other was a girl, equally slim, equally tall. Her eyes were a slightly darker shade of blue. She had long black hair.

Kerris stiffened. No instructor, he thought, got that kind of instant obedience.

"How long have you been practicing?" Charin said.

The girl glanced at the sun. "About two hours, skayin," she said.

"I thought so. You're tiring. Go take a walk, the both of you. Gerri, tie your hair back. Long hair in a fight will get your throat

266

cut, unless you're so good that it doesn't matter. You're not a cheari yet."

The girl caught at her thick loose hair and twisted it on top of her head. She pinned it there with a bone comb. "It fell."

"Tie it so it won't fall. Go."

They started to run to the gate. "Walk!" he called after them. Gerri looked back, grinning. They slowed to a walk, and strolled to the street, looking very sedate.

Kerris said, "They're twins?"

"Yes," said Charin. "Gerri loves the Yard. For her the knife and the dance are fun, a delight, a game. One day she'll waken to the art of it." He made a sunburst with spread fingers.

"And then?"

"And then she will start to be a cheari."

Charin's tone did not change. But Kerris felt a shadow in the words, a subtle and silent longing. "Was that what you wanted?" he asked. And could have bitten out his tongue. Even from a friend, which he was not, the question was both cruel and rude.

But the Yardmaster merely raised his thick dark eyebrows. "I didn't know it showed."

"I'm sorry," Kerris said.

"I'll be walking to the East Yard to see the chearas in a little while. Would you like to come with me?"

Kerris said, "Thank you, yes. I would."

Charin nodded to him. "It's easy to get lost in a strange place. Excuse me." He walked back toward the fighting circles, and Kerris could see now that he limped slightly on his right leg. Aside from that, he walked like a cheari, graceful, crisp, and perfectly controlled.

Kerris walked.

He wanted to get away from the Yard. He was annoyed at himself. Two blocks into the big town's noise, a skein of melody stopped him in his tracks. It was not a human sound. He'd never heard anything like it: a soft, urgent, blurry wail. He followed it round a corner.

He came to an alley behind a shop. Within the alley he found a pile of rotting vegetables, a dog rooting in a crevice, and three children, sitting on a stack of dusty, broken bricks. A piece of ivy trailed up the wall behind them. The scent in the alley was pleasant, if steamy. He recognized two of the children at once: they were the twins, Gerri and Danu. They stood up, shielding the third child with their shoulders.

"I'm sorry," Kerris said quickly. "I'll go away if you want me to. But I really like that sound—the music."

The children moved apart. "We thought you were Ree," said Gerri. "He doesn't like Suya." Suya was the third child. He was smaller than the twins, thin, dusky, and wary. His hair was black as Gerri's, but his skin was brown. His clothes were dusty, but then so were the twins'. His feet were bare. He looked older than the other children, and more ragged.

Kerris hunkered down in the dust. The dog came to sniff him. He pushed its muzzle away from his pack, knowing it would smell the jerky. "Git!" said Gerri. She bent to pick up a shard. The dog slunk away at the threat.

Gerri scowled. "It isn't fair. Even if it is the back of his old shop." Suya muttered at her, and she stopped talking.

Kerris said, "Would you show me how you made that sound?"

Suya opened his hand. His fingernails were ragged, and dark with dirt. On his small palm sat a wooden box. It was long and narrow and there were holes in it. He lifted it to his mouth and blew. He ran it along his mouth, and the wail went higher. He moved it the other way, and the wail grew deep and sad. Kerris listened, fascinated. It sounded like a lot of voices all singing together in different keys, but it blended, somehow.

"What is it?" he asked.

Suya sat on the brick. "A *sho.*"

"How does it work?"

The boy shrugged.

"Do it more."

He lifted it to his lips and played something slow and dreamy. Kerris closed his eyes, trying to remember where he had heard it. It was the lullaby Ilene sang. *"Sleep my babe, sleep my child, nothing restless, nothing wild..."* He sang it softly.

"That's nice," he said.

268

Suya smiled.

Over Kerris' head, a voice yelled, "Damn it!" A hard, dark face thrust through a square. The children jumped. Kerris grabbed Suya by one thin wrist as the boy made ready to run.

"I told you I didn't—" The man saw Kerris and the shout stopped. "Them kids botherin' you?"

"No," Kerris said, "I asked to hear the music."

"Huh. Music you calls it. Cat-talk I call it." But the head popped back within the brick building.

Kerris dropped Suya's wrist. Gerri clapped her hands. "Now we can stay here!"

Suya stayed on his feet. "He beat me last time he found me sleeping here."

Kerris glanced around the alley. "You sleep here?"

Suya shrugged.

Gerri hissed. "He's no right to beat you. Uglyface Ree. He's no kin to you."

"I'd like to kill him," said the boy evenly. "But I don't know how, and nobody will teach me."

Danu looked shocked. "You don't want to kill him," he said. "Killing people breaks the chea. You want him to stop beating you." Gerri nodded approval. But Suya looked at the dust.

A white bird slanted down into the alley. Its wings were like knives. It folded them neatly against its fat sleek body and pecked at the carrots and turnips. Kerris said, "What's that bird called?"

The children stared at him. Gerri finally answered. "A gull."

Kerris put his bedroll between his knees. "I'm from the north," he said. "I've never been this far south before. Why do you have to sleep in the alley?"

Suya scrubbed his heel in the dust. "No kin."

"Are they dead?"

Suya shrugged again. "Don't know. Don't know who they are."

Kerris leaned back against the rough stone. It seemed impossible to him that a child would have no family, no kin.

Suya spoke. "My mother was Asech." He turned his head, so that Kerris could see the fine holes in his small earlobes. "Don't know what happened to *her*. My father was a towny. Don't know *him*."

"Where do you live?" Kerris said.

"In the streets."

"Where do you eat?"

"They feed me sometimes, in the Hall. That's supposed to be for strangers, but they let me."

"How old are you?"

"Don't know." The boy's stolid face darkened a little. "I think fourteen."

Kerris remembered a small boy that he had once known very well, watching his friends circle and thrust and parry and circle again in the Yard of Tornor. "That's not very fair," he said.

Suya's thin shoulders twitched in that bitter, defensive shrug.

Kerris shook his head. "You need someone," he said. "Some kin. If not a mother or father, then aunt or uncle, or brother." He thought of how lonely his life would have been in Tornor without Paula, Josen, Tryg—even Morven. Even Kili.

Gerri said, "I tell him he should come to the Yard with me, and we'll show him how to beat Ree into splinters! But he won't come."

"Can't."

"Why not?" asked Kerris.

Suya kicked a bit of brick across the alley. The soles of his feet were dusty and looked hard as horn. "No knife." He touched his belt, fingering the place a knife would hang. "Besides, they don't want me."

There was terrible isolation in that little sentence, and pain, and need. Kerris felt it touch the wall in his mind and fall away. It seemed unfair that he, of all people, had happened upon this child, he who was a stranger to this town and to the south. Suya was looking at him sullenly, as if angry that this stranger had broached his privacy, intruded into his hurt....

An idea niggled at Kerris' mind.

"You want to go to the Yard?" he said slowly.

Suya nodded. "Can't," he repeated.

Kerris stood, and the boy tensed. "You don't have to be afraid of me," Kerris said. "If you want to go to the Yard, I'll help you."

Suya's dark eyes enlarged. "How?"

"I know the Yardmaster." It was, he thought, a necessary lie. "I think I can talk him into letting you into the children's circles."

Suya's face tightened in suspicion. But Gerri let out a loud, exuberant whoop. She leaped abruptly to the alley floor. She seized Suya's shoulder. "Yes," she coaxed, "It's a good idea. Charin's nice. He'll let you come to the Yard even if you don't have a knife!"

It took a deal of persuasion before Suya was willing to leave the alley. Gerri and Danu did most of it. Kerris waited. He could not help thinking of Kel, remembering the night in the garden, the day by the pool. . . . He remembered Kel's description of their mother. "She used to come home tired all the time. I never understood why visiting people made her tired until I realized she was using her gift, mediating, mending quarrels." The first thing he had ever done for the chearas was mend a quarrel.

Now what can I do?

Anything you like. He heard Sefer's voice, saying it. His throat prickled. Whatever he did, whatever he learned to do—Sefer would never know.

The Yard was empty. Charin was standing at the gate. He put up a hand when he saw Kerris walking toward him. "Get lost?" he called. "I was starting to wonder whether I should wait for you."

He was wearing Yard clothes: a thick shirt, breeches, boots. A wide leather belt cinched his waist. A short sword in a decorated scabbard hung at his left thigh. Outside the Yard he looked bigger than he had within it. Kerris felt Suya's steps begin to lag.

He laid his palm more firmly on the boy's bony shoulder. Gerri skipped ahead of them. Danu marched on Suya's other side. He had insisted on carrying Kerris' bedroll.

Charin looked at the odd quartet. "What's this?" he said. He gazed at Suya.

Kerris said, "His name is Suya. He is part Asech and part of Arun, he tells me, but neither people will take him. He cannot come to the Yard because he is kinless, with no one to give him a knife. He sleeps in alleys and is beaten by shopkeepers. He's fourteen years old. It seems to me that this is no way for a person to have to live. A Keep would have treated him better."

Charin's face did not change. "Why do you bring him to me?" he said.

Kerris felt Suya stiffen. The boy cast one eloquent look upward. You see, said his eyes. You see? He started to twitch his shoulder out of Kerris' grip.

Kerris held on. He extended his mind to the big man, brushing aside the surface resistance, *feeling pride, love, pity, compassion*—Delicately, he gathered his talents together. Then he sent his thought—like a beam of sunlight—playing over the Yardmaster's conscious mind. *Because you are a decent man*, he spoke, *and because you know what it feels like to want and not to have, to desire and to be denied because of an accident, a flaw no fault of your own....*

Yes, answered Charin, *yes, I do know*—and then his mind reacted to the invasion—*Damn it, you have no right to walk into my mind like this! Get out. Get out!* But Kerris was already out. He held onto Suya, watching the Yardmaster's great hands clench and open. The man's face had whitened, and his eyes were squeezed shut. He swayed a little. Finally, he opened his eyes and drew a deep breath.

He looked at Kerris, and then quickly away. His glance found Suya's face. He held out his right hand, palm up. "Come here."

The boy moved from under Kerris' hand. He took a step forward.

"You want to learn to fight?"

Nod.

"You know who I am?"

"Yardmaster."

"Yes. If I say you may come to the Yard, then you may, and no one can keep you out. Do you get enough to eat?"

"Sometimes."

"Fighters must eat. I will talk to the cooks in the Hall. And you can sleep in the weapons shed. It's big enough to hold a pallet and it's out of the rain."

Gerri, at Charin's back, turned a joyful cartwheel. Her hair flopped from its hold; the comb clattered to the brick.

Without turning, Charin said, "Gerri, stop that."

She scooped the comb up and coiled her hair on her head.

Charin glanced again at Kerris. "You children get out of here," he said. "You'll be late to watch the chearas."

"There'll be too many people," said Danu mournfully. "They won't let *us* in."

"Have you never climbed a fence?"

Gerri seized Suya's hand. "Come on," she said. "I know a back way. They won't ever see us." Danu dropped Kerris' bedroll at his feet. They scampered off, but Suya hung back to press something small, hard, and cool into the palm of Kerris' hand.

Kerris gazed at it. It was the sho.

He faced Charin. "I owe you an apology." His fingers closed tightly on the music-maker. "There was no way to warn you."

"How did you do that?"

"I lived fourteen years in the north," Kerris said. "But I was born in the witch-town, Elath."

The Yardmaster rubbed his shaven chin. "I see," he said. He ran his hand over his hair. "I've never—no one ever—"

"I understand," Kerris said. "I'm sorry." He fingered the satiny wood of the sho. He could not believe Suya meant him to have it. "It seemed important."

"It must have." Charin glanced at the angle of the sun. "We'd best hurry," he said.

Kerris stuck the sho in his belt and picked up the bedroll. He tucked it under his arm again. Slowly they moved southeast, toward the river. Gulls flew over their heads, mewing as if requesting them to drop something to eat.

Charin said, "I had heard of such things. But I never—" Again he stroked his fingers over his dark hair.

"I won't do it again," Kerris said. The words made him think of Riniard.

The bridge was wide enough for two carts to pass each other. It stood on four stone arches. It was built of gray stone, with dark lines curling and threading through it like veins in a leaf. Gulls hovered over it. Green stems grew up the arches. The river smelled of fish.

There were people fishing on both banks. Pole-barges and sailboats and rowboats moved along the flat green water. In the south a soft mist was rising. The sun was dropping westward. Lights spangled the streets of the quarter they had left and the quarter they were going to.

The east side of the city seemed softer, newer, less cramped. The streets were wider, and many of them had trees growing along them, shading the house doors. A street sweeper moved along the bricks, collecting the dung left by the horses. In one house people were singing, and Kerris heard through walls the soft sweet harmony of a flute. He took the sho from his belt and held it in his hand.

The East Yard was bigger than the West Yard. It had a wooden fence around it. A city guard at the gate was counting people as they walked in. Charin said, "Follow me." He walked straight for the gate. Kerris grinned to see the people push out of his way.

His heart was thundering. He gripped the sho until its edges marked his hand, and kept at Charin's heels. The Yardmaster moved to the very front of the audience. Kerris saw a familiar face. It was the man he had seen at the inn at the Shanan crossroads. All around him came the rustle of silk and velvet. A woman in a crimson shirt stared at him, as if wondering who he was. She smelled of flowers. She saw him looking at her and smiled. The big space began to blaze with light as torches flared on their iron poles.

He saw them. They stood in a circle. Kel's shining hair swung long and loose. Ilene had threaded her scarf through her hair; it gleamed like a coronet. Elli was talking to Arillard. Jensie and Riniard stood side by side; Jensie's thumb was crooked through Riniard's belt loop. Calwin was kneeling, tightening a bootlace. His hair stood up on his head like brush bristles. Kerris trembled. He sat. He wanted to call to them—and he wanted, too, to wait, concealed, watching, as if they were strangers.

He brushed the sho against his lips. He was so close to them.

They would see him, sooner or later. The crowd quieted. It didn't matter which. He leaned forward, resting his bedroll in his lap.

Kel's head lifted. His booted foot stamped to set the beat of the dance. The chearas moved.

The people murmured with pleasure. Kerris smiled. Joy sustained him. Later would do.

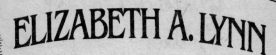

THE FANTASTIC
WORLD OF FANTASY

____**FAITH OF TAROT**	05054-8 – $2.25	
Piers Anthony		
____**VISION OF TAROT**	04441-6 – $1.95	
Piers Anthony		
____**ALL DARKNESS MET**	04539-0 – $1.95	
Glen Cook		
____**OCTOBER'S BABY**	04532-3 – $1.95	
Glen Cook		
____**A SHADOW OF ALL NIGHT FALLING**	04260-X – $1.95	
Glen Cook		
____**MALAFRENA**	04647-8 – $2.50	
Ursula K. Le Guin		
____**THE MERMAN'S CHILDREN**	04643-5 – $2.50	
Poul Anderson		
____**PEREGRINE SECUNDUS**	04829-2 – $2.25	
Avram Davidson		
____**THE SHAPES OF MIDNIGHT**	04567-6 – $2.25	
Joseph Payne Brennan		